Bibliotheca
Classica
B. H. Johnsonis

THE WORLD THE ROMANS KNEW

Also by N. H. H. Sitwell

ROMAN ROADS OF EUROPE

THE WORLD
THE ROMANS KNEW

by

N. H. H. SITWELL

HAMISH HAMILTON

LONDON

First published in Great Britain 1984
by Hamish Hamilton Ltd
Garden House, 57–59 Long Acre, London WC2E 9JZ

British Library Cataloguing in Publication Data

Sitwell, N. H. H.
   The world the Romans knew.
   1. History, Ancient
   I. Title
   930   D57
   ISBN 0-241-11318-0

Typeset by Rowland Phototypesetting Ltd
Bury St Edmunds, Suffolk
Printed in Great Britain by
St Edmundsbury Press, Bury St Edmunds, Suffolk

IN PIAM MEMORIAM
I.W.H.S.

CONTENTS

ILLUSTRATIONS

MAPS

ACKNOWLEDGEMENTS

The quotations at the beginning of each chapter are all from the works of Rudyard Kipling. The author and publishers wish to thank Macmillan London Ltd, and the National Trust for Places of Historic Interest or Natural Beauty, for permission to reproduce them.

Most of the translations of Greek and Latin writers are from the Penguin Classics series (Herodotus, *Histories*, by Aubrey de Sélincourt; Josephus, *Jewish War*, by G. A. Williamson; Livy, *History of Rome*, by Henry Bettenson; Pausanias, *Guide to Greece*, by Peter Levi; Polybius, *Histories*, by Ian Scott-Kilvert; Tacitus, *Agricola* and *Germania*, by H. Mattingly; Tacitus, *Annals*, by Michael Grant).

The author also wishes to thank the staff of the London Library, the Institute of Archaeology Library (London), and the Library of the Societies for Promotion of Hellenic and Roman Studies.

PREFACE

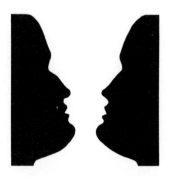

Illustrated above is a well-known optical illusion. Do you see it as two black faces, or as one white urn? By jogging some internal mental switch, can you change from one of these perceptions to the other? Can you do this faster and faster (faces – urn – faces – urn – faces . . .) to the point where the picture seems neither the one thing nor the other, yet also both at once? And if so, have you achieved a small mystic vision, a miniature of what the world's great saints and swamis experience, or are you merely wasting time that could more profitably be spent observing something other than yourself?

My father, the late I. W. H. Sitwell, to whom I have dedicated this book, loved questions of this kind, and all questions whose theme is 'What is inside and what is outside?' Independently of Edward de Bono, he developed by himself several principles of what is now called 'Lateral Thinking' – the gaining of new insight into a problem by jumping from one view of it to another, as with the faces and the urn. It was he who produced the idea on which this book is based. There have been many books about the Roman Empire, and all too often they treat it as if it existed in complete isolation. Even their maps often show it surrounded by blank space, as if the non-Roman world had no existence except when barbarians emerged from it to make a nuisance of themselves. As a counterpoise to such works, this one starts with the opposite assumption: here it is the Empire that appears as the blank space, and its 'barbarian' neighbours who receive attention.

'And who is my neighbour?' Some of the people described were contiguous neighbours of the Roman Empire, but others were not. Others again, such as the Huns, were first recorded at a great distance from the nearest Roman territory, but later approached it and finally irrupted into it. To have dealt only with the contiguous neighbours would still have been biased, over-emphasizing the western side of the Ancient World at the expense of the eastern. I have aimed instead to portray a 'Known World' stretching in a diagonal band across three continents, from Ireland in the far north-west to Java in the far south-east; Rome, seen thus, lies not at the centre of affairs but well out to one side. I have taken a similarly generous view of the time-scale: the main object of attention is the age of the early Roman Empire (first and second centuries AD), but to complete the picture it was often necessary to consider earlier and later events, sometimes casting back to a time when Rome was little more than a village, and at other times forward to when it was mostly in ruins.

The Ancient World was at once a larger and a smaller place than is generally supposed. Larger, because many parts of it were neither Greek nor Roman, and so are left out of the standard history books; smaller, because people could and did travel to these foreign parts and gain considerable information about them. When Ethiopians went to Palestine, Greeks to India, Chinese to Persia and Romans to China, what then was inside and what was outside?

N. H. H. SITWELL
Kew, 1983

CHAPTER ONE

THE CELTS

Rome never looks where she treads.
   Always her heavy hooves fall
On our stomachs, our hearts or our heads;
   And Rome never heeds when we bawl.
Her sentries pass on – that is all,
   And we gather behind them in hordes,
And plot to reconquer the Wall,
   With only our tongues for our swords.

A Pict Song

In 1961, the population of Europe was approximately six hundred million. Of these, some 80,000 regularly spoke Irish Gaelic; about as many spoke the closely related Scots Gaelic; some 660,000 spoke Welsh; and rather more, it is thought, spoke Breton. (The French census-takers have paid little attention to the subject.) Altogether, perhaps, Europe had a million and a half Celtic-speakers – one quarter of one per cent of her total population. Appropriately was the region where they lived called the 'Celtic Fringe'.

It was not always so. In the last centuries before Christ the Celts were probably the most numerous, certainly the most widespread, people in Europe. They occupied all the British Isles, all France and most of the Low Countries, the northern parts of Spain and Italy, and all the Danube lands from the Black Forest to the Black Sea. One group had even crossed from Europe into Asia, establishing itself in the heart of what is now Turkey. Greeks and Romans alike clashed repeatedly, and sometimes disastrously, with these fierce warriors of the north; writers of both nations reckoned them among the most imposing and formidable of all the 'barbarians'.

The centre from which Celtic expansion began was the land of the upper Danube, shared today by Germany, Switzerland, Austria and Czechoslovakia. Here, starting in about 700 BC, flourished what is known to archaeologists as the Hallstatt culture, named after an important salt-mining settlement in the Austrian Alps. It was succeeded, in about 450 BC, by the La Tène culture, which takes its name from a settlement on Lake Neuchâtel in Switzerland. Both Hallstatt and La Tène Celts travelled widely, and through their skill in forging and wielding iron weapons were able to dominate their neighbours in several directions. Only on the north, where their lands marched with those of the early Germans to be described in Chapter Two, did they fail to make headway – at the last, indeed, losing to the Germans even their original territory. In a westward direction, however, the Celts were more successful. All France, with its neighbours up to the river Rhine, passed into their hands and became peculiarly their own. Classical writers refer to it as Keltica, Galatia or Gallia – three different spellings of the same word, which means neither more nor less than 'the country of the Celts'. France replaced the upper Danube as the heartland and powerhouse of the Celtic-speaking peoples.

From Gallia (or Gaul, as Englishmen call it) groups of Celts made repeated crossings to the British Isles. At first they came in small numbers, carving out supremacy for themselves with their iron swords (new to the islands) and creating a society somewhat like that of Norman England many centuries later. Celtic military aristocracies ruled over a large non-Celtic subject populace. But as time went on the Celts grew more numerous and their influence more pervading. When the Romans reached Britain in the last century BC, virtually all trace of the pre-Celtic language and culture had disappeared except in the far north of the island, among the people later to be known as Picts.

While some Celts crossed the Narrow Seas to Britain, others crossed the Pyrenees to Spain. Here their dominion over the previous inhabitants (the Iberians) was less complete than in Britain. In the north and west of the peninsula the Celtic language became predominant, as is shown by numerous place-names ending in the word *briga* (Celtic for 'hill', related to *Berg* in German and *brae* in Lowland Scots). But in the south and east Iberian culture persisted with little change.

The southern Celtic expansion was more limited in extent than the western, and started later, in the fifth century BC. Celtic tribes overran the plain of northern Italy, defeated the Etruscans who had previously ruled there, and made the land their own. Romans of the Republic were regularly to call it Gallia Cisalpina – 'Gaul on this side of the Alps', as much a part of the Celtic world as Gallia Transalpina on the further side. One tribe, the Insubres, established the city of Milan (ancient Mediolanum, meaning 'in the middle of the plain'). The city of Felsina was captured by the Boii, and took from them the name of Bononia; it is now Bologna. A third tribe, the Senones, advanced even further, reaching the Adriatic Sea and giving their name to Sena Gallica (Senigallia). In 390 BC a far-flung warband of this last tribe crossed Tuscany, destroyed a Roman army on the river Allia and went on to sack Rome itself. (Only the Capitol held out, so the famous story goes, saved by the cackling of the sacred geese when the Gauls tried a

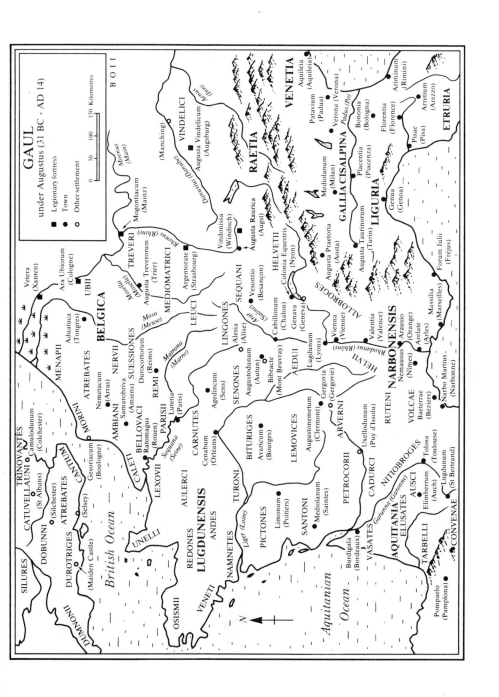

GAUL
under Augustus (31 BC - AD 14)

■ Legionary fortress
● Town
○ Other settlement

0 50 100 150 Kilometres

surprise attack on it by night.) For some time thereafter the Celts of northern Italy were a continuous menace to their more civilized southern neighbours.

The eastern advance of the Celts, down the Danube, came last of all. Alexander the Great encountered some of the leaders of this movement on the lower course of the river in 335 BC; he asked them what thing in the world they most feared, and received the surprising answer that it was the possibility of the sky falling down upon them.[1] Half a century later the movement reached its apogee with a Celtic invasion of Greece (including an unsuccessful attack on the holy and very rich city of Delphi) and an invasion of Asia Minor. The central part of this peninsula (thereafter known as *Galatia*, which means the same as *Gallia*) became the base from which three tribes, in exactly the same manner as their kinsmen in Italy, launched repeated raids on their neighbours in all directions. They were decisively beaten by the Romans in 189 BC, and brought under direct Roman rule by the emperor Augustus in 25 BC; but even then some of them preserved their own language and special character. A hint of their fiery nature appears in St Paul's letter to them, warning them against 'Adultery, fornication, uncleanness, lasciviousness, idolatry, witchcraft, hatred, variance, emulations, wrath, strife, seditions, heresies, envyings, murders, drunkenness, revellings, and such like'.[2]

*

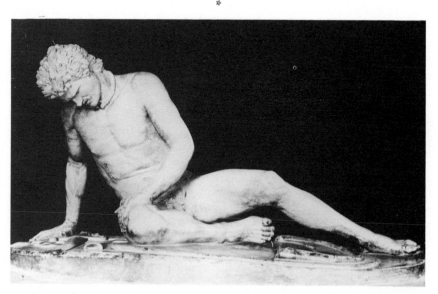

The 'Dying Gaul' (Capitoline Museum, Rome): a romantic Celt as pictured by the ancients.

Several ancient writers, some using Latin and some Greek, describe for us the physical appearance of the early Celts. Their accounts all agree, and add up to a very different picture from that of the 'typical Celt' as he is usually seen today.

The Celtic warrior was taller, heavier and stronger than most men of the Mediterranean world. He had a loud voice, and used it frequently. His skin was fair, and so was his hair, which he wore in abundance; northern France was known to the Romans as Gallia Comata, which means 'Hairy Gaul'. It was often lightened still further in colour by mixing it with a paste of chalk and water. Many warriors also wore large moustaches of the soup-strainer type, similarly treated. (All the above description, except for the moustaches, applied equally well to the womenfolk; many of them proved as formidable in battle as their husbands – Queen Boudica or 'Boadicea' being the best-known example.) The whole picture more resembles that of the Complete Germanic Hero, as made famous by Wagner and infamous by Hitler, than anybody one is likely to meet in the streets of Dublin or Cardiff today; and it was indeed remarked that in physical type Celts and Germans were very similar.

The Celt wore elaborate and decorative clothes. He liked bright colours, and he liked them to be combined in patterns, forerunners of

'Boadicea': a romantic Celt as pictured by the nineteenth century. Scythe-bearing chariots were not used in Britain.

the present-day tartans. The kilt, however, was not generally worn, the usual male attire being a tunic and trousers known as *bracae* (whence the modern English word 'breeches'). Those who could afford it wore ornaments of precious metal and jewelry, and these too were decorated in elaborate patterns. To Celtic taste, a plain colour or a plain surface seemed almost abhorrent; and this attitude to design reflected a similar attitude to general life.

Ancient descriptions of Celtic character find more of an echo in modern times than do the descriptions of Celtic appearance. The nobles at least (nothing is said about the common people) were mercurial types, passing quickly from joy to sorrow and from sorrow to rage, proud, touchy, with a strong sense of their own dignity, and apt to become belligerent in maintaining this. (To modify an old joke: if a Greek, a Roman and a Celt were each left alone on three separate desert islands, the Greek would start a philosophical discussion, the Roman would start a government and the Celt would start a fight.) Classical writers were reminded of the Greek world described by Homer many centuries earlier – the world in which Achilles sulked in his tent, and Ajax quarrelled with Odysseus, and even the gods took violent sides in the conflict between Greece and Troy.

Nor was this estimate of the Celtic character confined to writings by the Celts' enemies. Here, for example, is an extract from the Irish saga called *Mac Da Tho's Pig*:

'Move off from the pig', said Conall.
'And what would bring thee to it?' said Cet.
'Truly', said Conall, 'to seek admission of battle-victory for myself . . . I have never slept without a Connachtman's head beneath my knee'.
'It is true', said Cet, 'thou art a better warrior than I. But if it were Anluan who were here, he would match thee with victory for victory. It is bad for us that he is not in the House'.
'But he is', said Conall, drawing Anluan's head from his belt; and he hurled it on to Cet's chest so that blood flowed over his lips.
Then Cet left the pig, and Conall sat down by it.[3]

So, as in heroic Greece, the best warrior received the best cut of the joint.

This reference to a severed head is far from unique. Head-hunting was as much a part of the Celtic warrior's world as scalp-hunting among the Red Indians. Human heads were fastened up at the gates of settlements, in temples and in private houses, sometimes even being placed on the table during meals. On other occasions they were cast into water as a kind of thank-offering. In the Walbrook, which used to

Shrine at Rocquepertuse in Provence: human skulls set in niches.

flow through the City of London, numerous skulls were found, probably belonging to Roman Londoners decapitated during the sack of the city by Queen Boudica's forces. In the same revolt the head was hacked off a bronze statue of the emperor Claudius (probably at Colchester) and flung into the river Alde, whence it was recovered in 1907. Vestiges of the custom still survive – in the large stone balls sometimes found at the entrances to historic houses, for instance, and in the lanterns carved from turnips or pumpkins and carried by small boys at Hallowe'en, an important Celtic festival. Guy Fawkes' Night, five days later, preserves in symbolic form another unpleasant custom associated with the same festival, the burning alive of prisoners in wicker cages. Even the Romans, by no means a soft-minded people, found this practice disgusting; one of their first acts on taking over Gaul was to outlaw it.

*

The Celt's characteristic temperament, with its swings between frenzied courage and black despair, became particularly noticeable when he was engaged in his favourite occupation of warfare. From the earliest times, armies containing *some* Celts and some non-Celts (the officers, preferably, being mostly non-Celtic) have proved themselves first-rate upon the battlefield. The army of Hannibal, in which Celts fought alongside Africans and Spaniards, defeated the Romans in four devastating battles. Later, in the service of their former enemy, Gallic troops (cavalry in particular) proved themselves invaluable in maintaining and enlarging the Roman Empire. More recently still, the history of the British Empire is full of the exploits of regiments from Wales, Ireland and the Scottish Highlands. The all-Celtic army, however, has had a more varied and unstable record in warfare, its occasional spectacular victories being matched by equally spectacular defeats, from Telamon in 225 BC to Culloden in AD 1746. Either a Celtic army carried all before it, or else it wavered, dispersed and was lost. Drawn battles and fighting retreats were alien to it. To command such a force was like riding a bicycle: if you did not go forward the whole time, you began to wobble and eventually fell off – and the bicycle disintegrated beneath you.

The fierce pride of its warriors, none of whom wished to take the second place, meant that a Celtic tribal army seldom had more than one battle-line, nor yet any kind of useful reserve. In recent times, and probably in ancient times too, the line was drawn up on the basis of kinship; families formed units within clans, and small clans formed units within larger ones. Conflict generally opened with every warrior making as much noise as possible. Some relied upon their unaided lung-power; others, in the ancient world, blew horns and trumpets with mouths shaped like those of animals. At some later, uncertain date, the Scots developed an even more terrifying psychological weapon in the bagpipes. Some warriors might work themselves up into a state similar to that of the Viking berserkers, and tear off all their clothes. Here, for example, is Polybius writing of the battle of Telamon, where the Romans gained their revenge for the disaster on the Allia:

> The Insubres and the Boii wore their trousers and light cloaks, but the Gaesatae had been moved by their thirst for glory and their defiant spirit to throw away these garments, and so they took up their positions in front of the whole army naked and wearing nothing but their arms. They believed that they would be better-equipped for action in this state, as the ground was in places overgrown with brambles and these might catch in their clothes and hamper them in the use of their weapons.[4]

Celtic trumpeters, on the cauldron found at Gundestrup in Denmark.

And here is Livy, writing of a battle between Romans and Gauls in Asia Minor, in 189 BC:

> [The Gauls'] wounds were plain to see because they fight naked and their bodies are plump and white since they are never exposed except in battle ... But they are not worried about such open gashes; sometimes indeed they cut further into the skin, when the wound is broad rather than deep, and imagine that thus they are fighting with greater glory. On the other hand, when the point of an arrow or a sling-bullet has buried itself in the flesh ... these same men become maddened and ashamed at being destroyed by so small an affliction; and they throw themselves prostrate on the ground.[5]

(A medical argument could be presented in favour of this practice. In an age without antibiotics, fragments of not-very-clean clothing carried into a wound could cause complications more dangerous than the wound itself. A likelier explanation, however – likelier too than the one offered by Polybius – is that the warriors believed themselves to be protected by some kind of personal magic. A similar belief was held by the Red Indian 'Ghost Dancers' in 1890, also by the French high command in 1914; many lives were lost in vain attempts to show that the 'offensive spirit' could overcome barbed wire and machine-guns).

Next came the most intimidating part of a Celtic battle, the charge. The principal weapon used in this was the long slashing sword, later to be known in Scotland as a claymore; the Romans called it a *spatha*, a word which has given rise to Spanish *espada*, French *épée*, and the 'spades' in a pack of cards. Like its wielder, the spatha was not wholly reliable. Though iron-working standards among the Celts were above average for the time, the whole process was still somewhat haphazard. Without going too deeply into the physics and chemistry of the subject, we may say that the behaviour of iron is profoundly affected by the presence in it of relatively small amounts of carbon. Pure iron, or iron with only a very little carbon in it, is not a useful material; a sword made from it would be too soft, and would bend 'plastically' – that is, bend and stay bent until forcibly straightened, with results very unpleasant for its user in a battle. Adding a little more carbon turns the iron into a form of steel; it becomes much harder, and now bends 'elastically' – springing back into shape when the applied force is removed. This was the ideal towards which ancient smiths strove, with many prayers to Vulcan and several nasty semi-magical practices. But though a moderate amount of carbon is beneficial a larger amount is not. It hardens the metal still more, but at the cost of making it brittle; and a sword liable to break in use is even more dangerous than one liable to bend. Perhaps for such metallurgical reasons, the Roman legionaries rejected the long sword altogether; they used instead a shorter and thicker weapon, said to be of Spanish origin, designed for stabbing rather than slashing. This Roman sword, or *gladius*, had the further advantage that much less room was needed to wield it.

The screaming war-cries, the whirling swords, the flying hair, the moustaches like the tusks of wild boars, the huge bodies wearing outlandish clothes or no clothes at all, combined to make the Celtic charge a terrifying spectacle. Many ancient and modern armies confronted with it simply turned and ran. But should it ever be halted, whether by the javelins and thrusting-swords of Roman legionaries or by the musketry of English redcoats, the battle was as good as lost.

One other feature of some ancient Celtic armies deserves a mention, the famous war-chariot. This device had a long and widespread history. Originating in the Near East in about 2000 BC, it was soon taken up by the Egyptians and a little later by the Greeks. In the heroic world of Homer's *Iliad* the chariot plays an important part, as it does in the very similar heroic world of the Irish bards about fifteen centuries later. It was also found in the armies of China, Assyria and Persia; the Persians used a force of chariots (with no success at all) against Alexander the Great in 331 BC. But by this time horses had been bred much larger and stronger than they had been when the chariot made its début, and were able to carry men wearing a substantial amount of armour. Cavalry, being easier to manoeuvre, replaced chariotry except in two regions remote from the centre of affairs – the Sahara Desert and the British Isles.

The purpose of the chariot in battle has often been misunderstood. There is a strong general tendency to see it as the ancient equivalent of a tank, used for breaking through enemy formations by sheer weight and impetus. Horses, however, cannot be induced to behave in this way. Any attempt to drive a chariot straight into a hostile formation of troops would produce what the show-jumping fraternity calls a refusal, quickly followed by a spectacular crash. The true function of a chariot resembled that of a jeep, or even a helicopter, on the modern battlefield. It was for moving soldiers rapidly from one place to another, and it went out of use because bigger horses made it possible for cavalry to do the same job better. The British chariot, thus designed with the object of making smallish horses move biggish men as fast as possible, was deliberately made extremely light, little more than a basket on wheels. The wheels themselves, however, were a considerable triumph of technique. Their various parts were made of different sorts of wood, each carefully chosen to suit the work it had to do; and in their method of fitting the parts together the Celts were more sophisticated than the Greeks or Romans. Contrary once again to popular belief, scythe-bearing chariots were *not* used in Europe (though they are recorded in Asia, in Africa and in a curious late Roman military work known as the Anonymous *De Rebus Bellicis*.[6]

*

The failure of the Celtic-speaking peoples (for, with apologies to those alive today, it must be admitted that they have failed in comparison with their Latin- and Teutonic-speaking neighbours) has often been ascribed to their political disunity. From Vercingetorix via King Arthur down to Bonnie Prince Charlie, the romantic hero turns up again and again in their history – always trying to unite his people a little too late, and always going down in a glorious but futile fight against overwhelming odds.

At one early stage in their history, however, the Celtic peoples did achieve considerable unity. Some of their tribes were among the largest political groupings in Europe – much larger, for example, than the city-states of classical Greece or early Italy. The Brigantes of northern England occupied a territory shared by five (pre-reform) counties: Cumberland, Durham, Westmorland, Lancashire, and the North and West Ridings of Yorkshire. The Pictones of western Gaul occupied, and gave their name to, the mediaeval county of Poitou, which was almost as big as present-day Northern Ireland. The Boii of central Europe likewise occupied and gave their name to the mediaeval kingdom of Bohemia (now called Czechy by its inhabitants; it forms the western end of the nation of Czechoslovakia); and so huge was this tribe that it was able to send one offshoot into Italy and another into France, apparently without noticing the slightest deficiency. Julius Caesar maintained that the two largest tribal assemblages in Gaul (those of the Aedui in Burgundy and the Arverni in Auvergne) could each easily produce 35,000 fighting men, the equivalent of some seven Roman legions, or of the entire army of classical Athens.[7] The force raised by Vercingetorix, of which these Aeduan and Arvernian contingents formed only a small part, is said by Caesar to have numbered more than a quarter of a million. He was nevertheless able to defeat and disperse it – and with it collapsed Gallic independence.

There are some examples, however, of multi-tribal Celtic states that enjoyed a longer life. One such is the realm of Cunobelinus (Shakespeare's Cymbeline) in south-eastern England. Cunobelinus reigned from about AD 5 to about AD 40, not only over his own tribe (the Catuvellauni of the south Midlands) but also over the Trinovantes of Essex and several small tribes in Kent. At the height of his power he also encroached upon the territories of the Iceni in Suffolk, the Dobunni in the West Country, and the Atrebates south of the Thames.

The Roman writer Suetonius even describes him as *Britannorum rex* – 'King of the Britons', anticipating by many centuries the equivalent title of *Bretwalda*, much contested among the Saxon kings of England.[8] Ireland in due course reached a still greater though more nebulous degree of unity, first with the establishment of the famous 'Four Provinces' of Ulster, Connaught, Leinster and Munster, and then with the appearance of a High King with his capital at Tara, predominant (in theory) over all four.

It may not be a coincidence that these movements towards unity took place in regions remote from Roman influence and separated by water from the main body of the Roman world. (Britain was not conquered by the Romans till AD 43, and never became so thoroughly Romanized as Gaul. Scotland came under Roman rule only for short periods, Ireland never). Alongside the official history of the Empire, with its emphasis on emperors, generals and great battles, there runs a diplomatic history about which much less is known – a history of great battles avoided, of tribes judiciously played off against each other, of pro-Roman leaders in a tribe secretly or openly supported against their rivals. In the words of Tom Lehrer, 'They've got to be protected, All their rights respected, Till somebody we *like* can be elected!'

Caesar mentions a good example of this kind of power-politics in

Aerial view of Tara in County Meath, the residence of the High Kings of Ireland.

the conflict between the brothers Diviciacus and Dumnorix for leader-
ship of the Aedui; the former was pro- and the latter anti-Roman.
Dumnorix was eventually killed by Caesar's orders.[9] About a century
later, governors of Britain backed the pro-Roman queen Cartimandua
against her anti-Roman husband Venutius in a similar way; and at the
same time tribes in Germany were being played off against each
other.[10] So the failure of the Celts to achieve greater political unity
may have been largely due to the Romans' taking deliberate steps to
prevent them. But this particular river of ancient history runs mostly
underground, and only now and then appears in the surviving records.

*

Celtic society, like many others in the history of the world, was divided
into four groups: the nobles, the priests, the artists and artisans, and
the common people. The nobles we have already met; it was they who
led the tribes in battle, and it is they who receive the greatest attention
from ancient writers. The precise nature of the government varied.
Sometimes we hear of the 'chief men' of a tribe, without any suggestion
that one is superior to the rest; sometimes we find the nobles electing a
leader from among themselves; and there are also examples of something approaching a hereditary monarchy. (Cunobelinus in Britain,
for instance, had succeeded his father Tasciovanus and was in turn
succeeded by his sons Caratacus and Togodumnus.) But the strict
hereditary principle, that the eldest son always succeeds his father, was
unknown in the Celtic world. It was common practice for a ruler to be
succeeded by his uncle, brother or cousin, with his own son becoming
perhaps the next ruler after that. Such an arrangement had the great
advantage of avoiding rule by minors, though it could at times produce usurpations and faction-fights of the kind immortalized by
Shakespeare in *Macbeth*. At all times personal ability was important in
bringing a man to the top, regardless of his exact relationship (if any)
to the ruling family (if there was one).

The Celtic priesthood, the famous Druids, caught the imagination
of scholars in the sixteenth century, since which time a fair amount of
nonsense has been written about them. They had nothing whatever to
do with Stonehenge, a monument built many centuries before the Celts
ever reached Britain, by an entirely different set of people with
different religious beliefs. Celtic religion did not produce monumental
buildings. It was of a naturalistic kind, paying attention to sacred
groves and springs; in this respect it had much in common with the
religion of the early Germans, that of the early Romans, and the system
of beliefs called Shinto which is still an official religion of Japan.[11] The
word 'Druid' itself is derived from a word meaning 'oak-tree', and

Pliny records the famous rite in which mistletoe was cut from the sacred oak-tree with a golden sickle.[12]

Woods and forests played a large part in Celtic religion. The Druids of Gaul used to meet in a forest in the territory of the Carnutes (somewhere near modern Chartres); the British Druids had an important wooded shrine on the island of Anglesey.[13] Right across Europe we find ancient place-names containing the element *nemetum*, which means 'grove', hence 'sacred grove', and hence in turn 'temple'. There was even one named after the Emperor – the city of Clermont, capital of the Arverni, whose name in Roman times was *Augustonemetum*.[14]

Partly from a genuine distaste for the Druids' practices (human sacrifice in particular), partly because in effect they formed an anti-Roman secret society, the Romans opposed Druidism and suppressed it wherever they could. In Gaul the idea of a pan-Gallic meeting was preserved, but its venue was changed from the remote forest of the Carnutes to the city of Lyons, right under the eye of the Roman authorities, and an affirmation of loyalty to the emperor became the central feature of the meeting. The site has been excavated: it was found to have had numerous trees, as if in memory of things past, and also a large amphitheatre – implying, as it were, that the Celts' worst form of brutality had been officially replaced by the nearest Roman equivalent.[15] Druidism survived in Britain for some time longer, but was finally suppressed there by armed force. Here is Tacitus on the storming of Anglesey in AD 60:

> The enemy lined the shore in a dense armed mass. Among them were black-robed women with dishevelled hair like Furies, brandishing torches. Close by stood Druids, raising their hands to heaven and screaming dreadful curses.
>
> This weird spectacle awed the Roman soldiers into a sort of paralysis. They stood still – and presented themselves as a target. But then they urged each other (and were urged by the general) not to fear a horde of fanatical women. Onward pressed their standards and they bore down their opponents, enveloping them in the flames of their own torches. Suetonius garrisoned the conquered island. The groves devoted to Mona's barbarous superstitions he demolished. For it was their religion to drench their altars in the blood of prisoners and consult their gods by means of human entrails.[16]

Below the Druids, but above the ordinary peasant or humbly, stood various other people. Chief among these was the bard. In an illiterate society, he was not only poet and musician, but historian, genealogist and public-relations expert besides. Alexander the Great once remarked that Achilles was unusually fortunate in having Homer to praise him; and Celtic heroes similarly relied on their bards for immortality in legend and song. The British monk Gildas noted and deplored this practice in the sixth century AD: 'When the attention of thy ears has been caught, King Maelgwn, it is not the praises of God that are heard, but thine own praises . . .'[17]

The skilled metal-worker was also a man of consequence. Every community probably had its blacksmith, able to make the iron objects required in everyday life; but objects like the shield found in the Thames at Battersea, or the bowl from Gundestrup in Denmark, or the gold torcs and other adornments found throughout the Celtic world, imply the existence of some much more distinguished craftsmen probably working under noble or royal patronage. Their productions are very beautiful, and quite different from anything found in the classical world. Both Greek and Roman art aim at representing things, and the further they develop the more faithfully they succeed in doing so – sometimes too faithfully for modern tastes. Even fabulous creatures such as the Minotaur and the Centaurs are portrayed in a realistic, almost matter-of-fact, manner. Celtic art, by contrast, makes even the real appear imaginary. Foreground merges into background; human, animal, plant and abstract forms merge into one another. Even with a classical original, Celtic artists changed it into something characteristic of themselves. Some British coins, for example, have a design based on a gold coin of Philip of Macedon; but as in the game where a sentence is whispered from person to person till it becomes unrecognizable, so the existence of a Greek original could never have been guessed from the final form of the British copy. The Celtic way of looking at things largely disappeared under Roman rule, and was replaced by a somewhat dull provincialism. It survived, however, in the remoter parts of the British Isles, and eventually produced some of its greatest masterpieces in the so-called 'Dark Ages'.

*

The Celts had a variety of different settlements, some of them very large. The simplest type, known as a 'ring-fort', consisted of a tract of level ground, usually circular, surrounded by a defensive enclosure. In Ireland, where ring-forts are especially common, the ones with stone walls are called 'cashels' while those with earthen banks are called 'raths'. Both words often appear in modern Irish place-names.

More impressive are the 'hill-forts', of similar design but set on high ground for extra defensive strength. These again can be classified as rocky or earthy, 'cashel-type' or 'rath-type'. A good example of the former is the city still called Cashel, the chief place of ancient Munster, which owed its early importance to the precipitous rock on which it

BRITISH ISLES
(4th century AD)

● Roman fort or fortified town

○ Non-Roman fort or fortified town

0   50   100   150 Kilometres

N

German Ocean

ORCADES
(Orkneys)

DUMNA
(Lewis)

(Burghead)

Tuesis (Spey)

SCITIS
(Skye)

CALEDONII

(Dunkeld)

MALAIUS
(Mull)

VERTURIONES
(Dunadd)

Tava (Tay)

(Dumbarton)

Bodotria (Forth)

(Edinburgh)   (Traprain Law)

Clota (Clyde)   (North Eildon)

SELGOVAE

VOTADINI

NOVANTAE

(Hadrian's Wall)

ULAID
(Ulster)

Ituna (Solway)

Luguvalium
(Carlisle)

CARVETII

Emain Macha
(Navan Rath)

BRIGANTES

Isurium
(Aldborough)

CONNACHTA
(Connaught)

MANAVIA
(Man)

(Downpatrick)

MIDE
(Meath)

*Buvinda
(Boyne)*

Irish Ocean

Eburacum
(York)

PARISI

Cruachain
(Rathcroghan)

MÔNA
(Anglesey)

Abus (Humber)

Senos (Shannon)

(Tara)

Eblana?
(Dublin)

Deva
(Chester)

CORITANI

Lindum
(Lincoln)

*Metaris
(Wash)*

Dun Aillinne
(Knockaulin)

Segontium
(Caernarvon)

Ratae
(Leicester)

ICENI

(Cashel)

LAIGIN
(Leinster)

ORDOVICES

Viroconium
(Wroxeter)

CATUVELLAUNI

Venta
(Caistor)

MUMU
(Munster)

Manapia?
(Wexford)

CORNOVII

TRINOVANTES

*Birgus
(Barrow)*

DEMETAE

Glevum
(Gloucester)

Corinium
(Cirencester)

Camulodunum
(Colchester)

Verulamium
(St Albans)

Moridunum
(Carmarthen)

Venta
(Caerwent)

SILURES

DOBUNNI

*Tamesis
(Thames)*

Londinium (London)

Sabrina (Severn)

ATREBATES

Venta
(Winchester)

Calleva
(Silchester)

CANTIACI

Durovernum
(Canterbury)

Isca
(Exeter)

DUROTRIGES

BELGAE

REGNI

Noviomagus
(Chichester)

(Boulogne)

DUMNONII

Durnovaria
(Dorchester)

VECTIS
(Wight)

British Ocean

stands. Edinburgh and Dumbarton developed in a similar way. Of the 'rath' type of hill-fort, with earth banks for defence, the two best-known examples are probably Tara in County Meath (the former seat of the High Kings of Ireland) and Maiden Castle in Dorset; but a glance at the Ordnance Survey's *Map of Southern Britain in the Iron Age* will show many others, all over the hillier parts of England and Wales.

Similar fortified sites can be found on the Continent. The chief place of the Aedui, Julius Caesar's allies, was a hill-fort called Bibracte (now Mont-Beuvray); his enemies the Arverni had a capital of similar type, called Gergovia (now Gergovie).[18] The crucial battle of the Gallic War, ending any possibility of Gallic independence, was fought in 52 BC round the hill-fort of Alesia (probably the Mont-Auxois, near Alise-Sainte-Reine).[19] Caesar on this occasion was both besieger and besieged, containing Vercingetorix within the fort and at the same time defending himself against a large Gallic army outside it. The walls of such places often had a more sophisticated construction than that generally found in Britain: it was known as the *murus Gallicus*, and consisted of a timber latticework with the spaces between the baulks filled up with stones. Caesar made a note of this type of defence while besieging the stronghold of Avaricum (Bourges); he remarks that the stonework protected the timber from fire, while the timber gave the stones reinforcement and stopped them from being knocked aside by the Roman battering-rams.[20]

Another kind of fortified Celtic site, often looking like a ring-fort cut in half, was the promontory-fort. These are numerous on the Irish coast, where they seem to symbolize the tragic side of Celtic history.

Aerial view of Hod Hill in Dorset, one of the largest Iron Age hill-forts in Britain. The small enclosure inside the large one is a Roman fort.

One seems to see the last defenders of the Celtic world turning to bay within them, at a Dunkirk with no friendly ships at hand; 'the barbarians drive us to the sea,' as Gildas wrote, 'and the sea drives us back to the barbarians'. In fact, however, the enemy against whom these works were built was not the foreign invader, but the rival tribe living a few miles away down the coast. Warfare, as already mentioned, was endemic within Celtic society.

For traces of yet another type of settlement we must visit a different type of landscape, the lowlands of eastern France, Belgium and south-east England. This was the country of the people collectively known as Belgae. Perhaps because of the terrain on which they lived, perhaps through an admixture of Germanic blood from further east, they seem to have had a more practical, a more earthy, one might almost say a more English character than the Celts of more westerly lands. They were good farmers, who worked assiduously at clearing the dense forest cover of the Lowlands, and may have developed a new type of plough heavier than that in general use elsewhere. They were formidable fighters, not only in pitched battle but also in making use of the terrain against their enemies. The Nervii, against whom Caesar fought in 57 BC, showed themselves adept in the European equivalent of jungle warfare, blocking the roads with thick thorny hedges and on one occasion concealing a complete army in a forest to surprise the Romans just as they were making camp.[21] This use of plant material for defensive works appeared also in the design of Belgic settlements. In Caesar's second British campaign (54 BC) we hear that his arch-enemy Cassivellaunus had a 'town' protected by forests and marshes: 'The Britons call it a town [*oppidum* in Latin] when they have fortified thickly wooded spots with a rampart and ditch'.[22] Archaeologists have borrowed the term from Caesar, and settlements of this kind are regularly known to them as *oppida*. The one attacked by Caesar was probably Wheathampstead, near St Albans; other places of the same type included St Albans itself, Colchester, Canterbury, Selsey Bill and Silchester (whose ancient name, Calleva, means 'town in the woods').[23]

The last kind of Celtic settlement to be considered here is the kind protected by water. Once again, these are exceptionally numerous in Ireland; the marshier parts of that country are full of artificial islands known as crannogs, some of which were used (against the English) as recently as the sixteenth century. By far the most successful example of a water-guarded Celtic settlement, however, is the city of Paris (known to the ancients as Lutetia, which means 'town in the mud'). The Celtic settlement here occupied the Ile de la Cité in the middle of the Seine; the Romans later built an extensive new town on the Left Bank, but during the third century AD this was abandoned again, and thereafter Paris remained within its old Celtic limits for a long time. Besançon, the capital of the Sequani in eastern France, was also defended by water, in this case the river Doubs which flows in a loop round three sides of the old town. At Strasbourg, which became a Roman legionary base under the Empire, the Romans may have been influenced in their choice by the defensibility of the pre-Roman site, surrounded as it was by many channels of the river Ill just above its junction with the Rhine. And Sisak, far to the east in what is now Yugoslavia, became an important pre-Roman and Roman stronghold for the same reason; it was surrounded on all sides by branches of the rivers Kulp and Save.[24]

*

Preoccupation with the impressive outer works of Celtic settlements has left investigators in some ignorance of the equally important question: what kind of buildings did the occupiers construct inside? This is understandable. The sheer size of some of these enclosures is daunting. Maiden Castle covers some 45 acres; Silchester, about 100; Mont-Beuvray, 330 acres, which makes it equal in extent to the Roman city of London. Moreover, archaeologists have naturally been reluctant to spend time and money looking for something that may not be there at all; for large tracts of the interiors would have been used as grazing for animals, not for human habitation. At Maiden Castle, a small part of the interior was excavated, and yielded traces of huts and pits scattered about with no clear pattern. Silchester was dug in the nineteenth century, by methods that would not be acceptable today, and little is known about the Celtic settlement that underlay the more imposing Roman city. Mont-Beuvray, however, yielded more interesting results. Though the street plan was highly irregular, there were signs that different sorts of worker had worked in different parts of the settlement; there was also an area that may have been the central market-place, analogous to the *forum* of a Roman town or the *agora* of a Greek one.[25]

But the most impressive of all Celtic settlements in this respect is Manching, on the upper Danube in what is now Bavaria. This town (for it can with justification be called a town, rather than a fort or overgrown village) was surrounded by a *murus Gallicus* enclosing over nine hundred acres, which makes it larger than any walled city built by the Romans in northern or western Europe; only late Roman Trier, at about seven hundred acres, even begins to approach such a figure. Naturally, only a small fraction of this huge area was built up; but that fraction was laid out in a formal and regular manner quite unlike anything that one commonly associates with the Celts. Within it lived workers in iron, bronze and gold, makers of jewelry, strikers of coins, potters and glass-manufacturers. Finds of amber, tin, porphyry and wine-jars indicate the range of trading contacts between Manching and the rest of the world.[26]

Though Celtic settlements on hilltops tended to go out of use under Roman rule, their defensive purpose being lost, many settlements in more accessible places survived the conquest to become flourishing cities of the Roman Empire. Manching, however, did not. There are signs that it was taken by force of arms, perhaps in the Roman campaign on the Danube in 15 BC, and thereafter it never revived. The surrounding area was established as the Roman province of Raetia, and its capital was not Manching but Augsburg, some distance further south. Manching fell into decay, its site marked only by a Roman fort called Vallatum, 'the walled place' – a last memory of a stronghold that lacked a Vercingetorix to defend it or a Caesar to record it.[27]

Places like this make us wonder what would have happened if the course of history had been a little different. Could Napoleon have won at Waterloo? and if so, what would have come about? Could the Celts, influenced rather than conquered by Rome (as they had already been influenced by the Greeks based at Marseilles) have developed a literate civilization of their own, with large cities, roads joining them, and a government linking the tribes into new and larger confederations? Could Welsh have become the predominant language of Europe? – and Gaelic, perhaps, the predominant language of North America? Or are we merely saying that if the Celts had been a different sort of people, and the Romans also, then the clash between the two would have turned out otherwise? This is a true remark, but hardly one to make a new contribution to the theory of history.

Furthermore, the Romans cannot be given all the blame for suppressing the Celtic way of life. It was to receive an even more serious blow from the people described in the next chapter.

CHAPTER TWO

THE GERMANS

... And that is called paying the Dane-geld;
But we've proved it again and again,
That if once you have paid him the Dane-geld
You never get rid of the Dane!

Dane-geld

The past two thousand years have witnessed, alongside the decline of the Celts, a corresponding increase in the importance of their old neighbours and enemies the Germans. From their original home in North Germany and Scandinavia, Germanic-speaking peoples overran the whole of the Western Roman Empire, crossed the Atlantic to discover a new world, played a large part in founding the Russian nation, and finally spread themselves into every part of the globe. English and German have become two of the most important languages in the history of human speech.

The origin of these Germanic peoples is a controversial subject, in which many authorities have deceived both themselves and others. Julius Caesar, the first writer to tell us anything in detail about them, creates a thoroughly disingenuous atmosphere at the start. Though he had conquered all Gaul and expelled various German tribes from it, his attempts to carry the war into the enemy's country east of the Rhine had led to nothing in particular. As a result he portrays the Germans as much fiercer, much more barbarous and much more different from their neighbours than was probably the case. The Rhine in his view formed a political, ethnic and cultural barrier: on one side of it lived the Gauls, on the other side the Germans, and there was no contact between the two save on the battlefield. Even if this situation ever existed it can only have been a short-lived one. Caesar himself states that in the past the Gauls had occupied large tracts of German territory, and other sources both written and archaeological amply confirm this. (After Caesar's time the situation was reversed: several German tribes eventually took up permanent quarters west of the Rhine in what had formerly been Gallic territory.) Moreover, some tribes of Gaul such as the Nervii and Treveri claimed to have some German blood, while conversely some German tribes such as the

THE GERMANS
(Late 2nd century AD)

- - - - Roman frontier
■ Legionary fortress
● Town

0   50   100   150 Kilometres

SUIONES
(Swedes)

SCANDIA

German
Ocean

GAUTAE
(Goths)

TEUTONI

CIMBRI

HARUDES

EUDOSES
(Jutes)

DAUCIONES
(Danes?)

Suebic Sea

HERULI

ANGLII
(Angles)

RUGII

Amisius
(Ems)

Visurgis
(Weser)

SAXONES
(Saxons)

VARINI

LEMOVII

GOTONES
(Goths)

Vistula
(Vistula)

FRISII
(Frisians)

CHAUCI

SUEBI
LANGOBARDI
(Lombards)

BURGUNDIONES
(Burgundians)

ANGRIVARII

AMSIVARII

Lake Flevo

CHAMAVI

CHERUSCI
(Teutoburger Forest, AD 9)

SUEBI
SEMNONES

Suebus or Viadua?
(Oder)

N

BATAVI

Vetera
(Xanten)

Albis
(Elbe)

BRUCTERI

Aduatuca
(Tongres)

UBII

Colonia Agrippinensis
(Cologne)

Mosa
(Meuse)

Bonna
(Bonn)

TENCTERI

USIPETES

CHATTI
(Hessians)

(Mt Zobten)

LUGII
(Vandals?)

SUDINI
(Sudetens)

TREVERI

Augusta
Treverorum
(Trier)

Mogontiacum
(Mainz)

Moenus
(Main)

MARCOMANNI

Marus
(Morava)

COTINI

QUADI

Mosella
(Moselle)

VANGIONES

Noviomagus
(Speyer)

Borbetomagus
(Worms)

HERMUNDURI
(Thuringians?)

Castra Regina
(Regensburg)

OSI

Rhenus
(Rhine)

NEMETES

NARISTI

Carnuntum
(Petronell)

Argentorate
(Strasbourg)

Danuvius (Danube)

Augusta Vindelicum
(Augsburg)

Lauriacum
(Lorch)

Vindobona
(Vienna)

Brigetio (Szony)

Vesontio
(Besançon)

Aenus
(Inn)

NORICUM

PANNONIA

Aquincum
(Budapest)

RAETIA

Juvavum
(Salzburg)

Augusta Raurica
(Augst)

Nemetes and Usipetes had names which were not German but Celtic. (*Nemetes* means 'nobles'; *Usipetes* means 'good horsemen'.)

The problem of distinguishing early Celts from early Germans is more difficult than might at first sight appear. If the Time Machine were in existence, it could be solved by sending a philologist back in time to listen to the conversation of the tribes concerned. Celts spoke Old Celtic, akin to modern Welsh; Germans of the Rhineland spoke Old West German, the ancestor not only of modern German but also of Dutch, Flemish, Frisian and English. The two types of language are distantly related, both being members of the great Indo-European family that includes nearly all the languages of Europe; but it would not have been difficult to tell them apart. In the absence of a Time Machine, however, linguistic studies are of little help, since both Celts and Germans were illiterate and all that we can work on is a fairly short list of proper names preserved for us by Greek and Roman writers. Nor are theories based on 'racial type' of any use. Celts and Germans were physically similar even in life, and certainly cannot be told apart by study of their skeletons. Nor, more surprisingly, do their other material remains provide a clear diagnosis. In the archaeological record one can recognize a culture in (say) Brittany which differs from that found in (say) Saxony or Thuringia, but the two merge into each other without any sharp dividing line along the Rhine or anywhere else.

*

The next writer to describe the Germans in detail, about 150 years after Caesar, is Tacitus; and here again it is necessary to read between the lines of what is written. But whereas Caesar's underlying theme is glory – for Rome in general and for himself in particular – Tacitus is biased the other way. He is the supreme historian of inglorious Rome, vicious Rome, the Rome of the wicked Emperors; his work inspired Gibbon and indirectly inspires numerous people in the film industry today. It was Tacitus who made the famous remark about his fellow-countrymen, *Solitudinem faciunt, pacem appellant* – 'they make a desert and call it peace'. This is put into the mouth of a Caledonian chief, addressing his men before leading them to disaster in the battle of Mons Graupius in AD 84.[1] But as idealized enemies of Rome the Britons were not exactly what Tacitus was seeking. In the southern part of the island, they were already learning the Roman way of life with indecent haste.

> The Britons were gradually led on to the amenities that make vice agreeable – arcades, baths and sumptuous banquets. They spoke of

such novelties as 'civilization', when really they were only a feature of enslavement.[2]

The Gauls were even worse. Once held up to the whole Mediterranean world as an example of fierce independence, they had taken to 'the amenities that make vice agreeable' almost immediately after their conquest by Caesar. By Tacitus' time, some of them had attained positions of the highest wealth and power at Rome itself. The mantle of the Noble Savage was now being correctly worn only on the farther side of the Rhine. In AD 9 the Germans had freed themselves from Roman rule, in the battle of the Teutoburger Forest; and thereafter they successfully resisted not only Roman arms but also, apparently, the whole process that now goes by the name of 'neo-colonialism'. We are told, for instance, that usury was unknown among them, and that only the tribes nearest the Roman frontier used money at all.[3] (Roman coins have in fact been found all over Germany; but they may have been valued for their own sake, as gold sovereigns and silver dollars are valued today, rather than passing from hand to hand as money must pass if it is to function as money.) Tacitus also tells us that Germans liked the old Roman coins best – though he omits to add the reason, which was that the weight and fineness of Roman silver coins had a distressing (and at length catastrophic) tendency to fall.

It is when he deals with sexual life and morals, however, that Tacitus is most obviously contrasting an ideal Germany with an all-too-real Rome. Young men in this virtuous land, he says,

are slow to mate, and their powers, therefore, are never exhausted. The girls, too, are not hurried into marriage. As old and full-grown as the men, they match their mates in age and strength, and the children reproduce the might of their parents.[4]

One thinks of the emperor Augustus, who tried to boost the falling birthrate of the Roman nobility by insisting that all its members should marry and produce children as soon as they were physically able; or of Claudius, whose fourth and last wife was his own niece. Marriage in Germany is for life:

Clandestine love-letters are unknown to men and women alike. Adultery in that populous nation is rare in the extreme, and punishment is summary and left to the husband . . . No one in Germany finds vice amusing, or calls it 'up-to-date' to debauch and be debauched . . . To restrict the number of children or to put to death any born after the heir is considered criminal. Good morality is more effective in Germany than good laws in some places that we know.[5]

Here it is the Empresses and noble ladies of Rome who are occupying the author's thoughts. As for sexual practices of a less straightforward kind, they receive even more summary treatment. In classical Greece male homosexuality was a normal feature of life. In Rome it was disapproved but not actively persecuted. In Gaul it was commonplace. But in Germany:

> The traitor and deserter are hanged on trees, the coward, the shirker and the unnaturally vicious are drowned in miry swamps under a cover of wattled hurdles. The distinction in the punishments implies that deeds of violence should be paid for in the full glare of publicity, but that deeds of shame should be suppressed.[6]

Tacitus' *Germania*, from which come all the above quotations, is one of the most valuable works on ancient anthropology that we possess; but it cannot, any more than Caesar's *Gallic War*, be read as if it were straightforward reporting.

*

Let us now consider the material remains of early German society, and the way in which archaeology sometimes complements and sometimes contradicts the evidence from written sources.

The greatest drawback of archaeology as a means for studying the past is the number of things that fail to survive. As a general rule, hard substances such as bone, stone, brick, pottery, glass and metal will be preserved, but flesh, wood, leather, cloth, basketry and paper will not. In many parts of northern Europe, however, the soil is acid and waterlogged; such conditions discourage the growth of bacteria, and thus preserve much that would normally have rotted away to nothing. It is possible to find timber foundations, boats, clothing and – most spectacular of all – complete human bodies deliberately buried in exactly the manner described by Tacitus. (It remains uncertain, however, whether this was done as a punishment for shameful crimes, as he states, or as a sacrifice to the 'Spirits of Place' comparable with the Celtic practice of casting human heads into rivers and springs.) The famous Tollund Man, excavated from a Danish bog in 1950, is the most distinguished member of a group numbering several hundred.

Combining the evidence from these bodies with that from Roman writings and inscriptions, we can say that the average German was similar in physique to the average Celt, a larger and more powerful man than the southerner. His hair was of lightish colour, and often worn shorter than that of the Celts. (Tollund Man's hair was cropped noticeably short – as a mark of degradation?) Some Germans were clean-shaven. From Tacitus again we learn that young men of the Chatti let their hair and beards grow until they had killed their first enemy, and that the Suebi grew their hair long and tied it into a knot (as was observed on a body found at Osterby in Schleswig).[7]

German clothing was simpler than Celtic. Some Germans wore only a cloak, others only a pair of trousers, whereas Celts normally had both. Women wore long dresses; the mini-skirt, popular in northern Europe in the Bronze Age, had gone out of fashion. Colours were generally plain, in contrast to the bright and sometimes garish hues favoured by the Celts. Ornamentation was also plain, though more from necessity than choice; at a later period, by which time they had taken over much of the Roman Empire, Germanic leaders combined Celtic, Roman and East European styles to produce some of the most magnificent jewelry ever made.

The Germans obtained their food in various ways. There was game to be hunted in the forests which then covered much of the land, and fish to be caught in the sea and the numerous rivers. Many animals were kept for eating. There was also agriculture, though Germans of the warrior class disdained it.

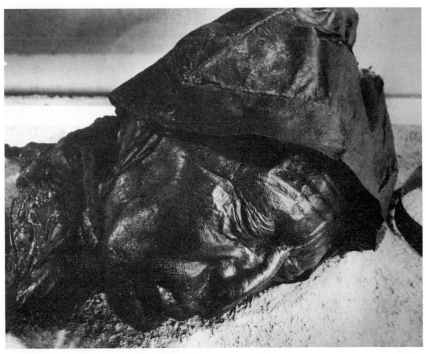

Head of Tollund Man.

> You will find it harder to persuade a German to plough the land and
> to await its annual produce with patience than to challenge a foe and
> to earn the prize of wounds. He thinks it spiritless and slack to gain
> by sweat what he can buy with blood.[8]

Tollund Man's last meal had been a depressing sort of gruel, made
from a mixture of wild and cultivated plants. No trace was found in it
of any kind of meat.

The same simplicity, whether primitive or merely impoverished, is
also found in German settlements.

> It is a well-known fact that the peoples of Germany never live in
> cities, and will not even have their houses set close together. They
> live apart, dotted here and there, where spring, plain or grove has
> taken their fancy.

Thus Tacitus; while Caesar notes that the same thing applied on a
larger scale, since each tribe liked to surround itself with a belt of
uninhabited territory.[9] The early Germans apparently resembled the
early Boers, who began to feel crowded if they could see a neighbour's
smoke on the horizon. Archaeology has shown that they did in fact
have groups of houses; but these settlements are very small and
primitive, not only by comparison with cities of the Roman world but

*German prisoners, on a
Roman monument at
Mainz.*

also when compared with the larger settlements of the Celts. The Germans built no Manchings or Maiden Castles; some of their villages were defended only by a simple palisade, others not at all. Only on rare occasions do we hear of anything bigger, as for example the capital built by king Maroboduus of the Marcomanni at about the time of Christ. This place, probably somewhere in Bohemia, became an important centre of Roman trade and may have looked more like a true town than most other German settlements. But it is not known exactly where it was, or by how long it outlived its founder.[10]

War as well as peace was conducted with simple equipment. Whereas the weapon most closely associated with the Celts was the long sword, that of the Germans was a kind of thrusting-spear known as a *framea* (vividly translated by Robert Graves in the *Claudius* books as 'assegai'). At times this amounted to no more than a sharpened stick without even a metal head. Swords did exist, but were confined to the richer and more important warriors in a tribe. The story of Siegfried and the sword Nothung gives an idea of the tremendous magic and prestige that such weapons must have possessed. Body-armour was also rare, the metallurgy of the early Germans being rudimentary. In fact, since a Roman legionary possessed a helmet, a mail coat, a shield, a sword, a dagger and two javelins, it becomes hard to see how his German enemies ever managed to win a battle at all; and it is true that their great victory in the Teutoburger Forest was mainly due to gross incompetence on the part of the Roman commander. As time went on, however, the Germans began to use more effective arms and armour, much of it at first probably bought or captured from the Romans. Eventually we find some of them using weapons peculiar to themselves – such as the *francisca*, a kind of throwing-axe used by the Franks on the lower Rhine, and the *sax* or *scramasax*, a dagger-like weapon favoured by the Saxons of the North Sea coast.

Most Germans fought on foot. A horse, even more than armour or a sword, was the mark of a nobleman; consider for example the German word *Ritter*, the French *chevalier* and the English *knight*, all implying a man riding figuratively as well as literally higher than his fellows. (The Romans had a similar word, *eques*; but the knightly tradition of the West, as exemplified by Charlemagne and Coeur-de-Lion and the Cid, owes far more to Germanic than to Latin sources. An *eques* of the Roman Empire did not have to be a warrior at all.) In Tacitus' time only a few of the Rhineland tribes, such as the Usipetes and Tencteri, had any cavalry worthy of the name. This was probably due to their close contact with the Gauls, who were generally richer than the Germans in material possessions and in particular made a greater use of horses. Later, at the other end of the German-speaking world, the

Goths learned the habit of riding from their neighbours in the country north of the Black Sea; among these people horsemanship was an integral part of life, as will be related in Chapter Three. The battle of Adrianople, in AD 378, has sometimes been presented as a victory of Gothic heavy cavalry over Roman heavy infantry – as ushering in, so to speak, the Age of the Knight which was to last throughout the Middle Ages till it perished in the mud of Crecy and Poitiers. But even on this occasion the Gothic infantry played a part at least equal in importance to that of the cavalry. And among some other tribes (the Anglo-Saxons included) the horse seems hardly to have been used at all.

*

The society which organized this kind of warfare was likewise a straightforward one, though it grew less straightforward as time went on. In Caesar's description, the life of the Germans is communistic: all land is held in common, and though we are told about councils of the leading men in a tribe there is hardly any indication of such men being richer or more powerful than their fellows. In wartime special leaders (at least two, and sometimes more) were elected, but their powers were strictly limited to the duration of the war. In peacetime the tribes managed themselves with a minimum of government of any kind.

Tacitus' description is more complex. In his time the elected war-leader still existed, but there were also rulers of a more monarchical kind, elected from a recognized royal family and holding power for life. A similar change had overtaken the Roman Republic somewhat earlier. Originally it had had its council of elders (the Senate) and its elected war-leaders (the Consuls); there were always two consuls, and they were not supposed to hold office for more than a year at a time, so as to prevent any one man from seizing supreme power and going back to the bad old days of the kings. The system, however, had broken down: whatever legal fictions might be invented to make the Empire look like a continuation of the Republic, the fact remained that in practice it was an absolute and usually hereditary monarchy.

These parallel developments in Rome and Germany may have had the same underlying cause, the increasing power of the armed forces and their leaders. The early Germans, like most tribal societies, had probably engaged in regular bouts of cattle-stealing and woman-stealing from their neighbours; but we also sometimes find the same game being played for higher stakes. As early as 105 BC two German tribes, the Cimbri and Teutoni from northern Denmark, destroyed a Roman army at Orange in the Rhône valley and went on to threaten Italy itself. Again, in 58 BC, Gaul was attacked by a group of tribes whose leader, Ariovistus, speaks more like an absolute monarch than any kind of elected representative. (However, since it is Julius Caesar who tells us what Ariovistus said, this may be a case of the pot calling the kettle black.)[11] The result of these and other raids was to create a new German upper class in the form of a body of men who lived entirely by fighting. When not fighting, in Tacitus' words,

> . . . they spend some little time in hunting, but more in idling, abandoned to sleep and gluttony . . . They love indolence, but they hate peace.[12]

These men would naturally be the best equipped members of the tribe, and each successful raid would make them better equipped still. The ordinary German with his simple wooden spear would have had no chance of joining such a warband.

As well as fighting the Romans, German tribes frequently fought each other. In AD 58, for example, the Hermunduri defeated the Chatti in a great battle, and afterwards sacrificed their beaten enemies to Tiw and Woden (or, as the Romans called them, Mars and Mercury).[13] Somewhat later a tribe called the Bructeri was almost annihilated by its neighbours in a battle where 60,000 men are said to have perished.[14] What became of the survivors is not recorded, but it is likely that they were enslaved, many of them perhaps ending life as slaves within the Roman Empire. For it has been plausibly suggested that the appearance of Roman power on Germany's borders had the same effect as the appearance of European traders in West Africa many centuries later; warfare ceased to be desultory and became a form of business, whose object was to take as many prisoners as possible and sell them to the foreign slavers.

Though the life of a German war-leader offered great scope for self-enrichment, it had also its precarious side. Apart from the obvious danger of stopping a Roman javelin, power-politics within a German tribe could be as complex and bloodthirsty as those of the Roman imperial court. Even the great Arminius, who saved his country in the battle of the Teutoburger Forest and holds a position in modern German hearts analogous to that of 'Boadicea' in Great Britain, was killed by his own relations for displaying too much kingly power. Maroboduus of the Marcomanni was deposed and exiled for the same reason, as were his successors Catualda and Vannius. Such internal strife was of course highly advantageous to Rome, whose settled policy was to keep all the German tribes and factions at loggerheads.

*

Early German and early Celtic religion had much in common, most notably an interest in sacred woods and springs. The tribes of Jutland worshipped a goddess called Nerthus (Mother Earth), whose statue was kept in a sacred grove on an island and never allowed to be seen.[15] The Semnones had a grove which no one could enter unless he was bound; and should he happen to fall over he had to roll out of the grove without rising to his feet again.[16] The wooded mountain known to modern Germans as Zobten and to Poles as Sobotka, in Silesia, was an important religious centre of the Vandal folk, and retained its import-ance well after the conversion of the region to Christianity.[17] And when Germanicus Caesar led his army through the Teutoburger Forest in AD 15, six years after the fateful battle there, this is what they found:

> On the open ground were whitening bones, scattered where men had fled, heaped up where they had stood and fought back. Frag-ments of spears and of horses' limbs lay there – also human heads, fastened to tree-trunks. In groves nearby were the outlandish altars at which the Germans had massacred the Roman colonels and senior company-commanders.[18]

The gods honoured in this unpleasant fashion are well known from later sources (the Icelandic sagas in particular), but they seem as time went on to have changed their attributes and relative importance, and we cannot be certain how much of the Icelandic material already existed in the time of Tacitus nearly a thousand years earlier. The principal German god was Woden, identified by the Romans with Mercury – somewhat oddly at first sight, since Woden is generally portrayed as an old man and Mercury as a young one. They had in common, however, a concern with the life of the mind, especially with the crafty, cunning, subtle side of human nature. The god Tiw, more straightforwardly, was equated with Mars: for though he had origi-nally been a sky-god (his name being related to *Zeus* in Greek) he had become specifically the god of battle. It was to him above all that the Germans sacrificed their enemies. Thor, or Thunor, was the storm-god, his hammer symbolizing the power of thunder and lightning; he thus resembled Jupiter, although the earlier Roman writers refer to him as Hercules. Frigg, like Nerthus and several other deities, was a goddess of fertility.

One consequence of this is still with us. When the seven-day week, originally a Babylonian institution, became current in the Latin-speaking part of the Roman Empire, its days were known as *dies Solis* (or *Domini* among Christians), *dies Lunae*, *dies Martis*, *dies Mercurii*, *dies Iovis*, *dies Veneris* and *dies Saturni* – the days respectively of the

Sun, the Moon, Mars, Mercury, Jupiter, Venus and Saturn. In modern English they have emerged as the days of the Sun, the Moon, Tiw, Woden, Thor, Frigg and Saturn, with four Roman deities replaced by their Germanic equivalents.

*

G. K. Chesterton once remarked that the great destiny of Empire was in four acts: 'Victory over barbarians. Employment of barbarians. Alliance with barbarians. Conquest by barbarians.' Although the speaker (in *The Flying Inn*) is an Irishman referring to the imminent conquest of the British Empire by Turks, the general principle has something to be said for it. Applied to the Roman Empire, it is certainly better than the popular picture which concentrates entirely on the first and last acts of the drama and omits the intervening two.

The first act, 'Victory over barbarians', was short as far as Germany was concerned. Even Julius Caesar, as we have seen, achieved little there. The emperor Augustus was at first more successful. A series of campaigns by his stepsons Tiberius and Drusus established Roman rule over most of the country between the rivers Rhine and Elbe. But this was ended by the disaster of AD 9, which almost lost to Rome the whole of Gaul as well as Germany. Between AD 14 and 16 Germanicus Caesar, the son of Drusus, covered some of the same ground as his father, but ran into a difficulty often found by those who fight an elusive enemy in thickly wooded country – that enormous forces are needed to produce a disproportionately small result. In the second half of the first century AD the emperors Vespasian and Domitian annexed some land between the upper Rhine and upper Danube, which was later enclosed with defences and given a flourishing Roman life; but its area was minute compared with Germany as a whole. The Roman army by this time was still able to paint the map red, but had abandoned the brush of the house-painter for that of the Academician.

'Employment of barbarians' was meanwhile well under way. The Roman Imperial Army possessed two main types of soldier: legionaries, who fought on foot in heavy armour, and auxiliaries, who could be light or heavy, cavalry, infantry or mixed. Recruits to the legions had to have Roman citizenship, which under the early Empire usually meant that they had to come from Italy or one of the more civilized provinces. Auxiliaries, however, could come from anywhere – on the whole, the wilder the better – and were rewarded with Roman citizenship on completion of their term of service. And the Germans, one of the finest fighting races in Europe, were soon allowed to set their feet upon this road to preferment. A strong but impoverished young German tribesman might well have given himself a better start in life by walking into the Roman recruiting-office at Cologne or Mainz than by trying to join a warband of his own tribe; the Romans, unlike the Bructeri or the Chatti, provided their recruits with equipment and regular pay. The emperor Caligula (the son of Germanicus Caesar, and thus only two generations removed from the great invasions of Germany under Augustus) had a German bodyguard. Doubtless he felt that a group of warriors speaking no Latin would have some immunity from involvement in the plots that repeatedly threatened his life. Much later, the Byzantine emperors were to use the Varangian Guard (also largely Germanic) with the same idea in mind.

The number of Germans in the regular army also increased. When Augustus fixed the frontier of the Empire on the Rhine, some of them were already on the Roman, or western, side of it, despite Caesar's efforts to keep them out, and became recognized citizens of the Empire. The Batavi at the mouth of the river were even granted a special privilege, common in the early days of the Republic but rare in Imperial times, of only contributing armed men to Rome instead of the standard tribute of money or goods. It was thus with an unusual sense of shock, as if their favourite dog had turned out to be a wolf, that the Romans received the news of a Batavian revolt (in AD 69, when civil war throughout the Empire was setting its subjects a thoroughly bad example). The moving spirit behind the revolt bore the purely Roman name of Julius Civilis: as with some more recent empires, the chief enemies of Rome were not utter backwoodsmen but people who had learned something of Roman civilization. The revolt was suppressed, but only after four Roman legions had disgraced themselves – a foretaste of what lay in the Empire's future.[19] Fifteen years later we hear of a smaller but grimmer example of German insubordination; a cohort of Usipetes murdered their Roman officers in Britain, then sailed round the island, becoming so starved on the way as to take up cannibalism, and finally landed on the North Sea coast of Germany, where they were at once taken prisoner and sold as slaves.[20] But other German cohorts gave the Roman army more faithful service.

'Alliance with barbarians', *pace* Chesterton, is not in itself a sign of weakness. From their very beginnings as a nation the Romans were constantly making alliances with others, and their skilful use of these did much to increase their power. And though the earlier alliances were mostly made with states superior to Rome in civilization, others were made with people who were undoubtedly 'barbarians'. Rome's alliance with the Numidian tribesmen, for example, helped her to acquire the province of Africa in 146 BC. Her alliance with the Aedui in what is now Burgundy proved invaluable to Caesar in his conquest of Gaul. The 'client' or tributary king was a recognized feature of the early Empire, examples ranging from Herod in Palestine to Cogidub-nus in Sussex. Among the Germans a tribe called the Ubii showed themselves unusually friendly to Rome, from Caesar's time onward; the chief place of this tribe, Cologne, was intended by Augustus to be the capital of his new province of Germany, and maintained its importance even though the province failed to materialize. The Her-munduri, whose territory marched with Rome's along the upper Danube, were also generally friendly; they were even allowed to cross the river and penetrate Roman territory as far as the city of Augsburg. Though it is not stated whether they received active Roman support in their war with the Chatti (page 31), the result of the war must have given the Romans much relief, since the Chatti were not only fiercely hostile but also the best disciplined and organized of the German tribes. And at a later period we hear of the emperor Domitian sending Roman troops to help the Lugii against the Marcomanni.[21]

In such alliances Rome was able to lead from strength. The time was to come, however, when she had to lead from weakness, something at which Romans were not good. (Greeks were better; this may be one reason why the western, Latin-speaking Empire fell while the devious Byzantines were able to carry on.) An early sign of Roman weakness appeared in the 170s AD, when all the Danubian tribes (including the once-friendly Hermunduri as well as the habitually hostile Marco-manni) rose against Rome. Some of them penetrated Italy itself, and besieged the city of Aquileia; they were defeated and expelled by Marcus Aurelius, but only with great difficulty.[22] Another German crisis occurred in AD 251, when the emperor Decius was killed by the Goths in the marshes of the lower Danube. Twenty years later the province of Dacia (roughly corresponding to modern Romania) had to be abandoned to them. This was not in itself especially serious, since Dacia was one of the last Roman provinces to be acquired and there had always been some doubt about the wisdom of holding it at all; but its loss to Germanic tribesmen clearly showed which way the wind was blowing.

A much stronger blast from the same direction came in the late fourth century AD. The pattern of Germanic settlement, having settled down somewhat since the confused migrations of the third century, was thrown into fresh disorder by the arrival of a new people – the Huns from the far east, regarded by Roman and German alike with dread and disgust. The Ostrogoths in the Black Sea country collapsed altogether, and for the next century had no existence except as vassals of the Huns. The Visigoths in Dacia asked and received permission to escape the menace by crossing the Danube into Roman territory. Soon, as might have been expected, a quarrel broke out between 'hosts' and 'guests'. At Adrianople in 378 the emperor Valens and his army perished at the hands of the Visigoths. Theodosius, the next emperor, brought the situation partly under control, but was not strong enough to push the invaders back beyond the river. Henceforth there was a large and independent-minded body of Germans within the Empire – a spanner that at any time might smash the works altogether.

The disaster at Adrianople leads us into the last act of the drama, 'Conquest by barbarians'. The events which inspired the work of Gibbon can hardly receive justice from a few paragraphs; three of them, however, seem to stand out particularly – the event which began the destruction of the Western Empire, the event which at the time had the greatest effect on human minds, and the event which may be taken as completing the melancholy process.

On the last day of AD 406 a mixed force of Suebi, Vandals and Alans crossed the frozen Rhine and overran Gaul. Now was revealed a terrible weakness of the Western Empire compared with the Eastern, brought about by the facts of geography. Gaul was the linchpin of the whole western system. It was the richest of the western provinces, both in agriculture and in industry; and the Rhineland, the first area to be overrun, was at this time probably the richest part of Gaul. Its excellent communications, moreover, meant that a hostile force there, like a well-placed queen on a chessboard, could exert a powerful influence in several directions. The years after 406 saw a steady Germanic advance from Gaul to Spain, and from Spain to North Africa, as if in some horrible parody of the Mad Hatter's Tea Party.

The Gothic sack of a single city in 410, however, had more impact on people's feelings than the sacking of a whole country four years earlier: for the city was Rome itself. In Gibbon's words: 'Eleven hundred and sixty-three years after the foundation of Rome, the Imperial city, which had subdued and civilized so considerable a part of mankind, was delivered to the licentious fury of the tribes of Germany and Scythia'. But as the same author points out, the damage done on this occasion was probably less than that of the Gallic sack in 390 BC or that of Charles V in 1527.[23] Our own times, moreover, have shown how speedily a city can rise from its ashes even when destroyed by powers greater than the ancient world could have imagined. Settlements may decay for many reasons, but armed violence is not so common a reason as one might have supposed. The Vandals, in North Africa, did more than the Goths to force Rome into decline, by the indirect method of cutting off the African corn-supply on which its citizens depended.

The last date in this grim sequence is AD 476, when the last Roman to reign (one cannot say 'rule') in Italy was quietly told to cease from doing so. By an odd irony he bore the name Romulus; history refers to him contemptuously as Romulus Augustulus, 'the Little Emperor'. The real ruler of Italy at the time, a North German chief named Odoacer, received *de jure* what he already held *de facto*, being confirmed as King of Italy and official ally of the eastern emperor Zeno. Roman rule in the west thus ended not with an explosion of violence, but in an atmosphere more suggestive of a takeover bid. The Germans had come to stay.

CHAPTER THREE

EASTERN EUROPE

There's never a law of God or man runs north of Fifty-Three.
Rhyme of the Three Sealers

What is now called European Russia was known to the ancient Greeks as Scythia and to the Romans as Sarmatia, after two tribal groups that at different times dominated it (though neither ever occupied the whole of it). An outstanding physical feature of this land is its division into two parts, along a line roughly following the fiftieth parallel of latitude. North of this line the natural landscape is forest, and the inhabitants on the whole have had a fairly settled and stable existence. South of the line forest gives way to grassland, the famous steppe-country, which reaches westward as far as Hungary and eastward as far as Mongolia. This was the land of the nomadic horsemen, succeeding one another in seemingly endless advance like the procession of kings in *Macbeth*. At the beginning of its recorded history the Scythians had made their appearance by superseding a mysterious people called the Cimmerians (from whom the Crimea takes its name). The Scythians in turn were to give place to the Sarmatians; then came Huns, Avars, Bulgars, Petchenegs, Cumans and finally Mongols, the most formidable of them all. Only in recent times, with the expansion of Russian power into Siberia, was this river of humanity dried up at its source.

*

Let us now consider the people of the forest zone, who being less mobile than the steppe-dwellers have a history somewhat easier to unravel. The most northerly of these, on the fringe of the known Ancient World, were the people known to modern linguists as the 'Finno-Ugrians'. They are represented today by two main groups, the Finns of Finland and Estonia and the Magyars (or 'Ugrians') of Hungary (or 'Ugria'); but there are also closely related peoples – Meryas, Mordvins, Cheremiss, Ostyaks and others – living in what is now the USSR.

The Magyars of Hungary did not enter that land until about the tenth century AD. The Finns of the far north were already well established there in ancient times, but not surprisingly receive only an

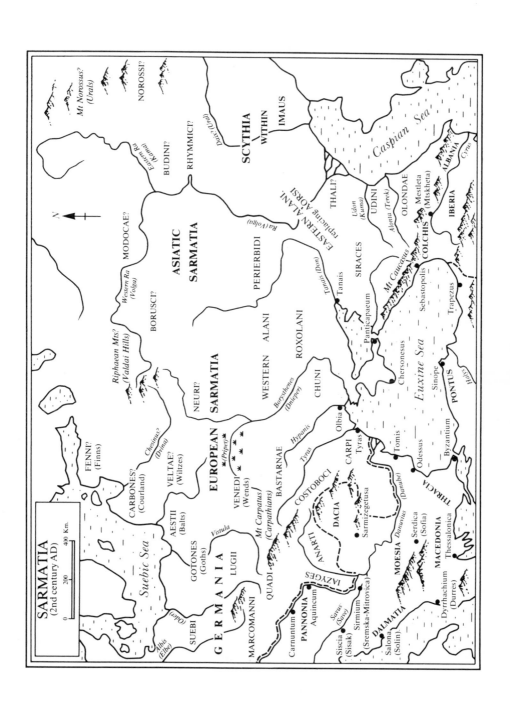

SARMATIA
(2nd century AD)

0 200 400 Km.

GERMANIA

MARCOMANNI
SUEBI
QUADI
LUGII
GOTONES (Goths)
AESTII (Balts)
CARBONES? (Courland)
FENNI? (Finns)
VELTAE? (Wiltzes)

Albis (Elbe)
Viadus (Oder)
Vistula
Chesinus? (Dvina)

Suebic Sea

EUROPEAN SARMATIA

VENEDI (Wends)
Mt Carpatus (Carpathians)
NEURI?
Mt [Pripet]
Riphaean Mts? (Valdai Hills)
BORUSCI?
MODOCAE?
BUDINI?
RHYMMICI?

Western Ra (Volga)
Eastern Ra (Kuma)

ASIATIC SARMATIA

PERIERBIDI

SCYTHIA WITHIN IMAUS

Dâix? (Ural)

Caspian Sea

WESTERN ALANI
ROXOLANI
CHUNI
BASTARNAE

Borysthenes (Dnieper)
Hypanis
Tyras
Tanais (Don)
Ra (Volga)

EASTERN ALANI, replacing AORSI

SIRACES
Tanais
Panticapaeum

THALI?
Udon (Kuma)
UDINI
Alonta (Terek)
OLONDAE
Mestleta (Mtskheta)
ALBANIA
Cyrus
IBERIA
COLCHIS
Sebastopolis
Mt Caucasus

Olbia
CARPI
Tyras
COSTOBOCI
Tomis
Odessus
Byzantium
Chersonesus
Sinope
PONTUS
Trapezus
Halys

Euxine Sea

ANARTI
IAZYGES
DACIA
Sarmizegetusa
Serdica (Sofia)
MOESIA
Danuvius (Danube)
THRACIA
MACEDONIA
Thessalonica

Carnuntum
Aquincum
PANNONIA
Siscia (Sisak)
Sirmium (Sremska-Mitrovica)
Savus (Save)
DALMATIA
Salona (Solin)
Dyrrhachium (Durres)

occasional mention in ancient writings. Herodotus, the 'Father of History' who has some claim to be also regarded as the 'Father of Geography', seems to mention them under the name of *Androphagi* – the Cannibals, or more precisely the Eaters of Men.[1] (Eaters of human beings regardless of sex would have been called *Anthropophagi*. Perhaps these early tribesmen, like some others in other parts of the world, believed that by eating a dead warrior they could take into themselves a part of his manly spirit.) The name of the Mordvins, preserved in a district called the Mordovian ASSR some three hundred miles south-east of Moscow, can be interpreted as meaning 'man-eaters'.

The first ancient writer to mention the Finns by their modern name is Tacitus. He does so in terms hardly more flattering than those of Herodotus:

> The Fenni are astonishingly wild and horribly poor. They have no arms, no horses, no homes. They eat grass, dress in skins, and sleep on the ground. Their only hope is in their arrows, which, for lack of iron, they tip with bone. The same hunt provides food for men and women alike; for the women go everywhere with the men and claim a share in securing the prey. The only way they can protect their babies against wild beasts or foul weather is to hide them under a makeshift network of branches . . .[2]

Some Finns have been so incensed at this description of their ancestors (which, it must be admitted, does not well agree with the archaeological record) as to claim that Tacitus was not referring to the Finns at all but to the Lapps, who are of related stock but live even further north. Probably, however, the historian was never aware of such a nice distinction.

During Tacitus' own lifetime, in the late first and early second centuries AD, some person or persons unknown, in circumstances also unknown, acquired new knowledge about the Finno-Ugrian peoples. We learn of this in an indirect way, by studying the treatment given to the Caspian Sea by different geographers at different times. Although Herodotus was wrong about the shape of this sea, he at least made clear that it was an *inland* sea, and gave an interesting account of the tribes living north and north-east of it (of which more will be said in Chapter Ten). Later, however, a belief grew up that the sea was really a bay, linked with the mysterious and largely hypothetical 'Northern Ocean'. This was the view taken, for example, by Pliny in the seventies AD. About eighty years later, on the other hand, Ptolemy gives us an entirely different picture. He still portrays the Caspian Sea with the wrong shape, but he has rightly surrounded it on all sides with dry land. More interesting still, he shows with very fair accuracy a large river flowing into its northern end – the river Volga, making its first appearance in written records under the name of Ra.[3] Somebody, sometime, must have explored the course of this river and made contact with the Finno-Ugrian tribes that lived along it. But unfortunately we are not told who he was or what he was trying to do.

Next to the Finns, along the shore of the sea that bears their name, lived the Balts. Two groups of them, the Latvians (or Letts) and the Lithuanians, live there still, though now incorporated into the USSR. A third group, the Old Prussians, was overwhelmed in the Middle Ages by the eastward advance of the Teutonic Knights; its land became an outpost of the Germanic world and its language disappeared by about 1700.

The people whom Herodotus calls Neuri, who were reputed to turn themselves into wolves, may have been Balts (though some authorities maintain them to have been Slavs). They lived somewhere on the upper Dnieper or one of its tributaries. The 'Baltic' Balts are first mentioned by Tacitus, under the name of Aestii; he praises their skill at growing crops, 'with a patience quite unusual among the lazy Germans'.[4] Of more general importance was that the land of the Aestii produced (and still does produce) most of the world's supply of amber. Beads of this substance made their apperance in Greece as early as 1500 BC, and were also exported to many other parts of the world. The Roman Empire, as usual, operated on a larger scale than anything done before. From Pliny, for example, we hear that in Nero's reign (AD 54–68) a Roman businessman visited the amber country and brought back enough amber to decorate all the equipment for a large gladiatorial show. The biggest piece obtained weighed thirteen pounds.[5]

Not only have the Balts maintained themselves for a long time in the same place, but they have been conservative in two other ways besides, in language and in religion. The Baltic languages belong to the Indo-European family, which includes most of the tongues of Europe (though not Hungarian, Estonian or Finnish, which as already mentioned belong to the Finno-Ugrian family). A characteristic of Indo-European languages is that they are inflected: that is, a word has a stem giving its fundamental meaning, to which are added endings giving its grammatical signification. In Latin, for example, the stem *ama-* conveys the idea of 'love': from this are derived not only the famous *amo*, *amas*, *amat* ('I love; you love; he, she or it loves') but also more complex words such as *amaverunt* ('they have loved'), *amandarum* ('of lovable women') or *amabiliter* ('lovingly'). In general, the older an Indo-European language is, the more of these inflexions it has. Classical Greek has more than Latin, and Sanskrit more still. Of all such languages, English has gone the furthest in dropping its inflexions. Lithuanian stands at the other extreme, having kept a remarkably full set, and is thus of the greatest interest to philologists interested in the origin and development of other members of the Indo-European group.

The historian of religion has likewise much to interest him in the Baltic states. They were almost the last part of Europe to be converted to Christianity; it has even been said, sarcastically but with only moderate exaggeration, that they had hardly become Catholic when it was time to think about becoming Protestant. All kinds of religious practice commonly associated with the ancient world – the worship of sacred groves and stones, the worship of fire, the cremation of great men with all their goods, and the setting up of animal heads in prominent places to ward off evil spirits – survived in Baltia quite openly until the thirteenth and fourteenth centuries AD, and in an undercover form for even longer. In the monkish chronicles describing them we seem to hear strange distant echoes of Strabo and Tacitus, saying much the same about Celts and Germans over a thousand years earlier.

By contrast with the stay-at-home Balts, the next group of people to be discussed has spread itself considerably since ancient times. The rise to power of the Germanic-speaking peoples in Western Europe has its counterpart in the rise of the Slavonic-speakers further east; and if the USA is a living monument to the former, then the USSR is to a still greater extent a monument to the latter.

The origin of the Slavs is as controversial and vexatious a question as the origin of the Germans, with the further difficulty that while the 'German Question' is plagued by contradictory evidence from ancient sources, the 'Slav Question' can hardly be illuminated by ancient evidence at all. Nineteenth-century German scholars, arguing mainly on linguistic grounds, maintained that the Slavs originated in the Great Pripet Marsh – an unprepossessing region, formed by the river Pripet before it joins the river Dnieper. To have one's origins in a marsh, however, seems almost as repugnant to common sense as to national pride; and twentieth-century Slavonic scholars have made repeated attempts to claim a larger and more interesting territory for their ancestors. A reasonably acceptable modern hypothesis is that the early Slavs occupied what is now the western Ukraine, between the present-day cities of Lvov and Kiev. On the north, the Great Pripet Marsh separated them from their kinsmen the Balts; on the south, the Carpathian mountains separated them from the Dacians, whose territory was for a time to be a province of the Roman Empire. To east and west, however, were no such convenient natural boundaries, and the early Slavs were influenced by peoples arriving from both these directions. From the east came the nomads of the steppe, the Scythians and Sarmatians, who may at times have exercised an overlordship upon the Slavs as the Mongols are known to have done later; it has indeed been suggested that Herodotus refers to the Slavs as 'Scythians', though distinguishing them from the main body of the Scythians – a nomadic people – by adding the epithet *Georgi*, which means 'farmers'.[5] From the north-west, Slavonic territory was under continual pressure from the early Germans. The course of the river Dniester (in the south-western USSR, near the frontier with Romania) was occupied in the time of the early Roman Empire by a large tribe called the Bastarnae, who may have been Germanic; later almost the whole of the Ukraine was conquered by the Goths, who certainly were; and annexation of the same rich area was an important target of the German high command during both World Wars.

The early Slavs, however, could gain territory as well as lose it. Pliny, for example, mentions a people called the Venedi, and seems to place them on the southern shore of the Baltic, well away from the putative original home of the Slavs. Tacitus describes them in more detail:

> The Venedi have borrowed largely from Sarmatian ways; their plundering forays take them over all that wooded and mountainous country that rises between the Peucini and the Fenni. Nevertheless they are to be classed as Germans, for they have settled houses, carry shields, and are fond of travelling – and travelling fast – on foot, in all these respects differing from the Sarmatians, who live in waggons or on horseback.[7]

The Peucini, according to Tacitus, were the same as the Bastarnae: his description of eastern Europe, if correct, would thus allow to the Venedi an enormous tract of country, reaching right across Russia from the frontier with Romania to the frontier with Finland. Ptolemy's account is less generous to the tribe (he limits them to the neighbourhood of the 'Venedic Gulf', probably the Gulf of Danzig), but he does dignify them with the status of a 'major' tribe, their neighbours the Goths and Finns being merely 'minor' ones. And these Venedi, or 'Wends' as they later came to be called, are generally regarded as a Slavonic people. Jordanes, writing in the sixth century AD, specifically states that the *Sclavini* (Slavs) were one of the two branches of the *Venedi* (the other branch being called the *Antes*).[8]

Soon after Jordanes' time the Slavs began to expand their influence, eventually achieving a predominance in Eastern Europe equal to that of their old enemies the Germans in the West. But whereas the German expansion is described in terms of blood and thunder, with Thor riding the whirlwind to bring battle and murder and sudden death, the Slavs moved more in the manner of snow – a flake here and a flake there, nothing very spectacular at first, until the whole land was covered with them. The 'Western Slavs' crossed the Vistula and entered a country that was almost uninhabited; its earlier, Germanic occupants had all gone to seek their fortunes within the Roman Empire. Two of the incoming tribes, the Poles and Czechs, were destined to found nations that survive to this day and still speak Slavonic languages. Other groups, such as the Wiltzes, Obotrites and Lusatians, are now known only to the specialist. The result of their activities, however, remains detectable on the map of Germany; across this country runs a line, roughly coinciding with the Iron Curtain, to the west of which the place-names are mostly Germanic, while to the east of it they are mostly Slavonic.

The 'Southern Slavs', meanwhile, were acquiring territory at the expense of the Byzantine Empire. In alliance with the Avars (a tribe of Central Asian origin, related to the Huns), they took the city of Sirmium (Sremska-Mitrovica, near Belgrade) in AD 582. Fifty years later they had overrun the whole Balkan peninsula, which they still dominate. The name *Yugoslavia* means 'Land of the Southern Slavs', and its neighbour Bulgaria is also Slavonic-speaking though it takes its name from a non-Slavonic tribe. Even the Greeks of today probably have more Slav blood in their veins than they would care to admit.

Though it was ultimately to produce the most spectacular results of all, the advance of the 'Eastern Slavs' was slow in starting – perhaps because it entailed going the wrong way down a one-way street, the movement of tribes across Europe having almost invariably been from east to west. By about AD 900 the Slavs had reached north-east from their original home about as far as the site of Moscow, driving a wedge between the Baltic and the Finno-Ugrian tribes; but like their ancestors they were exposed to repeated attacks by Germans on one side of them and steppe-dwellers (Mongols in particular) on the other. The Russia that we know today, ruled from Moscow or 'Muscovy', did not become important until the reign of Ivan III in the late fifteenth century.

In an earlier book (*Roman Roads of Europe*) I remarked that the clash between Gauls and Germans, first heard in Julius Caesar's time, has been ringing down the ages ever since. The conflict between Germans and Slavs has almost equally early beginnings and an even greater importance today. Though at one end of the story we have the seemingly aimless meanderings of obscure tribes with improbable names, at the other end we have an entire German army lost at

Stalingrad and the threat of still more terrible battles to come. Those who cannot remember the past, as Santayana said, are condemned to repeat it.

*

Whatever their potential for the future might be, in ancient times the Slavs, like the Balts and Finns, were an elusive and ill-documented folk. As with many forest-dwellers, we sometimes feel their presence or get a glimpse of them flitting among the trees, but cannot see them clearly in the round. The forefront of the East European stage was occupied by an entirely different and much more spectacular group of people – the nomads of the steppe, whose customs were so completely unlike those of the civilized world as to attract constant attention, and who repeatedly proved themselves a menace to that civilized world right across Eurasia.

As might have been expected of dwellers in a tract of country nearly five thousand miles long, the nomads varied widely in physical type and language. The Sarmatians, who dominated the Black Sea steppes in the time of the early Roman Empire, were of Iranian stock, akin to the Persians whose territory they often attacked. They were big men with distinguished features, often bearded, and probably with skin no darker than that of southern Europeans. The Cimmerians and Scythians, who had occupied the same region somewhat earlier and are described for us by writers in classical Greece, were also of Iranian stock. By contrast the Huns, who arrived on the scene towards the end of the fourth century AD, were Mongoloid – small of stature, with the yellow skin and slant eyes characteristic of the Far East, and regarded by ancient western writers as hideously ugly. Some of them were made to look even more peculiar by the custom of putting bindings round children's heads, thus deforming the skull and giving the impression of some horrible disease of the brain. Victims of the Huns in the Roman Empire described them as hardly human at all, more like wild beasts or demons. Later Mongoloid invaders of the West were regarded in the same way; the tribe correctly called Tatars, for example, came to be commonly known as 'Tartars' after Tartarus, the classical Hell, whence God had sent them to chastize the sins of Europe.

Despite such profound differences between various nomadic tribes, however, they all had a striking number of features in common, from the Cimmerians of about 800 BC to the Mongols of AD 1300 or even of today. The genus 'mounted nomad' is easily recognizable whether met in Europe, Asia or North America.

All steppe-dwellers were superb riders. Possession of a horse, among Celts and Germans the mark of a nobleman, was to the Sarmatians and

Huns practically the mark of a human being. On the rare occasions when Huns dismounted, they were observed to be so bandy-legged that they could hardly stand upright. The women could ride as well as the men; it was probably the female members of early tribes on the Black Sea steppe who launched the famous Greek legend of the Amazons. Objects too bulky to be carried on horseback (in particular the tents, usually made of felt, in which the nomads set up camp) travelled in waggons similar to the 'prairie schooners' with which the American West was won; even the method of disposing them in a circle for protection against attack was the same. The Sarmatians are often mentioned in Greek and Latin writings under the general name of *Hamaxobii* or *Hamaxoeci*, both of which terms mean 'waggon-dwellers'. It was this feature of their life that made the nomads such a difficulty and danger to the civilized lands on their southern flank. None of the usual techniques for dealing with a 'barbarian' enemy would work against them. They would not come to a pitched battle unless the odds were strongly in their favour; you could not force them to battle, for their army moved faster than yours; you could not even damage them by destroying their settlements, for they had none.

They had no agriculture, either. Given time and opportunity, they enjoyed hunting wild game on the steppe and in the forest which bordered it; but their chief source of food was the livestock which accompanied them, to provide the meat and milk that formed their staple diet. (To this day Chinese cooks, though able to make a delicious dish out of almost anything, reject cheese and other milk products, which they think fit only for 'northern barbarians'). The usual drink was mare's milk, sometimes fermented to produce what the Mongols called *koumiss*; but like all northerners the nomads drank wine with eagerness whenever they could get it.

To protect themselves from the intense cold of the Russian winter they wore many clothes, usually made of leather, felt or fur. Though unproductive in many ways, they can at least claim to have invented one vital institution of the modern world – trousers. These, essential if one is to ride a horse efficiently, found favour in Persia at an early date, but Greeks, Romans and Chinese alike all insisted that some form of robe-like garment was more dignified. Trousers, to them, were the unmistakable mark of a barbarian.

The principal weapon, used in hunting as well as in war, was the bow. This was not of English 'long-bow' type, which would have been far too unwieldy to use on horseback, but a more subtle 'composite' bow in which wood, horn and sinew were combined to produce a power almost equal to the longbow's for only about one-third of its length. A favourite tactic of Scythians, Huns, Turks and Mongols alike was to use their superior speed to keep always at some distance from the enemy, sometimes feigning retreat to lure him into a rash counter-attack, and all the time pouring into him a continuous stream of arrows. When Darius of Persia invaded their country in about 512 BC, the Scythians sent him the cryptic present of a bird, a mouse, a frog and five arrows. Darius was at first inclined to see these as a token of surrender, but one of his companions read the riddle aright: 'My friends', he said, 'unless you turn into birds and fly up in the air, or into mice and burrow under ground, or into frogs and jump into the lakes, you will never get home again, but stay here in this country, only to be shot by the Scythian arrows'. And that is what very nearly happened.[9]

Besides the bow, most nomads had some additional weapons. Daggers and short swords are often found in their graves, as are battle-axes. From Herodotus we learn that one extremely formidable

Scene from Trajan's Column, Rome: Roman cavalry attacking a force of armoured Sarmatians.

type of axe was called a *sagaris*, also that certain tribes added an extra touch of the Wild West to their appearance by being skilled with the lasso.[10] The most remarkable type of military equipment, however, was that used by some of the Sarmatians. Greek and Roman illustrations of them show a group of people who would hardly have looked out of place at the Battle of Hastings. Their heads, their bodies, their legs and their horses were all protected, apparently by leather armour with many small metal plates fastened to it. In fact, since the stirrup was not used, they were probably wearing as much armour as it was physically possible to wear. Their principal offensive weapon was the lance rather than the bow, while for close-quarters work they also carried tremendous two-handed swords. And a tomb at Kerch, in the Crimea, has yielded a wall-painting that seems to show two Sarmatian 'knights' engaged in single combat.[11] (But on the other hand the Sarmatians, like the Celts, practised the unchivalrous custom of head-hunting. They were fond of making their enemies' skulls into drinking-cups).

Again like the Celts, the Scythians and Sarmatians must have had some highly skilled workers in metal; for some of the gold-work found in their royal tombs has an impressive artistic style of its own. Animals were a favourite subject for portrayal – not so much the animals of the steppe, surprisingly, as those of the forest country further north, such as the stag, the boar, the bear and the wolf. The griffin, too, seems to have had a special significance. As well as often appearing in the art of the steppes, it is mentioned in an interesting passage of Herodotus.

> [Aristeas of Proconnesus] tells us that 'inspired by Phoebus' he journeyed to the country of the Issedones, and that beyond the Issedones live the one-eyed Arimaspians, and beyond them the griffins which guard the gold, and beyond the griffins the Hyperboreans, whose land comes down to the sea.[12]

It has been suggested that this refers to the gold of the Altai Mountains in Mongolia, and that Aristeas' 'Hyperboreans' were the Chinese under the Chou dynasty. More will be said of this in Chapter Ten; meanwhile, it is perhaps worth noting that not only was Phoebus, the sun-god, supposed to have a temple in the country of the Hyperboreans, but he was also regarded by alchemists as the special patron of gold.

In parts of Siberia the intense cold has the same happy consequences for archaeology as the waterlogging in the marshes of north-western Europe, described in the last chapter; all kinds of things that would normally have decayed are preserved as if in a vast deep-freeze. And the 'animal-style' of art is as prevalent on these perishable objects as on those made of metal. A carpet, probably made in Persia but clearly designed for the nomad market, depicts stags and griffins; masks representing the same two animals were found on the heads of sacrificed horses; and the body of a man had its arms and legs completely covered with animal tattoos. From other sources besides we know that when a great man of the steppe died he was regarded as going on a journey for which he needed suitable equipment and companions. Bodies were treated with preservative (as in Egypt, though less efficiently) and men and horses were strangled and fastened up on stakes around tombs, as if to serve as ghostly outriders.[13]

The religion of the steppe-dwellers, like that of the Greeks, had two sides, which may be called masculine and feminine, or *Yang* and *Yin*. On the masculine side the chief deity was the universal 'Skyfather'. To the Sarmatians he was also the sun-god; to the Mongols he was *Menke Koko Tengri*, 'the Eternal Blue Heaven'. The god of war, aptly enough,

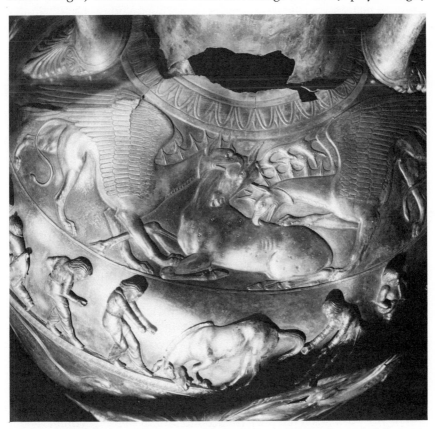

Griffins, on a vase found at Chertomlyk on the river Dnieper.

also received special attention, often in the form of a sword set upright in the ground. The Sarmatians, like the Persians, worshipped fire. But there were feminine beliefs alongside these masculine ones. Besides 'Skyfather' there was also 'Earthmother' who gave increase to the flocks and herds on which nomadic life depended; and the cult of the dead already mentioned, with animals as guides to the afterworld, also belonged to the *Yin* side of existence. Beliefs of this sort, collectively known as shamanism, were widespread in Siberia down to recent times.

Political life on the steppes, as in other parts of the non-civilized world, was based on the tribe – but with one special feature not found elsewhere. Western European tribes possessed a fair degree of permanence: some of them, such as the Cantiaci of Kent and the Parisii of Paris, have given their names to features that still appear on the map today. Tribal life on the steppes, by contrast, was always much more fluid. Repeatedly we hear of peoples gathering together, usually under the banner of some charismatic leader, and for a time sweeping all before them – only to disperse again, like a magic spell at midnight, when the centripetal force was removed. The great Hunnish empire of Attila, which ravaged northern Italy and at one time threatened to reach the Atlantic, outlived its founder by a mere two years. Genghis Khan was more fortunate; his descendants remained important in Russia, Persia and China for more than a century after his death. But even with the Mongol Empire, and still more with the nomadic tribal groups of ancient times, it is advisable to remember that we are dealing with an entity similar to the knife that had had three new blades and two new handles, and that a single tribe cannot be systematically traced through history any more than a single cloud can be systematically traced through a thunderstorm.

The recorded history of the Russian steppes, like that of many other parts of Europe, begins with the Greek colonization of their shores. Byzantium, the gateway to the Black Sea, is supposed to have been founded in 660 BC, and at about the same time other Greek cities began to develop further north. The river Danube, known to the Greeks as the Istros, gave its name to the town of Istros near its mouth in what is now Romania. Further north still, Tyras took its name from the river Tyras, the modern Dniester. Northward again was Olbia, 'the prosperous one'; it occupied a commanding position at the mouth of the large river Bug, with easy access to the even larger Dnieper. Herodotus, who visited Olbia, had high praise for this:

> The Borysthenes [Dnieper], the second largest of the Scythian rivers, is in my opinion the most valuable and productive not only of the

THE BLACK SEA
COUNTRY
(2nd century AD)

- - - - Roman frontier
■ Legionary fortress
● Town

0   100   200 Kilometres

(Future site
of Moscow)

(Moscow river)

ALANI
(Alans)

PERIERBIDI

(Pripet)

(Future site
of Kiev)

Borysthenes (Dnieper)

Tanais (Don)

OPHLONES

BASTARNAE

Hypanis
(Bug)

CHUNI
(Huns ??)

ROXOLANI

(Donetz)

DACIA

Hierasus (Sireti)

Tyras (Dniester)

TYRAGETAE

AXIACAE
Olbia
(Sto Mohil)

Taphrae
(Perekop)

AGARI

Tanais
(Nedvigovka)

TANAITAE

CARPI

Tyras
(Belgorod)

TAURI

Neapolis

Lake Maeotis

Panticapaeum
(Kerch)

MAEOTAE

Phanagoria
(Sennaya)

SIRACES

Anticites
(Kuban)

Troesmis
(Iglitza)

Istros
(Caranasuf)

Durostorum
(Silistra)

Tomis
(Constanza)

(Danube)

Chersonesus
(Sebastopol)

Theodosia
(Theodosia)

SINDI

Mt Caucasus

Odessus
(Varna)

Euxine Sea

Sebastopolis
(Sukhumi)

COLCHIS

THRACIA

Byzantium

Heraclea
(Eregli)

Amastris
(Amasra)

Halys

Sinope
(Sinop)

Amisus
(Samsun)

Trapezus
(Trebizond)

Phasis
(Poti)

Phasis
(Rion)

HENIOCHI

Acampis
(Coruh)

Nicomedia (Izmit)

Nicaea (Iznik)

Cerasus
(Giresun)

PONTVS

ARMENIA

BITHYNIA

Ancyra
(Ankara)

Amasia
(Amasya)

Sebastia (Sivas)

N

rivers in this part of the world, but anywhere else, with the sole exception of the Nile with which none can be compared. It provides the finest and most abundant pasture, by far the richest supply of the best sorts of fish, and the most excellent water for drinking – clear and bright, whereas that of other rivers in the vicinity is turbid; no better crops grow anywhere than along its banks, and where grain is not sown the grass is the most luxuriant in the world.[14]

In the Crimea two cities were outstanding, one on each side. On the west, near modern Sebastopol, stood Chersonesus, 'the peninsular city'. (It should be noted that modern Russian place-names ever hardly match the ancient ones – ancient and modern Theodosia do stand on the same site, but modern Sebastopol is not the same place as ancient Sebastopolis, nor modern Odessa the same as ancient Odessus, nor yet modern Kherson the same as ancient Chersonesus.) The chief city on the eastern side of the Crimea was Panticapaeum (still important today under the name of Kerch). To ancient geographers it had a special significance, because of its position on the strait known as the 'Cimmerian Bosporus' – an exact match to the position of Byzantium on the better-known 'Thracian Bosporus'. Both straits were regarded as separating Europe from Asia, and given a greater importance than they really deserved. Though Panticapaeum lacked access to a great river such as the Dnieper, it possessed equally good fishing-grounds in the Sea of Azov (the ancient *Maeotis Palus*) immediately north of the Cimmerian Bosporus. Even today this water is far richer in fish than either the Black Sea or the Mediterranean; there are indications, indeed, that parts of these had already been over-fished in the days of classical Greece. Fishing must also have been an important industry for the town of Tanais, at the mouth of the river Tanais (Don). This had the distinction of being the most northerly Greek-speaking settlement in the world, also the coldest and the most isolated; the Maeotis regularly freezes in winter.

Though these ice-bound northern settlements might at first sight seem to have had no great importance for the sunnier world of classical Greece, they were in fact as important as bread and butter, or at least (since the Greeks did not eat butter) as important as bread and kippers. Mainland Greece, though not as bleak in ancient times as it is today, has always been a barren land whose small pockets of fertile ground have suffered from chronic overpopulation; it was this that had caused the classical Greeks to found colonies in the first place. And the outposts on the Black Sea, with their wealth of agriculture and fisheries, were at times essential to the economy of the Greek homeland.

The history of these regions, as already mentioned, begins with the writings of Herodotus. In his day most of the country north of the Black Sea was occupied by Scythians; they seem to have been organized in the manner of a Mongol khanate, the ruling branch being distinguished by the epithet *basileis* or 'royal'. North of the Scythians lived other tribes, of different origin and somewhat hard to identify – the Neuri (Balts?), the Androphagi (Mordvins?), and the Budini (Permians?) who had the nasty habit of eating lice. Further east, beyond the river Don, lived the Sauromatae, with customs similar to those of the Scythians except that they gave a higher position to women. To explain this there was a tradition that they were descended from Scythian fathers and Amazon mothers.

> The women of the Sauromatae have kept to their old ways, riding to the hunt sometimes with, sometimes without, their menfolk, taking part in war and wearing the same sort of clothes as men. The language of these people is the Scythian, but it has always been a corrupt form of it because the Amazons were never able to learn to speak it properly.[15]

For some time after Herodotus the historians give us only a few scattered references to events on the steppe. In about 350 BC, it is thought, the Sauromatae began to cross the Don and put pressure on the Scythians. Two centuries later they had completely superseded them as the dominant power north of the Black Sea; the 'Scythia' of Herodotus became the 'Sarmatia' of writers in the Roman period. In the light of what has already been said, we should see this as a stirring-up and mingling of peoples, rather than the physical extermination of one people by another; a change at the top of society, rather than through it as a whole. Some Scythians, moreover, were able to preserve their identity from the Sarmatian takeover. One such group emigrated to the Dobruja, the land south of the mouths of the Danube; Pliny mentions them here under the name of *Scythae Aroteres*, 'the Scythian Ploughmen',[16] and under the late Roman Empire their territory formed the province of Scythia Minor. Another group of Scythians entered the Crimea and similarly took to an agricultural life. They even built themselves a capital (Neapolis, near modern Simferopol) which was no mere collection of huts but a true city in the Greek style, with a massive stone defensive wall and many stone buildings.

The conflict between Scythians and Sarmatians brought hard times for many of the Greek cities in their neighbourhood. An inscription from Olbia shows the city being threatened by Celtic, Germanic and Scytho-Sarmatian tribes, and on occasions having to pay them large sums of money.[19] The Olbiopolites were to have various ups and downs in the years ahead, but never again were they to enjoy the prosperity they had known in Herodotus' time. At Chersonesus the inhabitants seem to have played off one tribe against another, anticipating in miniature the policy of the late Roman Empire. Such a game, however, needs at least two pieces other than one's own; and the powerful Scythian kingdom, immediately next to Chersonesan territory, must usually have dominated the board. Panticapaeum was in the strongest position: whereas the other coastal cities operated as individual units, this one had fairly early in its history become the capital of a hereditary monarchy which controlled many smaller communities on both sides of the Cimmerian Bosporus.

This Bosporan kingdom was indirectly responsible for bringing Roman influence into the Black Sea. In about 110 BC the Bosporans, looking for a strong ruler to help them against the surrounding tribesmen, called upon Mithradates VI of Pontus, who ruled most of what is now the northern coast of Turkey. At the height of his power this vigorous king controlled an enormous horseshoe of lands reaching nearly two-thirds of the way round the Black Sea; only its south-west corner, by Byzantium, was denied to him. But he fell foul of the Roman Republic, was defeated (though only after a prolonged struggle) and finally, in 63 BC, was killed by his own orders in his northern capital of Panticapaeum.

Rome already possessed part of Turkey's northern shore in the province of Bithynia, bequeathed to her by its last king in 74 BC. The fall of Mithradates gave her some more of it, the name of the province being changed to Bithynia-et-Pontus. Further territories were added later; the Roman frontier on the European side of the Black Sea came to be marked by the river Danube, on the Asian side by a river called the Acampsis (the modern Çoruh, on the frontier between Turkey and the USSR). The northern side of the Black Sea remained outside Roman direct rule (the Bosporan kingdom, for example, kept its own monarchs down to the mid-fourth century AD) but the indirect influence of the Empire was all-pervading. The Jewish historian Josephus, describing the armed forces of Rome in the sixties AD, remarks:

> Need I mention the Heniochi, the Colchians, and the Tauric race, the peoples near the Bosporus, the Black Sea, and the Sea of Azov? At one time they recognized not even a native ruler, and now they submit to 3000 legionaries, while forty warships keep peace on the sea where before none but pirates sailed.[18]

The Heniochi lived on the south-eastern shore of the sea; the Colchians at its extreme eastern end, in the fabled land of the Golden

Fleece; the 'Tauric race' in the Crimea, often known to the ancients as the 'Tauric Peninsula'. Inscriptions confirm the presence of Roman garrisons at Olbia, Chersonesus, Charax (Ai-Todor, near Yalta) and sometimes at Panticapaeum itself.

The Sarmatians meanwhile had been expanding their own power. The spearhead of their advance was a tribe called the Iazyges. In the seventies BC these people had had their first clash with Rome, fighting in alliance with Mithradates. By the beginning of the Christian era they had reached the mouths of the Danube; here they encountered the poet Ovid, who had offended the emperor Augustus with his licentious poem, *The Art of Love*, and been banished to the Black Sea port of Tomis – the nearest equivalent to Siberia that the Empire at this time possessed. He paints a vivid picture of the 'Sauromatae', with icicles hanging from their beards, crossing the frozen Danube to plunder.[19]

Not long afterwards, probably in the twenties AD, the Iazyges moved still further west, to occupy what is now called the Great Plain of Hungary, the last westernmost outlier of the Eurasian steppe belt before it gives way to the wooded and hilly country of Austria and Slovakia. Their former place on the lower Danube was taken by another Sarmatian tribe, the Roxolani. Rome was thus confronted along the river by a formidable set of potential enemies: Germans on its upper course, then Iazyges, then Dacians in the mountains of Transylvania, and finally Roxolani. Each group, moreover, could contribute something different to an anti-Roman coalition. The Germans had perhaps the greatest physical courage and *furor barbaricus*, the Dacians had the greatest political cohesion, while one weakness of these two forest-dwelling peoples, lack of cavalry, was amply repaired by the light horsemen of the Iazyges and the heavily-armoured 'knights' (page 48) which were a speciality of the Roxolani. Whereas in the early first century AD there was a general feeling that the Rhine was the most dangerous frontier of the Empire, from about AD 80 onwards attention (and military garrisons) shifted steadily away from the Rhine and towards the Danube. The emperors Domitian (AD 81 –96), Trajan (98–117) and Marcus Aurelius (161–180) all had to fight Danubian wars; the two last set up columns at Rome in honour of their victories, and these give us a valuable record of the Sarmatians' appearance and mode of fighting.

So great was the spread of Sarmatian power at this time that some branches of the same people became involved with Rome in Asia, at the other end of her Empire. On the river Kuban, to the east of the Bosporan kingdom, lived a people called the Siraces. They were less purely nomadic than most Sarmatians; they knew something of agriculture and possessed some settlements (Tacitus mentions the name of one of these, Uspe, which was captured by the Romans in AD 49).[20] But this did not prevent the Siraces from going on plundering expeditions northward to the river Don and southward over the Caucasus.

North of them lived a larger tribe, the Aorsi, who had also taken part in the campaign of AD 49, but on the Roman side. Soon afterwards, however, they disappeared from the records. The reason is given by a Chinese source: 'the kingdom of the Yen-ts'ai', it writes, 'has changed its name to A-lan'.[21] That is to say, in European terms, that the tribe of the Aorsi had been taken over by the tribe of the Alans; that some anonymous precursor of Attila and Genghis Khan had shaken the kaleidoscope of nomad politics into a new pattern. Like the Siraces and Aorsi, the Alans were to make repeated crossings of the Caucasus, harassing Persian and Roman Empires alike. The writer Arrian, best known for his life of Alexander the Great, had to contend with them in Cappadocia during Hadrian's reign; he defeated them, and wrote a book explaining how he did it.[22] But for some time longer the Alans remained the dominant power in south Russia, the 'master-tribe', like the Royal Scythians before them, to which lesser tribes had to pay homage.

*

Success in the steppe-lands is fleeting. All the Sarmatian peoples – Iazyges and Roxolani, Siraces and Aorsi, Alans and many smaller ones – were to vanish almost without trace from the world, and the name 'Sarmatia' to become as obsolete as the name 'Scythia'. All this was to happen, too, in a remarkably short time.

The first blow to Sarmatian power came in about AD 200. The Goths, a Germanic people, migrated from their earlier home on the lower Vistula and came down to the Black Sea with devastating results. Olbia was sacked, the Scythian and Bosporan kingdoms overrun, the Alans dispersed. Some of them stayed on as subjects of the new Gothic kingdom; others moved south-eastward, into the Caucasus; others again moved westward, in which direction the Goths very soon followed them.

The final blow, however, came from the east. Like some enormous wave that seems to gather up lesser waves in its path for a mighty assault on the land (and then breaks, leaving behind nothing but flotsam and jetsam), so in AD 375 did the Huns fall upon an unsuspecting Europe. Alans and Slavs, Goths and Vandals, the remnants of the Roxolani and Iazyges – all were swept along by them, as unwilling allies or terrified refugees. Attila, their greatest leader, called himself 'King of the Huns, Goths, Medes and Danes' and even claimed to rule islands in the northern Ocean;[23] on one occasion his armies reached as far as Orléans, only 200 miles from the Atlantic and more than 3000 from the putative original home of the Huns near the Great Wall of China. But in AD 453 he died, and the wave broke. The Huns were never again a power in the land, and the Sarmatians even less so. The steppe-dwellers ceased to be a menace to civilization, and became once more merely a nuisance.

CHAPTER FOUR

AFRICA

Then Kolokolo Bird said with a mournful cry, 'Go to the banks of the great grey-green, greasy Limpopo River, all set about with fever-trees, and find out'.

Just So Stories

Communications in Africa are generally difficult, and throughout its history ideas and techniques have taken a long time to spread. Even the Egyptians, contrary to popular belief, were slow starters in the race to civilization, not taking up agriculture till after it was established all over the Near East, in Greece and in parts of Central Europe. And though they afterwards made a 'Great Leap Forward' (being able to build the Great Pyramid by about 2500 BC) very little of this new-found civilization rubbed off on their western and southern neighbours. The Phoenicians (starting as early as 1000 BC according to tradition – in fact probably much later) planted a string of colonies along the North African coast; but for most of the time these turned their faces to the sea and their backs to the land. Life in the interior continued much as before. The Romans advanced inland with more vigour and effectiveness; but even their best efforts, when drawn on the map of Africa as a whole, make up little more than a decorative red edging to a very large white tablecloth.

The main cause of this slow communication was of course the Sahara Desert. Though at one time this was grassland, as we know by finding rock-carvings of wild animals and their hunters in the middle of it, these remains date from the prehistoric period, probably about 5000 BC. The desert explored by Phoenicians, Greeks and Romans is thought to have been about as arid as it is today. There are four main ways of traversing the Sahara to reach the more fertile land on its further side – by sea, along the west coast; by land, through the desert itself; by land and water, up the Nile; or by sea again, along the east coast. All four routes were used by the ancients, with varying degrees of success.

*

In exploring the west coast of Africa, as in exploring the Nether Regions, the difficulty lies not so much in the setting out as in the

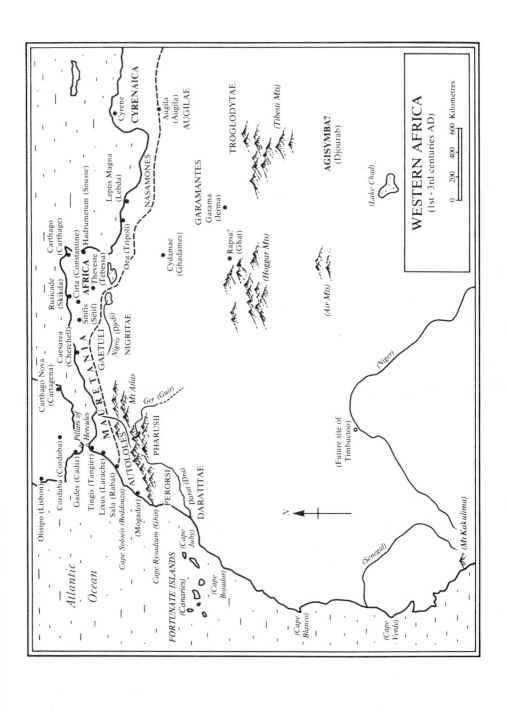

WESTERN AFRICA
(1st - 3rd centuries AD)

0   200   400   600 Kilometres

Atlantic

Ocean

Olisipo (Lisbon)

Corduba (Cordoba)

Gades (Cadiz)
Pillars of
Hercules
Tingis (Tangier)
Lixus (Larache)
Sala (Rabat)
(Mogador)
Cape Soloeis (Beddouza)

Cape Rysadium (Ghir)

FORTUNATE ISLANDS
(Canaries)

Cape
Juby)

(Cape
Bojador)

(Cape
Blanco)

(Cape
Verde)

Carthago Nova
(Cartagena)

Caesarea
(Cherchell)

M A U R E T A N I A

Mt Atlas

AUTOLOLES

PHARUSII

PERORSI

Darat (Dra)

DARATITAE

Ger (Guir)

(Senegal)

(Mt Kakulima)

N

Rusicade
(Skikda)
Carthago
(Carthage)
Cirta (Constantine)
AFRICA
Sitifis   Theveste
(Sétif) (Tebessa)
GAETULI
Nigris (Djedi)
NIGRITAE

Cyrene
CYRENAICA

Augila
(Augila)
AUGILAE

Hadrumetum (Sousse)

NASAMONES

Leptis Magna
(Lebda)

Oea (Tripoli)

Cydamae
(Ghadames)

GARAMANTES

Garama
(Jerma)

Rapsa?
(Ghat)

(Hoggar Mts)

(Air Mts)

TROGLODYTAE

(Tibesti Mts)

AGISYMBA?
(Djourab)

(Lake Chad)

(Niger)

(Future site of
Timbuctoo)

(Niger)

returning. The prevailing wind along this coast is the famous North-East Trade Wind, blowing fairly continuously in the same direction, and supported by an offshoot of the Gulf Stream called the Canaries Current. The ancient world had two types of ship, neither of them well suited to voyages in such conditions. The round ship, used for cargo, was a tub-like vessel normally equipped with only one mast, one yard and one large square sail, and thus incompetent at beating against the wind. The long ship or galley, used mainly in battle, had the advantage of being oar-driven and independent of the wind, but also had two grave disadvantages: its long narrow shape and low freeboard made it liable to suffer in bad weather, and it was extremely tiring to work. (Slaves were not used in ancient galleys nearly as often as is generally supposed; moreover, even slaves have to eat, and a galley had very little space in which to store their food for a long voyage.) It would be unwise on such theoretical grounds alone to say that a long-range expedition round West Africa was impossible in ancient times, for someone may yet prove it possible by making it; but it is worth noting that even Thor Heyerdahl, that famous maker of 'impossible' voyages, has always travelled with the prevailing winds and currents, never against them.

On the whole, moreover, records of what was done in West Africa confirm the theoretical analysis of what was possible. Most ancient explorers seem not to have gone beyond Cape Juby, opposite the Canary Islands and near the southern boundary of modern Morocco. Arab ships of the Middle Ages, though equipped with the lateen sail which is handier to windward than the square rig, did little better; the usual mediaeval limit to navigation was Cape Bojador, only about 170 miles south of Cape Juby. When the Portuguese finally broke the barrier of Bojador in the fifteenth century, they did so by never trying to return the way they had come; instead they used to swing away to the west, sometimes as far as Brazil, to catch a wind that would bring them back to Portugal. And their ships were better rigged and more seaworthy than those of the Ancient World.

One ancient document, however, describes an expedition that may have gone far beyond the boundaries of Morocco. Its leader was a Carthaginian called Hanno: his original account of what he did has (like almost everything else connected with ancient Carthage) utterly perished, but a Greek translation survives. The gist of it is as follows. At an uncertain date (round about 500 BC?) Hanno set off with sixty galleys and 30,000 people (an unlikely start to the story, unless he had sailing-ships with him as well; no galley at this time could have carried 500 people). He was commissioned to found colonies on the Atlantic coast of Africa, which he did, the most southerly of these being on an island called Cerne. Instead of then returning home, however, he ventured still further south, apparently exploring the land in search of pure knowledge – a rarish event in ancient history. On this further voyage he reached a bay . . .

> which according to the interpreters was called the West Horn. In it lay a large island, and in the island a marine lake containing another island. Landing on the smaller island, we could see nothing but forest, and by night many fires being kindled, and we heard the noise of pipes and cymbals and a din of tom-toms and the shouts of a multitude. We were seized with fear, and our interpreters told us to leave the island.[1]

But they still went on, and passed a very high mountain which the Greek text calls *Theon Ochema* – usually, though perhaps incorrectly, translated as 'Chariot of the Gods'. A great flame shot up from its centre, and covered all the land around with fire. Last of all came another island, with the same configuration as the previous one – a lake in it, and in that lake a smaller island. This time Hanno's men not only saw but captured some of the local inhabitants, hairy people whom the interpreters called *Gorillae*. (This is the first recorded mention of a word now familiar in many languages.) The account concludes abruptly: 'This was the end of our journey, owing to lack of provisions'. No mention is made of any difficulties on the way back.

The story of Hanno has had a profound influence on modern as well as ancient writers, on poets and story-tellers as well as geographers. But what, if anything, it means is very hard to interpret. There have been three main schools of thought about it, distinguished mainly by their attitude to the high burning mountain called the 'Chariot of the Gods'. What one might call the 'long-distance' school would identify this with Mount Cameroon, which as an active volcano more than 13,000 feet high is eminently suited for the part. But so long a voyage is hardly possible in the time given by the account; it would have involved leaving the belt of Trade Winds for a region that often has no wind at all, not to mention passing the dreaded Bight of Benin where 'one comes out when forty go in'. The more modest 'middle-distance' school of thought generally identifies the mountain with Mount Kakulima in Sierra Leone, postulating a large grass-fire to explain the flames seen by Hanno's party.

It is possible, however, to take an altogether more destructive attitude to the text. The 'short-distance' or 'no-distance' school main-tains that it is a forgery, not translated from the Carthaginian language at all, but made up by some unknown ancient Greek out of odd snippets of knowledge mixed with legend. (If so, it has a claim to be the most successful forgery in existence, having deceived layman and scholar alike for some 2400 years.) There are several points about the narrative that do not inspire confidence. In an official inscription, as the original account is said to have been, would not the commander have been called 'Hanno, son of . . . Such-and-such' instead of just 'Hanno'? Would he have admitted being 'seized with fear'? And the style is too flowery, too poetic, as if a work supposedly by Captain Cook came out sounding like *The Ancient Mariner*. On the geographical side, too, the account is questionable. Though the Greek word *ochema* can mean 'chariot' it can also mean 'anything that bears or supports'; so the real name of the burning mountain may have been not the Chariot, but (like Olympus) the '*Pillar* of the Gods'. And this calls to mind a statement made by Herodotus:

> In shape [Mount Atlas] is a slender cone, and it is so high that according to report the top cannot be seen, because summer and winter it is never free of cloud. The natives . . . call it the Pillar of the Sky.[2]

(Was it like the Lord in the wilderness, 'a pillar of cloud by day, and a pillar of fire by night'?) Then there is Pliny's description of the same mountain, written in the first century AD but drawing on older sources:

> A religious horror steals imperceptibly over the feelings of those who approach, and they feel themselves smitten with awe at the stupendous aspect of its summit, which reaches beyond the clouds, and well nigh approaches the very orb of the moon. At night, they say, it gleams with fires innumerable lighted up; it is then the scene of the gambols of the Aegipans and the Satyr crew, while it re-echoes with the notes of the flute and the pipe, and the clash of drums and cymbals. All this is what authors of high character have stated . . .[3]

Here four of the phenomena of Hanno's voyage – the fires, the music, the people not quite human, and the onlookers overtaken by panic terror – are all associated not with Sierra Leone but specifically with the Atlas. Are Hanno's Gorillae, one wonders, any more real than Pliny's 'Aegipans and Satyrs'?

As the reader will already have noticed, ancient accounts of North-West Africa contain a large amount of fable and fantasy. Mount Atlas itself was regarded in legend as the petrified body of Atlas the giant, turned to stone by a glance from the Gorgon's head which Perseus had captured somewhere in the same region. Hercules had also passed that way, seeking the golden apples of the Hesperides; while off the coast lay the Islands of the Blest where heroes went when they died. The

Carthaginians, who from about 500 BC onward held a monopoly of trade in the western Mediterranean, did everything they could to encourage such rumours and muddles in the minds of their Greek rivals; and even after the fall of Carthage neither Greek science nor Roman horse-sense ever quite succeeded in straightening things out again. Other explorers of the west coast, besides the mysterious Hanno, included a Persian prince named Sataspes (about 470 BC); the Greek historian Polybius (about 146 BC); another Greek, Eudoxus of Cyzicus (whose last expedition, in about 110 BC, failed to return); and a party sent out by king Juba of Mauretania at about the time of Christ.[4] This last did produce one indisputable addition to knowledge: the Canary Islands ceased to be the half-legendary 'Islands of the Blest' and received a precise position on the map. For the rest, however, one can argue at length about the reported doings of these explorers without coming any nearer to a conclusion. As with the Hanno story, the 'long-distance' school of thought postulates voyages right past the Saharan coast, reaching to the river Senegal or even further, while the 'short-distance' school continues to insist that no ancient expedition passed beyond the boundaries of present-day Morocco. The archaeological evidence, such as it is, favours the second hypothesis. The most southerly known outpost of Mediterranean civilization in western Africa lay on an island near Mogador, only a little more than halfway down the Moroccan coast. It earned its living mainly by extracting purple dye from shellfish, for which reason the Romans called it Purpuraria Island; but it has also been put forward as the site of Cerne, the elusive island on which Hanno founded his south-ernmost colony.[5] Other sites further south may still remain to be discovered, but until then the 'short-distance' party would seem to have the advantage.

Ancient journeys through the Sahara itself are somewhat easier to understand than journeys round its western side. The crossing was harder in ancient than in mediaeval times, because of the lack of camels (more of this later); but at least no one has ever claimed that it was impossible. And though legendary and fantastic peoples are sometimes mentioned in the desert, they are not so inextricably entangled with the main story-line as they are further west.

Little is known about ancient exploration in the western Sahara. This region is cut off from the Mediterranean by the peaks of the Atlas, a barrier both physical and spiritual, and cannot have been often visited. The Romans did not acquire a foothold in the neighbourhood until AD 42, when the kingdom of Mauretania was annexed and made into two provinces. In the same year Suetonius Paullinus (the future conqueror of Boudica in Britain) became the first Roman to lead an army over the Atlas. Passing first through forests 'full of all kinds of elephants, wild beasts and serpents', then through deserts of black sand, he came at last to a river called the Ger – probably the one now called the Guir, which rises in the High Atlas and flows for some distance into the desert before losing itself.[6] But this expedition was an isolated *tour de force*: Roman direct rule in Mauretania was confined to a coastal strip not much more than fifty miles wide, and large tracts of fertile ground remained independent. (The statement often found in textbooks, that the Empire's southern frontier lay on the desert, is untrue for this part of Africa though true for the regions further east.) Paintings of chariots found in the western Sahara suggest that there was a route across it, from the Guir river in the north to the Niger in the south; but we have no direct evidence that the Romans used it or even knew about it.[7]

The central Sahara was better known. It was dominated by a powerful tribe called the Garamantes (regarded by some as the ancestors of the Tuareg, those sinister veiled nomads who form an indispensable background to the stories of Beau Geste and his comrades). Their homeland was the region now called the Fezzan, in southern Libya; but already by Herodotus' time they were making long-distance raids through the desert.

> The Garamantes hunt the Ethiopian hole-men, or troglodytes, in four-horse chariots, for these troglodytes are exceedingly swift of foot – more so than any people of whom we have any information. They eat snakes and lizards and other reptiles and speak a language like nothing upon earth – it might be bats screeching.[8]

The troglodytes may have been the ancestors of the Tibu, who live in the Tibesti Mountains about four hundred miles south-east of the Fezzan and still speak a language peculiar to themselves.

By Roman times the Garamantes had become civilized enough to have a capital city of their own, called Garama (modern Jerma), and many smaller settlements; but they were still a highly mobile folk, and a lasting threat to the Roman Empire further north. In 19 BC the governor of Roman Africa, Cornelius Balbus, was awarded a triumph for his campaigns against them (a particularly high honour at this time, since the emperor Augustus disapproved of any military activity not carried out under his own auspices).[9] In the reign of the next emperor, Tiberius, the Roman province was repeatedly harassed by a guerrilla leader named Tacfarinas. Though this man was not himself a Garamantian (he belonged to a tribe called the Musulamii, in what is now Tunisia) he had active support from the Garamantes, as well as from the Moors in Mauretania and other tribes all along the northern fringe of the desert.[10] There was further trouble in AD 69. Two cities of the Libyan coast, Oea and Leptis Magna, took advantage of the civil war raging in the Empire at the time to stage a small private war of their own; the Oeans, getting the worst of this, called in the Garamantes, who ravaged the territory of Leptis until a Roman army drove them off again.[11]

One incident in this last campaign may shed some light on an important but obscure feature of Saharan history, the introduction of the camel. The one-humped camel (or dromedary) was first domesticated in Arabia; it had become common in Egypt by about 500 BC, but its introduction to the lands further west dates only from the Roman period. Two recorded figures show the beginning and end of the process: in 46 BC we hear of Julius Caesar capturing twenty-two camels from the king of Numidia, whereas in AD 370 a governor named Romanus was demanding no less than 4000 of them from Leptis Magna alone.[12] The campaign of AD 69–70 hints at one of the intermediate stages, for Pliny tells us that a new road was discovered into the country of the Garamantes, bearing the name of *Iter Praeter Caput Saxi* – 'Past the Head of the Rock'. (It was probably the route called in Arabic *Bab Ras el-Hamada*, which means the same thing.) It is tempting to suppose that this new route was usable only by camels and not by horses, and that for a time the Romans were able to dominate the Garamantes by means of their superior new form of transport. At all events, relations between the two peoples seem to have improved, for Ptolemy mentions two Roman expeditions made with Garamantian assistance. Septimius Flaccus travelled south from Garama for three months, Julius Maternus for four; Maternus eventually emerged into the land of Agisymba, 'where the rhinoceri gather'.[13] The position of this region is uncertain, but it must surely have lain on the southern side of the desert.

Maternus' expedition, however, was far from being the first recorded crossing of the Sahara. He had been anticipated by several centuries. Herodotus tells us the story of five young men of the Nasamones (a tribe of the Libyan coast) who set off through the desert 'in a westerly direction' and at length encountered

> some little men – of less than middle height – who seized them and carried them off. The speech of these dwarfs was unintelligible, nor could they understand the Nasamonians. They took their captives through a vast tract of marshy country, and beyond it came to a town, all the inhabitants of which were of the same small stature, and all black. A great river with crocodiles in it flowed past the town from west to east.[14]

The identity of this river is disputed. It could have been the Niger, or the Komadougou Yobe which flows into Lake Chad, or a watercourse called the Bahr el-Ghazal which runs out of Lake Chad into what is called the Djourab Depression. (This last at present seldom carries any water, but in ancient times may have carried more.) Herodotus himself, however, believed that the crocodile-river was the upper Nile. Like many Greek thinkers, he tended to see more symmetry in Nature than really existed; he argued that since the Danube, that other super-giant among rivers known to him, rose in the far west of Europe, so as if to balance it the even more impressive river Nile had to rise in the far west of Africa.

This theory of Herodotus' was to generate one of the most complex riddles in the history of geography. Pliny, quoting from a work by king Juba, describes at some length the course of a river called the Nigris, which was said to rise in Juba's own country of Mauretania and make its way by devious means right across Africa to become the upper Nile – on occasions adding to the geographer's confusion by running for long stretches underground.[15] Ptolemy also mentions this river, under the name of Nigeir, but rejects its link with the Nile; instead he makes it into a self-contained system somewhere in the heart of Africa, described in terms apparently more precise than Pliny's but in practice no easier to understand.[16]

In the Middle Ages some more information about an Inner African river filtered through to Europe. There were tales of powerful Negro kingdoms along its banks, of a great wealth of gold, and of a wonderful city called Timbuctoo (which subsequently proved a re-peated disappointment to those who succeeded in reaching it). The cause of pure knowledge received a setback, however, in the notion that the river flowed not from west to east as the ancients seemed to have maintained, but from east to west so that it eventually reached the Atlantic. Not until the very end of the eighteenth century did Mungo Park clear up this problem, and the final destination of the river was only discovered (by the Lander brothers) thirty years later still.

Nineteenth-century geographers could thus say that a problem first posed by Herodotus had at last been solved in their own time. But is the river we now call the Niger really the same as the Nigris of the ancients? Almost certainly not. The Niger does not rise in Mauretania or anywhere near it, nor at any point in its course could it ever have formed the boundary of Rome's African province, which Pliny says the Nigris did.[17] The latter river is in fact probably the watercourse now called the Djedi, which flows through Algeria on the northern, not the southern, side of the desert – its connexion with the Nile being merely a piece of wishful thinking by king Juba. As for Ptolemy's map, it

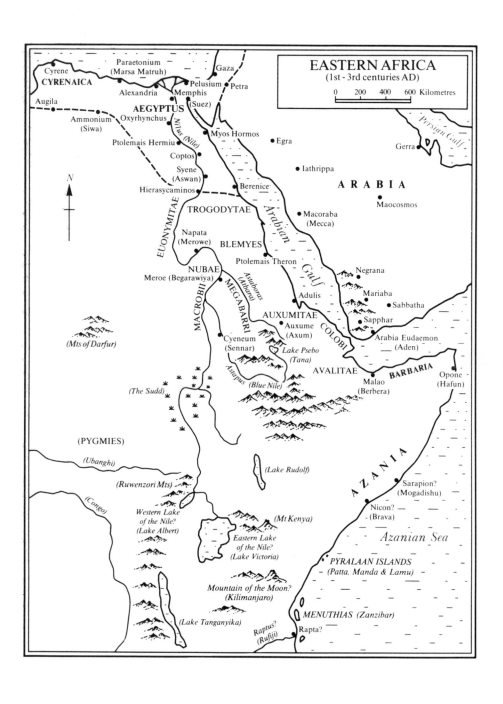

EASTERN AFRICA
(1st - 3rd centuries AD)

0   200   400   600 Kilometres

N

Cyrene
CYRENAICA
Paraetonium
(Marsa Matruh)
Gaza
Pelusium   Petra
Alexandria   Memphis
Augila   (Suez)
AEGYPTUS
Ammonium   Oxyrhynchus
(Siwa)
Ptolemais Hermiu
Myos Hormos
Egra
Gerra
Coptos
Iathrippa
Syene
(Aswan)
Hierasycaminos   Berenice
ARABIA
Maocosmos
TROGODYTAE
Macoraba
(Mecca)
Napata
(Merowe)
BLEMYES
EUONYMITAE
Ptolemais Theron
Negrana
NUBAE
Meroe (Begarawiya)
Mariaba
Sabbatha
MACROBII
MEGABARRI
Astaboras (Atbara)
Adulis
Sapphar
AUXUMITAE
Auxume
(Axum)
Cyeneum
(Sennar)
Lake Psebo
(Tana)
Arabia Eudaemon
(Aden)
(Mts of Darfur)
Astapus (Blue Nile)
AVALITAE
BARBARIA
Opone
(Hafun)
Malao
(Berbera)
(The Sudd)

(PYGMIES)
(Ubanghi)
(Lake Rudolf)
AZANIA
Sarapion?
(Mogadishu)
(Ruwenzori Mts)
Nicon?
(Brava)
(Congo)
Western Lake
of the Nile?
(Lake Albert)
(Mt Kenya)
Azanian Sea
Eastern Lake
of the Nile?
(Lake Victoria)
PYRALAAN ISLANDS
(Patta, Manda & Lamu)
Mountain of the Moon?
(Kilimanjaro)
MENUTHIAS (Zanzibar)
(Lake Tanganyika)
Raptus?
(Rufiji)
Rapta?

Nilus (Nile)
Arabian Gulf
COLOBI
Persian Gulf

appears to have suffered some strange dislocation, as if the author had mixed up two different sets of units when he made his measurements. Everything west of the Nile on this map tends to be placed too far south; features on or near the sea are pushed inland, and features on the north side of the Sahara are pushed into the desert itself, two victims of this push being the river 'Nigeir' and its equally confused companion the river 'Geir'. In the geography of the Sahara, as in the geography of the West African coast, ancient sources do not always mean what at first sight they would appear to mean.

*

When we move from the Sahara to the Nile, the picture becomes somewhat clearer and certainly more detailed. Most of the places mentioned by ancient sources must have stood on the river itself, so that the historical geographer needs to work only in one dimension instead of the usual two. The sources, besides, cover a much longer time-span than they do further west (though this presents its own difficulties; a really thorough account of the region would need to draw on material in seven different languages, Ancient Egyptian, Greek, Latin, Meroitic which is as yet undeciphered, Coptic, Old Nubian and Arabic).

The country of the upper Nile came to the attention of foreigners at a very early date. To the Greeks it was Aethiopia, 'the land of burnt faces' – but also the land of some of the wisest, justest and noblest men on earth.[18] To the Egyptians, by contrast, it was 'wretched Kush', to be treated in the violent manner depicted by Verdi in *Aïda*.[19] The traditional southern limit of Egypt proper was the set of rapids known as the First Cataract, near Aswan; but Egyptian military expeditions repeatedly invaded the country beyond. The most successful of these, under the Eighteenth Dynasty between about 1550 and 1400 BC, reached beyond the Fourth Cataract to within striking distance of the southern fringe of the desert. By about 750 BC, however, the situation was reversed and a Kushite dynasty (the Twenty-Fifth on the Egyptian list) ruled the whole Nile valley from their capital at Napata. They later lost Egypt, which was then dominated in turn by Assyrians, Persians, Greeks and Romans; but the upper Nile preserved its independence. Attempts to overrun it from Egypt met with 'qualified success', plain failure, or disaster. Its capital was now at Meroe, more than 300 miles upstream from Napata and 800 from the Egyptian frontier.[20] Here a king of Ethiopia defied a king of Persia:

'The king of Persia has not sent you with these presents because he puts a high value on being my friend. You have come to get information about my kingdom; therefore, you are liars, and that king of yours is a bad man. Had he any respect for what is right, he would not have coveted any other kingdom than his own, nor made slaves of a people who have done him no wrong. So take him this bow, and tell him that the king of Ethiopia has some advice to give him: when the Persians can draw a bow of this size thus easily, then let him raise an army of superior strength and invade the country of the long-lived Ethiopians. Till then, let him thank the gods for not turning the thoughts of the children of Ethiopia to foreign conquest.'[21]

So says Herodotus, also remarking that a Persian invading army was reduced to cannibalism before coming anywhere near the enemy's headquarters.

The Romans fared little better. They occupied Egypt in 30 BC after the suicide of Antony and Cleopatra, and only five years later had to deal with an invasion from the south. Petronius the governor of Egypt at once counter-attacked, reaching as far as Napata and sacking it; but the whole campaign sounds like a blow directed at nothing. Pliny's description of it is almost apologetic:

The farthest point he reached was 870 miles from Syene [Aswan], but nevertheless it was not the arms of Rome that made the country

Pyramids at Meroe.

a desert; Ethiopia was worn out by alternate periods of dominance and subjection in a series of wars with Egypt.[22]

Rome's only lasting gain from this was the tract of land known as the Dodecaschoenus, south of Aswan; a *schoenus* was a Greek unit of length, and twelve (*dodeca*) of them made not 870 miles but a mere seventy-five.

Roman relations with Meroe were afterwards fairly peaceful, each side perhaps thinking it futile to attack the other. Egypt was unique among Roman provinces in having its main garrison not on the frontier or even near it, but instead just outside the capital (Alexandria, where many thousands of Greeks and Jews constituted a far greater threat to peace than a few tribesmen in the south). In about AD 61, during Nero's reign, there was further Roman activity in Ethiopia, but it is uncertain whether its object was exploration, trade or spying; nor was the spying, if any, followed by an invasion. Instead of the dusty answer given to the Persian envoys, the Romans received active help from the rulers of Meroe, and penetrated far up the Nile until they were stopped by swamps – the dreaded *sudd* in the southern Sudan, whose barrier was not broken until the nineteenth century.[23] But even this Roman feat may have been anticipated by Egyptian explorers many centuries earlier.

As a result of these and other expeditions up the Nile, the 'Nubian slave' with his bulging muscles and midnight complexion became a well-known figure in European art and literature. Like most stereotypes, this is only part of the truth. The Nubian of today forms a distinct physical type, more negroid than the Egyptian but less so than the people to the south of him. In the past, Nubian racial make-up must often have changed, as the tide of invasion flowed up and down the river. There may also have been large individual differences; ancient Egyptian artists portrayed some of the Kush as black, but others with the same brownish-red skin colour that they used for their own people. And Egyptians and Greeks alike knew that Africa produced some of the world's smallest people (the famous Pygmies) as well as some of its tallest. One noticeably 'Negro' feature of society in Meroe, however, was that fatness in women was apparently a sign of beauty: whereas Egyptian queens are always shown with the most elegant figures, Meroitic ones display a more matronly *embonpoint*.

The queens of Meroe were important persons, so much so that some writers of the Roman Empire wrongly believed that the country was matriarchal. Among them was the author of the *Acts of the Apostles*:

> ... And behold, a man of Ethiopia, a eunuch of great authority under Candace queen of the Ethiopians, who had the charge of all

her treasure, and had come to Jerusalem for to worship, was returning, and sitting in his chariot read Esias the prophet.[24]

'Candace' was in fact not a name but a title, and Meroe did have kings as well as queens; but the Meroites do seem to have given a higher position to women than most other peoples of the ancient world.

Meroitic society would be easier to understand if we could interpret the Meroitic language. This, unfortunately, presents the same problem as ancient Etruscan: we can read the script (it was usually written in hieroglyphics, similar in general appearance though not in detail to those of Egypt) but though we thus know what the words sounded like we do not know what most of them mean. Meroitic does not seem to show much affinity with any other known language of Africa – not even with Nubian, which has been used in the same region in mediaeval and modern times. Perhaps the rulers of Meroe, like those of Norman England, spoke a different language from that of their subjects. But the problem may never be solved unless a longish bilingual text (in Meroitic and Greek, say) should happen to turn up.

Though it sometimes shows signs of Iranian and even Indian influence, reminding us that the kingdom had contacts with the Red Sea as well as with Egypt, Meroitic art gives to the non-specialist viewer an overwhelmingly Egyptian impression. The whole convention, the way in which the figures are portrayed, is Egyptian; so are many of the themes, two popular ones for instance being the ruler smiting his enemies and the ruler receiving the favour of the gods. (Some of these, such as Amun the sky-god, are themselves of Egyptian origin.) Wild animals, especially elephants and lions, are more often shown in Meroe than in Egypt – not surprisingly, since they existed on the upper Nile long after they had become extinct further downstream. The lion was very important, being associated with a god called Apedemek who has no parallel in Egypt. One thinks rather of the animal's tremendous importance in Black Africa as a symbol of kingly power, rulers in this region often wearing the skins of lions as part of their regalia and sometimes even trying to walk like one.

Two important industries, pottery and iron-working, are amply attested in the kingdom. The pottery was finely made, attractively decorated, and has been regarded as Meroe's greatest contribution to art. The style, again, is partly Egyptian and partly Black African; there seem to have been two different levels of production, the more sophisticated pots being turned on a wheel by men while simpler ones with a more conservative tradition behind them were hand-made by women. Evidence of iron-working, in the form of large slag-heaps, is abundant at Meroe itself – so much so that the city has been called 'the

A Meroitic temple at Naqa, about halfway between Meroe and Khartoum.

Relief from the Lion Temple at Naqa: Queen Amanitare smiting her enemies.

Apedemek, the
lion-god of Naqa.

Birmingham of ancient Africa'. This is important historically, for it is likely that the knowledge of iron reached sub-Saharan Africa by way of the Meroitic kingdom.[25]

The third century AD was a time of violent and world-wide political upheaval. The Han dynasty collapsed in China, as did the Kushans in India and the Parthians in Persia. The Roman Empire was racked by chronic civil war, parts of it at times breaking away from the central government altogether; it also had to face attacks by its neighbours in Ireland, Scotland, Germany, Russia, the Near East and the Sahara. And the Meroitic kingdom also fell into difficulties. In the north, where it marched with Roman Egypt, two tribes previously waiting in the wings now began to occupy the centre of the stage. They were called the Blemyes and the Nobatae, and both are something of a mystery. The Blemyes in classical writings lead a double life, sometimes real and sometimes mythical. In their mythical form they are the original of Othello's 'men whose heads do grow beneath their shoulders', living in some ill-defined part of Inner Africa alongside the Himantopodes or 'Strapfeet', the Aegipans, the Satyrs, the Dogheads, and other peculiar folk. The name was also given, however, to a real people who lived in the desolate country between the Nile and the Red Sea. The ancient Egyptians called them Medju; their name today is Beja; the British Army was at one time familiar with them as 'Fuzzy-Wuzzies'. It is possible that, like the nomads further west, they had begun to use the camel in the third century AD and thus made themselves more mobile; at all events, by this time they were established along the river and making repeated raids into the Roman province.[26]

The Nobatae also pose a problem. A name of this sort (Nubae, Nobatae, Noba) appears in several sources at various times, but it is uncertain whether it refers always to the same people or to different ones.[27] The name seems somehow to be connected with the west bank of the Nile: though this river is now usually regarded as a highway, the ancients often regarded it as a frontier (sometimes, rather perversely, as the frontier between Africa and Asia); and in the third century it might have been a political dividing-line, with Blemyes on one side and Nobatae on the other, each trying to dominate the settlements on the river itself. The archaeological record, however, does not confirm this. The post-Meroitic material in Nubia shows not two cultures but one, known as the X-group (the letter, as in 'X-rays', having been deliberately chosen to convey a sense of the unknown). Whatever its origins, the X-group shows a remarkable mixture of splendour and squalor. Rulers were buried with fantastic amounts of treasure; human sacrifice, long ago made symbolic in the civilized world, reappeared in its crudest and most literal form; writing virtually disappeared, as did the attractive Meroitic pottery; and unpleasant rubbish that should have been decently buried was instead left littering the X-group houses. It was a foretaste, so to speak, of what was to overtake large parts of western Europe a century or so later.

The final collapse of Meroe, however, was probably not due to the Blemyes and Nobatae, but to another group of people coming from a different direction. To place these in their context it is necessary to consider the lands east of the Nile.

*

The eastern side of Africa is easier to explore by sea than the western. The Red Sea does present the same difficulty as the Atlantic off Morocco, a prevailing wind from the north, but this is nothing like as strong or as persistent as the North-East Trade. And when one leaves the Red Sea for the Indian Ocean, the situation becomes surprisingly straightforward, since the wind here is of the 'monsoon' type (named from an Arabic word meaning 'seasonal'). From May to September the South-West Monsoon blows from Africa to India; from November to March the North-East Monsoon blows back again, so that by choosing the right time of year a ship can sail a very long way without ever having to beat against the wind.

Voyages along the East African coast are known to have started early. In about 1500 BC Queen Hatshepsut of Egypt sent expeditions to a country called Punt, probably in what is now Somalia; they returned with incense-trees, ivory, ebony, tortoiseshell and several kinds of wild animal for the queen's zoo. In about 950 BC King Solomon was collecting gold from a mysterious land called Ophir, which has been variously located in Africa, Arabia, India or even Malaya. In the reign of Necho of Egypt (610–595 BC) some Phoenicians claimed to have circumnavigated the entire African continent. Herodotus tells us of this:

> The Phoenicians sailed from the Arabian Gulf [the Red Sea] into the southern ocean, and every autumn put in at some convenient spot on the Libyan coast, sowed a patch of ground, and waited for next year's harvest. Then, having got in their grain, they put to sea again, and after two full years rounded the Pillars of Hercules [the Straits of Gibraltar] in the course of the third, and returned to Egypt. These men made a statement which I do not myself believe, though others may, to the effect that as they sailed on a westerly course round the southern end of Libya, they had the sun on their right – to northward of them.[28]

As with Hanno's voyage, there has been much controversy over Herodotus' account, some authorities accepting it while others treat it as impossible. It was certainly never repeated in ancient times, and had little effect on geographical thinking. Most ancient writers regarded Africa as a relatively small continent, with little more than a quarter of its true size.

Ptolemy son of Lagos, one of Alexander the Great's generals, seized Egypt in the confused fighting that followed his leader's death in 323 BC; and his descendants, also bearing the name Ptolemy, actively promoted exploration of the Red Sea coast. New towns were founded there, bearing the names of members of the royal family. At the head of the Gulf of Suez, not far from Suez itself, was a town called Arsinoe; further south, near the southern frontier of Egypt proper, was Berenice; further south still was Ptolemais, distinguished from other places with that name by the epithet *Theron*, 'of the hunts'. Alexander's Indian campaigns had introduced the Greeks to the use of elephants in battle, and Ptolemais Theron was the chief base from which expeditions went out to capture them – though these sub-Saharan elephants were neither as large nor as reliable as the Indian ones used by the Ptolemies' rivals in Asia.[29] Through such expeditions the Greeks learned something about the tribes of the eastern Sudan and Abyssinia, and often described them in accordance with Brillat-Savarin's dictum – 'Tell me what you eat and I'll tell you what you are'. The coast-

Obelisk at Axum.

dwellers were naturally called Ichthyophagi or 'Fish-eaters', while inland we hear of tribes known as Agriophagi, Moschophagi, Ophiophagi, Struthiophagi and Pamphagi – these being respectively eaters of wild beasts, shoots, snakes, ostriches and everything. There were also inevitably some Anthropophagi or cannibals.

The most interesting work on ancient eastern Africa, however, dates from the Roman period. It is called the *Periplus of the Erythraean Sea* (*Periplus* being the Greek for 'circumnavigation', and 'Erythraean Sea' the ancient name for all the waters between Africa, Arabia and India).[30] The precise date of the work is disputed, but it should probably be placed in the late first or early second century AD. The author's name is likewise unknown, but he was clearly no armchair geographer but a man with close personal knowledge of the places he described. The *Periplus* is in effect an East-Indiaman's guide or *vade-mecum*, giving full details of the approaches to eastern ports, the goods bought and sold there and sometimes even the personal characters of the local rulers.

The African section of the work begins with the harbours of Myos Hormos and Berenice, both within the Roman province of Egypt. Then comes Ptolemais Theron, somewhat declined from its earlier importance: the Romans did not use elephants in battle, and had handier places than the Red Sea coast from which to fetch them for other purposes. Further south still was Adulis, not much of a place in itself, but the port of a powerful kingdom: three days' journey inland was the large town of Coloe, and five days further still brought one to the still larger town of Auxume – modern Axum, the first capital of the Abyssinians.[31]

The Axumite kingdom, mentioned here for the first time, had a distinguished future before it. At the height of its power it ruled not only the greater part of Abyssinia, but also parts of south-western Arabia and much of the Sudan – in all, an area nearly as big as the western Roman Empire though nothing like as populous. The *Periplus* names its ruler as Zoscales, a man 'mean in his way of life and with an eye on the main chance, but otherwise high-minded, and skilled in Greek letters'.[32] Perhaps because of his 'eye on the main chance' and his valuable trading contact with the Graeco-Roman world, he bequeathed to his successors a position of increasing power. In about AD 350 an Axumite king named Ezana was able to conquer (or perhaps reconquer) the kingdom of Meroe, the only other sub-Saharan state with a comparable civilization. He set up a long inscription at Axum announcing the fact:

> Through the might of the Lord of Heaven, who is victorious in Heaven and on earth over all! Ezana, the son of Ella-Amida, of the tribe Halen, the king of Axum and Himyar and of Raidan and of Saba and of Salhen and of Siyamo and of Bega and of Kasu, the King of Kings . . .[33]

'Kasu' is the same as Kush, the Meroitic kingdom. Curiously enough the inscription, though it goes on to describe the conquest of this region in some detail, does not mention either the town of Meroe or its rulers; most of the opposition to Ezana came from a people called the Noba, who as already mentioned may or may not be the same as the Nobatae on the Roman frontier far to the north. The general impression given is that Ezana did not take over the kingdom as a going concern, but imposed his authority on a region where the central government had already broken down. When and how this happened is uncertain.

Ezana has another claim to distinction, as the first Abyssinian ruler to become a Christian. His country retains a strong Christian tradition today, the only nation in Africa to have maintained that religion continuously since ancient times. It was largely for this reason that it came to be regarded as the home of Prester John, the mysterious champion of Christendom against Islam who was at first supposed to live somewhere in the far east of Asia.

Beyond the Axumite kingdom, in the Horn of Africa, were several marts involved in the famous spice trade between the Indies and the Roman Empire. Cape Guardafui, the easternmost point of the continent, was known as the Cape of Spices, and the surrounding region was often given the name of 'the Cinnamon Country'.[34] In fact it produced no cinnamon (this, like most spices, came from South-East Asia) but the Arabs who handled much of the spice trade concealed this from their customers in the Western world. Guardafui itself had for some time been regarded as the southern limit of Africa, the coast thereafter being supposed to turn to the north-west and continue in this direction till it reached the Straits of Gibraltar. The *Periplus*, however, is better informed. It describes the coast as continuing southward, as far as the port of Rapta. The exact site of this place is disputed, but it undoubtedly has the honour of being the most southerly settlement recorded in ancient writings – at least five degrees south of the equator and possibly more.[35] In the time of the *Periplus* it was controlled by the ruler of Mapharitis, a district of south-western Arabia; and Arab influence on East Africa has remained noticeable ever since. Rapta was also visited by people in 'sewn boats' (*rhapton ploiarion* in the Greek, from which the place was supposed to take its name). Most probably these were local craft, though it has been suggested that they had come all the way across the Indian Ocean from Indonesia, bringing with them the spices of that region for redistribution by the Arabs.[36] This seems unlikely. Indonesians certainly visited Africa (Madagascar especially) at some early date, but probably not before the fifth century AD; and the *Periplus* says nothing about spices being bought at Rapta, only ivory and tortoiseshell.

One other discovery in East Africa was to have a particularly long-lived effect on people's imaginations. Somewhere inland from Rapta, according to Ptolemy, stood the famous Mountain (or Mountains) of the Moon, and close by were lakes or swamps which formed the true source of the Nile, some 3500 miles from its other postulated source in the mountains of Mauretania.[37] Once again, as with the 'Nigris' river, an ancient geographical remark was to set off a tremendous modern controversy, not fully resolved till Stanley made his great expedition of 1874–77. And once again the problem arises: how much did the ancients really know? The name 'Mountains of the Moon' is now commonly given to the Ruwenzori range, but it seems unlikely that Ptolemy's informants ever penetrated so far inland. They were more probably referring to Kilimanjaro – the highest mountain in Africa, always snow-capped, and only 200 miles from the sea. They may also have heard that the country beyond was full of lakes, but the idea that these were the source of the Nile sounds like no more than an inspired guess. Ancient travellers in Africa did make some remarkable discoveries, but not quite such remarkable ones as the nineteenth century was willing to credit to them.

CHAPTER FIVE

ARABIA AND THE INCENSE ROUTES

... from which the rays of the sun were always reflected in
more-than-oriental splendour.

Just So Stories

Ancient descriptions of Arabia sound very strange to the modern ear.
Not only is there the mental effort needed to imagine Arabs without
Islam and all the customs that go with it, but the whole landscape
seems different from anything we associate with Arabia today. There
was indeed a region called *Arabia Deserta*, which to most Westerners
would seem to be a fair name for the whole country; but this name was
given only to the relatively small tract of land that lies between the
Levantine countries and Mesopotamia. Everything south of this, the
whole peninsular part of Arabia, bore the name *Arabia Eudaemon* in
Greek and *Arabia Felix* in Latin, both epithets meaning 'happy' or
'fortunate'. Ancient Arabia, like the Canary Islands, was the Land of
the Blest.

Consider, for example, the account given by Herodotus:

It would seem to be a fact that the remotest parts of the world are the
richest in minerals and produce the finest specimens of both animal
and vegetable life ... The most southerly country is Arabia; and
Arabia is the only place that produces frankincense, myrrh, cassia,
cinnamon and the gum called ledanon ... the whole country
exhales a more than earthly fragrance.[1]

(Nothing in this world is perfect, however, and Herodotus also
remarks that Arabia was troubled by some mysterious creatures,
found nowhere else, which he calls 'flying snakes'.) Pliny's *Natural
History* is full of extraordinary remarks, but the following must be
among the most extraordinary of all:

[Arabia] is by a kind of design, apparently on the part of Nature,
surrounded by the sea in such a manner as to resemble very much the
form and size of Italy, there being no difference either in the climate
of the two countries, as they lie in the same latitudes.[2]

Ptolemy's map of Arabia teems with peoples and settlements. There
even appear to be some in the 'Empty Quarter' of the south-east, now
one of the most horrible deserts in the world.

Could there have been some great natural disaster between Ptolemy's time and our own, causing Arabia to dry out? Are there perhaps great ancient cities buried in the sands of the Empty Quarter, awaiting rediscovery by archaeologists of the future? Possibly, but probably not. When the ancients said these complimentary things about Arabia, they were thinking not of the peninsula as a whole but of a small region in its south-west corner, now shared by the nations of North and South Yemen. This is mountainous country (its highest peaks reach above 10,000 feet) and, as often happens in the world's desert belt, the mountains catch rain and create a habitable region round themselves. South-western Arabia thus became the seat of an advanced civilization while all the rest of the country was still living a more primitive, pastoral existence (unchanged in some parts until quite recent times).

Though isolated from other parts of the civilized world, the ancient Yemenis were by no means living in a vacuum. Like some Arab countries today (though not in the same region of Arabia) they possessed a valuable commodity that all the rest of the world wanted to buy. This was incense, vital for obtaining the favour of the gods and thus as essential in its way to ancient economies as petroleum is to modern ones. As Pliny said:

> They are the richest nations in the world, seeing that such vast wealth flows in upon them from both the Roman and the Parthian Empires; for they sell the produce of the sea or of their forests, while they purchase nothing whatever in return.[3]

The two chief kinds of Arabian incense, both best known to the West through the story of Jesus and the Three Wise Men, were myrrh and frankincense. Myrrh (Greek *smyrna*, Latin *myrrha*) is a gummy substance extracted from a smallish tree known to botanists as *Balsamodendron myrrha*. In ancient times this tree was grown in most of south-western Arabia, and also in the Horn of Africa which lies immediately opposite. (From Pliny we learn that the African or 'Trogodytic' myrrh was considered to be the finest of all.)[4] Frankincense (Greek *libanos*, Latin *tus* or *thus*) is also a gum; it is derived from a plant called *Boswellia*, more of a large bush than a tree, and with a more restricted distribution than the myrrh-plant. Once again, it could be found in the Horn of Africa as well as in Arabia; but the frankincense-country *par excellence* was the region now called Dhofar, belonging to the Sultanate of Oman and lying some way to the east of the myrrh-country and the main area of South Arabian settlement. Incense is extracted in much the same way as rubber, by making cuts in the bark of the tree and allowing it to ooze out; the early Arabs, however, seem to have concealed this prosaic fact from the West, for Herodotus tells some ludicrous stories about the stratagems needed to obtain the precious stuff. The frankincense country, he says, suffered especially badly from the 'flying snakes' already mentioned; they had to be smoked out, like so many bees or wasps, by burning a gum called storax. Cinnamon, of which more will be said in Chapter Eight, reached Europe *via* but not *from* Arabia, and Herodotus seems to have had some inkling of this – but then he goes on to tell a crazy tale about its being brought to Arabia by birds. Another sort of gum, called ledanon, was supposedly collected by a still odder method; it had to be combed out of the beards of goats, which browsed on the bushes that produced it. (The final product, one would have thought, would when burnt have been more suitable for repelling deities than attracting them.)

But despite such stories, with their strong suggestion that someone's leg was being pulled, the incense itself was real enough, and so was the

Myrrh, from a nineteenth-century engraving.

civilization to which it gave rise. Despite their physical isolation, the southern Arabs were as technically and socially advanced as any other people in the Ancient World. The alphabetic system of writing, thought to have been first developed in Phoenicia in about 1000 BC, quickly spread southward; the angular, runic-looking signs of the South Arabian alphabet are found carved on stone throughout the region, in forms ranging from monumental inscriptions to the humblest type of 'Kilroy-was-here' graffito. In all forms of stonework the southern Arabs excelled. Working on a small scale they produced numerous figurines, of which the ones in alabaster are especially attractive. They were equally capable when they turned from the smallest to the largest scale. Like the Romans, they were great builders of irrigation works – dams, canals and the like – to make the best possible use of the limited rainfall. The greatest of all such works was the dam at Marib, mentioned in the Koran and therefore familiar to every pious Muslim; its remains are some 1800 feet long and in places still stand more than fifty feet high.[5] Again like the Romans, the southern Arabs were great road-builders, often taking immense trouble to hack their way through the extremely mountainous and rocky country in which they lived; roads meant tolls, and tolls on the rich incense-bearing caravans were the governments' chief source of revenue.

The mason's craft was as important in religious as in secular

The great dam at Marib: northern sluice-gate.

buildings. One of the few buildings to have been systematically studied at Marib is popularly known as the 'Temple of Bilqis'; here the temple itself proved impressive, but the massive wall of the forecourt was even more so. It was thirteen feet thick and at least thirty feet tall, as if the local priests expected an attack by the anti-clerical party.[6] The town of Shabwah, smaller than Marib, was said by Pliny to have had more than sixty temples.[7] The principal deity worshipped in them was Ilumquh, the Moon-god; the Sun-goddess was his consort, and the god of the Morning Star their offspring.

*

Prosperity in South Arabia did not bring peace. As in Ireland, there was at times a kind of High King, with real or imaginary powers over other tributary kings; but the written records of the country show that it never possessed much political unity, and was the scene of almost continuous local warfare.

Five principal states were involved. The most northerly of them was called Ma'in; westerners referred to its inhabitants as the Minaei. Its capital was called Qarnawu. Immediately south of Ma'in lay the kingdom of Saba or Sheba; to westerners it was the kingdom of the Sabaei. Through its queen's visit to King Solomon, 'to prove him with hard questions', Saba has become by far the best known of the five states, the only one whose existence can be said to belong to general

The so-called 'Temple of Bilqis' (in fact a temple of the moon-god 'Ilumquh) at Marib.

rather than specialized knowledge. The Sabaean capital was Marib, the city with the great dam and Moon-temple mentioned above. Next to Saba lay Qataban, whose name European writers found hard to spell; sometimes they reproduced it fairly accurately as 'Catabani', but sometimes it was spoonerized into the form 'Gebbanitae'.[8] The chief place of this kingdom, Timna, is one of the most fully studied sites in South Arabia. To the south-west, in the heel of the Arabian boot, lay the kingdom of Himyar (the Homeritae); its capital was Zafar. The last of the five was called Hadhramaut, a name which still survives as a geographical expression though not as a political one; to Europeans it was the land of the Chatramotitae. In more than one way it was the odd man out among the five; it was much the largest in area, though perhaps not in population, and it spread itself over a large tract of country to the east of the other four. Its capital was Shabwah, on the Wadi Hadhramaut which gave the kingdom its name; but its power extended as far as the frankincense country of Dhofar, nearly five hundred miles further east. Thus whereas myrrh could be produced by all five of the states, frankincense was a speciality, almost a monopoly, of the kingdom of Hadhramaut.

Warfare among the five was endemic. Its details are by no means fully understood even by the specialist, and tend to make the non-specialist feel like the Spartan who after listening to a long speech said that he had forgotten the first half and could not understand the second. It is known, however, that for a long period the kingdom of Saba was predominant. This seems to be implied in the Biblical story of Solomon and Sheba, which if true must be dated to about 950 BC. Sabaean supremacy is also implied in much of the earlier Greek writing about South Arabia. In about 100 BC, however, the kingdom of Himyar began to make the running. Its rulers, like the Royal Family in Great Britain today, took their name from their principal residence; they were called the House of Raydan. At some uncertain date they succeeded in conquering their rivals the Sabaeans, and began to refer to themselves in inscriptions as 'Kings of Saba and Dhu-Raydan'. Later still, however, this united kingdom broke up again – with the odd result that we find two sets of rulers, one in Saba and one in Himyar, each clinging to the older title and claiming suzerainty over the other. (The history of England again provides a parallel: its rulers claimed the throne of France in 1340 and continued to do so, on their Royal Arms at least, till as late as 1801.)

The other three kingdoms had equally complex and eventful histories. The northern kingdom of Ma'in flourished in the third century BC, handling much of the caravan trade up the west side of Arabia; in about 115 BC, however, it was conquered and annexed by Saba. The kingdom of Qataban was the 'Cockpit of Arabia', well placed for peaceful or warlike contact with any of the other four. It eventually succumbed to an attack by its eastern neighbour Hadhramaut; its capital, Timna, is known to have been sacked, but the date of this event has been put as early as AD 10 and as late as AD 280.[9] The Hadhramauti kings did not greatly profit from their conquest, rather the contrary: the removal of Qataban lost them a useful buffer-state and exposed them all the more to attacks from the Himyarites.

So much, in brief outline, for the internal history of the 'Five Kingdoms'. There also exists, however, an external history of them, derived from their customers in the Graeco-Roman world. Two of these outside accounts are of especial interest; one is the story of a Roman military officer, the other of a Roman merchant.

The officer's name was Aelius Gallus.[10] He was governor of the Roman province of Egypt, and in 25 BC he launched an invasion of southern Arabia under orders from his immediate superior, the emperor Augustus. This ruler's foreign policy is sometimes difficult to understand. He has often been regarded as an apostle of 'Peace, Retrenchment and Reform', and that is certainly how he liked to see himself. He was also the first Roman ruler to express a definite idea about what size and shape the Empire should have, rather than seizing everything seizable in the manner of most late Republican governors. And towards the end of his life he strongly advised his successors not to try annexing any more territory. Yet earlier in his reign his plans had sometimes sent Roman commanders into the most outlandish places – Drusus Caesar into Germany (page 33), Cornelius Balbus into the Sahara (page 64) and Petronius up the Nile (page 69), and the expedition of Aelius Gallus was the most extraordinary of all.

The chief reason for it was probably an economic one. Augustus expressed repeated concern about the Empire's balance of payments; rich Romans had begun to consume vast amounts of exotics – silk from China, spices from the Indies, incense from Arabia – all of which had to be paid for in coin, usually gold, since the mysterious foreign producers of these goods would accept nothing else. Though the Roman Empire had access to large supplies of gold (in Spain particularly) these could not be expected to last for ever. Something had to be done, and Augustus set about doing it in the directest possible way. In the matter of silk he was powerless: practically nothing was known about this substance except that it came from the 'Silk-land' far to the east, and nobody knew how big this land was or precisely how to get there. A campaign against the 'Silk-land', moreover, was almost certain to involve war with the Parthians in Iran, which Augustus was anxious to avoid. The trade in spices and incense, however, offered

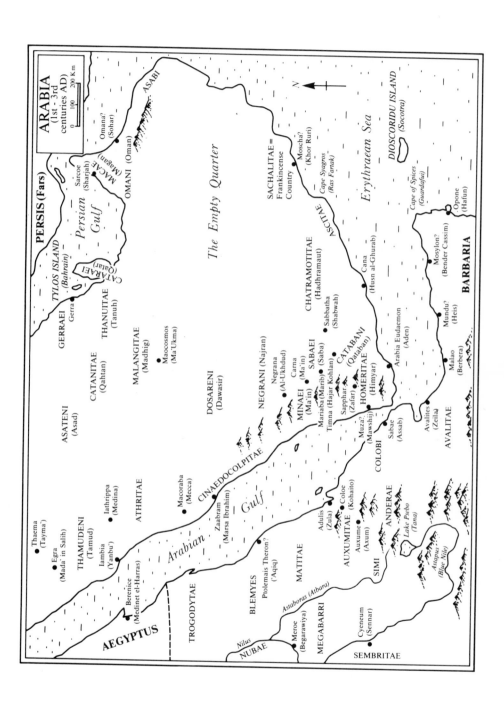

ARABIA
(1st - 3rd centuries AD)

0 100 200 Km

N

PERSIS (Fars)

ASABI

Omana?
(Sohar)

Sarcoe
(Sharjah)

OMANI (Oman)

MACAE
(Magan)

Persian
Gulf

TYLOS ISLAND
(Bahrain)

GERRAEI
Gerra

CATARAEI
(Qatar)

THANUITAE
(Tanuh)

CATANITAE
(Qahtan)

MALANGITAE
(Madhig)

Maocosmos
(Ma'Ukma)

The Empty Quarter

SACHALITAE =
Frankincense
Country

Moscha?
(Khor Ruri)

Cape Syagros
(Ras Farak)

Erythraean Sea

DIOSCORIDU ISLAND
(Socotra)

ASATENI
(Asad)

DOSARENI
(Dawasir)

NEGRANI (Najran)

ASCITAE

Cape of Spices
(Guardafui)

Thaema
(Tayma')

Egra
(Mada'in Salih)

THAMUDENI
(Tamud)

Iambia
(Yanbu')

Iathrippa
(Medina)

ATHRITAE

Macoraba
(Mecca)

CINAEDOCOLPITAE

Zaabram
(Marsa Ibrahim)

Arabian

Gulf

Negrana
(Al-Ukhdud)

Carna
(Ma'in)

MINAEI
(Ma'in)

SABAEI
(Saba)

Mariaba (Marib)

Timna (Hajar Kohlan)

Sapphar
(Zafar)

HOMERITAE
(Himyar)

CATABANI
(Qataban)

Muza?
(Mawshij)

COLOBI

Sabae
(Assab)

Avalites
(Zeila)

CHATRAMOTITAE
(Hadhramaut)

Sabbatha
(Shabwah)

Cana
(Husn al-Ghurab)

Arabia Eudaemon
(Aden)

AVALITAE

Malao
(Berbera)

Mundu?
(Heis)

Mosylon?
(Bender Cassim)

BARBARIA

Opone
(Hafun)

Berenice
(Medinet el-Harras)

AEGYPTUS

TROGODYTAE

BLEMYES

Ptolemais Theron?
('Aqiq)

MATITAE

Adulis
(Zula)

AUXUMITAE
(Kohaito)

Coloe
(Kohaito)

Auxume
(Axum)

SIMI

ANDERAE

Lake Psebo
(Tana)

Astapus
(Blue Nile)

Cyeneum
(Sennar)

MEGABARRI

Meroe
(Begarawiya)

Astaboras (Atbara)

Nilus

NUBAE

SEMBRITAE

greater scope for direct action. Both were reputed to come from Arabia, which was not very far from Egypt, which since 30 BC had been a special province treated almost as the emperor's personal property. It seemed worth while to send out a small expedition that might make an extremely valuable conquest.

In 25 BC, accordingly, Aelius Gallus set out. He took with him ten thousand Roman legionaries (infantry in heavy armour – by no means the troops best suited for a desert campaign); for guides he had five hundred Jews and a thousand Nabataean Arabs. These last, as we shall presently see, handled most of the trade between South Arabia and the Roman Empire: as guides they had the advantage of knowing all about the country to be traversed, but the disadvantage (from the Roman point of view) that they had everything to lose and nothing to gain from a Roman takeover of their valuable business contacts. Their leader was called Syllaeus; on him, justly or unjustly, was to be placed all the blame for the expedition's ultimate failure.

It began in a curiously disorganized way. On the one hand, it would have been possible (though difficult and dangerous) to make the attack almost entirely by sea, sailing down the whole length of the Red Sea to Aden or one of the other great incense-exporting ports, and then marching inland. On the other hand, and more in keeping with the usual Roman way of organizing a campaign, it would also have been possible to go overland all the way, down the western side of the Arabian peninsula. Gallus, however, used a mixed strategy involving land and sea journeys, and got the worst of both worlds. He embarked from Cleopatris, near Suez, and sailed down the Red Sea to make his first Arabian landing at a place with the Greek name of Leuce Come ('White Village').[11] The site of this is disputed, but it cannot have been much more than 500 miles from Suez, and perhaps less. Yet numerous ships were wrecked even on this short voyage; and the army on landing was so worn out and diseased that it needed the better part of a year to recuperate.

The Romans then advanced into the desert interior, with no clear idea of where they were or where they intended to go. All the signals seemed to be set for one of the world's great military disasters, comparable with the destruction of Crassus' army at Carrhae in 53 BC or Elphinstone's at Kabul in 1842. Syllaeus, however, must have been a more reliable guide than he was afterwards made out to be; instead of abandoning the Romans in the desert, as he could easily have done had he wished, he led them to the comparative safety of an oasis called Negrana (modern Najran, in Saudi Arabia just north of the frontier with the Yemen). From here it was no great distance to the most northerly of the 'Five Incense-Bearing Kingdoms', that of Ma'in;

and it is reported that the Romans captured two of its cities, Nesca and Athrula.[12] (Oddly enough, however, the account does not mention Carna or Qarnawu, the earlier capital of Ma'in. It is uncertain whether this is because it surrendered at once, or because it was no longer a place of consequence.)

Aelius Gallus by this time must have been feeling a disenchantment comparable with Dick Whittington's on finding that the streets of London were not paved with gold, or Cinderella's when the magic coach turned back into a pumpkin. He had been sent out to conquer one of the most romantic-sounding parts of the known world, and had passed through terrible privations to reach it; now that he was there at last, it seemed quite an ordinary place, not in the least like the *Arabia Felix* he must have expected to find. He marched on to a place called 'Marsiaba', besieged it for six days, but had to give up for lack of water; this in itself might not have deterred him, since reports came to him at just this time that the true 'Incense-Country' was only two days' journey away. But many travellers, not only in Arabia, have found out to their cost just how elusive that expression 'two days' journey' can be. The Roman army remained in South Arabia for a further six months, working hard to achieve nothing in particular, before Gallus at last concluded that the real Arabia could never be made to approximate to the ideal one. He and his army then returned northward (making better time on this journey than on the southward one) and at length reached Egypt imbued with a profound mistrust of Arab guides in general and of Syllaeus in particular.

The other story of Roman contact with South Arabia is very different: it is the *Periplus of the Erythraean Sea*, the salesman's guide whose account of East Africa was mentioned in the last chapter. Immediately after the East African section comes one on Arabia – described at first in most uncomplimentary terms:

> . . . along the sea occur the enclosures of the Ichthyophagi; and higher up are villages and nomadic encampments inhabited by scoundrelly people who speak two languages; and those who stray from the middle course and fall into their hands are either plundered or, if they survive from shipwrecks, are carried into slavery . . . the country being without harbours, with bad anchorages and a foul shore, unapproachable by reason of rocks, and in every way formidable.[13]

Better conditions were available, however, at the southern end of the Red Sea. Here lay the substantial port of Muza, visited by seafarers who sometimes sailed as far as India. It belonged to the king of

Ma'afir, or Mapharitis; but he was only a petty chief, subordinate to a more powerful inland ruler whose royal line we have already met:

> . . . Charibael, the lawful king of two tribes, the Homerite [Himyar] and that lying beside it called Sabaite [Sheba]; he is called 'Friend of the Emperors' on account of his continual embassies and gifts.[14]

(This mention of a 'lawful king' gives a hint of the turbulent political life of ancient South Arabia: Charibael's 'embassies and gifts' had convinced the Roman authorities that he was 'lawful', but there may well have been pretenders in the region who would have disagreed.) Charibael also controlled a large port at Aden further round the coast; the Greek name for this was the same as that given to the whole peninsula, Arabia Eudaemon or 'Araby the Blest' – a singularly inappropriate name, as more recent visitors to Aden have often pointed out.

> Eudaemon Arabia was called Eudaemon when in former days it was a city, when men had not voyaged from India to Egypt, and those from Egypt had not ventured to sail to the places further inside the sea-corridor, but came here where the cargoes from both India and Egypt were received, just as Alexandria receives them, both from overseas and from Egypt itself. But now, not very long before our time, Caesar destroyed it.[15]

The last sentence of this confused and confusing passage has aroused much controversy. Some authorities assert that 'Caesar' is a mistake for some other name, such as Charibael or Elisar, and those who take the word to mean what it says disagree about the identity of the 'Caesar' concerned; suggestions range from Augustus in 23 BC to Caracalla in AD 196.

Just as Charibael was the 'Myrrh King', so his eastern neighbour Eleazus was the 'Frankincense King'; the *Periplus* even refers to him as such, rather than by his official title which would have been 'King of Hadhramaut'. He ruled the island of Socotra as well as Hadhramaut, and like Charibael had far-reaching trade contacts, 'with Barygaza and Scythia and Omana and the neighbouring regions of Persis'.[16] His chief port was called Cana, and to it was brought the produce of the 'Frankincense Region' proper. Gathering incense was neither an agreeable nor an honourable task:

> The incense is handled by the royal slaves and men who have been sent there as punishment. The place is fearfully unhealthy, and pestilential even to those who sail past it; to those who work there it is always fatal; and in addition they are killed off by sheer lack of food.[17]

(Once again, as in Herodotus' account, one seems to hear the voice of the Arab monopolist determined not to let foreigners discover the true sources of his wealth.)

*

The rest of Arabia, outside the incense-bearing countries of the south, was sparsely inhabited and seldom mentioned by ancient writers. It was a land of passage, through or around which the incense had to be carried on its way to its principal consumers in the Roman and Parthian empires. It was a dangerous land, too, a place of heat and drought and oppression, of bad roads and shoal waters and 'scoun-drelly people' who practised brigandage on land and piracy at sea. The foreign traveller's chief object on entering it was to leave it again as quickly as possible.

The sea route between South Arabia and the Roman Empire has already been briefly mentioned. From such ports as Cana, Aden and Muza, ships regularly sailed up the Red Sea despite the obstacles to navigation mentioned by the *Periplus* and other ancient sources. Sometimes they went right up as far as Suez, which was linked with the Nile by a Roman road and also by a canal (though the canal had an irritating habit of silting up and becoming unusable). More often the ships ended their voyage at a port further south on the coast of Roman Egypt, such as Myos Hormos or Berenice. The goods were then carried across the desert to the Nile and shipped downstream, which was safer than using the open sea.[18] Whichever route they took they were likely to pass through Alexandria, the capital of Egypt and the second largest city in the Roman Empire; such trade with Arabia (and also, as we shall see in later chapters, with India and even China) was one of the city's chief sources of wealth.

There was also an overland route, with some flourishing commer-cial towns on it, leading up the western side of the Arabian peninsula. On leaving the Incense-Country by this route, the caravans came first to Negrana (Najran), as Aelius Gallus had done. Further north lay Macoraba (Mecca), not a large settlement but already an important religious centre; its principal shrine, the Ka'bah, eventually came to contain 360 idols, as well as the famous Black Stone (a piece of meteoritic rock) which is still there and still venerated. The other great holy place of Islam, Medina, is also of pre-Islamic origin; its early name was Yathrib or Iathrippa, and it too was on an important caravan-route.[19]

Further north still was the kingdom of the Nabataeans, a people with numerous trading connexions. From their famous capital at Petra they sent caravans westward down to Gaza and other ports on the

Mediterranean coast, from which the incense was dispatched by sea to reach its final consumers; northward, they spread their commercial and political influence through the desert sometimes as far as Damascus; eastward, they crossed Arabia Deserta to make contact with the Parthian Empire; southward, they controlled the land of Midian as far as the town of Egra (Mada'in Salih) and sometimes further.[20] Nabataean art displays a remarkable mixture of Greek, Arab and Persian styles; Nabataean technical skill was able to plant flourishing towns in some very remote and desolate places. These were no Bedouin like their southern neighbours, but a settled people growing rich through their control of an established trade route.

'Some men of noble stock are made; some glory in the murder-blade; Some praise a Science or an Art; but I like honourable Trade!

Rock tombs at Mada' in Salih (ancient Egra) near the southern frontier of the Nabataean kingdom.

Sell them the rotten, buy the ripe! Their heads are weak, their pockets
   burn.
Aleppo men are mighty fools. Salaam Aleikum! Safe return!'

But in AD 106 the sands ran out for the Nabataean kingdom; it was
annexed by the emperor Trajan, and made into the Roman province of
Arabia. Petra, isolated in the middle of a desert, did not even get the
consolation prize of becoming the provincial capital; this honour went
instead to Bostra (Busra), some distance further north and more
accessible from other parts of the Roman world. The lines of trade
were redrawn so as to pass more often through other Eastern centres
such as Alexandria, Antioch and Palmyra, and less and less often
through Petra.

*

The Parthian Empire, in Iraq and Iran, was as eager to buy South
Arabian incense as was the Roman Empire. So, while some caravans
travelled up the west side of the peninsula in the direction of Rome,
others turned in a north-easterly direction and aimed for the Parthian
capital of Ctesiphon. Unfortunately we know very little about this East
Arabian trade-route. Surviving Parthian geographical writings are
rare, and none deals with Arabia. From the westerners' point of view,
commerce between Arabia and Parthia was of no special importance
and not worth describing in detail. The author of the *Periplus* says
practically nothing about it; Pliny's account is long, involved and
largely incomprehensible; Ptolemy's map, though promising at first
sight, is not of much use when it comes to pinning down a particular
ancient name on to a particular modern place.

   It is known, however, that the island of Bahrain played an important
part in East Arabian history from early times. Greek and Latin writers
knew it as Tylos, which they often regarded as a variant of 'Tyros' or
Tyre; this led them to the implausible conclusion that the Phoenicians
had sailed round Arabia, founded Bahrain and named it after their
own principal city. But the underlying idea that Bahrain was a very
ancient place has been confirmed by archaeologists. It was probably
the headquarters of a state called Dilmun, which was already
flourishing by about 2000 BC as the middleman in trade between the
civilizations of Mesopotamia and the Indus Valley.

   In the time of the Roman and Parthian Empires there was a large
port called Gerra on the mainland somewhere opposite Bahrain. Its
exact site is unknown, but was extensive (Pliny mentions that it had a
wall with towers, five miles in circumference) and advantageously
placed.[21] Caravans from South Arabia, having skirted the sands of the

*The Khazneh or
'Treasury' at Petra.*

Empty Quarter, normally stopped at Gerra rather than continue northward up the coast and through Kuwait; instead their cargoes completed the journey to Parthian territory by sea. The Gerraeans, like their opposite numbers the Nabataeans, grew rich by means of their trans-shipment facilities. They had also a valuable resource of their own; the pearls of the Bahrain region were the second most famous in the Ancient World, outclassed only by those of Ceylon.

The lands east and south-east of Bahrain (the modern United Arab Emirates and Oman) were the least well-known of all to geographers in the Roman Empire. Unlike South Arabia, they produced nothing of intrinsic value; unlike western, central or eastern Arabia, they were not on any of the routes by which any commodity was brought to better-known parts. Even the trade between Mesopotamia and India often sailed past them without stopping. There was apparently one substantial mercantile town in the neighbourhood, called Omana; but this is even harder to locate than Gerra, and has a claim to be the most elusive site in ancient geography. Ancient accounts of it are wildly at variance. Some place it in Arabia within the Gulf, others outside, and others again (including the usually reliable *Periplus*) on the Persian coast opposite. The name has survived to the present day, but only as the name of a region – which raises a further disturbing possibility, that 'Omana' in ancient writings may have meant 'the capital of Oman' without implying that this was always in the same place.[22]

*

The Romans were neither the first nor the last people to invade ancient Arabia. On the contrary, it seems to have been a point of honour among all the great powers in the neighbourhood to demonstrate their greatness in the same way. As early as the seventh century BC we hear of Assyrian armies attacking the town of Al Jawf, in the heart of Arabia Deserta; and in about 550 BC king Nabonidus of Babylon occupied Tayma, still farther south on an important route between the Incense-Country and the Levant. Darius I of Persia sent an expedition from the Indus along the Iranian coast, then round Arabia and up the Red Sea. Alexander the Great had both sides of the Persian Gulf explored, and made a plan to conquer the whole Arabian peninsula – but died before he could try to put it into practice. And Pliny states that there had once been Greek cities in Arabia (Arethusa, Larisa and Chalcis), afterwards 'destroyed in various wars'. Unfortunately his account is so vague that there is no way of telling where these might have been.[23]

The Parthian kings, with their many domestic and foreign troubles, were unable to afford the luxury of Arabian adventures. Their successors the Sasanians, however, had a more aggressive policy towards the Arabs, as towards their other neighbours. Shapur II (AD 309–79) campaigned all along the western side of the Gulf, from the Euphrates to Oman; his barbarous treatment of prisoners caused the Arabs to nickname him Dhu'l-aktaf, 'the dislocator of shoulders'.

At about the same time the ancient rivalry between East and West for domination of Arabia was complicated by the appearance of a new power. This was the kingdom of Axum, mentioned at the end of the last chapter. The inscription of king Ezana at Axum (page 77) calls him 'king of Himyar and Raidan and Saba' which were all districts of south-western Arabia; just as the Persians had succeeded in controlling both sides of the mouth of the Gulf, so the Axumites had done the same at the mouth of the Red Sea.

Alongside this political struggle was fought a still more complex religious one. The Persians promoted Zoroastrianism, the Axumites promoted Christianity, and both had to contend not only with the native paganism but also with a strong force of Judaism. King Dhu Nuwas of Himyar, for example, was a convert to Judaism, and demonstrated the old rule that converts are more fervent than those born in the faith; in 523 he seized the Christian town of Najran, offered its inhabitants the choice between Judaism and death, and had the non-recanters burned alive in a trench.[24] This action caused the Christian Axumites to invade, and once again most of South Arabia came under their rule. One Axumite expedition reached as far north as Mecca, but failed to take it, supposedly because their elephants refused to co-operate. Muslim tradition has it that this 'Year of the Elephant' was also the year of Mohammed's birth, and fell in AD 570.[25]

Though the birth of the Prophet is a convenient point at which to end Arabian ancient history, it is worth noting the circumstances in which he grew up. Mecca was almost exactly equidistant from the Byzantine, Persian and Axumite centres of operations, and the young Mohammed was well placed to observe the machinations of three political powers and four religions. It was an appropriate origin for the founder of a new religion that was rapidly to become a new political movement as well.

CHAPTER SIX

THE PARTHIANS AND SASANIANS

We have spent two hundred million pounds to prove the fact once more,
That horses are quicker than men afoot, since two and two make four;
And horses have four legs, and men have two legs, and two into four goes
  twice,
And nothing over except our lesson – and very cheap at the price.

The Lesson
(On the Boer War, 1899–1902)

Most of the territory that once formed the Parthian Empire is shared today by Iraq and Iran, two nations which despite their similar names have never had much in common; the war in progress between them as these words are being written is only the latest display of a very old tradition of hostility. Iraq is flat; Iran is mountainous. Iraq is watered by two of the world's greatest rivers, the Euphrates and Tigris, along whose banks at a very early date developed an advanced civilization using dykes and canals to control the water-supply and grow great quantities of grain. (Similar riverine civilizations were to develop somewhat later along the Nile in Egypt, the Indus in Pakistan and the Yellow River in China.) Iran has no such great rivers (parts of it, indeed, have hardly any water-supply at all) and in ancient times was the home of a more footloose people. From their eyries in the Zagros mountains the early Iranians often cast covetous eyes upon their richer neighbours in the plain below; on perceiving the slightest sign of weakness, they would drop down hawklike upon it – only to become the captives of their captives, to learn settled civilization in their turn, to lose their military prowess and finally to fall victims to a fresh group of invaders pressing down from the east. Iraqis today speak Arabic, a language of the Semitic family related to Hebrew, Ancient Egyptian, Phoenician and Aramaic (the speech used by Jesus Christ). Iranians speak Persian, which though usually written in the Arabic script is not related to Arabic at all: it is a member of the Indo-European language family, and thus a distant cousin of most of the languages used in Europe. In religion, too, there are long-standing differences. Ancient Iraq, like most other ancient countries, was polytheist, worshipping the Sun, the Moon, the God of Battle, the Goddess of Love and all the rest of the pantheon best known today in its Roman form, but by no means confined to the Roman world. The Iranians, by contrast, had at an early stage in their history taken up the beliefs of Zoroaster, according to whom all such multiple gods were trivial; the world in his view contained only two important forces, those of Light and Darkness. (For this reason the early Persian kings often expressed a kind of fellow-feeling towards the Jews, the only other people in the Ancient World whose thought had run on anything like the same lines.) Even today, though both countries are Muslim, they profess different varieties of Islam, most Iraqis being Sunnite and most Iranians Shi 'ite. In other respects too Iran has often been the maverick among Islamic nations, the only one in which the great flood of Islam did not entirely cover the land, but left a few peaks of older belief still standing up above it. (Mediaeval Iran, for example, produced a distinguished school of painting, which the orthodox condemned as 'worshipping graven images' and thereby breaking the Second Commandment.)[1]

*

Iraq and Iran were first united by Cyrus the Great. This remarkable world-conqueror, who perhaps deserves a higher place in history than he has generally received, began life as a prince of Persis – not, in those days, merely another word for 'Iran', but meaning specifically a smallish part of Iran, on its south-western side and somewhat isolated

Relief from Palmyra: the Phoenician god Baalshamin, flanked by the gods of the Moon and Sun, all in Greek military uniform.

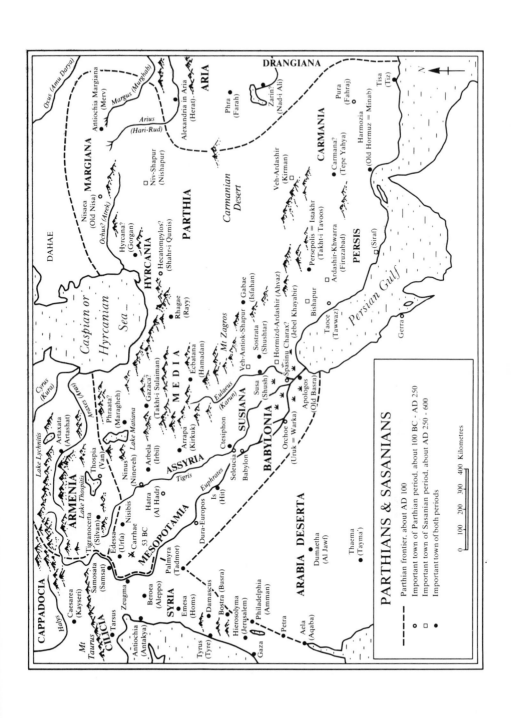

PARTHIANS & SASANIANS

- - - - Parthian frontier, about AD 100
○ Important town of Parthian period, about 100 BC - AD 250
□ Important town of Sasanian period, about AD 250 - 600
● Important town of both periods

0 100 200 300 400 Kilometres

N

DRANGIANA

ARIA

Oxus (Amu Darya)
Margus (Murghab)
Antiochia Margiana (Merv)
Arius (Hari-Rud)
Alexandria in Aria (Herat)
Phra (Farah)
Zarin? (Nad-i Ali)
Tisa (Tiz)
Pura (Fahraj)

MARGIANA
Ochus? (Atrek)
Nisaea (Old Nisa)
Niv-Shapur (Nishapur)
Carmana? (Tepe Yahya)
Harmozia (Old Hormuz = Minab)

PARTHIA

CARMANIA

Carmanian Desert

DAHAE

Hyrcana? (Gorgan)
Hecatompylos? (Shahr-i Qumis)
Veh-Ardashir (Kirman)

Caspian or Hyrcanian Sea

HYRCANIA

Rhagae (Rayy)
Persepolis = Istakhr (Takht-i Tavoos)
(Siraf)

PERSIS

Cyrus (Kura)
Araxes (Aras)
Lake Lychnitis
Lake Thospia
Artaxata (Artashat)
Thospia (Van)
Phraata? (Maragheh)
Lake Matiana
Gazaca? (Takht-i Sulaiman)

Gabae (Isfahan)
Veh-Antiok-Shapur
Sostrata (Shushtar)
Hormizd-Ardashir (Ahvaz)
Spasinu Charax?
Jebel Khayabir
Ardashir-Khwarra (Firuzabad)
Bishapur
Taoce (Tawwaz)

Persian Gulf

Gerra

ARMENIA

MEDIA

Mt Zagros

Ecbatana (Hamadan)

Eulaeus (Karun)

SUSIANA

Susa (Shush)

CAPPADOCIA

Halys
Caesarea (Kayseri)
Mt Taurus
Tarsus
CILICIA
Antiochia (Antakya)

Tigranocerta (Silvan)
Samosata (Samsat)
Edessa (Urfa)
Nisibis
Carrhae
53 BC
Ninus (Nineveh)
Arbela (Irbil)
Arrapa (Kirkuk)
Zeugma

MESOPOTAMIA

Hatra (Al Hadr)

ASSYRIA

Tigris

Dura-Europos
Is (Hit)
Euphrates

Ctesiphon
Seleucia
Babylon

BABYLONIA

Orchoe (Uruk = Warka)
Apologos (Old Basra)

Palmyra (Tadmor)

SYRIA
Beroea (Aleppo)
Emesa (Homs)
Damascus
Bostra (Busra)
Hierosolyma (Jerusalem)
Philadelphia (Amman)
Tyrus (Tyre)
Gaza
Petra
Aela (Aqaba)

ARABIA DESERTA

Dumaetha (Al Jawf)

Thaema (Tayma')

from the main stream of history.[2] He died (in 530 BC) as ruler of all Iran, Iraq, the Levant and Asia Minor; he had also conquered most of what is now Afghanistan, and in the last years of his life was fighting the nomadic steppe-dwellers in what is now Soviet Central Asia. His son Cambyses conquered Egypt; his cousin Darius conquered the Indus Valley to create the largest and most powerful empire that the world had ever seen. Posterity, however, was to keep a special place in its heart for the first and greatest of the Persian High Kings: 'Cyrus', it was said, 'ruled his country like a father, Cambyses like a tyrant, Darius like a shopkeeper'.

Whereas Cyrus has received less than his due from the modern world, Alexander (also called the Great) has perhaps received more. Cyrus *made* the Persian Empire from diverse elements; Alexander merely *annexed* it as a going concern, and died (in 323 BC) before he had come to the difficult task of driving his ill-assorted team in a constant direction. His death was soon followed by the break-up of what even the most incompetent Persian rulers had been able to hold together. After much confused fighting, the short-lived empire of Alexander found itself divided into three principal parts: the Antigonid family ruled Greece, the Ptolemies ruled Egypt and the Seleucids ruled most of the rest. Seleucid territory, however, soon began to disintegrate in its turn. India, the most easterly of the former Persian territories, was given up by Seleucus I (the founder of the dynasty) as early as 304 BC; and he and his successors thereafter paid more and more attention to the 'Fertile Crescent' of Syria and Mesopotamia, less and less to the mountainous lands of Iran with their hostile climate and even more hostile inhabitants. It was against this background, of a vast country being ruled by absentee landlords, that the Parthians began their rise to power.

East of the Caspian Sea lies a land of steppe and semi-desert. In ancient times it was occupied by nomadic horsemen, closely akin to the Scythians of the Black Sea steppe described in Chapter Three. One of these Caspian tribes was called the Dahae, and one branch of it was called the Parni. In about 238 BC these people crossed the mountains which now separate the USSR from Iran, and overran the land of Parthia to the south of them. Western writers accordingly came to call the Parni 'Parthians', though Parthia was not their original home.

The Seleucid kings fought repeatedly against the Parthians, but with little success. Antiochus III defeated them and apparently reduced them to vassalage, but was then laid low by a disaster at the other end of his empire: in 190 BC the Romans defeated him at Magnesia (now Manisa, in western Turkey) and imposed peace-terms that left him seriously and permanently weakened. Some thirty years later the

Parthians began to take the offensive again. Under their great king Mithradates I they conquered the whole of Iran, then like the Persians before them dropped from the heights of the Zagros on to the plains of Mesopotamia. In 141 BC they entered Seleucia-on-the-Tigris, one of the twin capitals of the Seleucid kingdom (the other being Antioch on the Orontes) and at the time one of the largest cities in the world. Two years later the Seleucid king himself, Demetrius II, became Mithradates' prisoner. A counter-attack by his brother, Antiochus VII, began well but ended in even worse disaster, this king being killed in battle in 129 BC. Thereafter the Seleucids dwindled into obscurity. In 92 BC, like the jaws of a giant vice, Roman and Parthian empires closed together on the line of the Euphrates, and the last heirs of the once-mighty Greek dynasty ended their days as helpless pensioners of Rome.

The Romans at this time had a low opinion of the Parthians, regarding them as a mere disorganized rabble of 'wild men from the East'. It was the misfortune of Marcus Licinius Crassus to find out the hard way that there was more to them than that.

Crassus was one of the three men known to history as the 'First Triumvirate', who from 59 BC shared supreme power at Rome.[3] Of the other two, Pompey the Great was at the time Rome's premier general, the conqueror of large parts of the Near East; Julius Caesar, the youngest of the three, had first come to prominence as a politician rather than a soldier, but more recently in his conquest of Gaul had shown military ability as impressive as that of Pompey. Crassus' main contribution to the group was his enormous wealth; but he too had military ambitions, and in 55 BC he attempted to realize them by means of an attack (totally unprovoked) on the Parthian kingdom. Right from the start things went badly. Most of Rome's keenest young soldiers, eager for glory and booty, were in Gaul with Caesar; most of her veterans, who knew a soft job when they saw one, were in Spain with Pompey. Crassus' army contained a disturbingly large number of raw recruits and bad characters whom the other two had rejected. As it left Rome the expedition was solemnly cursed by one of Crassus' political rivals; and with hindsight even the cries of the costermongers came to be taken as unlucky. (They were selling figs from Caunus, in Asia Minor, and their *Cauneas, Ca-u-ne-as* sounded like *Cave ne eas* – 'Look out! Don't go!')

The army in due course reached Syria, and spent the year 54 BC in minor operations. The opening of the next year's campaign, however, called upon Crassus to make an important decision. The heart of Parthian territory (if it could be said to have a heart at all) was Ctesiphon, on the Tigris opposite the older Greek city of Seleucia. The most direct way of reaching it from Syria would have been to follow first the Euphrates, and then the Royal Canal which linked it with the Tigris.[4] On this route there would be no danger of losing the way or running out of water, and the citizens of Seleucia itself were known to be friendly to Rome. So too was the king of Armenia, and it would also have been possible to advance through his country in an eastward direction, strike the Tigris further upstream, and then descend it. This had the further advantage that the mountains of Armenia would have made it hard for the Parthians to deploy their cavalry. Crassus, however, rejected both plans: instead he played straight into the enemy's hands by marching directly into the desert.

Near the town of Carrhae (Harran) the Roman and Parthian armies made contact. In appearance and tactics they made a striking contrast. The Roman army as usual consisted mostly of heavy infantry – seven legions of them, about 40,000 men whose standard tactic was to close with the enemy, hurl their heavy spears (*pila*) at him, then close further still and finish off with the short sword. On crossing the Euphrates the Romans had also had 4000 horsemen; but most of these, contributed by 'allied' local kings, deserted before the battle.

The Parthian army, by contrast, numbered a mere 10,000 men; but every single one of these was mounted. About 1000 of them were heavy cavalry; they rode some of the largest and finest horses in the world, bred on the Nisaean plains of Media and strong enough not only to carry a man in full armour but also to wear armour all over themselves. These horsemen, rather than the flimsy chariotry of a few centuries earlier, were the 'tanks' of the Ancient World. They could stride through the smallest gap in the enemy's formation, and only the most desperate man, with the dagger of a Welsh mountaineer and the courage of a Japanese *kamikaze* pilot, could dodge under the horse's belly and kill it by striking upwards. The remaining 9000 Parthians rode smaller horses and wore little or no armour; their chief weapon was the bow, which they could shoot forwards, sideways and even backwards over the horse's rump – the famous 'Parthian shot'.

It was these archers who destroyed the army of Crassus. Roman after Roman fell; even their last hope, that the wretched ponyboys would soon run out of arrows, was frustrated – the Parthian commander, Surena, had thought of this and brought up a fresh supply on the backs of camels. A short stay in Carrhae itself only delayed their fate until they ran out of food. On their march back towards Syria Crassus himself was killed while negotiating with the enemy; tradition has it that his head later formed a gruesome 'prop' in a performance of Euripides' *Bacchae*, watched by the kings of Parthia and Armenia. In all, some 20,000 Romans perished with him; another 10,000 were taken prisoner and sent to the oasis of Merv, far to the east; only 10,000 (among them Cassius, the future murderer of Caesar) escaped to the safety of the Euphrates frontier.

Terrible as were the immediate results of Carrhae, its long-term results were worse still. Although (or perhaps because) they had been the aggressors, the Romans never forgot or forgave Carrhae: it stirred in them a desire for *revanche* as burning as that of the French after Sedan. Again and again Roman leaders strove to overthrow the power that had so insulted them. Julius Caesar's plan for a Parthian campaign, in 44 BC, was halted only by his death. Mark Antony made that plan an actuality; with a force about twice as large as Crassus', he successfully crossed Armenia to enter the region of north-western Iran known as Atropatene. But the mountains of this land proved as formidable an obstacle as the deserts further south. Antony failed to take the local capital, Phraata or Phraaspa; and though on the return march he avoided the total disaster of Crassus, he nonetheless left behind many dead men and prisoners – men who might have been useful in his forthcoming clash with his rival Octavian.[5]

The latter, on achieving supreme power and taking the title Augustus, took a more peaceful attitude to the 'Eastern Question'. He was able to recover, by negotiation, the standards lost under Crassus and Antony (an important piece of face-saving, since a Roman legion had even stronger feelings about its Eagle than a British regiment has about its colours) and also some of the prisoners. But the dream of great eastern conquests was still there, put forward repeatedly by the court poets.

> Caelo tonantem credidimus Iovem
> regnare: praesens divus habebitur
>   Augustus adiectis Britannis
>   imperio gravibusque Persis.

> 'Jove reigns in heaven, the thunder seems to say,
> And we believe: but Jove is far away:
>   On earth Augustus shall be held divine
> When Briton and dread Persian own his sway.'[6]

Under the emperor Nero this dream took tangible form once more. Domitius Corbulo, one of Rome's most distinguished commanders, attacked Armenia and captured its two largest cities, Artaxata and Tigranocerta; but his incompetent colleague Caesennius Paetus threw away the advantage and was driven out in the most humiliating fashion by the Parthian counter-attack. Though an honourable peace was then agreed (page 107) the Parthians had once again come off best in practice whatever the situation might be in theory.[7]

In the second century AD the Romans were superficially more successful. Ctesiphon, the Parthian capital, was taken no less than three times: by the armies of Trajan in 116, of Lucius Verus in 165 and of Septimius Severus in 198. But each time the victory proved to be fairy gold. Trajan for a brief period was able to call himself ruler of Armenia and all Mesopotamia right down to the Persian Gulf; but widespread revolts in his older Eastern provinces forced him to turn back to the Mediterranean, and on his death soon afterwards his successor Hadrian restored the *status quo*. Lucius Verus' campaign acquired the city of Dura-Europos, on the middle Euphrates – also an unusually virulent form of plague, which spread through the Roman Empire at just the time when it needed all its manpower to withstand the growing threat from the German tribes in the north. Septimius Severus did gain something more permanent, in the form of the 'Province of Mesopotamia'; but this was not the whole land between the rivers Euphrates and Tigris, but only a small part of it in what is now eastern Syria. By doing even this much, as we shall presently see, he may have created more problems for Rome than he solved.[8]

*

Fresco from the Temple of the Palmyrene Gods, Dura-Europos.

The Parthians have been poorly treated by posterity. Even their own country, Iran, has been unkind to them: standard Iranian history tends to pass quickly from the glories of Cyrus and Darius round about 500 BC to the equal glories of Ardashir and Shapur round about AD 250, dismissing the intervening few centuries as an unpleasant interlude best forgotten. The European layman knows the Parthians only for their unsportsmanlike habit of shooting backwards. And even when one looks into the subject more deeply, it is still hard to form a true and fair view of these people, since almost everything written about them comes from their enemies the Greeks and Romans.

After Carrhae, Roman writers regularly referred to the Parthians as 'the fierce', 'the troublesome', 'the implacable'. (*Cet animal est très méchant; quand on l'attaque il se défend*). But when observed without bias they show themselves to have been unusually relaxed and go-as-you-please in their political life. For example, their territory was full of Greek cities, from Dura-Europos in the west to Antiochia-Margiana in the east, founded by Alexander and his Seleucid successors. Though the Greekness of some of these communities consisted of little more than a new name, others really were inhabited by people of Greek origin and Greek habits of thought; and it was noticeable that whenever the Romans invaded Parthian territory, most of the Greek communities came out in their support. Yet it never seems to have occurred to the Parthian kings to exterminate the Greeks, or deport them to some remote spot in the Carmanian desert where they would be less of a nuisance, or even disperse them from their cities into the countryside; when this is contrasted with the fate of the Jews, who had an analogous position within the Roman Empire, the tolerance and humanity of the Parthians seem remarkable.

Whereas Romans always look as if they know where they are going, even when it is to disaster, Parthians give the impression of being completely disorganized even when they win. As in pre-Mao China, described by Bertrand Russell, 'Industry was too inefficient to produce either automobiles or bombs; the State too inefficient to educate its own citizens or to kill those of other countries; the police too inefficient to catch either bandits or Bolsheviks.'[9] And this inefficiency, this floppy organization, may paradoxically have helped the Parthian state to persist. What country with a centralized bureaucratic government could have survived having its capital city occupied three times within a century?

The relationship of the Parthian king to his subordinates likewise seems loose-knit and untidy when compared with the Roman system. Many rulers of Iran, from Cyrus the Great to the twentieth century, have borne a title meaning 'King of Kings'; the Parthian rulers were among them, and in their case the title was unusually apt. Pliny tells us that the High King of Parthia ruled eighteen vassal kings, eleven being 'upper' or northern and seven 'lower' or southern.[10] He does not go on to enumerate them, and it has not been possible to work out the full list. As a small sample, however, I propose to describe three of these sub-kingdoms to give some idea of the variety of peoples that lived under the Parthian umbrella.

The kingdom of Armenia was among the largest and most important of all. It was a tract of mountainous country, about the same size as England with Wales, reaching from the Black Sea to the Caspian. Like the Garden of Eden, which some people believe was situated there, it was the source of several great rivers: the Acampsis flowing into the Black Sea, the Cyrus and Araxes into the Caspian, and the Tigris and Euphrates into the Persian Gulf. Parts of it, again like the Garden of Eden, were very fertile, and produced flowers, fruit and vegetables in great abundance. To men from the drier countries to the south and east it seemed like a paradise; on the other hand, trying to cross it in winter could be more like trying to cross the lowest circle of Dante's Hell.

Civilization in Armenia has a long history. In about 900 BC it became the seat of a kingdom called Urartu, with its capital at Tushpa (modern Van, on Lake Van).[11] The Urartians, however, had to contend with powerful neighbours on several sides – Assyrians to the south, Scythians in the steppe-country to the north and Medes in the mountains of Iran to the east. By about 600 BC the kingdom had collapsed; its territory became subject first to the Medes, then to the Persians, and finally to the Macedonians.

The gradual weakening of Macedonian power allowed Armenia to take a more independent line once again. In 188 BC a dynast called Artaxias was officially confirmed in his power by the Roman Senate, and at once took advantage of his valuable new status by attacking his neighbours. His descendant Tigranes II (the son-in-law and ally of Mithradates of Pontus, whose meteoric career was described in Chapter Three) was even more successful, and extended his power over all of eastern Asia Minor, Syria and parts of Phoenicia. But this brought him up against the Romans, first Lucullus and then Pompey; in 69 BC his new capital of Tigranocerta was sacked, and though he kept his throne he was forced to give up all his conquests.

From then on Armenia, like Urartu before it, was a small power placed between two much larger ones, and had to walk delicately. The son of Tigranes, Artavasdes II, at first did this well: it was he who, having offered his services to Crassus (page 102), changed sides in time to congratulate the Parthian king on a splendid victory. An attempt to take the same line with Mark Antony, however, saved the Armenian state but not its ruler. Artavasdes was captured, sent to Egypt and finally murdered.

The year AD 53 saw a change of dynasty, the new king being a brother of the king of Parthia. This was the signal for renewed war with Rome, which ended in a compromise in which the emperor Nero himself placed the crown on the head of his former enemy. Despite a painful interlude in Trajan's reign, when king Parthamasiris was murdered by the Romans and his kingdom annexed, the Parthian dynasty managed to survive in Armenia till as late as AD 428, by which time the senior branch of the family had long been extinct. The nation itself survived longer still; and even today, though the Armenians are no longer independent or even politically united, they still possess a clear identity of their own.

Another Parthian vassal-kingdom, smaller than Armenia but just as independent-minded, was that of Hatra. It lay in a landscape very different from the mountains of the north, consisting in effect of the city of Hatra (modern Al-Hadr, some thirty miles west of the Tigris) plus an ill-defined tract of surrounding desert. It was this desert that made Hatra strong: the best water-supply for miles around was within the walls of the city, so that in any attack the besiegers were likely to suffer more than the besieged. The armies of Trajan, Lucius Verus and Septimius Severus all attacked it without the slightest success. Only in about AD 240, by which time it had gone over to the Roman side, was it finally taken (supposedly through treachery) by the Sasanian king Shapur I. It was then destroyed and abandoned – but as often happens the 'destruction' has left behind much more impressive remains than a long period of peaceful rebuilding would have done. The Hatrans, like the Palmyrenes on the other side of Arabia Deserta, had waxed rich on the caravan-trade between the Roman, Parthian and Arab worlds, and with the proceeds had built a colossal temple for their local sun-god and many other large buildings. Greek, Roman, Arab and Persian styles mingled here with imposing, though sometimes clumsy, results.[12]

For a third important vassal-kingdom we visit a country whose physical features are different yet again. The rivers Tigris and Euphrates have changed their lower courses many times in recorded history, and it is not certain just how they flowed in the Parthian period. At all times, however, they have caused large tracts of country to be covered with marsh and swamp. Parts of Iraq are still like this today, inhabited by the interesting fenlanders described by Wilfred Thesiger in *The Marsh Arabs* and by Gavin Maxwell in *A Reed Shaken by the Wind*. In ancient times the marshes were more extensive, and

The Great Hall (iwan) of the Sun-Temple at Hatra.

protected a kingdom called Characene or Mesene, just as Armenia was protected by its mountains and Hatra by its desert. The capital of the region bore different names at different times. Alexander the Great, its founder, named it Alexandria; one ward of the city, reserved for Macedonians, was called Pella after his birthplace. Antiochus IV, the last Seleucid king to exercise real authority in the region, rebuilt the city after flood-damage and changed its name to Antioch. Later still it had to be rebuilt yet again, this time by a local ruler named Spasines or Hyspaosines; he protected it with great embankments, like the levees on the lower Mississippi, so that it came to be known as Spasinu Charax, 'the Stockade of Spasines'. Its exact site is uncertain: a promising candidate is the place now called Jebel Khayabir, on the banks of the Shatt-el-Arab, but this site has never been properly explored and for political reasons is likely to remain unexplored for a long time.[13]

Like Venice at the head of another large gulf, Spasinu Charax was a great centre of seaborne trade. Ships from here sailed regularly down the Gulf to fetch incense from Gerra, the chief port of eastern Arabia; and some went out of the Gulf, to follow the Iranian coast eastward and fetch the even more valuable spices of India. Unloaded at Charax, the goods were sent along a network of routes throughout the Parthian Empire – up the Tigris to the capital, Ctesiphon; up the Euphrates to Dura-Europos and the frontier with the Roman Empire; or via Hatra and Palmyra and other caravan-cities in the heart of Arabia Deserta. One of the few surviving works by a Characene citizen is the description of a great trade-route – the *Parthian Stations*, by Isidore of Charax, which begins at Antioch in Syria and guides the traveller to Ctesiphon and thence up to the Iranian plateau and so eastward as far as Kandahar. In AD 116 the emperor Trajan himself visited Charax – the newest, most easterly and most short-lived possession of his empire – and saw the great ships setting sail for India, and wished that he were a little younger, like Alexander, so that he could go there himself.

*

Over these and other kingdoms, all on the lookout for greater independence and at times ready to negotiate with the enemy to get it, the Parthian kings presided with a strange mixture of simplicity and sophistication. Unlike other great rulers of the Ancient World, from Rome to China, they never took to wearing robes; they kept instead to tunics and trousers as worn by their ancestors on the steppes, as if ready at any moment to jump on a horse and spend the rest of the day hunting or raiding. On the other hand, this simple costume was adorned with a great amount of jewelry – torques, belts, rings, and lesser jewels sewn on to the clothes themselves. The king and the great nobles wore elaborate jewelled headdresses, and there were strict rules about who was entitled to wear what sort. Surena, the Parthian commander at Carrhae, even wore make-up on his face. Roman writers often remarked how odd it was that these virile and warlike people could go about looking so effeminate. As time went on, however, Rome was to give the Easterners the sincerest form of flattery: not only did the Roman army adapt itself to a Parthian model by using more and more cavalry, but the Emperor himself came to dress (and act) more and more like an Oriental despot. Late Roman and Byzantine emperors used to appear in a blaze of jewels that would have delighted the Parthian kings, but made Julius Caesar feel slightly sick. And other features of the Byzantine court – the protocol, the seraglio, the eunuchs and the great difficulty of meeting or even seeing the ruler – are also derived from the tradition of 'the Great King, the King of Kings' in the East.

*

All dynasties come to an end, and the ramshackle Parthian dynasty was lucky to have lasted as long as it did. All through the second century AD it was troubled by faction-fights among its members and rebellion among its subjects, aided and abetted by two powerful outside enemies, the Kushan kingdom in the east and the Roman Empire in the west. The campaigns of Septimius Severus in 197–8, and his conquest of northern Mesopotamia, seem to have been the last straw; within thirty years the Parthians had gone, but from their fall Rome derived no benefit whatever.

Of all the Parthian vassal-kingdoms the proudest was that of Persis in south-western Iran. Persian kings had been ruling most of the civilized world at a time when Rome was still a village and the Parthians' ancestors an insignificant sub-tribe roaming the steppes of the Caspian. The old capital of the region, Persepolis, had been devastated by Alexander (in 330 BC) and left in ruins; but a new capital soon appeared not far away, also known as Persepolis to Western writers although its real name was Istakhr.[14] Here stood a great temple of the goddess Anahita, burning one of the everlasting fires which were important in early Iranian religion. One of the high priests at this temple bore the name of Sasan; he himself is not important in history, but his descendants – the Sasanid dynasty – certainly are. His grandson Ardashir launched a successful revolt against Parthian rule; his forces defeated and killed the last Parthian king, Artabanus V, in about AD 224, and thereafter defended themselves against attacks by Kushans, Romans, Armenians (for the royal house of Armenia was related to that of Parthia) and even 'Scythians' from beyond the Caucasus.

The underlying theme of Dame Freya Stark's interesting book *Rome on the Euphrates* is the way in which every effort by the Romans to secure their eastern frontier led to a result just the opposite of what they had intended. The Roman war with Antiochus III, back in 190 BC, had permanently weakened the Seleucid kingdom (which was at least of European origin and shared with Rome the traditions of the Western world) and led to its replacement by a set of Iranian nomads whose native traditions were altogether different. The Parthians might pay lip-service to the Greek way of life but they never really understood it; Greek writing appears on the coins of even the last Parthian kings, but by this time so barbarized as to be almost meaningless. Now Rome had helped to bring down the Parthian kingdom in turn – but only to see it replaced by a new state still more set in ways that were not the ways of Europe, and ready to take an aggressive policy in imposing these ways upon the outside world.

Shapur I, the son and successor of Ardashir, soon showed himself to be an even more vigorous new broom than his father. He began his reign with an attack on the Kushan kingdom to the east, seizing its capital Peshawar and deposing the ruling dynasty. He then turned his attention to his other great enemy, the Roman Empire. Cities of Roman Mesopotamia and Syria were overrun, among them the Syrian capital of Antioch, the third city of the Empire. Three Roman emperors were humbled – Gordian III, killed in battle; Philip the Arabian, forced to make a shameful peace; Valerian, captured in about AD 260 with all his army and led off to some unknown fate in Iran. Rock-carvings show the Persian king, dressed like someone out of Buffalo Bill's Wild West Show, triumphing over his Roman enemies. Some of the prisoners were further insulted by being settled in a new city with the name of Veh-Antiok-Shapur, 'Shapur's City, Better than Antioch'.[15] The Roman Empire fell into a decline from which it very nearly failed to recover.

Though at length it did recover, holding its own against the new power in the east and at times even seizing some extra territory, it never again became quite what it had been before. Once again Iran had led the way in changing her customs and Rome had followed. The accession of the emperor Diocletian (in AD 284) is commonly taken by historians to mark the end of the 'Early Empire' (in French, *le Haut-Empire*) and the start of the 'Late Empire' (*le Bas-Empire*); and

Rock-carving at Naqsh-i Rustam, near Persepolis. Triumph of Shapur I over the Roman emperors Philip (kneeling) and Valerian (standing behind him).

one of the chief differences between the two was the growth in the later period of governmental officiousness. The number of emperors, with associated imperial courts, was increased from one to four. Bureaucracy in the provinces increased to match. New laws governed prices, people's occupations, where they were to live. Officials appeared with the innocent-sounding name of *agentes in rebus*, 'agents of business': they were in fact secret policemen. In religion the indifference of earlier emperors gave way to an ugly fanaticism. We enter a world whose motto is 'Everything not forbidden is compulsory'.

With the rise of the Sasanians a similar change had already taken place in the Roman Empire's eastern neighbour. Its effects there were somewhat less distressing, for two reasons: first, Iraq and Iran already had behind them a long tradition of absolute government, in a way that the West had not; and even more important, the Sasanian kingdom had a vigour and self-confidence that the third-century Roman Empire noticeably lacked. The change of government in Iran certainly had its bright side. From being weak and divided, a laughing-stock to her eastern and western neighbours, the nation now sprang back to the position of a first-class power. The loot of Antioch and Peshawar must have made some people (though almost certainly not the general populace) much richer than before. In the arts of peace there was likewise an exciting expansion. Great new cities were built, with such names as Ardashir-Khwarra and Bishapur and the already mentioned Veh-Antiok-Shapur, honouring the new rulers. Surveys in Iraq have shown that large tracts of land previously unused now came under cultivation (just the opposite of what was happening in much of the Roman Empire at the same time).[16] Commerce flourished, particularly in the trade with Arabia and India, and sophisticated new banking systems grew up to deal with it. (The word 'cheque' is of Persian origin.) Coins now bore inscriptions in good Persian instead of bad Greek.

But all this took place under a highly rigid and authoritarian government. As in the Late Roman Empire, the orders of society became more and more fixed – at the top, the king; then the great nobles (not as numerous or as independent as in Parthian times, though their rulers were still never able to control them as fully as they wished); then an army of bureaucrats; and at the bottom a mass of people in a state little removed from slavery. Taxes were high, trade strictly controlled and new enterprise frowned upon.

In religious affairs too there was a greater rigidity than before. The religious practices of the Parthians are not at all well known. They were vaguely Zoroastrian, giving honour to the great Ahuramazda, creator of the world and supreme principle of the Good; but they also honoured at least two other major deities. Mithra, or Mithras, had originally been a sun-god but was converted into the St Michael of Zoroastrianism, leading the forces of Ahuramazda in their assault on the powers of Darkness and Evil. His cult became popular in the Roman army, eventually reaching places as far afield as Hadrian's Wall. Anahita was the Great Goddess, worshipped under a variety of names by all ancient Near Eastern peoples except the Jews; her fire-temple at Istakhr, served by the ancestors of the Sasanian kings, has already been mentioned. Besides these Iranian cults, however, the Parthians seem to have had others dating back to the time when they were nomads of the steppe: in particular they used to sacrifice horses, a practice of which Zoroaster would have thoroughly disapproved. And among their subjects could be found Babylonians worshipping Bel and Marduk, Jews worshipping Jehovah and Greeks worshipping the Olympic pantheon, all in perfect freedom.

The Sasanian rulers took a stricter attitude. Ardashir made Zoroastrianism the official religion of the state, destroying a great number of pagan temples and replacing them with the fire-temples that were among the most characteristic features of this belief. Shapur I was somewhat more open-minded, perhaps not so much through genuine tolerance as because he wanted a universal religion but was uncertain what form this should take. He took especial interest in the thoughts of a prophet called Mani, whose system took in a variety of ideas from older religions: it included the struggle between good and evil (of Zoroastrian origin); the transmigration of souls (Buddhist); a celibate, vegetarian priesthood (possibly Hindu); baptism, communion and absolution (Christian); and the rejection of idols (ultimately Jewish – though Jews themselves he regarded as servants of the Devil). Soon after Shapur's death, however, the court reacted violently against the Manichaean creed, and its founder was executed. Some rock-inscriptions of the time tell us of a man named Kartir, who became father-confessor to Shapur's grandson Bahram II and launched a violent attack on Jews, Buddhists, Hindus, Christians, Manichaeans and some other sects which we cannot identify.[17] Zoroastrianism had become the compulsory religion of the Sasanian state, some decades before Christianity became the same for the Roman Empire.

*

Meanwhile warfare between the two powers continued, sometimes blazing and sometimes smouldering. Shapur II (who reigned for seventy years, from AD 309 to 379, and is said to have had the unusual distinction of being crowned before he was born) proved himself as formidable in battle as his ancestor and namesake Shapur I. He sent expeditions southward against the Arabs of the Gulf (page 95), and eastward against the Kushan kingdom, which he utterly overthrew. Sasanian influence now began to reach right through Central Asia to the borders of China.[18] On his western front Shapur was equally successful against the Romans; in AD 363 the emperor Julian was killed in battle, and to avoid a second Carrhae his successor Jovian had to make a hasty peace and abandon some territory.

Thereafter the situation became more settled. Though there were further wars between Byzantium and Persia, they usually centred on single cities or forts (the region round Nisibis, modern Nusaybin, being a frequent centre of strife) rather than involving whole provinces as they had done before. There was a feeling, observable in such writers as Procopius, that the whole frontier region was now so devastated as to be hardly worth fighting over. There was a last flare-up in the early years of the seventh century: for a short time the armies of Chosroes II held Egypt, the Levant and Asia Minor, regions which had not been under Iranian rule since the destruction of the first Persian Empire by Alexander. Then came the counter-attack of the emperor Heraclius: passing through Armenia and Assyria, he was able to threaten the Sasanians' capital, Ctesiphon, as dangerously as they had previously threatened his. Chosroes was deposed and killed; his successor made a peace based on the *status quo*.

Sasanian silver dish, possibly of Bahram V (AD 421–39).

But it was too late. In 633, about a year after Mohammed's death and five years after that of Chosroes, the great Arab invasions began. Within little more than a decade they had shorn from the Byzantine Empire its provinces in Egypt, Cyrenaica and the Levant, and wiped the Sasanian kingdom out of existence altogether. The faith of Zoroaster vanished almost completely from the land of its birth, surviving only among the Parsees of India. The two great powers of the Near East, the two 'Eyes of the World' as they sometimes called themselves, had looked askance at each other once too often.

CHAPTER SEVEN

INDIA

All good people agree,
   And all good people say,
All nice people, like Us, are We
   And every one else is They:
But if you cross over the sea,
   Instead of over the way,
You may end by (think of it!) looking on We
   As only a sort of They!

We and They

When we speak of 'India', as when we say 'Holland' for the Nether-
lands or 'Persia' for Iran, we are naming a whole country after one part
of it. The original India (also called Hind or Sind) was the land watered
by the river Indus (or Hindus, or Sindus). This region, the nearest part
of the sub-continent to Europe, was naturally the first to come to the
Europeans' attention. Herodotus, for instance, states correctly that
beyond the Indus lies a desert, but goes on to say that beyond this one
comes to the Outer Ocean that washes the shores of the world.
Alexander the Great's conquests revealed the error of this idea, and
gave the name 'India' a much greater geographical scope than before.
In Roman times it was extended still further; the peninsula of South-
East Asia was known to Ptolemy as 'India beyond the Ganges'. Marco
Polo referred to Abyssinia as 'Middle India', and Columbus' famous
misunderstanding planted the name on the far side of the Atlantic. And
by a final irony the original 'India' is today not called India but
Pakistan.[1]

*

A large part of Indian history is the story of people and ideas entering
the country from the north-west, the direction in which its protective
mountain wall is most easily surmounted. The people and ideas then
overrun the Indus valley fairly rapidly, often go on to the Ganges valley
and sometimes to the southern regions as well, but hardly ever make
themselves dominant throughout the sub-continent. The oldest Indian
traditions, going back to about 1000 BC, describe just such an invasion: a people calling themselves Aryans (a word with the same root as

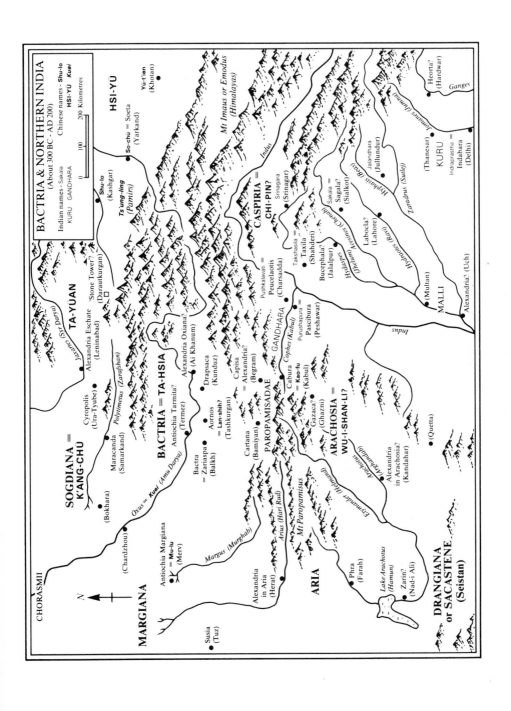

BACTRIA & NORTHERN INDIA
(About 300 BC - AD 200)

Indian names - Sakala
Chinese names - **Shu-lo** *Kuei*
KURU GANDHARA
HSI-YU **HSI-YU** *Kuei*

0   100   200 Kilometres

HSI-YU

Yu-t'ien
(Khotan)

So-chü = Soeta
(Yarkand)

Shu-lo
(Kashgar)

Ts'ung-ling
(Pamirs)

Mt Imaus or Emodus
(Himalayas)

Heorta?
(Hardwar)

Ganges

Jomnos (Jumna)

Zaradrus (Sutlej)

Jalandhara
(Jullundur)

(Thanesar?)

KURU

Indraprastha =
Indabara (Delhi)

CASPIRIA =
CHI-PIN?

Srinagara
(Srinagar)

Pushkalavati =
Peucelaotis
(Charsadda)

Takshasila =
Taxila
(Shahderi)

Sakala =
Sagala?
(Sialkot)

Labocla?
(Lahore)

Bucephala?
(Jalalpur)

Hydaspes
(Jhelum)

Hydaspes (Jhelum)

Acesines (Chenab)

Hydraotes (Ravi)

Hyphasis (Beas)

(Multan)

Alexandria? (Uch)

MALLI

CHORASMII

N

Jaxartes (Syr Darya)

'Stone Tower'?
(Daraukurgan)

TA-YUAN

Alexandria Eschate
(Leninabad)

Cyropolis
(Ura-Tyube)

Polytimetus (Zarafshan)

SOGDIANA =
K'ANG-CHÜ

Maracanda
(Samarkand)

(Bokhara)

(Chardzhou)

Oxus = **Kuei** *(Amu Darya)*

Antiochia Tarmita?
(Termez)

Alexandria Oxiana?
(Ai Khanum)

Drapsaca
(Kunduz)

BACTRIA = TA-HSIA

Bactra
= Zariaspa
(Balkh)

Aornos
= **Lan-shih?**
(Tashkurgan)

Cartana
(Bamiyan)

Capisa
= Alexandria?
(Begram)

PAROPAMISADAE

Mt Paropamisus

Cabura =
Cophes (Kabul)

Kao-fu
= (Kabul)

Gazaca?
(Ghazni)

GANDHARA

Purushapura =
Pascibura
(Peshawar)

Cophes (Kabul)

ARACHOSIA =
WU-I-SHAN-LI?

Alexandria
in Arachosia?
(Kandahar)

Arachotus (Arghandab)

Etymandrus (Helmand)

(Quetta)

Indus

Indus

MARGIANA

Antiochia Margiana
= **Mu-lu**
(Merv)

Margus (Murghab)

Arius (Hari Rud)

Alexandria
in Aria
(Herat)

ARIA

Phra
(Farah)

Zarin?
(Nad-i Ali)

Lake Arachotus
(Hamun)

DRANGIANA
or SACASTENE
(Seistan)

Susia
(Tuz)

'Iranians') crossed the Hindu Kush and destroyed the flourishing ancient civilization of the Indus valley so thoroughly that its very existence was forgotten until the twentieth century. The division of India into an 'Aryan' north and a 'non-Aryan' south has persisted ever since: most ancient and modern languages of the north (including Sanskrit, Hindi and Urdu) belong to the Indo-European family, while such languages of the south as Tamil and Telugu belong to an entirely different family, the Dravidian.

A better-documented invasion, though smaller in extent and importance, was that of Alexander the Great. In 327 BC he conquered Gandhara, the valley of the Kabul river which flows into the Indus from the west; in the following year he crossed the Indus and began to advance through the Punjab, the 'Land of the Five Rivers'. On one of these, the Hydaspes (Jhelum), he won an impressive victory. But on reaching the river Hyphasis (Beas) his troops refused to go any further. They must have realized by this time that the Indus system was *not* near the eastern limit of the world, and they may well have guessed that their commander had no more idea where that limit was than they had themselves. The force accordingly returned to the Hydaspes and sailed downstream, meeting with various adventures on the way, until it reached the mouth of the Indus. In the autumn of 325 BC the homeward journey began, through the waterless wastes of Gedrosia. In some three years Alexander had conquered almost all of what is now Pakistan, but hardly penetrated at all into the much larger territory that is now India.

The Greeks' hold on the Indus region was short-lived. One of the strongest kingdoms outside their frontier was that of Magadha, which dominated the middle Ganges from its capital at Pataliputra (Patna). Soon after Alexander's death (in 323 BC) the throne of Magadha was seized by a vigorous young adventurer named Chandragupta Maurya. He went on to conquer the whole Ganges basin, then advanced westward into that of the Indus. Seleucus I, who had acquired the eastern parts of Alexander's empire, sent a force against him, but with no success; in a treaty of 304 BC he accepted a corps of war-elephants, and in return left Chandragupta in control not only of all the Indus valley, but also of the mountainous lands west of it which now form Afghanistan. A Greek envoy named Megasthenes was sent to reside at the court of Patna, and has left us one of the best early accounts of India 'under western eyes'.[2]

The Mauryan dynasty founded by Chandragupta gave the northern Indians some of the most glorious pages in their history. His son Bindusara is thought to have conquered much of Central India; he was known to the Greeks as Amitrochates, from a title meaning 'Slayer of

Foes'. His son in turn, Asoka, campaigned in Eastern India and there overthrew the kingdom of Kalinga. But this conquest turned his mind away from the pomp and glory of war to its waste and suffering; he became a convert to Buddhism, and concerned himself with the sacredness of life and the importance of *Dharma* (meaning something like 'righteousness' but not exactly translatable). Among Buddhists he has come to be regarded as a saint – and as often happens with saints, many unlikely stories have gathered around his name. We are fortunate, however, in having numerous inscriptions on the subject of *Dharma* carved by order of the king himself. For example:

> The Beloved of the Gods considers victory by *Dharma* to be the foremost victory. And moreover the Beloved of the Gods has gained this victory on all his frontiers to a distance of six hundred *yojanas* [about 1500 miles], where reigns the Greek king named Antiochus, and beyond the realm of that Antiochus to the lands of the four kings named Ptolemy, Antigonus, Magas and Alexander . . .[3]

Asoka has been likened to Marcus Aurelius, another ruler who (some four centuries later) combined absolute power, love of mankind and a strong sense of religion. It might also be said of Asoka, as was said of Marcus, that his death changed an age of gold into one of iron and rust. The later Mauryan kings were obscure and ineffectual, presiding over an empire in disintegration, and threatened as in the days of their founder by enemies coming down from the north-west.

Indian sources called these newcomers 'Yavanas, Sakas and Pahlavas'. In the course of this book we have met them all under slightly different names. *Yavana* means 'Ionian' – that is, Greek. (Ionia, in what is now western Turkey, had been the westernmost province of the Persian Empire, just as the original 'India' had been the easternmost; both names in due course took on a more general meaning). Though deprived of power in India by Chandragupta Maurya, the Greeks had held control of Bactria to the north-west of it. More will be said of this land, and its interesting contacts with Europe, Persia, China and Siberia, in Chapter Ten; more important to the present chapter is that the Greek rulers of the region, having promoted themselves from satraps to independent kings in about 256 BC, thereafter intervened repeatedly in Indian affairs. The details of what happened were complex even at the time, involving three mutually hostile Greek dynasties, and are very controversial today. It is known, however, that some of the 'Indo-Greek' kings annexed parts of India that Alexander himself had failed to reach. On the south, they ruled the peninsula of Syrastrene (modern Kathiawar) for some time; on the east, they besieged and captured Patna, though they were probably not able to hold it for long. One of them, Demetrius, was eventually to come to the attention of Chaucer, who mentions him as 'grete Emetrëus, the kyng of Inde'.[4] Another, Menander, was still more successful and gained a still more remarkable reputation: as 'King Milinda' he became the central character of a Buddhist holy book called the *Milindapanha*.[5] This even states that he became a Buddhist himself, as Asoka had done before him; Menander's coins, however, suggest a generous acceptance of all religions available to him, whether Greek, Buddhist or Hindu.

The second group of people to harass India at this time was that of the Sakas, known in Western sources as the Sakai or Sacae. In race, language and customs they were closely akin to the Scythians of southern Russia described in Chapter Three – nomadic horsemen, without permanent settlements of their own, and ready at the slightest opportunity to overrun the civilizations on their southern border. The Sakas had been a thorn in the side of the Persian Empire ever since its foundation; Cyrus the Great had met his death fighting them on the river Oxus. Alexander had chastised them, but the dynastic quarrels of his successors gave them a fresh chance, and pressure from other nomadic tribes behind them urged them to take it. By about 130 BC they had overrun Bactria and suppressed the interesting but quarrelsome 'Graeco-Bactrian' kings there. Soon afterwards they occupied the arid and windy region where modern Iran marches with Afghanistan, and gave it their name: having previously been called Drangiana, it came instead to be called Sacastene and is now Seistan. In about 110 BC the Sakas occupied Sind, on the lower Indus, and began a war with the Greek successors of Menander further upstream. The most far-flung branch of the tribe was also the longest-surviving; it advanced south-eastward from Sind and at length formed what was known as the 'Great Saka Satrapy' with its capital at Ujjain and its chief port at Broach, a place often visited by merchants of the Roman Empire in the first two centuries AD.

'Yavanas' were Greeks and 'Sakas' were Scythians; the third people mentioned above, the 'Pahlavas', were Parthians. While one branch of this tribe was overthrowing Greek rule in Iran and Iraq, as described in the previous chapter, another branch was advancing eastward. Here the Surena family was active, expelling the Sakas from Sacastene and taking it over. Like so many Prussian Junkers in a barren land surrounded by enemies, they were to supply numerous fighting men for service on the 'Western Front' of their people against the Romans. It was a Surena who won the decisive battle of Carrhae – though his victory brought him no personal benefit, but merely caused the High King of Parthia to suspect him of having dangerous ambitions and at length order his execution. Another member of the family, Gondopharnes, extended his power into north-west India, and like several of his predecessors in this region seems to have taken an interest in comparative religion. Christian tradition has it that St Thomas the Apostle visited his court, and though the details of this visit may be fictitious there is nothing impossible about the basic idea. Indeed Thomas, as an ex-Jew, may have felt more at home and less out of place among the Parthians than his friends Peter and Paul felt on their visits to Imperial Rome.[6]

The most successful of all these foreign invaders of India, however, were yet another set of people called the Kushans. At its height the Kushan kingdom was the third greatest state in the world, exceeded in power only by the empires of China and Rome; today the Kushans have become even more of a Lost Tribe than their neighbours and inveterate enemies of the Parthians, not even remembered for a picturesque detail like the Parthian habit of shooting backwards. The reason in each case is the same. The Kushans, of nomad origin like the Parthians, had few written records of their own, and these are now all lost. What little we know of their history comes from their coins and from a few casual records in the writings of people who either disapproved of them or else knew very little about them.

The ancestors of the Kushans were a people known to Western writers as the Tochari and to Chinese ones as the Yüeh-chih. They are first recorded as living near the Great Wall of China, far to the east of their later domain. In about 165 BC, however, these Yüeh-chih were defeated by their neighbours the Hsiung-nu (the ancestors of the Huns) and forced to move westward. One branch, the Lesser Yüeh-chih, climbed on to the plateau of north-eastern Tibet and remained there for several centuries; they are mentioned by Ptolemy under the name of Thaguri, still in the same place next to a mountain named after them.[7] The main body of the tribe, the Greater Yüeh-chih, went further west still, to occupy the tract of country where five modern nations (China, India, Pakistan, Afghanistan and the USSR) meet and frequently dispute their borders. Here one branch of the tribe, the Kuei-shang or Kushans, gained supremacy over the others and went on to make itself into a first-class power. In the first century AD king Kujula Kadphises conquered most of what is now Afghanistan; his son and successor, Vima Kadphises, defeated the Sakas and Parthians who had previously been fighting for control of the Indus valley, and annexed this too.

The greatest of the Kushan kings, Kanishka I, is also one of the most mysterious. It is not known now (if at all) he was related to the Kadphises family, nor is there any certainty about his dates. There are strong arguments for believing that he began to reign in AD 78 (certainly an important date in Indian history, since it was used for long afterwards as a standard zero-point, the equivalent of AD 1 in Christendom); but equally strong arguments suggest that he should be placed at least fifty years later. A recent conference on the subject reached the conclusion that no conclusion could be reached.[8] Whatever its dates, Kanishka's kingdom was certainly very large, taking in

Headless statue of king Kanishka, found near Muttra on the Jumna.

great tracts of land on both sides of the Hindu Kush. It covered all the Indus valley, and that of the Ganges as far east as Benares; in the opposite direction it reached through Afghanistan into what is now Soviet Central Asia, putting the Kushans in a commanding position astride the famous 'Silk Road' between China and Rome. Kushans and Romans were usually on good terms with each other, united by a common dislike of the Parthian kingdom between them. Kanishka also had interests in what is now Chinese Central Asia, and at one time may have controlled the towns of Kashgar, Yarkand and Khotan. This, however, brought him into conflict with the powerful Chinese empire of the Han, which regarded this part of the world as lying exclusively within its own sphere of influence. In the fighting that resulted the Chinese seem to have come off best.

The capital of Kanishka's kingdom was Purushapura (Peshawar), a city well placed for ruling hillmen as well as plainsmen. (Under British rule, it was to become the capital of the North-West Frontier and the centre from which the 'Great Game' was played against the emissaries of Russia.) The second city of the kingdom was Mathura or Muttra, on the river Jumna. Both these places were adorned by Kanishka with many new buildings, chiefly temples and monasteries, to such an extent that Muttra came to be mentioned by Ptolemy as 'Modura of the Gods'.[9] For Kanishka, like Asoka and Menander before him, was interested in Buddhism and became recognized as one of that religion's principal worthies. He resembled Menander rather than Asoka, however, in not accepting Buddhism to the exclusion of other beliefs; the Kushans were ready to take up ideas from all over the known world. It was in the Kushan period, for example, that the remarkable 'Gandharan' or 'Graeco-Buddhist' school of art flourished, working in the style of Greece and Rome and portraying the Buddha almost as a second Apollo. The royal titles also drew inspiration from all the corners of the world. One monarch gave himself the mouth-filling title of *Maharaja Rajatiraja Devaputra Kaisara* – 'the Great King, the King of Kings, the Son of Heaven, the Caesar' — as if he felt himself equal to the combined sovereigns of India, Persia, China and Rome.[10]

The shape of the Kushan kingdom, however, laid it open to hostile as well as friendly contacts and put its kings in the position of a man trying to ride two horses at once. Despite their exalted titles, the power of Kanishka's successors steadily declined. In the third century the kingdom was almost completely destroyed by Shapur I of Persia (page 111), and India entered a period of confused fighting (neither the first nor the last in her history) about which practically nothing is known. The fourth century saw a revival of civilization, under the Gupta dynasty. Its founder, Chandragupta I, had the same name as the great

A Buddha in the 'Gandharan' style (1st century AD?). The Gandharan artists are thought to have been the first to portray the Buddha as a person.

founder of the Maurya dynasty six centuries earlier, and came from the same region (Magadha, with its capital at Patna.)[11] The most successful of the Gupta kings controlled or claimed to control almost as much territory as the Mauryas had done, and the Gupta period is regarded as one of the golden ages of Indian history. But Gupta rule was noticeably less organized and more loose-knit than that of Chandragupta Maurya or Asoka, differing from it somewhat as the Holy Roman Empire differed from the original Roman one. In the fifth century, moreover, the Guptas were threatened by yet another set of invaders from the north and north-west – the ubiquitous Huns. By about AD 500 the empire had collapsed, whereupon northern India fell into disorder once again.

*

India, like Italy, has a flat northern part and a hilly southern part, with different traditions behind them, and histories that have as often as not run independently of each other. This was noted long ago by Indian geographers, who contrasted *Uttarapatha* ('the North Country' – that

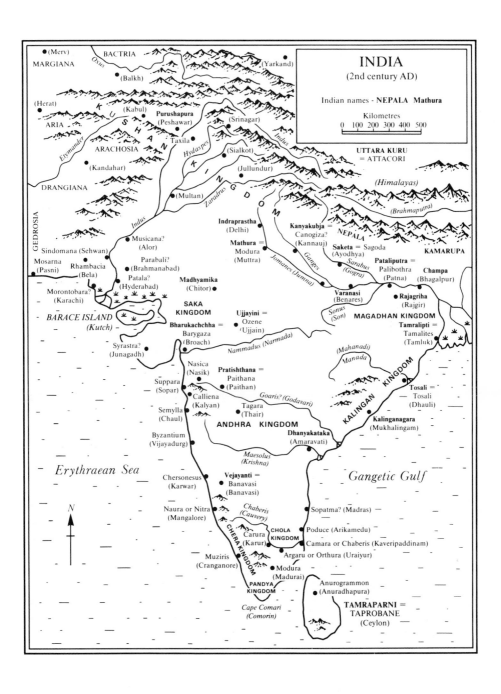

INDIA
(2nd century AD)

Indian names - **NEPALA** Mathura

Kilometres
0   100 200 300 400 500

(Merv)
MARGIANA
BACTRIA
Onus
(Balkh)
(Yarkand)

(Herat)
ARIA
(Kabul)
K U S H A N
Purushapura
(Peshawar)
(Srinagar)

ARACHOSIA
Taxila
(Sialkot)

(Kandahar)
Hydaspes
(Jullundur)

DRANGIANA
Etymander
K I N G D O M
Zaradrus
(Himalayas)

GEDROSIA
Indus
(Multan)
(Brahmaputra)

UTTARA KURU
= ATTACORI

Indraprastha
(Delhi)
Kanyakubja =
Canogiza?
(Kannauj)
NEPALA
KAMARUPA

Sindomana (Sehwan)
Musicana?
(Alor)
Mathura =
Modura
(Muttra)
Ganges
Saketa = Sagoda
(Ayodhya)
Sarabus
(Gogra)
Pataliputra =
Palibothra
(Patna)

Mosarna
(Pasni)
Rhambacia
(Bela)
Parabali?
(Brahmanabad)
Jomanes (Jumna)
Champa
(Bhagalpur)

Morontobara?
(Karachi)
Patala?
(Hyderabad)
Madhyamika
(Chitor)
Varanasi
(Benares)
Rajagriha
(Rajgir)

BARACE ISLAND
(Kutch)
SAKA
KINGDOM
Ujjayini =
Ozene
(Ujjain)
Sonus
(Son)
MAGADHAN KINGDOM

Syrastra?
(Junagadh)
Bharukachchha =
Barygaza
(Broach)
Nammadus (Narmada)
(Mahanadi)
Manada
Tamralipti =
Tamalites
(Tamluk)

Nasica
(Nasik)
Pratishthana =
Paithana
(Paithan)
Goaris? (Godavari)
K A L I N G A N
Tosali =
Tosali
(Dhauli)

Suppara
(Sopar)
Calliena
(Kalyan)
Tagara
(Thair)
K I N G D O M

Semylla
(Chaul)
ANDHRA KINGDOM
Dhanyakataka
(Amaravati)
Kalinganagara
(Mukhalingam)

Byzantium
(Vijayadurg)
Maesolus
(Krishna)

Erythraean Sea
Gangetic Gulf

Chersonesus
(Karwar)
Vejayanti =
Banavasi
(Banavasi)

N
Naura or Nitra
(Mangalore)
Chaberis
(Cauvery)
Sopatma? (Madras)

CHOLA
KINGDOM
Poduce (Arikamedu)

Carura
(Karur)
Camara or Chaberis (Kaveripaddinam)

Muziris
(Cranganore)
C H E R A   K I N G D O M
Argaru or Orthura (Uraiyur)

Modura
(Madurai)

PANDYA
KINGDOM
Anurogrammon
(Anuradhapura)

Cape Comari
(Comorin)
TAMRAPARNI =
TAPROBANE
(Ceylon)

is, the plain watered by the Indus and Ganges and their tributaries) with *Dakshinapatha* (The 'South Country' – the peninsular part of India, known today as the Deccan). But whereas civilization entered Italy from the south and gradually worked northward, so that the northern plain of 'Cisalpine Gaul' was not regarded as a true part of Italy until the time of Augustus, in India the movement was the other way. Civilization had first appeared there in the Indus valley, and then spread to the Ganges valley and also round the coasts of the peninsula; but in ancient times the inner parts still contained many wild tribes, ignorant of agriculture and living instead on the wild animals and plants of the forest. (Some of them, such as the Gonds, continued to live like this till recent times.) To the sophisticated scribe in a great city of the north such as Delhi or Benares, *Dakshinapatha* seemed a savage land, a country of half-Aryans with half-manners and non-Aryans with no manners at all. But it was also a land of opportunity. It was southern rather than northern India that produced 'the wealth of Ormuz and of Ind' – the precious metals, the gemstones, the pearls, the ivory and the spices; and it was to southern rather than northern India that merchants came from the West in the days of the Roman Empire.

The early history of the Deccan is even more confused and fragmentary than that of the northern plain, and no continuous account can be given of any part of it. The effect is like watching a play in a thunderstorm when all the stage lights have failed: every now and then a lightning-flash illuminates some figure in a heroic attitude, but we never learn his real importance in the play or how he is related to figures that appear earlier or later.

One such figure is king Kharavela of Kalinga, whose career is recorded by an inscription found at a place called Hathigumpha ('Elephant Cave').[12] His kingdom of Kalinga lay on the east side of the peninsula in the region now called Orissa; its heartland was the delta of the river Mahanadi. It had been conquered with great slaughter by the armies of Asoka, but apparently regained its independence soon after his death. The Hathigumpha inscription mentions that Kharavela was able to take the offensive against the north; on one occasion he reached as far as the important-town of Rajgir, only about forty miles from the northerners' capital at Patna. He was also active in the opposite direction, defeating the king of the Pandyas in the extreme south of India and capturing 'hundreds of thousands of gems and pearls'. And he spent large sums of money on public works and even larger ones on entertaining his subjects. But nothing is known of his successors, and it is unlikely that Kalingan power long survived the great man's death.

South and west of Kalinga, and often at war with it, was a state

Scenes in the life of the Buddha, from Amaravati in south-east India. Here the artists have kept to the old convention of not portraying the Buddha. He is represented by his footprints (above) or by his seat under the Bo-tree (centre).

sometimes known as the Satavahana and sometimes as the Andhra kingdom. 'Satavahana' was the name of its ruling dynasty; 'Andhra' was the name of the region which probably contained most of its inhabitants and most of its wealth, the region round the mouths of the rivers Godavari and Krishna, still called Andhra Pradesh today. (Pliny notes that the *Andarae* could put into the field 100,000 foot, 2,000 horse and 1,000 elephants; the corresponding figures for their rivals the *Calingae* were 60,000, 1,000 and 700.)[13] The capital of the 'Andhra' kingdom was not in the Andhra country itself but much further to the west, at Pratishthana (Paithan) on the upper Godavari and closer to the western than the eastern coast of India. Precisely how this arrangement came about is unknown; but it is clear that the rulers at Paithan controlled a considerable area, and that some of them ruled from the Indian Ocean to the Bay of Bengal. Their title of 'Lords of the Deccan' was not undeserved.

The third main power in central India was that of the Sakas, on the west coast in and around what is now Gujarat. As with Kalinga, so among the Sakas only one ruler has left any substantial record of his career. This was Rudradaman, who flourished in the mid-second century AD and set up an inscription near the town of Junagadh.[14] He fought successfully against the Andhra kings, seizing from them the region round present-day Bombay. Like Kharavela of Kalinga, he also took an interest in irrigation-works, restoring a large artificial lake near Junagadh that had recently burst its banks. The inscription says a fair amount about his personal character, and shows that an ideal Indian king had to be like an ideal Renaissance prince. Rudradaman is proficient not only in 'the management of horses, elephants, and chariots, and wielding of sword and shield' but also in 'grammar, music, logic and other great sciences'; he composes 'prose and verse which are clear, agreeable, sweet, charming, beautiful, excelling by the proper use of words'; and 'his beautiful frame owns the most excellent marks and signs, such as auspicious height and dimension, voice, gait, colour, vigour and strength'. Even the most manic of Roman emperors, however much he might privately agree with such a description of himself, would have hesitated to have it set up on a public monument. Claudius wrote books, Nero played the lyre, Hadrian designed buildings and Commodus was a first-class gladiator; but Roman public opinion regarded such accomplishments as debits rather than credits, likely to distract rulers from their real business of ruling.

The extreme south of India was occupied by non-Aryan, Tamil-speaking peoples, who had remained outside Asoka's empire and for some centuries afterwards continued to resist Aryan ideas as well as Aryan armies. The three chief Tamil nations were the Cheras in the west, the Cholas in the east and the Pandyas most southerly of all.[15] Their early epic poetry shows that these three kingdoms fought each other repeatedly, with a violence and bloodthirstiness seldom found in the north. Whereas northern Indians had for some time been considering what was and what was not a 'righteous conquest', and eventually produced a code of chivalry similar to that of mediaeval Europe, the early Tamils preferred what the northerners called 'demoniac conquest' – a total war in which each side applied to the other the principle that the only good Indian was a dead Indian.

*

From the earliest times Western accounts of the Indian sub-continent always portrayed it as somewhat larger than life – bigger than any other country, more populous, with more rivers and more cities, and inhabitants who all seemed either incredibly rich or spectacularly poor. The attitude which gained for Marco Polo the nickname of 'Marco Milione' was already well established among Westerners writing about the East many centuries before he was born.

India is indeed an extensive country (the seventh largest in area in the world today, even after the separation of Pakistan and Bangladesh) and to inhabitants of the Greek world inevitably seemed super-colossal. Greek geographers, however, regularly described it as even larger than it was, one of them going so far as to assert that it formed a third of the inhabited world. Traditional Indian geography exaggerated still more: it was believed that *Bharatavarsa*, the land south of the Himalayas, had a diameter of 9000 *yojanas*, which would give it an area about equal to that of the *whole* world.[16]

India produced remarkable treasures of the mineral, vegetable and animal kingdoms alike. Herodotus reports that the north-west alone contributed to the Persian exchequer the annual sum of 360 talents of gold-dust, worth about 130 million dollars at today's prices; being Herodotus, he adds a story of how it was dug up in the desert by giant ants 'bigger than foxes, but not as large as dogs'.[17] India also produced precious stones, including diamond, ruby, sapphire, garnet and aquamarine, and the waters between India and Ceylon contained the finest pearl-fisheries in the Ancient World.

The plants of India also impressed visitors from the West. In striking contrast to the situation today, the northern plain was seen as an immensely rich agricultural land; it was noted with admiration that the climate made it possible to grow two crops a year, usually rice in summer and wheat or barley in winter. Two other useful crops were sugar-cane and cotton, while the forest regions yielded fine timber, including teak, sandalwood and ebony. The spices of southern India, the most valuable export of all, will be described in the next chapter.

Even more impressive were some of the wild animals of India – the giant snakes, the tigers, and above all the elephants. Though the Greeks had had first-hand knowledge of ivory since the Mycenaean period (about 1500 BC) and of African elephants since about 600 BC when they founded their first settlements in Libya, the domestication of these animals was unknown to them until Alexander came to India. The battle of the Hydaspes was nearly lost when the Greek cavalry refused to face the Indian war-elephants; and the successors of Alexander used elephants, both Indian and African, in large numbers (the Indian ones always being thought superior). The Romans encountered elephants in their war with king Pyrrhus of Epirus, and again in their war with Hannibal; but after the initial surprise had worn off they soon realized that the new weapon was expensive and unreliable, and never made much use of it in their own armies. The Indians themselves might have done better to follow the same policy; as it was, their attitude towards elephants came to resemble the Royal Navy's attitude for many years towards battleships, and they went on using them long after new techniques of warfare had made them dangerously obsolete.

After animals, people: the human inhabitants of India also had characteristics that interested the West. One well-known feature of the land today, its immense population, was noted at an early date; Herodotus calls the Indians 'the most populous nation in the known world' and he had no knowledge of anything east of the Indus valley.[18] The Ganges region was probably even more populous, as it is today; the Mauryan army is said to have had 600,000 infantry – the equivalent of about 120 Roman legions, four times as many as the Roman Empire normally had – plus 30,000 cavalry and no fewer than 9000 elephants.[19] Though these figures are surely exaggerated (estimates of the sizes of foreign armies are notoriously unreliable) it is at least clear that Europeans were again seeing India as a country where everything happened on a larger scale than at home.

Another feature of Indian life today, the caste system, is also mentioned by the ancients, though not in its present form. Like many other peoples in history, the Aryan invaders of about 1500 BC seem to have been divided into three great classes: the nobles or *kshatriyas*, the priests or *brahmanas* ('Brahmins') and the ordinary people or *vaisyas*. The pre-Aryan inhabitants of India, conquered by the newcomers, were then added to the bottom of society as serfs or *sudras*. The resulting four classes are still the basis of the Indian caste system, though at some stage the Brahmins, as lords spiritual, managed to promote themselves to the first rank, over the heads of their former superiors the *kshatriyas* or lords temporal. But *classes* of this kind have existed in many parts of the world. What makes *caste* in India unusual is not that dukes fail to associate with dustmen, but that carters, carpenters, cobblers, cutlers, cordwainers and cooks form separate groups, each with its own strict rules about associating with any other. There is little trace of such a system in ancient India; it was certainly nothing like as complex as it has since become. The rulers could originate from any of the four main classes, even the lowest; one royal dynasty was said to be descended from a barber and a courtesan.[20] Moreover, caste was accepted only by the Hindu religion. Buddhism, formerly more influential in India than it is now, rejected all such distinctions as artificial and irrelevant.

This brings us to the complex subject of ancient Indian religion. Hinduism, like the pagan beliefs of ancient Greece, had its beginning in the conquest of a non-Indo-European agricultural people (the Indus Valley civilization) by an Indo-European pastoral one (the Aryans). The famous tradition of the 'Sacred Cow' is probably pre-Aryan and very old indeed. Model cows and bulls have been found at Indus Valley sites, and the cult may be linked with the well-known bull-cult of early Crete, both being derived from an Asian belief that has left traces from as early as 6000 BC. The warlike Aryans, on the other hand, paid greater honour to the horse. One of the most spectacular rites of ancient India was the *asvamedha*, by which the greatest rulers showed off the extent of their power. A specially consecrated horse was set free and allowed to wander for a year, while the king's men followed it and demanded homage from all chiefs whose territory it entered. At the end of the year the horse was brought back to the capital and sacrificed in a great ceremony.

The religion of the early Aryans at times shows remarkable similarities to that of their distant kinsmen, the earliest Greek-speakers in Greece. Both were dominated by 'Skyfather' – Indian *Dyaus-pitar*, Greek *Zeus pater*, Roman *Jupiter* and Germanic *Tiw* (destined to become the god of Tuesday). But Hindu deities, like modern limited companies, were subject to mergers and takeovers; the attributes and powers of one god could readily pass to another. (This is why they are often shown with more than one pair of hands: the extra ones are needed to hold all the various objects that symbolize their various abilities.) *Dyaus-pitar* long ago passed into oblivion. Conversely, the two chief gods of modern Hinduism, Vishnu and Siva, both arose from obscure beginnings, and neither can be described as the god *of* anything in the way that Jupiter, say, is the god of the sky, Neptune the god of the sea and Mars the god of war. Vishnu, called 'the Preserver', is believed by his followers to have saved the world in many different incarnations – as a fish, a boar, a dwarf who suddenly turns into a giant, the epic hero Rama, the tragic hero Krishna, and even the Buddha. His rival Siva has a still more complex (and more sinister) history. He seems to have begun as a non-Aryan fertility god, one of his emblems being the phallus (*lingam*) and another the snake. At the same time, though, he is a great ascetic and teacher; also the patron of dancing; also 'Siva the destroyer', the god of death and time and the end of all things. His consort Parvati has a similar multiple character: sometimes she is portrayed as a beautiful and contemplative young woman, sometimes as an Amazon riding a lion and killing monsters, and sometimes as a hideous hag with a necklace of skulls.

In ancient times Hinduism had to compete with two powerful rivals, Jainism and Buddhism. The founders of these were contemporaries, both flourishing in the second half of the sixth century BC. Jainism, developed by a sage named Mahavira, is notable for its extremely austere approach to life.[21] The early Jains were vegetarians and teetotallers, wore no clothes, had no personal property and vowed never to take life, not even that of an invisible microbe; to take one's *own* life, however, often in a most painful way, they regarded as no sin but a positive virtue. Mahavira starved himself to death, and the Jains claim that Chandragupta Maurya accepted their religion and did likewise. Alexander the Great met fifteen ascetics who may have been Jains; they told him that no man could learn their wisdom without first casting off the encumbrance of clothes, and one of them (named Calanus) accompanied the king on his travels and eventually burned himself to death on a pyre.[22] Later writers frequently mention the Indian *gymnosophistae* or 'naked philosophers', and sometimes compare them with other famous priestly groups such as the Persian Magi and the Celtic Druids. Even if they were not all Jains, they were certainly well established in the Indian tradition of holiness that is still producing a regular supply of *fakirs, saddhus, gurus, yogis* and *rishis* for the solace of the West.

Though there are still Jains in India, the religion has never been so successful as its rival Buddhism. This was founded by Prince Gautama, who came to be known as the Buddha or 'Enlightened One'. Its themes were that the world is full of suffering, a wheel of misery going round through endless rebirths; that this suffering is caused by desire, which must be set aside so that one may escape from the wheel and achieve the blessings of *Nirvana*; and that one does this by means of the 'Middle Way', avoiding the extremes of self-indulgence on the one hand and self-mortification on the other. In the period with which this book chiefly deals (*circa* 300 BC to AD 400) Buddhism scored some notable successes. As already mentioned, it was taken up by three of the greatest rulers of early India – Asoka, Menander and Kanishka. In

Asoka's time it was introduced to Ceylon, and somewhat later it appeared in South-East Asia (along with many other customs of Indian origin, as will be related in the next chapter). In the first century AD it began to influence China, whence it was to spread to Tibet, Korea and Japan. But, for no very clear reason, Buddhism was eventually to decline and almost disappear in the land of its origin. There are more Buddhists in India now than there were a few decades ago, but still not many compared with the number of Hindus.

In ancient India, as in the Graeco-Roman world, religious beliefs were seldom mutually exclusive. People could and probably did offer reverence to Vishnu, Siva and the Buddha in turn, as well as to foreign deities such as Apollo of Greece, the fire-god of Iran, the sword-god of Central Asia, and even the emperor Augustus of Rome (who had a temple dedicated to him at the port of Muziris in southern India)[23] – not to mention a variety of ghosts and demons who could not safely be specified. Gibbon's remark that the various beliefs of the Roman world 'were all considered by the people as equally true; by the philosopher, as equally false; and by the magistrate, as equally useful' can be applied to the ancient history of Asia as well as to that of Europe.

*

Noble *kshatriyas* wrote about war and government: pious brahmins wrote about the sorrows of this world and the superior importance of the next. Meanwhile ordinary life went on.

Though the land, then as now, was mainly rural, there were numerous large cities and some very large ones. Patna stretched for nine miles along the Ganges, and its walls had 570 towers and 64 gates.[24] It was the centre of a road system as impressive as that of the Roman Empire, reaching in one direction to the Indus and in the other to the Bay of Bengal. Several ancient inscriptions mention the importance of irrigation in the great river-valleys, and the steps taken by wise rulers to provide dams, canals and reservoirs. India produced some of the Ancient World's most skilful weavers, carpenters and metal-workers. The fine cottons of India were almost as highly prized at Rome as the silks of China; the Mauryan palace at Patna, made entirely of wood, was one of the wonders of the world; and a fourth-century iron pillar is still visible near Delhi and shows no sign of rust.[25]

Early Indians were fond of plants, and the richer ones, like rich Romans, laid out splendid gardens. They enjoyed dice-games and board-games; one of these, a four-handed game called *chaturanga* or 'Four Armies', was later adapted for two players by the Persians and eventually developed into modern chess. They cooked curry and rice, probably in much the same way as they still do; and though the devout had begun to frown upon meat and strong drink, it seems that the less devout enjoyed these things whenever they could obtain them. And besides tales of battle and tales of righteous living, ancient India has left us the *Kama Sutra* – a manual that deals not only with the art of sex, but also with the more general art of having a happy and leisurely time.

CHAPTER EIGHT

SOUTH-EAST ASIA AND THE SPICE ROUTES

Once there was a pirate-ship, being blown ashore —
  (*Plitty soon pilum up, s'posee no can tack.*
Seven-piecee stlong man pullum sta'boa'd oar.
  That way bling her head alound and sail-o back.)
But before, and before, and ever so long before
  Grand Commander Noah took the wheel,
The Junk and the Dhow, though they look like anyhow,
  Had rudders reaching deep below their keel — ahoy! akeel!
  As they laid the Eastern Seas beneath their keel!

The Junk and the Dhow

The region known today as South-East Asia was formerly often called Indo-China — an apt name in some ways, since in the past it was profoundly influenced by India to the west of it and China to the north. Older books on the region's early history make much of this, sometimes too much; more recent ones often start by emphasizing the opposite, that 'Indo-China' has a special character of its own, neither pure Indian nor pure Chinese nor yet a simple mixture of the two, and that at no time in the past was it a blank sheet on which the older civilizations could write just what they liked. Nevertheless, the ancient influence of India and China on South-East Asia was real and noticeable, and shows an interesting contrast. Chinese influence, most pronounced on the eastern side of the peninsula, was mainly military and (like most Chinese history) well documented; Indian influence, more widespread, was mainly religious and (like most Indian history) hardly documented at all, but no less important for that.

The early history of South-East Asia, like that of Western Europe, sometimes confuses the uninitiated by the way in which modern nations take their names from peoples who originally lived somewhere else. The Burmese, a people akin to the Tibetans, entered present-day Burma only in the eighth century AD; the Thais did not reach Thailand until the thirteenth century. The Malays, a widespread people found in the islands as well as on the Malayan mainland, have lived there since prehistoric times; but the *name* 'Malaya' has been highly mobile. It is of Indian origin, meaning 'a mountain' and found also in the name of the Himalayas; but when early Indian sources mention *Malayadvipa* or 'Mountain Island' they are probably referring not to present-day Malaya but to Sumatra. The name 'Java' (also of Indian origin, from *Yavadvipa* meaning 'Barley Island') was even more mobile, apparently being applied sometimes to modern Java, sometimes to Sumatra and sometimes to Borneo.

'Vietnam' is another old name that has not always meant what it means now. The word *Viet* (pronounced *Yüeh* in modern Mandarin) appears frequently in early Chinese writings as the name of a people who occupied not only Vietnam but also all the south-east coast of China up to the mouth of the Yangtze. *Nam*, or *nan*, means 'south'; the present-day Vietnamese are thus the 'southern Yüeh', the only part of this people to have avoided incorporation into the Chinese Empire. They have not, however, escaped wholly untouched by Chinese direct rule. Ch'in Shih-huang-ti, the first true Emperor of China (221–210 BC) and the first Chinese ruler to give his country the shape it has today, did this by conquering the whole of Nan Yüeh – all South China as well as North Vietnam – and bringing it for the first time under the rule of an Empire whose power had hitherto been confined to North China. The new dependency broke away in the confusion that fol-

Bronze figure from the kingdom of Tien (Yunnan province, China, circa 100 BC). The art of this region is thought to have influenced that of South-East Asia.

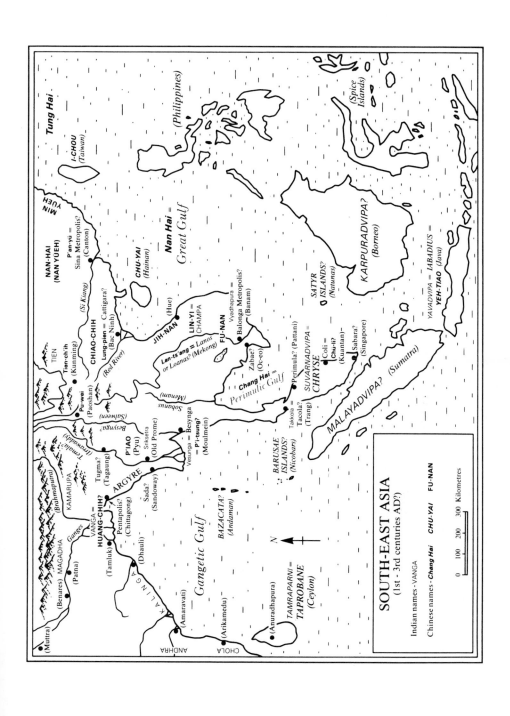

SOUTH-EAST ASIA
(1st - 3rd centuries AD?)

Indian names - VANGA

Chinese names - *Chang Hai* **CHU-YAI** **FU-NAN**

N

0   100   200   300 Kilometres

lowed the fall of the Ch'in dynasty, but was reconquered by Emperor
Wu (141–87 BC) of the succeeding Han dynasty. Census reports of
the Han Empire list its three southernmost territories as *Chiao-chih*
(modern North Vietnam, round the delta of the Red River, with its
capital not far from modern Hanoi); *Chiu-chen*, further south near the
recent short-lived demarcation-line between North and South Vietnam; and *Jih-nan*, the most southerly of all, with its capital near the
modern town of Hue. (The name *Jih-nan* is picturesque; it means
'South of the Sun' and indicates the surprise of the Chinese when they
passed the Tropic of Cancer and found the sun on the wrong side of the
sky.) Chinese rule in Vietnam had to contend with frequent rebellions
– including one led by two women, the Trung sisters, who were older
contemporaries of 'Boadicea' and have a place in Vietnamese tradition
similar to her place in the tradition of Great Britain. In the late second
century AD the declining Han dynasty was forced to abandon its
control of Vietnam; this was renewed, however, by the T'ang dynasty
in the seventh century, and has been claimed by Chinese rulers ever
since, whether or not they have felt strong enough to put their claim
into practice.

The earliest surviving record of travel in South-East Asia dates from
the Han period: it is a passage in the *Ch'ien Han shu* (*Annals of the
Early Han*) recording a voyage from the Chinese commandery of
Jih-nan to a country called Huang-chih.[1] The latter name would have
been pronounced with a G in ancient Chinese, something like 'Guang-
ji', and may refer to the river Ganges and the town of Gange in its delta,
mentioned by the *Periplus of the Erythraean Sea* and by Ptolemy.[2] The
intervening places on the voyage cannot be identified with certainty,
but it seems fairly clear that travellers from China to India had already
realized that two alternatives lay before them: either they could sail all
the way round the Malay peninsula, or they could shorten the voyage
by cutting across it.

Ancient Indian influence on South-East Asia, though at least as
important as that of China, is much harder to interpret. There are
several theories of how it came about. The oldest of these, now
discredited, called for physical migration of people on a large scale, as
if the Indianizing of South-East Asia had resembled the Europeanizing
of the Americas in more recent times. But though there were several
occasions when people *might* have left India in large numbers (for
example, Asoka's conquest of Kalinga in the third century BC, or the
Kushan conquest of northern India in the first century AD), there is no
evidence that this ever actually happened. A more promising theory is
that Indian influence was carried by traders; a European parallel is
provided by ancient Etruria, which took up many features of the Greek

way of life although it was never a Greek colony. This theory is likely to contain part of the truth, but not the whole of it. Religion was probably as important as trade, and recent works on the subject often propose that Indian customs were introduced to South-East Asia by Buddhist and Brahmin missionaries, analogues of St Patrick and St Columba. It is unknown what particular part of India, if any, led the way in spreading this influence (though local patriotism has sometimes stepped into the gap left by the absence of definite knowledge; northern Indian writers generally give predominance to the north, southern ones to the south). It is also worth noting that Malaya and Indonesia have a distinguished seafaring tradition of their own, and that their ancient inhabitants were perfectly capable of going to India themselves instead of waiting for the Indians to come to them. Buddhist and Hindu converts in the region, therefore, could well have visited India to see the holy places of their new religions, as Chinese Buddhists are known to have done.

Whatever the mechanisms behind it, the influence was certainly strong. Buddhism and Hinduism were both highly successful, though they were later to lose ground through the spread of Islam; Buddhism is still the chief religion of Burma and Thailand, while Hinduism survives on the Indonesian island of Bali. Some languages of South-East Asia, such as Malay and Javanese, contain many loan-words from Sanskrit. Dances and puppet-shows in the region often take their themes from the great Indian epics, the *Ramayana* and the *Mahabharata*. Buildings like Angkor Wat in Cambodia, or the Borobudur temple in Java, show the spread of Indian artistic ideas. Yet for all that, we are dealing with an *influence*, not the slavish imitation of one culture by another. Spain owes much to the influence of the Romans, and more to that of the Moors; but 'Romano-Moorish' is not an acceptable synonym for 'Spanish' in art, customs, ways of thinking or anything else.

*

One of the first states recorded in the region was also one of the most successful in its history. This was the kingdom of Funan, established probably in the first century AD, surviving until the seventh, and at times powerful enough to rank as an empire and even to challege the might of the Chinese Empire itself. 'Funan' is the modern Mandarin pronunciation of the name; it was originally *B'iu-nam*, meaning 'a mountain' – spelt *Phnom* in the modern language of Cambodia and found also in Phnom Penh, the name of the country's present capital. Like several other rich and powerful states of the Ancient World, Funan lay on a great river – the river Mekong. Its capital bore the name

Vyadhapura, meaning 'City of Hunters', but could also be called by the same name as the kingdom: Ptolemy seems to refer to it as *Balonga Metropolis*, 'The capital of B'iu-nam', and its modern name is Banam.[3] The chief port of the kingdom, at a site called Oc-eo, has been excavated; the finds included Indian jewelry and figurines, intaglios from Sasanid Persia and others from the Roman Empire, one coin of the emperor Antoninus Pius and one of his successor Marcus Aurelius.

Tradition has it that Funan was founded by a foreigner, perhaps from India, called Kaundinya (or in Chinese, Hun-t'ien.) He married a local queen called Liu-yeh ('Willow Leaf') after a curious episode in which he transfixed her boat with an arrow from his magic bow (some device similar to a Roman *ballista*, perhaps?). More definite information appears in the third century AD, when a ruler named Fan Shih-man founded a new dynasty and greatly increased the power of the kingdom. None of the neighbouring states conquered by him can be precisely located, but it seems likely that Funanese rule was established over most of southern Thailand, including the isthmian

Bronze lamp-holder of the Dong Son culture (North Vietnam, 4th century BC). The style is already distinctly 'South-East Asian', not Indian or Chinese.

region north of Malaya. Control of this isthmus and the trade-route across it would explain the importance of Funan as a middleman between India and China. The successors of Fan Shih-man sent embassies to both these lands, and received others in return; it is mainly from reports by Chinese ambassadors that we know what we do know about the kingdom's history.

Outside Funan, the ancient history of South-East Asia is very obscure, and does not clarify itself until well after the end of the 'Roman' period. The Vietnamese coast, north of Funan and south of the Chinese dependencies, was occupied in the third century AD by a kingdom called Lin-yi, later to be known as Champa; its early rulers took advantage of the increasing weakness and disunity of China to increase their power at China's expense. On the opposite side of the peninsula, much of Burma was occupied by a people called the Pyu (in Chinese writings, the P'iao) whose capital after about AD 500 was a city called Sriksetra (near modern Prome, on the river Irrawaddy.) The Pyu kingdom and its capital may be older than this (they have sometimes been claimed as much older, going back to the second century AD or even to the time of the Buddha) but at present the question of their origin cannot be answered. The same problem arises with the ancient history of Malaya and Indonesia. Important things certainly happened in both regions, but few of them can be interpreted.

*

Though religion may have been more important than trade in promoting early contact between India and South-East Asia, trade was certainly important too. The spice trade, in particular, linked together all parts of the Indian Ocean; and the demand for spices, above all in the Roman Empire, led to some of the Ancient World's most remarkable feats of seamanship.

Modern European cooks generally make a distinction between 'herbs', which can be grown in one's own garden, and 'spices', which come from far-away places, usually tropical, and have to be bought from the grocer or *épicier*. Herbs and spices alike are distinguished in their turn from 'perfumes' and also from 'medicines', both of which come from a different kind of shop altogether. The ancients, on the other hand, thought in more general terms, recognizing a large group of plant products collectively known as *aromata* or 'scented things'; some of these could find a place equally in the kitchen, the boudoir, the pharmacy and the temple.

Then as now, herbs and spices were used to modify the taste of food – though, then as now, gourmets had their doubts about the practice; they felt that good food needed to be cooked in the simplest possible way, and that strong flavours in a dish could indicate that the basic material was tough, putrescent or pretending to be what it was not. Many rich Romans, however, had less elegant tastes, and sometimes added vast amounts of expensive spice to food to show that they could afford it. Aromatics could also be added to drink, producing a great range of tisanes, punches, possets, cordials and metheglins; and the subtle art of disguising the badness of bad drink with additives – sometimes lethal ones – was already well established. The ancients had no tea, no coffee and no Pure Food Regulations.

Aromatics, including spices, were also important in the perfumery industry, the distinction between 'scents for cooking' and 'scents for wearing' being less clear-cut than it is now. Victors in the Olympic Games received crowns of wild olive; successful Roman commanders received crowns of bay-leaf. Pliny gives a list of perfumes fashionable in his time, and mentions not only flower-scented ones such as rosewater, but also others based on what we should now call culinary plants, such as marjoram, saffron and cinnamon.[4] These and many other aromatics were mixed with oil and wine to produce *unguenta* or unguents, the ancient equivalent of scented soap. The anointing ceremony in the Coronation is a reminder of a soapless age in which oiliness, cleanliness and godliness were closely linked – just the opposite of the more recent Anglo-American tradition of a close link between 'grease' and 'dirt'.

Gods as well as people enjoyed pleasant smells. The incense trade, the very lucrative export of myrrh and frankincense from southern Arabia to the rest of the world, has already been described in Chapter Five; but incenses and ointments for divine service could also contain other ingredients from still further afield. Chapter XXX of the Book of Exodus gives recipes for two aromatic mixtures especially favoured by the Lord. One is composed of myrrh, cinnamon, cassia (which is related to cinnamon) and a substance called calamus; the other of frankincense and three substances called stacte, onycha and galbanum. It is further commanded that neither mixture shall be used by any private individual. The Romans, with greater resources than the Israelites, consumed incense and spices together in enormous amounts, particularly at funerals. Pliny had a low opinion of the practice:

For what hath made Arabia blessed, rich and happy, but the superfluous expense that men be at, in funerals? employing those sweet odours to burn the bodies of the dead, which they knew by good right were due unto the gods . . . Cast then, how many funerals every year after were made throughout the world: what heaps of odours have been bestowed in the honour of dead bodies; whereas we offer unto the gods by crumbs and grains only.[5]

The last major use of aromatics, and one of the most important of all, was in medicine. Many spices found their first use here, at a time when they were still too expensive to be used for anything else. Lacking wonder-drugs from the pharmaceutical industry, the ancients turned to all the animal and plant products of the world they knew. Hope springs eternal in the human breast, and it was always tempting to believe that some strange new decoction, from the confines of Africa or Asia, could succeed where one's native herbal tea had failed. Some of these exotic mixtures, indeed, were reputed to have yielded results that no modern drug could yield. One such was the famous *Mithradatium*, taken by Mithradates of Pontus when as a young man he found himself surrounded by ambitious relations and began to notice peculiar tastes in his food. *Mithradatium* had thirty-six ingredients, including pepper, saffron, ginger, cinnamon, frankincense and myrrh; so powerful an antidote was it that when, defeated and deposed, the king wanted to poison himself, he was unable to do so and had to call on the sword instead.[6]

*

Spices have been carried over long distances since very early times. The greatest boost to the trade, however, came with the establishment of the Roman Empire under Augustus. The peace and prosperity brought by this greatly increased the demand for all kinds of expensive luxuries at Rome, and the Romans' failure to conquer Parthia set them looking for ways to by-pass that awkward country and avoid its heavy tolls on goods coming from India overland. The death of Cleopatra in 30 BC, moreover, had given the Romans control of Egypt, whose Red Sea coast was already the starting-point for many voyages to the East; and Alexandria, the capital of Egypt, was one of the world's chief centres of trade and must have contained many shippers and seamen with personal knowledge of the eastern sea-routes.

It was probably in Augustus' time that a new and more efficient way of crossing the Indian Ocean was discovered. Previous mariners had made the voyage by staying fairly close to the coast, even though parts of it were among the most unpleasant to be found anywhere in the world – the sea full of rocks and shoals, infested with pirates, the land waterless and uninhabited, or inhabited by people like the Ichthyophagi of the Makran coast. (These lived on fish, made their houses of fishbones and asserted that their ancestors had *been* fish.)[7] By using the monsoons, however, as described on page 74, it was possible to avoid this depressing country and instead sail direct from Arabia to India. A mariner called Hippalus is said to have been the first to do this, crossing some 1200 miles of open sea between Cape Syagros (Ras Fartak, in what is now South Yemen) and the mouth of the Indus. Later voyagers went still farther from land, one of their favourite targets being the mouth of the Narmada and the port of Barygaza (Broach). This was the chief port of the Sakas, who at the time dominated much of western India (page 120). Among its exports was Indian spikenard, used to anoint Jesus Christ on a famous occasion.[8]

The approach to Barygaza, however, was difficult and could be dangerous.

> Because the violent movement of the water when the tide is already rising cannot be withstood, and anchors do not hold, ships are caught by its force and are turned sideways by the violence of the current, driven on to the shoals, and wrecked. The smaller boats indeed are capsized. Those that have turned into the creeks during the ebb of the tide, unless they are propped upright, are filled with water from the first head of the current when the rising tide suddenly returns.[9]

A further difficulty was that if a ship's navigation was faulty, so that it sailed north of its proper course, it might well enter the even more dangerous region now called the Rann of Kutch, where it was possible to run aground while still out of sight of land. Erring too far to the south was also serious, for it brought the voyager to a debatable land coveted both by the Saka kings and by their rivals the Andhras, and notorious for its pirates.

The extreme south of India was safer and more profitable to visit. It produced great quantities of pepper, which became enormously popular in the Roman world – so much so that the emperor Domitian had special warehouses, the *horrea piperataria*, constructed at Rome to handle it. By this time seamen had become still bolder about using the monsoons, and it was not unusual for ships to sail direct from the Gulf of Aden to the pepper-country, covering some two thousand miles in forty days.

The same method could also be used to reach Ceylon. Pliny records an early visit made by accident, when in the reign of Claudius a freedman of one Annius Plocamus was blown all the way from Arabia to Ceylon in the space of fifteen days.[10] He was received by the king, who was impressed by the standardization of the Roman coins he had on him; in due course an embassy was sent from Ceylon to Rome, and the Romans acquired new information about the island – not all of it accurate. Ceylon had had a special place in the minds of Western geographers ever since they first came to hear of it in the time of Alexander. It shared with the British Isles and the Canaries the distinction of being, so to speak, a world in its own right, cut off by Oceanus from the everyday world of Europe, Asia and Africa. There was a feeling that in such lands the laws of nature might not be the same as they were in other places, and this feeling was especially strong about Ceylon because of the mistaken belief that it was the largest island in the known world. (In fact Great Britain and Ireland are both larger.) The *Periplus* describes it as almost touching the shore of Azania, in eastern Africa; Pliny and Ptolemy both mistakenly assert that it extends into the southern hemisphere, and Ptolemy spreads it over no less than fifteen degrees of latitude and twelve of longitude – which would make it bigger than France and Spain put together.[11]

Ceylon was well placed to be the meeting-point of people coming in several different directions, and meeting on the battlefield as often as in the market-place. To this day it is inhabited by two different groups of people: the Tamils, mostly Hindu, whose language resembles that of the Indian mainland opposite the island, and the Sinhalese, mostly Buddhist, whose language is Indo-European and related to the tongues of northern India. Though they had the greater distance to travel, it was the Sinhalese who arrived first (traditionally in the sixth century BC); it was they who built the first capital of the island, Anuradha-

The Ruvanveli Dagoba at Anuradhapura.

pura, mentioned by Ptolemy as 'the royal city of Anurogrammon'.[12] Buddhism came to Ceylon in the reign of a king called Devanampiya Tissa, a contemporary and friend of Asoka in the north. Ceylonese Buddhists claim to possess one of the Buddha's teeth, and a *pipal*-tree (or *Bo*-tree) grown from a cutting of the original tree under which he achieved enlightenment. The Tamils are thought to have arrived shortly after king Tissa's time (*circa* 200 BC), and the following centuries saw frequent wars between the two groups. Perhaps for this reason, Greek and Roman mariners did not visit the island as often as they might have done, despite its great wealth (above all in pearls) and its reputation in legend.

*

Though a meeting-place in one sense, Ceylon and southern India were also a barrier. From such evidence as there is, it would seem that each of the two seas bordering India (the Erythraean Sea on the west and the Gangetic Gulf, or Bay of Bengal, on the east) had its own dominant set of carriers. The two sets would meet each other at certain recognized trans-shipment points, but only rarely would they enter each other's territory. Thus, though commodities travelled often enough from South-East Asia to the Roman Empire, they did not normally do so in one ship going all the way.

Even after allowance for bias (since almost all the known evidence comes from Greek sources) it remains likely that trade in the Erythraean Sea was dominated by the Greeks of the eastern Roman Empire, and above all by those of Alexandria. Their chief rivals were the Arabs of southern Arabia, who are known to have been active along the East African coast and would have been equally capable of making voyages to India. Further north, the old coastwise trade between the Persian Gulf and northern India continued as before, building up the prosperity of such cities as Spasinu Charax (page 108); but it is uncertain what sort of people handled it. They could have been Greek, Arab or Jewish; they are less likely to have been Iranian, since the Iranians habitually thought of themselves as a land rather than a sea power. Nor do the Indians, at least on the western side of the peninsula, seem to have done much travelling: Indian sources speak often of foreign ships coming into Indian ports, but less often of Indian ships going out.

On the other side of the peninsula, Indians may have taken a more active part in trade and exploration. As already mentioned, they certainly had a profound influence on South-East Asia, even though no one is certain how this came about. But the South-East Asians themselves, and the Malays in particular, may have been equally active carriers. A hint about this is given in the *Periplus*:

> [There] are the marts of Camara and Poduce and Sopatma [on the Coromandel Coast of south-east India], where are local ships which sail along the coast as far as Limyrice, and others which are very large vessels made of single logs bound together and called *sangara*; those that cross over to Chryse and the Ganges are called *colandiophonta* and are the largest.[3]

Both the *sangara* (whose name means 'outriggers') and the *colandiophonta* were probably Malayan or Indonesian rather than Indian. Chinese sources describe the *colandiophonta* in more detail, under the name of *K'un-lun p'o*, and confirm that they were indeed exceptionally large. Some of them could be over 200 feet long, and carry six or seven hundred men and some nine hundred tons of cargo – which makes them perhaps a shade larger than those other leviathans of the Ancient World, the grain-ships that plied between Alexandria and Rome. They were also probably faster: even the largest Roman ships usually managed with a single enormous square sail, whereas a *K'un-lun p'o* had four sails and may even have arranged them in the fore-and-aft rig, like a schooner.[14]

South-eastern India has also produced one of the most interesting tangible examples of trade with the Roman world. At a place called Arikamedu, near Pondicherry, have been found brick buildings that may have been warehouses, and objects of Graeco-Roman origin including an intaglio, part of a lamp, fragments of amphorae and fragments of Arretine pottery (from Arezzo in Tuscany) dating from the first century AD. This settlement is almost certainly the place mentioned by the *Periplus* and by Ptolemy as *Poduce*, from the Tamil name *Pudu-chcheri*, meaning 'New Town'.[15]

Spices of several kinds would certainly have been among the goods carried from South-East Asia in the *colandiophonta*. Cinnamon and its close relation cassia are thought to have originated in Vietnam, and ginger possibly in Java. Two other familiar spices, cloves and nutmeg, had a still more remote origin; they came from the Moluccas, the famous 'Spice Islands' over which Europeans were to fight fiercely in the sixteenth and seventeenth centuries. To bring them even as far as Singapore took a voyage of nearly 2000 miles, farther than from Singapore to India and almost as far as from India to the Roman Empire.[16]

*

The rarity of Graeco-Roman voyages beyond India meant that ancient geographers (with one striking exception) had very little knowledge of how the land was shaped in these parts. The general belief was that on reaching the mouth of the Ganges one had already reached the eastern side of the world, and that quite a short voyage from here would take one to the coast of the *Seres* in China. The detailed and informed part of the *Periplus*, for example, ends with the description of 'Limyrice' (the Tamil country, in southern India). The final sections of the work (dealing with Ceylon, China and an island called *Chryse* or 'the golden' which is probably the Malay peninsula) are based on hearsay and altogether vaguer. *Chryse* is mentioned by several other ancient geographical writers, and often coupled with another island called *Argyre* or 'the silver'. This presents a problem, since silver is rare in South-East Asia; perhaps, as Paul Wheatley has suggested, *Argyre* was introduced merely because 'the two metals, gold and silver, ought to be associated in any good fairy story'.[17] But the gold really did exist, and was also noted by Chinese and Indian writers. The former mention a kingdom called *Chin-lin* or 'Frontier of Gold', while the latter write frequently of *Suvarnabhumi*, 'The Land of Gold', and *Suvarnadvipa*, 'the Island of Gold'. It may well have been this gold, in the Malay peninsula, that led the Indians to establish contact with South-East Asia in the first place.

The one striking exception to the general Western ignorance of lands east of India is the *Geography* of Ptolemy.[18] By this time, it would appear, mariners from the West were passing beyond India more often than before. Where previous writers mention only capes and islands that could be almost anywhere, and tribes that are obviously mythical, Ptolemy devotes a whole chapter to what he calls 'India beyond the Ganges' and gives an enormous amount of information about it. Unfortunately, as often happens with Ptolemy, his figures are not accurate enough for modern scholars to determine exactly where his places should be put; but the broad outline is clear, and very creditable considering how little had been known about the region before. The coast of Burma is easily recognizable, part of it still bearing the name *Argyre* but no longer treated as an island. Further south, the island of *Chryse* has similarly been corrected into a peninsula, *Chryse Chersonesos*, the 'Golden Chersonese'. The theme is further emphasized by the mention of a 'golden river' (the *Chrysoanas*) and a 'golden town' (*Sabara* or *Sabana*, from the Indian word *suvarna*). This last, from its given position at the extreme southern tip of the Chersonese, should be on or near the site of modern Singapore, though as yet no remains of the right age have been found here.

On the other side of the Chersonese, the coastal outlines of Thailand, Cambodia and South Vietnam can be recognized without difficulty. The river Menam, the chief river of Thailand which flows past modern Bangkok, appears as the *Sobanus* ('the golden one', again); and the larger river Mekong is given its due importance as the *Doanas*.[19] Oc-eo, the chief port of Funan (page 140), seems to be shown under the name of *Zabae*.

Altogether, this must be called a very distinguished piece of work by Ptolemy and his informants. Only on two matters have they made serious errors: they have drawn the Malay peninsula much too short and too thick (though many Europeans trying to draw it from memory might do the same today); and, though they show Java as *Iabadius* and correctly state that this means 'Island of Barley', they have omitted the nearer and larger island of Sumatra. In its place appear several small islands, said to be inhabitated by cannibals.

But though Ptolemy is good on 'India beyond the Ganges', his next chapter on the *Sinae* of South China goes all to pieces, making one of the worst errors in the whole of his book. Instead of carrying the Chinese coast eastward and northward (it is in fact very close to an arc of a circle), he makes it turn round and run south again. Eventually it joins a hypothetical southern continent, the notorious *Terra Australis Incognita*, whose non-existence was not finally demonstrated until Captain Cook's voyages in the 1770s; this in turn joins southern Africa, so as to make the Indian Ocean into a basin entirely surrounded by land. A place called *Sina Metropolis* ('the capital of the Sinae', perhaps modern Canton) is given a latitude three degrees south of the equator, as if it were in Borneo; and Cattigara, the port of the Sinae, takes a latitude of eight and a half degrees south, as if it were in Java.[20] How Ptolemy came to make this error is unknown, and probably never will be known. I myself have sometimes entertained the fanciful idea that he or his informants had obtained a Chinese map, and failed to realize that this was drawn with south at the top and north at the bottom.

There is no doubt, however, that Ptolemy's *Sinae* were a real people, not a fictitious one, and did live in southern China. (He himself goes out of his way to deny one tall story about them – that their capital had walls made of bronze.) There was a well-established seaborne trade between South-East Asia and China; and though we do not know who were the chief carriers in the South China Sea, we do know that by the second century AD some of them were coming all the way from the Roman Empire. This is revealed by a note in the Chinese annals:

In the ninth year of the Yen-hsi period [AD 166, a little later than Ptolemy's time], in the reign of Emperor Huan, king An-tun of

Ta-ch'in sent an embassy. From the frontier of Jih-nan this offered ivory, rhinoceros horn and tortoiseshell; from that time began direct trade relations with this country – but their tribute contained no jewels whatever . . .[21]

'An-tun' was the Emperor of Rome, Marcus Aurelius Antoninus (AD 161–80); 'Ta-ch'in' was the standard Chinese name for the Roman Empire. Jih-nan (mentioned above on page 138) was the most southerly of China's possessions, in what is now the middle part of Vietnam; and this indicates that the 'embassy' had arrived by the new-found sea route, rather than by the better-known overland route (the 'Silk Road') which would have brought it to a much more northerly part of the Chinese Empire. At least one European expedition thus did what Columbus later devoted his life to doing, and to the end of that life believed that he had indeed done. A direct link had been established between Europe and the wonderful kingdoms of the Far East, avoiding all the intervening states with their insistence on the mean advantage of the middleman.

Whether the so-called embassy set out with the official backing of 'An-tun' is doubtful. It could well have been a private trading enterprise rather than a true embassy, bringing in the name of the Roman emperor 'to give artistic verisimilitude to an otherwise bald and unconvincing narrative'. Emperor Huan, at all events, was unimpressed by the gifts; ivory, rhinoceros-horn and tortoiseshell were substances which he knew perfectly well already. The givers had made the elementary mistake of assuming that what seemed exotic to them must also seem exotic to the recipient. A present of Baltic amber, Phoenician glass, Mediterranean coral or Roman cameos would at least have had the advantage of novelty; but these too might well have failed to arouse the Emperor's enthusiasm. Much later, when Western merchants really did have valuable and useful things to sell, the Chinese continued to infuriate them by taking precisely the same attitude that their ancestors had taken. As Emperor Ch'ien Lung explained to Lord Macartney at the end of the eighteenth century;

> Our Celestial Empire produces everything that the human race could possibly require, in profuse abundance. We therefore have no need to purchase the goods of barbarians, however interesting and curious these may be.

And in ancient times a boast of this sort was no mere chauvinism. China under the Han dynasty had a claim to be the most civilized nation in the world, as well as the largest and most powerful. Something about these distant *Seres* and *Sinae* – as seen by themselves, now, instead of by outsiders – will be the subject of the next chapter.

CHAPTER NINE

CHINA

Cities and Thrones and Powers
   Stand in Time's eye,
Almost as long as flowers,
   Which daily die:
But, as new buds put forth
   To glad new men,
Out of the spent and unconsidered Earth
   The Cities rise again.
'Cities and Thrones and Powers'

The usual Chinese name for China is *Chung-kuo*, which means 'The Middle Kingdom' or 'The Central Kingdom'. A tendency to see oneself in the middle of things, and to treat everyone else as aliens, 'furriners' or 'barbarians', is by no means peculiar to China: it can be observed in Persepolis, Penzance and Peoria as well as in Peking. In China, however, this feeling has been unusually intense, unusually enduring, and for many centuries almost wholly justified. Ancient China was a great and distinguished civilization, and its inhabitants had to travel a long way before coming to any other civilization that could begin to compare with it. All that made Greeks feel themselves superior to Romans or *vice versa*, all that makes Europeans feel superior to Americans or *vice versa*, combined to make Chinese feel superior to everyone else with no converse. In the ancient Far East, China combined the military supremacy of Rome with the cultural supremacy of Greece. And so it had always been, apparently, since the beginning of the world.

The founders of Chinese civilization, in the valley of the Yellow River, saw 'barbarians' on all sides of them. Eastward lay the ocean, seemingly endless; there were a few islands in it, but their inhabitants clearly had everything to learn from China and nothing to teach in return. Southward lay a land of swamp and jungle and steamy heat, full of snakes and leeches and people who seemed little better than snakes or leeches themselves; one word often used by the early north Chinese about the southerners has the basic meaning of 'squirmy'. There was a road of sorts linking south-west China with north-east India, but this was one of the most difficult and dangerous routes in the world, repeatedly climbing over snow-clad mountain passes and plunging down again into the jungly valleys of great rivers – a botanist's dream, but a traveller's nightmare. West of China the mountains are even higher, and beyond them lies the barren plateau of Tibet with hardly any inhabitants at all. North of China the cultivable land gradually merges into steppe, and this in turn into desert. Here lived the people whom the Chinese out of all their neighbours found most utterly detestable – the nomadic tribes, who unlike the people of the east and south and west were numerous and warlike enough to be a constant threat to the Empire. As early as the third century BC, the Great Wall of China had to be built to keep them out. Even after this, any lack of vigilance south of the Wall was likely to lead to invasion, and probably to a takeover of the Chinese government by the nomads. The Mongol conquest in the thirteenth century AD, which made Kublai Khan emperor of China as well as Great Khan of Mongolia, is the best-known example of something that has happened many times in China's history.

Between the mountains of Tibet and the deserts of Mongolia ran one route which, if followed far enough, could bring an ancient Chinese into contact with other great civilized nations. This was the famous 'Silk Road', of which more will be said in the next chapter. Along this route a few ideas and techniques may have reached China from the ancient civilizations of the Near East – the idea of agriculture, for

The Great Wall of China.

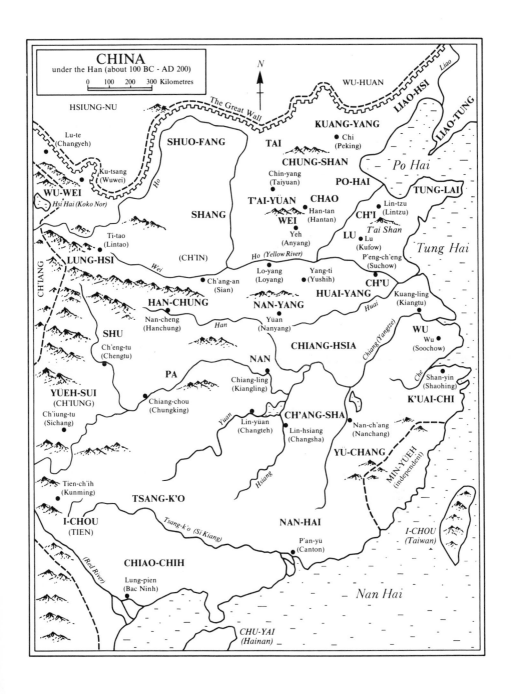

CHINA
under the Han (about 100 BC – AD 200)

0   100   200   300 Kilometres

N

HSIUNG-NU

WU-HUAN

LIAO-HSI

Liao

LIAO-TUNG

Lu-te
(Changyeh)

The Great Wall

SHUO-FANG

TAI

KUANG-YANG

Chi
(Peking)

Po Hai

Ku-tsang
(Wuwei)

CHUNG-SHAN

PO-HAI

TUNG-LAI

WU-WEI

Chin-yang
(Taiyuan)

Hsi Hai (Koko Nor)

Ho

SHANG

T'AI-YUAN

CHAO

Han-tan
(Hantan)

Lin-tzu
(Lintzu)

CH'I

Ti-tao
(Lintao)

WEI

Yeh
(Anyang)

T'ai Shan

LU

Lu
(Kufow)

Tung Hai

(CH'IN)

Ho (Yellow River)

P'eng-ch'eng
(Suchow)

LUNG-HSI

Wei

Lo-yang
(Loyang)

Yang-ti
(Yushih)

CH'U

CHIANG

Ch'ang-an
(Sian)

HUAI-YANG

Kuang-ling
(Kiangtu)

HAN-CHUNG

NAN-YANG

Huai

Nan-cheng
(Hanchung)

Han

Yuan
(Nanyang)

WU

Wu
(Soochow)

SHU

NAN

CHIANG-HSIA

Ch'eng-tu
(Chengtu)

Chiang (Yangtze)

Che

Shan-yin
(Shaohing)

PA

Chiang-ling
(Kiangling)

YUEH-SUI
(CH'IUNG)

Chiang-chou
(Chungking)

Yuan

Lin-yuan
(Changteh)

CH'ANG-SHA

K'UAI-CHI

Ch'iung-tu
(Sichang)

Lin-hsiang
(Changsha)

Nan-ch'ang
(Nanchang)

Tien-ch'ih
(Kunming)

YU-CHANG

MIN-YÜEH
(independent)

I-CHOU
(TIEN)

TSANG-K'O

Hsiang

NAN-HAI

I-CHOU
(Taiwan)

Tsang-k'o (Si Kiang)

P'an-yu
(Canton)

CHIAO-CHIH

(Red River)

Lung-pien
(Bac Ninh)

Nan Hai

CHU-YAI
(Hainan)

example, the idea of wheeled transport, and possibly the idea of metal-working (though right from the start Chinese metalwork was distinctly different from anyone else's). Buddhism reached China by the same route in the first century AD; Nestorian Christianity followed later, as did Islam, but neither of these had anything like the effect on China that Buddhism had had. Apart from these occasional contacts, and the transport of luxuries like silk, China remained a world on its own. After Buddhism, no other foreign idea was to have any serious influence on Chinese thought until the nineteenth and twentieth centuries.

Chinese civilization first developed in the valley of the Yellow River, a formidable stream which offered early man an impressive combination of danger and opportunity. Though one of the world's longest rivers, it is not outstandingly large, because of the dryness of the North Chinese climate (it carries only about one-seventh as much water as the Yangtze, for example). Much of the land through which it flows is covered with a kind of soil called loess, formed in the Ice Ages when polar winds gathered up silt and dust from the Eurasian tundra and dumped it here on the eastern side of the continent. This loess gives the Yellow River and the Yellow Sea their colour; it also makes the river one of the muddiest in the world, much more deserving than the Mississippi of the wisecrack about being 'too thick to navigate and too thin to cultivate'. The lower river has changed its course repeatedly, sometimes coming out on the north side and sometimes on the south side of the Shantung peninsula; every time such a change occurs, great numbers of people are usually drowned, while others lose their livelihood because their water-supply is no longer there. But the loess is so fertile that the Chinese again and again have braved the fury of the river to reap its advantages. From very early times, embankments and dykes were built to control the water; large states could do this more efficiently than small ones, and quite large states developed along the river perhaps as early as 2000 BC. They look small only by comparison with China as a whole.

In Chinese tradition the first two imperial dynasties are those of the Hsia (*circa* 2000–1500 BC?) and the Shang (*circa* 1500–1027 BC). At one time both were rejected as mythical; the existence of the Hsia remains dubious, but excavations in the 1930s revealed that the Shang (or at least the later Shang) was genuine after all. The most important site of this period is near Anyang, some distance north of the Yellow River. Here, in about 1300 BC, was a substantial town, with a royal palace, some impressive royal tombs and many lesser buildings. Rulers of this period knew the use of bronze, and the use of the horse-drawn chariot; like Bronze Age chiefs in some other parts of the world, they were entombed with many of their personal possessions, and many of their retainers were sacrificed to give them a fitting escort into the afterworld. Diviners, meanwhile, were attempting to read the future by study of the cracks on heated animal bones; they have left behind their conclusions, written on the bones in a script that can be recognized as the ancestor of present-day Chinese writing; and among the names thus preserved are many names of Shang rulers, as noted independently in traditional Chinese history.

The remarkable thing about Chinese civilization is not its great age, for to the student of ancient Egypt or Babylonia 1300 BC is almost a modern date. It is rather that so many features of Chinese life have persisted from the beginning of the country's history down to the present day. There can be few if any other countries in the world where a three-thousand-year-old text uses essentially the same script and language as are used today.

*

More definite records appear with the establishment of the next dynasty, the Chou, perhaps in 1027 BC; and in what is called the Spring and Autumn Period[1] (722–481 BC) the outline of what happened is clear. By this time Chinese civilization had expanded beyond the confines of the Yellow River valley. Northward it reached about as far as Peking; eastward it was bounded by the sea, southward by the river Yangtze, and on the west it was beginning to approach the mountains of Tibet. The Spring and Autumn Period saw a great flowering of thought, above all in the realms of philosophy and religion. This was the age of Confucius, whose traditional dates are 551–479 BC, and of Lao Tzu, the founder of Taoism, whose career is more shadowy but who may have been Confucius' contemporary. Together with the Buddha (also alive at this time, in a different sub-continent) these two were to dominate Chinese religion with their ideas until the twentieth century. But in its political and social life the period was less inspired. The later Chou rulers, like some of the mediaeval kings of France, claimed a large dominion but had very little that they could truly call their own; on all sides they were surrounded by so-called vassals whose real power was greater than their so-called overlord's. Warfare among these was continual, and grew worse as time went on. Indeed the period after the Spring and Autumn, from 481 to 221 BC, is known to historians as the Period of Warring States.

This was ended by the remarkable Ch'in Shih-huang-ti, nicknamed the Tiger of Ch'in, who plays a part in Chinese history similar to that of Alexander the Great in the history of the Greek world. He lived about a century later than Alexander, at about the same time as

Hannibal. His native land, like Alexander's, lay on the fringe of civiliz-ation: the kingdom of Ch'in was the most westerly of the Warring States, a buffer between the 'Ch'iang barbarians' of Tibet and the rich lowlands of the Yellow River. Its heart was the valley of the river Wei; its capital stood on this river, not far from the modern city of Sian.

Prince Cheng, as he was originally called, became king of Ch'in in 246 BC, and by 221 had overthrown all his rivals and established his rule throughout northern China. In honour of this, he took the title by which he is known to posterity, *Ch'in Shih-huang-ti* meaning 'Ch'in, the First Sovereign Emperor'. Having acquired the north, he went on to conquer the south as well, bringing Chinese arms and Chinese government into regions that had hitherto been almost unknown. And, though some of the earlier states had already built lengths of wall to defend themselves against the northern steppe-dwellers, it was Ch'in Shih-huang-ti who first had these joined together and reinforced to form the original Great Wall of China.[2]

But beside these credits to the First Emperor there are many debits. Out of all the philosophic systems contending for official backing in his time, he had chosen the harsh creed known as Legalism, which anticipated many of the ideas of modern Fascism. 'The severe house-hold has no fierce slaves,' wrote one eminent Legalist, 'it is the affectionate mother who has the prodigal son. Awe-inspiring power can repress outrage; virtue and kindness are insufficient'.[3] Ch'in

Tomb of Confucius at Kufow (ancient Lu, *his native city).*

The meeting of Confucius and Lao Tzu. A stone bas-relief of the Han period.

Shih-huang-ti agreed, so much so that he proscribed all philosophic schools other than Legalism and had their books publicly burnt. For this he has been roundly cursed ever since by the scholarly class, while the common people still have terrible legends of how they suffered in the building of the Wall. Alexander the Great, despite his many personal weaknesses, became a hero: Chin Shih-huang-ti, despite his genuine achievements for his country, became one of its chief national villains.

His dynasty, which he had boasted would last ten thousand years, in fact hardly lasted long enough to constitute a dynasty at all. He died in 210 BC, and his son (the so-called Second Emperor) almost at once showed himself to be hopelessly incompetent. Revolts broke out, and for a time it seemed that a second Age of Warring States had begun and might last as long as the previous one. Instead, however, the fighting was short-lived, and from 202 BC to AD 220 the Han dynasty gave China one of the most distinguished periods in her history.

Emperor Kao-tsu, the founder of this dynasty, has some attributes in common with the Emperor Augustus, the founder of the Roman Empire. To begin with a trivial point, he resembles Augustus in confusingly having different names at different stages of his career. His family name was Liu, his given name was Pang; during his rise to power he became king of a region called Han, on the Han river, and from this his dynasty takes its name. Only after his death was he given the title by which he is now usually called – Kao-tsu, which means 'Exalted Ancestor'. His struggle with a certain Hsiang Yü for control of China resembles the struggle between Octavian-Augustus and Mark Antony for control of the Roman world; in each case, so to speak, the tortoise beat the hare and the fox beat the lion. And whereas the First Emperor had made himself hated by applying too rigid a system to everything, Kao-tsu and Augustus achieved lasting results by improvising their political arrangements as they went along.

After Kao-tsu's death in 195 BC, Chinese history becomes less eventful. Life at court continued to have its disturbances; the late emperor (once again like Augustus) had left a widow of powerful and unpleasant character, the Empress Lü, who virtually ruled the Empire using her son as a puppet. This culminated in a civil war between the Liu and Lü families, in which the latter were massacred. But the land as a whole was little touched by this palace revolution.

The reign of Emperor Wu[4] (141–87 BC), Kao-tsu's great-grandson, saw events of more general importance. *Wu* means 'martial' or 'military', and the emperor well deserved this posthumous title. He extended the power of the Empire in three different directions. In the north-west, the Hsiung-nu (Huns) were chastised, and expeditions and embassies entered what is now Chinese Central Asia (known in those days as Hsi-yü, 'the Western Regions'). Some of these even reached what is now Soviet Central Asia, to make contact with the Kushans and their relatives in the formerly Greek-ruled kingdom of Bactria. News began to filter through about still remoter countries such as Parthia, Mesopotamia and north-west India. Chinese power

One of the life-size pottery figures from Ch'in Shih-huang-ti's army, found outside his tomb near Sian.

was also extended southward, into Nan Yüeh (south China and north Vietnam; see page 136) which had been conquered by Ch'in Shih-huang-ti but made itself independent again soon after his death. P'an-yü (modern Canton), the capital of Nan-Yüeh, was captured by the Imperial armies in 111 BC. Most of the region soon became an integral part of China, and still is: to this day the expression *Han-jen*, 'Men of Han', is used to signify the Chinese of China proper, as opposed to the Mongols, Manchus, Tibetans and others who did not enter the Empire until post-Han times. And in yet another direction, the armies of Emperor Wu established Chinese authority in what is now North Korea.

Like Ch'in Shih-huang-ti, Emperor Wu had a complex character. Though not an out-and-out Legalist, he certainly did not believe in tempering justice with mercy. Curious and sinister events occurred in his reign, such as the Witchcraft Scandal of 91 BC, in which his son and heir was forced to commit suicide and many others were executed.[5] Moreover, much of what we know about him derives from the writings of a man whom he humiliated in a most painful way – Ssu-ma Ch'ien, the Grand Historian and 'Father of Chinese History', who was castrated on a trumped-up charge of 'attempting to deceive the Emperor'. But whatever may be said against Emperor Wu, no one can deny his immense energy and efficiency. His successors had less of these, and some were downright feeble.

This led to a hiatus in the rule of the dynasty. Between AD 9 and 23 the throne was held by a man from a different family, usually known as 'Wang Mang, the usurper' though he saw himself as the founder of a new dynasty which he called the Hsin. He introduced some interesting reforms, most notably a scheme to nationalize and redistribute land. For this he has sometimes been described as an early Socialist, though the avowed object of the scheme was to recreate the golden justice of the remote past. ('When Adam delved and Eve span, who was then the gentleman?') At all events, the reforms failed: not only did they alienate the nobles and most of the scholars, but through a mixture of bad luck and bad management they did not even benefit the peasants as had been intended. A general revolt broke out, Wang Mang was assassinated, and in AD 25 the Han was restored by another member of the Liu family, who became the Emperor Kuang-wu.

The resulting second period of Han rule is sometimes known as the Later Han, and sometimes as the Eastern Han (because the imperial capital was shifted eastward from Ch'ang-an, modern Sian, to Lo-yang on the river Lo, which still keeps its ancient name). Though not without its moments of glory, the later period never managed to equal the brilliance of the earlier. Dangerous weaknesses began to appear in the Empire, similar to those that were to threaten the Roman Empire some two centuries later. Great baronial families grew up, with thousands of retainers and myriads of serfs; free peasants lost their freedom through pressure of debt; the imperial court was increasingly dominated by eunuchs and bureaucrats. Most disturbing of all was the situation on the frontiers. Direct attack on the 'barbarians', as favoured by Emperor Wu and others of the early Han, had given way to a policy called *i-i-fa-i*, which means almost exactly the same as the Latin *divide et impera*. One barbarian tribe was now to be played off against another, which in practice meant that important frontier provinces came to be held by tribesmen whose loyalty could not be relied on. Though the official date for the fall of the Han is AD 220, government had practically collapsed in many regions some decades earlier.

The succeeding 'Three Kingdoms' period (AD 221–280) has an Arthurian flavour; it was to become a favourite subject of Chinese literature and drama, in which its chief characters were portrayed as men of more than mortal clay.[6] (One of them, the paladin Kuan Yü, was eventually to enter the Chinese pantheon as the God of War.) But, like the Arthurian age in the West, the period must have been far less pleasant to live in than to read about. A brief reunion was achieved by the Tsin dynasty in AD 280, but soon afterwards the Empire was torn apart once more by a fresh wave of invaders from the northern steppes. Not until the age of the Sui dynasty (AD 589–618) and its longer-lived and better-known successor the T'ang (619–906) did China again know the power and prestige she had known under the Han.

*

The Chinese Empire, like that of Rome, was an absolute monarchy. Its ruler was supreme in all political and legal matters; he was also commander-in-chief of the army, though this was not as important in China as in Rome; and he was also the religious head of his people. This, conversely, was far more important than in Rome. Although emperors there used the quasi-divine title *Augustus* (meaning something like 'sanctified' or 'hallowed') and the title of High Priest (*pontifex maximus*), the religious aspect of their power was normally kept in the background. In China it was paramount. One title commonly used by the emperor there meant 'Son of Heaven'; the principle from which he took his power was called the 'Mandate of Heaven'. Like the priest-kings found in several other parts of the Ancient World, he was expected to mediate between gods and men, by means of great official sacrifices recorded in profuse detail by the imperial annalists.

In this respect the Chinese emperor had a great advantage over his opposite number at Rome. A fundamental weakness of the Roman Empire was that, constitutionally speaking, it ought not to have existed at all. There had been priest-kings of Rome in the remote past, but the last of these had been forcibly expelled 'by the will of the Senate and People'. The date of this event (509 BC, according to tradition) had an importance in the Roman Republic equal of that of 1776 in the USA or 1789 in France. Julius Caesar was murdered for behaving like an absolute monarch; Augustus avoided the same fate by means of the fiction that he had 'restored the Republic' and was merely its *princeps* or 'First Citizen'. In China such wrapping-up of the truth was unnecessary. It was universally believed that there had always been an emperor, and that to have none, or more than one, was a terrible calamity. The rule of two rival emperors was likened by Confucius to 'two suns in one sky'.

The doctrine of the 'Mandate of Heaven', however, had a catch. The job of a righteous and rightful emperor was to secure the favour of the gods for himself and his people: if he failed – if drought and flood, famine and pestilence, civil strife and foreign invasion came instead – it logically followed that he was not rightful after all. Rebellion against the Son of Heaven was monstrous and sacrilegious – unless it succeeded, when the success proved that the new ruler had had the Mandate all the time and the old one had not.

> Treason doth never prosper: what's the reason?
> For if it prosper, none dare call it treason.

*

Below the emperor and his family, Chinese society has traditionally been divided into four classes. To this extent it resembles traditional society in India and Europe, but the arrangement of the classes was peculiarly Chinese. In order of precedence, they were the scholars and gentry (*shih*), the peasants (*nung*), the artisans (*kung*), and the merchants (*shang*). This is one feature of Chinese thought that has survived the Revolution; it was the scholars and peasants who did most to bring it about, and they continue to be the most highly regarded classes under Communism.

In ancient China the scholars did not have the predominance that they later acquired. Though promotion by merit was an established principle, as was promotion by success in examinations, there were powerful noble families who also put in their claims for preferment. Ancient Chinese history shows a continuing rivalry between these two groups: on the one hand the courtiers, with extrinsic importance through their access to the emperor; and on the other hand the barons with intrinsic importance as territorial magnates in their own right, but further removed from the centre of ultimate authority.

The relative strength of courtiers and barons depended mainly on the attitude and ability of the emperor himself. Courtiers increased their influence under a strong ruler, barons under a weak one. This can be seen in the changing political map of ancient China. In the Age of the Warring States, and above all in the first half of the third century BC, the barons were everywhere predominant, strong enough to ignore the central authority and at length even to suppress it. With the triumph of Ch'in Shih-huang-ti in 221 BC the pendulum swung to the opposite extreme. As First Emperor of a united realm, the new ruler abolished all the earlier kingdoms and set up an entirely new system, whereby the Empire was divided into thirty-six units called commanderies (*chün*), all under his own direct rule. Soon after his death, however, adventurers of the baronial type appeared. Some of them, including the founder of the Han, went so far as to call themselves kings; and after reuniting the Empire, Han Kao-tsu was unable or unwilling to restore the *status quo* completely. Instead he set up a mixed administration, under which fifteen commanderies came under his own rule and ten kingdoms (*kuo*) were given to his friends and relations. This type of arrangement, with two different kinds of administrative unit, persisted throughout the Han period. One of its beneficiaries, a brother of Emperor Wu's who became king of Chung-shan, bequeathed to posterity one of the most striking archaeological finds made in China: his tomb, found in 1968, contained more than 2800 grave-goods, including a pair of jade suits, sewn together with gold thread, in which he and his consort had been buried.[7]

On the whole, however, the pseudo-autonomous kingdoms proved a grave nuisance to the emperors. Many of their rulers had to be deposed or executed for rebellion. As time went on, their size was steadily reduced by subdivision. Thus a census of AD 1–2 (the oldest census in the world to have survived in detail) describes the Empire as containing eighty-three commanderies as against only twenty kingdoms; and the emperor's power was as strong (or as weak) in the one kind of territory as in the other. A second census, taken by the Later Han in AD 140, lists thirteen large units known as provinces (*chou*), these being subdivided into seventy-nine commanderies, twenty kingdoms (but not the same twenty as before), and six territories known as 'dependent states' (*shu-kuo*). This last expression was in practice a euphemism for '*in*dependent states'; by this time the Han Empire was already showing signs of fraying at the edges.[8]

A contrast between the upper classes of ancient China and those of

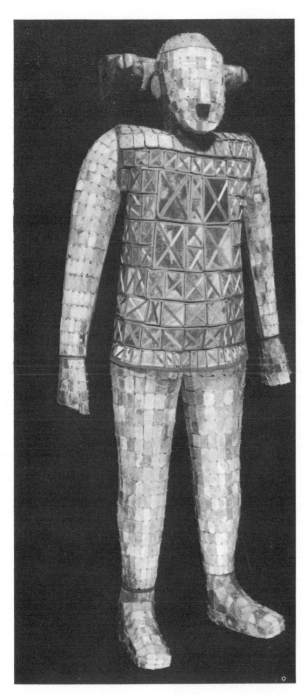

Jade burial-suit of Tou Wan, queen of Chung-shan and sister-in-law of Emperor Wu. She died in about 110 BC.

Rome was their opinion about the occupations proper to a gentleman. Romans such as Cicero believed the chief of these to be agriculture, the law and the army; most Chinese of similar status would have agreed about the importance of the first, but strongly disagreed about the other two. Confucian thought maintained that laws, ideally, should not be necessary; people were by nature good, and if they strayed from the path of goodness they needed to be brought back by benevolence and sincerity, not by force. The Legalists, as already mentioned, took the opposite view – that people were evil-minded donkeys who understood the stick better than the carrot. The controversy between the two schools ended in a compromise, the gist of which was that good people did not need laws but bad people did. Law, accordingly, never came to be seen in China as the framework of society, in the Greek or Roman manner; it was seen as something inflicted upon the dregs of society, and as often as not something 'lingering, with boiling oil in it'. Ordinary disputes were settled by custom or arbitration, not in the courts. There were no Ciceros.

For similar reasons, the army was not highly esteemed. It was necessary, and often successful; China did not become great solely by Confucian benevolence and sincerity. As early as the fourth century BC, Sun Tzu wrote a military classic called *The Art of War*, which has been highly praised by Captain Liddell Hart and also by Mao Tse-tung.[9] And Ch'in Shih-huang-ti so admired warfare that he had a whole army of life-sized pottery figures to stand guard over his tomb. But the general current of opinion flowed in the opposite direction. Mo Tzu, who like Sun Tzu lived in the fourth century BC, asked a question that still troubles thoughtful people today:

> . . . If a small crime is considered crime, but a big crime – such as attacking another country – is applauded as a righteous act, can this be said to be knowing the difference between righteous and unrighteous?[10]

Two Chinese words, *wu* and *wen*, illustrate the predominant attitude. *Wu* means 'martial' or 'military': *wen*, its opposite, means either 'civilian' or 'civilized'. Some emperors were called Wu, others Wen, and the latter were more esteemed than the former. And, on a more personal level, early Chinese verse is full of complaints about the misery of army life (for the Chinese army, unlike the Roman, was based on conscription):

> They fought south of the ramparts,
> They died north of the wall.
> They died in the moors and were not buried.

Their flesh was the food of crows.
'Tell the crows we are not afraid;
We have died in the moors and cannot be buried.
Crows, how can our bodies escape you?'[11]

The religion of ancient China had much in common with that of ancient Greece and Rome, and continued thus almost down to modern times. (The resemblance was noted with approval by several European visitors to China in the eighteenth century – and with strong disapproval by their more devout successors, the Christian missionaries of the nineteenth.) From the earliest times, many systems of thought and ritual had competed for attention in China, and a feeling grew up that to pay exclusive attention to any one of them showed an unbalanced mind. The idea of a 'jealous God', taken up by Christians and Muslims from Hebrew tradition, seemed to the Chinese not only alien but childish.

This sceptical attitude to revealed religion was intense in the works of Confucius (551–479 BC). His opinion on the world to come, for example, has been succinctly translated by Dr Lin Yutang as 'Don't know life: how know death?'.[12] But Confucius' turn of mind was conservative as well as sceptical: he liked ritual for its own sake, and he also liked what one may broadly call 'proper behaviour'; and he encouraged the one for the way in which it could stimulate the other. From Confucius, Chinese tradition traced its emphasis on filial piety, on reverence for one's ancestors and respect for the Emperor (with its corollary, that the Emperor's duty was likewise to respect his people). Many Romans, with their fondness for *pietas* and *gravitas*, would have agreed.

The golden rules of Confucius had to contend in ancient times not only with the iron and lead of Legalism, but also with the indiarubbery set of beliefs known as Taoism and ascribed to Lao Tzu. This man's life, conformably with his teaching, is almost entirely unknown. It has even been asserted, as with Homer, that he is a composite of several different people. Taoism takes its name from the word *Tao*, which literally means 'road' or 'way' but in this context cannot be easily translated. An essential principle of Taoism, indeed, is that all attempts to translate it are self-defeating: 'the Way that can be spoken of is not the true Way'. Taoism calls upon man to do what comes naturally, to use the heart rather than the head. Those who have to *think* how to act virtuously, like those who have to think how to tie their ties or change gear in their cars, it sees as taking a fundamentally wrong view of the situation.

Thus, while the schools of Confucianism and Legalism strove for control of the Chinese establishment, Taoism became a favourite belief of those outside the establishment or opposed to it altogether. (In the West today, it still is.) Professor C. Northcote Parkinson, from whose writings I have taken the notion of 'barons' and 'courtiers' contending for power in a great organization, has also noted the importance of the Fool or Jester, and pointed out that modern big businesses are the poorer for his absence.[13] In ancient China the role of King's Jester was habitually taken by the Taoist – the man as much as home in a tub as in a palace, able to dance Harlequin-like before the government, to needle it with dubious aphorisms, and to convince it that it, or he, or both, did not exist.

Taoism also became a favourite belief of those whose minds turned towards what used to be called 'natural philosphy' – those who found the behaviour of stars, or trees, or chemical substances, at least as interesting as the over-advertized behaviour of human beings. Lao Tzu was the patron of astrologers and alchemists, of geomancers and cheiromancers and all who sought to solve the Riddle of the Universe. It could be claimed, indeed, that all the world's great scientists have had a touch of Taoism in their character. The more successfully they explain things, the more they come to see how much remains unex-plained and maybe inexplicable, as when Isaac Newton likened himself to a boy playing on the seashore while the great ocean of truth lay all undiscovered before him. In China, however, this aspect of Taoism was eventually to bring about its decline. Instead of seeking new truths, the Taoists led themselves into a world of hey-presto and hocus-pocus, and their more sceptical countrymen refused to follow them.

Buddhism, the other main strand in the Chinese religious tradition, was the last to appear. It first came to the notice of the Chinese in the first century BC, as a result of Emperor Wu's operations in Central Asia; thereafter it gradually percolated into China proper, one of its devotees being Emperor Ming of the Later Han (AD 58–75). But throughout the Han period its importance was limited. The technical difficulties alone were a formidable obstacle to its spread; Buddhist sacred texts were written in Sanskrit, which differs from Chinese as much as any language can differ from any other. To Confucian orthodoxy, moreover, the Buddhist concern with individual salvation seemed selfish, while the practice of withdrawing from worldly life seemed idle and anti-social. Buddhism did not become important for China as a whole until after the fall of the Han, when the general disorder led people to think more often of the miseries of the world and the hypothetical superiority of the next. Under the T'ang, in the seventh century, it enjoyed a heyday; but it never achieved the success achieved by Christianity in similar circumstances on the other side of the world. The emperor, as Son of Heaven, remained the spiritual leader of China, and traditions at his court remained Confucian. There was to be no papacy, no body of clergy with a monopoly of learning, and no suggestion that the Church's law could overrule the State's.

*

Though the peasantry (*nung*) came second in order of precedence after the scholar-gentry (*shih*), the practical consequences of this were small. In China, as elsewhere, peasants seldom appear in the historical records except when they do something to annoy those set in authority over them. One such annoyance was the revolt of a peasant group called the Red Eyebrows in the twenties AD, which heralded the fall of Wang Mang; another was the revolt of the Yellow Turbans in the 180s AD, which lowered the power of the Later Han to a point from which it could no longer rise. Whereas English history acknowledges only one Peasants' Revolt, in 1381, Chinese history is full of them. Among the spiritual heirs of the Red Eyebrows and Yellow Turbans may be counted the T'ai-P'ing insurgents in the 1860s, the Boxers in 1900 and the Communists in the 1930s. In fairness to the Chinese historians, however, it must be admitted that they have always treated such revolts very seriously, as indicating something fundamentally wrong with the government of the time, and probably foretelling a transfer of the Mandate of Heaven.

Though silent about the peasants as individuals, the censuses of AD 1–2 and 140 have preserved some information about them collectively. The earlier census lists the total population of the Empire as

Pottery model of a farmstead (1st century AD).

59,594,978, the later as 49,150,220: an ominous change, for a declining population in the Ancient World usually meant that the Four Horsemen of the Apocalypse had been busy. Both figures should be taken as minima, since the Chinese had a strong and justified belief that census was the prelude to taxation, and many people may have succeeded in slipping through the census-takers' net. The population of the Roman Empire at its height, for comparison, was probably about 50–60 million; and it too is thought to have declined as time went on. Nobody knows why.

The Chinese censuses further show that the population was unevenly distributed. The highest densities were in the traditional heartland of Chinese civilization, the valley of the Yellow River; as one went away from this centre, they steadily decreased. (Here again there is a parallel with the Roman Empire, where the most populous provinces were those that bordered the Mediterranean.) But in AD 140 the contrast was less intense than in AD 1. Though the total population had fallen, that of the most southerly commanderies, the farthest from the Yellow River, had risen, sometimes by an impressive amount. In this respect the Chinese Empire was the inverse of the Roman. Expansion southward from the Mediterranean was soon halted by the dryness of the climate, and post-Roman settlement in North Africa was not more intensive than Roman settlement, but less. It was the opposite direction, northward, that showed the greater promise. In the Roman period itself we may see the beginnings of an important social and economic change, from the 'Mediterranean-centred' Europe of earlier times to the 'Rhine-centred' Europe of the Middle Ages and today.

In China the climate worked the other way round. North of China proper, the plains of Inner Mongolia were too arid to support the Chinese way of life, and the plains of Manchuria long remained almost unknown and unvisited. It was the south that attracted enterprising men of Han in search of new opportunities. With its warm climate and large rivers, it was eminently suitable for growing one of the world's most useful food-crops, rice, instead of the wheat and millet grown in the north. It also had a variety of more exciting and expensive natural products. There was the cassia-tree or *kuei*, whose product was as much prized in China as in the West; the name of the city of Kueilin, in Kuangsi province, means 'Cassia Forest' and derives from the name of a commandery first established by the founder of the Ch'in dynasty. Another kind of South Chinese tree was prized for the making of coffins. Among animal products were ivory, rhinoceros-horn and tortoiseshell, noted in the previous chapter as having disappointed Emperor Huan when he had expected something more exotic from the deputation of Rome. And Chinese pharmacists, who already had somewhat kill-or-cure ideas about what should be put into medicine, would pay high prices for such outlandish things as tiger's tendon and python's gall-bladder, which again could be most readily obtained in the south.

Mention of such commodities leads us to the last two classes of Chinese society, the artisans and craftsmen (*kung*) and the merchants (*shang*). Though held in lower esteem than the scholars, gentry and peasantry, both groups made remarkable contributions to Chinese life.

All ancient societies were rural by the standards of the industrial world today, but ancient China was at least as highly urbanized as anywhere else. The two largest cities of the Han Empire were Ch'ang-an and Lo-yang, the respective capitals of the Early and Late Han emperors. The population of Ch'ang-an in AD 1–2 was recorded as 246,200, an impressive figure, though not quite as large as one might have guessed from comparison with the Roman world. In the Roman Empire at its height (say about AD 150) Rome itself is thought to have had about a million inhabitants, Alexandria and Antioch perhaps half a million apiece. A city the size of earlier Ch'ang-an might have gained fourth place, slightly ahead of Carthage and Ephesus.

Other distinguished cities of the Han period were Ch'eng-tu, dominating the fertile Red Basin of the upper Yangtze, and P'an-yü (Canton), the chief city of the far South. These two have retained their importance to the present day. Among the numerous cities on the eastern side of China, in the flood-plain of the Yellow and Huai rivers, one of the most important was the city of Lu (the capital of a region also called Lu, renowned as the native land of Confucius); but its site today is not well known. Lin-tzu, another large city of eastern China, has likewise dwindled into obscurity. Peking, on the other hand, has risen in the world since ancient times; it is mentioned in the Han period as Chi, the capital of Kuang-yang commandery, but in those days was a modest town dangerously close to the northern frontier of the Empire. It became the capital of China only after the Mongol conquest, as a convenient place from which the new rulers could govern China and Mongolia at the same time.

Most Chinese cities, like many Roman ones, were laid out on a grid plan; but whereas in the Roman world this was usually done because the city had succeeded a military base, in China the chief reason was not military but mystical. The city, as a miniature world, had to imitate the plan of nature and align itself with the five cardinal points (North, South, East, West and Centre). But defence and security were also important. All Chinese cities have traditionally been walled, and some of them, including Peking, were maintaining and *using* their old walls within living memory. Ancient Ch'ang-an had internal as well as external walls, dividing it into wards, and the gates linking one ward with another were closed at night. In this respect the *Pax Romana* was at times more effective than the *Pax Sinica*; many cities of the early Roman Empire had no walls at all.

Cities and towns were linked by a network of roads as comprehensive as that of the Roman Empire, and also cheaper to construct, though less well known today. (Roman roads have survived for so long because they were built much more solidly than they needed to be.) And China, like Rome, had an efficient system of posting-stations for the use of imperial officials and messengers. Water transport was also important, and the age-old difficulties of contending with the Yellow River had made the Chinese expert in all aspects of water-control. Chapter 29 of Ssu-ma Ch'ien's *Historical Records* deals entirely with this subject, beginning with the thirteen-year plan undertaken by the legendary Emperor Yü to control the Yellow River, and ending with a note that the author himself had helped carry faggots to mend a dangerous breach in its embankment.

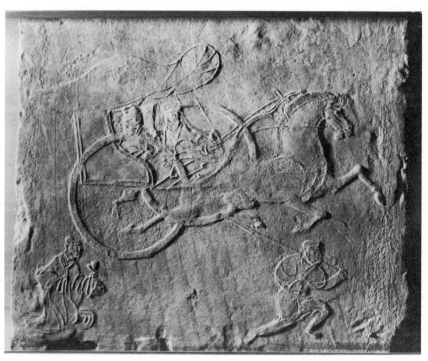

Horse and chariot, on a brick of the Han period.

The river rages on,
Its wild waters tossing.
It swirls back to the north,
A swift and dangerous torrent.
We bring the long stakes
And cast the precious jade.
The Lord of the River hears our plea
But there is not enough brushwood . . .[14]

Among other heavy industries in ancient China, iron-working and salt-working were of especial importance. Both were under government control, and in both some remarkable discoveries were made. Whereas the furnaces of the Western world were hot enough only to soften iron, so that it then had to be wrought by hammering with great labour, the Chinese furnaces (sometimes blown by water-powered bellows) were able to liquefy the iron completely, so that it could be poured off into moulds like bronze. The Han Chinese, in fact, had invented cast iron, a material not used in the West until the Industrial Revolution. Their search for salt led them to anticipate by many

Rural scene with drilling-rig in action, from a brick of the Han period.

centuries another well-known Western invention, deep drilling. The object of this was not petroleum, but the brine that is often found lying beneath it in underground deposits; the petroleum and associated natural gas may then have been used to heat vessels of brine and so produce salt by evaporation.

Three more specialities of ancient China also deserve mention – one animal, one vegetable and one mineral. The mineral was jade, a product of Central Asia rather than China proper, but known to the Chinese since Neolithic times. It was immensely prized, perhaps not least because it is immensely difficult to work. Unlike flint and obsidian, the other two best-known materials from which Neolithic tools were made, jade cannot be flaked or 'knapped' (a comparatively easy job for those who know the trick of it); it has to be ground into shape, and is so hard as to make this a very laborious task whatever technique is used. The jade-cutter was among the most distinguished of Chinese craftsmen.

The vegetable product was lacquer, the juice of the lac tree (*Rhus vernicifera*). This was useful as well as decorative, as the standard way of making objects waterproof – the ancient Chinese equivalent of mackintoshing, oilcloth or plastic laminates. It could be applied not only to the familiar boxes and bowls, but also to hats, shoes, umbrellas, parts of chariots, sword hilts and scabbards, and many other pieces of military equipment. So important was it to the armed forces that under the Han special government-controlled factories were set up to produce it.

The third product, of animal origin, was the most famous of all.

Collecting mulberry leaves for silkworms. (From a book published in 1696; but the technique of silk-making had remained almost unchanged for centuries.)

Chinese silk was, and still is, the finest natural fibre known to man; and in ancient times the techniques of breeding silkworms, of unwinding their cocoons, and of weaving the resulting fibres into cloth were all Chinese monopolies. The Romans were so ill-informed about silk that they could not even agree whether it was animal, vegetable or mineral. But whatever it was, they wanted it, as much of it as they could get, and were willing to pay enormous amounts of money for it. The methods by which this Roman desire was gratified form one of the most remarkable chapters in the history of ancient travel.

CHAPTER TEN

CENTRAL ASIA AND THE SILK ROUTES

Oh, East is East, and West is West, and never the twain shall meet,
Till Earth and Sky stand presently at God's great Judgement Seat;
But there is neither East nor West, Border, nor Breed, nor Birth,
When two strong men stand face to face, though they come from the ends
   of the earth!

The Ballad of East and West

The use of the plural above, 'Silk Routes' rather than the more familiar 'Silk Road', is deliberate. We are dealing not with a single entity like Watling Street or the Appian Way, but with a complex network of roads and tracks reaching right across Eurasia. There were some permanent nodes in the network, such as Ch'ang-an where much of the silk was produced and Rome where much of it was consumed; but the line taken by a particular caravan depended on the weather, the economic situation and the political situation, any of which might change with surprising suddenness.

Contact between China and the Near East was never impossible, but the route was a long one and messages passed down it were often garbled in transmission. It is possible, for instance, that the Greek legend of the Hyperboreans expresses some distant knowledge of the Chinese. The original Hyperboreans were a mythical race, wise, just and peaceful, supposedly living somewhere in the far north; their name means 'Dwellers beyond the North Wind'. The travels of Aristeas of Proconnesus, however, caused them to be regarded as a real people, dwelling near the sea beyond the country of the griffins (page 48) in a direction north-eastward rather than northward from Greece. It has been suggested that this idea may be based on genuine reports of China under the Chou dynasty, filtered through to Greece via the nomads of Central Asia. By comparison with the turbulent life of the steppes, the life of the Chinese would have seemed wonderfully rich, peaceful and well-governed.[1]

A similar belief existed in India. Here the equivalent of the Hyperboreans was a people called the Uttara Kuru, or 'Northern Kuru', living in a happy but inaccessible land somewhere north of the Himalayas. They are mentioned by Pliny under the name of Attacori, in a manner suggesting that once again reports of China formed the basis of the legend.[2] On the one hand, the Attacori are given a sea coast by Pliny, somewhere east of India; on the other hand, we are told that next to them live the Phuni or Thuni (possibly the Huns, in Inner Mongolia), the Focari (*i.e.* the Tochari, further west, in Chinese Central Asia), and the Casiri (probably the inhabitants of Kashmir).[3] These are exactly the three peoples whose territories would have been traversed on the most usual route from China to India.

On the other side of the Attacori, somewhere near the eastern edge of the world, Pliny places a people called the *Seres*. These again were the Chinese, and had been known to the Romans by that name since the time of Augustus. It is said to derive from the Chinese word *ssu*, meaning 'silk', the people being named after their most famous product – an unusual reversal of the normal arrangement. Much more often we find the product being named after its place of origin (arras from Arras, calico from Calicut, cambric from Cambrai, damask from Damascus, denim from Nîmes and many others). There may have been some confusion between *ssu*, which means 'silk', and *Ssu-li*, which means 'bureaucratic administration' and was the name of the metropolitan province of the Chinese Empire.

For a long time nothing was known in the West about these mysterious silk-people except that they produced silk. Under Augustus, for example, we find Virgil mentioning 'the delicate wool that the Seres comb from the leaves of their trees', and Horace more suspiciously saying that Maecenas must 'fear what the Seres may be plotting, and Bactra once ruled by Cyrus, and the discordant tribes on the banks of the Tanais'.[4] The word 'Seres' had come to replace the word 'Indians' as the standard expression for people who lived at the other end of nowhere. Pliny's account is slightly more detailed: he gives the Seres a sea coast and three rivers, all unidentified and bearing names that do not sound at all Chinese.[5] He also notes that 'the Seres are of inoffensive manners, but, bearing a strong resemblance therein to all savage nations, they shun all intercourse with the rest of mankind, and await the approach of those who wish to traffic with them'. Here he seems to be thinking not so much of the real Chinese as of the traditional Hyperboreans, who had likewise kept themselves strictly to themselves. And further on he has a highly misleading note derived ultimately from the Rajah of Ceylon: that the Seres 'exceeded the ordinary human height, and had flaxen hair and blue eyes'.[6] The inhabitants of China proper can never have looked like this at any stage in their history; the likeliest explanation is that these 'Seres' were some Central Asian tribe of Iranian stock, and that middlemen (not for the first or the last time in the history of trade) had been confused with manufacturers. A similar error, as we saw in Chapter Five, led

Herodotus to believe that Arabia produced cinnamon; and in more recent times there are such misnomers as 'Arabic numerals' which are really Indian, 'Indian ink' which is really Chinese, and 'turkeys' which are not Turkish but American.

Ptolemy, as usual, is at once more interesting and more irritating than any other source; interesting because he gives a great amount of authentic-looking information, irritating because there is no way of telling precisely what he means. He does, however, make a valid and important distinction between 'Scythia within Imaus' and 'Scythia beyond Imaus'; the former corresponds roughly to modern Kazakh-stan in the USSR, the latter to the western part of Chinese Central Asia. The name *Imaus*, used by most other ancient writers for the Hima-layas, here means the more northerly range now called the T'ien-shan or Celestial Mountains. Further east still is placed the land of Serica. It is given two rivers, probably representing the Tarim and the upper part of the Yellow River; but Ptolemy, more cautious than Pliny, refuses to say anything about Serica's hypothetical east coast, remarking instead that it is bounded on the east by *terra incognita*. Both Scythia-beyond-Imaus and Serica are given numerous towns, the most easterly of all being called Sera Metropolis, 'the capital of China'. But in identifying these it is hard to find any two modern authorities in agreement.[7]

*

Returning now from what the West thought of China to what the Chinese thought of the West, let us take an imaginary journey along the 'Silk Road' starting at the Chinese end and observing places of interest on the way. We may begin at the great city of Ch'ang-an, 'City of Eternal Peace', which was probably what Ptolemy meant by his Sera Metropolis. It was not in fact the capital of China in his time, though it had been before AD 25; but it was still a very large city, and probably the chief residence of merchants dealing with western trade (just as Alexandria and Antioch, rather than Rome, were the chief residences of merchants dealing with the eastern trade of the Roman Empire).

After leaving Ch'ang-an, the road climbed steadily up the valley of the river Wei, then turned in a more northerly direction to cross an outlying part of the Tibetan mountain mass. Here it passed through a town called Ti-tao; the ancient pronuciation of this name was some-thing like *Diek-dao*, and we may perhaps identify it with the place which Ptolemy calls *Daxata*.[8] It was the capital of a commandery called Lung-hsi, 'Western Dykes'. The *tao* part of its name is the same as the *tao* of Taoism, but here used with its literal meaning of 'road'.

Soon after Ti-tao the road descended somewhat, and entered a long panhandle of territory that jutted out from the main body of the

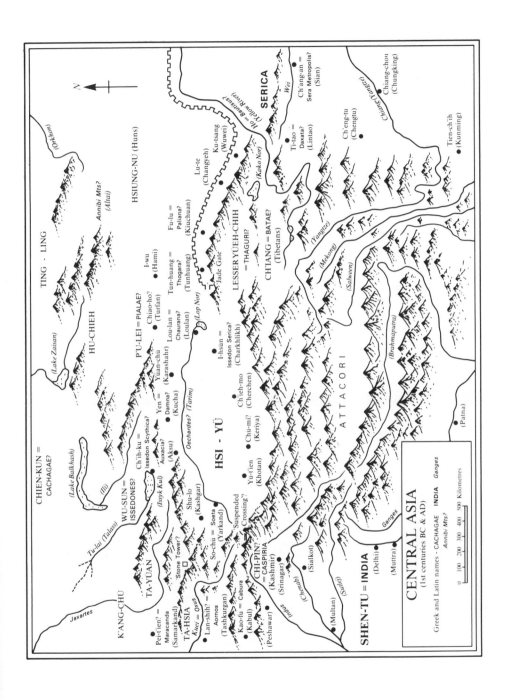

CENTRAL ASIA
(1st centuries BC & AD)

Greek and Latin names - CACHAGAE   INDIA   Ganges
                                   Annibi Mts?

0   100   200   300   400   500 Kilometres

CHIEN-KUN =
CACHAGAE?

(Orkhon)

TING - LING

Annibi Mts?
(Altai)

HSIUNG-NU (Huns)

SERICA

Wei

Ch'ang-an =
Sera Metropolis?
(Sian)

Chiang-chou
(Chungking)

(Lake Zaisan)

HU-CHIEH

(Yellow River)
Ho = Bautisus?

Ku-tsang =
Changyeh?

Ti-tao =
Daxata?
(Lintao)

Ch'eng-tu
(Chengtu)

Chiang (Yangtze)

(Lake Balkhash)

(Ili)

WU-SUN =
ISSEDONES?

PU-LEI = PIALAE?

I-wu
(Hami)

Fu-lu =
Paiana?
(Kiuchuan)

Lu-te
(Changyeh)

(Koko Nor)

Tien-ch'ih
(Kunming)

(Issyk Kul)

Ch'ih-ku =
Issedon Scythica?

Yen =
Damna?
(Kucha)

Yüan-chu
(Karashahr)

Chiao-ho?
(Turfan)

Auxacia?
(Aksu)

Tun-huang =
Thogara?
(Tunhuang)

Jade Gate

LESSER YUEH-CHIH
= THAGURI?

CH'IANG =
BATAE?
(Tibetans)

(Yangtze)

(Mekong)

K'ANG-CHU

TA-YUAN

Tu-lai (Talass)

Lou-lan =
Chaurana?
(Loulan)

(Lop Nor)

I-hsun =
Issedon Serica?
(Charkhlikh)

Oechardes? (Tarim)

HSI - YÜ

Shu-lo
(Kashgar)

Chieh-mo
(Cherchen)

(Salween)

Pei-t'ien?
Maracanda
(Samarkand)

Kuei = Oxus

Stone Tower?

So-chü =
Soeta
(Yarkand)

Suspended
Crossing?

Yu-t'ien
(Khotan)

Chu-mi?
(Keriya)

(Brahmaputra)

ATTACORI

Jaxartes

TA-HSIA

Lan-shih? =
Aornos
(Tashkurgan)

CHI-PIN? =
CASPIRIA
(Kashmir)

Kao-fu = Cabura
(Kabul)

(Srinagar)

(Chenab)

(Sialkot)

(Patna?)

(Peshawar)

(Multan)

(Sutlej)

(Chenab)

SHEN-TU = INDIA

(Delhi)

(Muttra)

Ganges

Ganges

Chinese Empire, narrowly confined between the mountains of Tibet on the south and the Great Wall on the north. This is one of the driest parts of China, and like several other arid regions of the world has been rich in archaeological finds. Near the town of Wu-wei (which takes its name from a commandery of Han times) was made a particularly famous discovery, a tomb containing 177 bronze figures, including the Flying Horse of Kansu which became the star piece in the Chinese Exhibition of 1973. It was an appropriate find for the region, because what Westerners call the 'Silk Road' was from the Chinese point of view the 'Horse Road'. The land of Ferghana, in what is now Soviet Central Asia, used to produce some of the finest horses in the world; and it was to seek out these, rather than to establish contact with the West for its own sake, that Chinese rulers put themselves and their subordinates to such repeated trouble in the Western Regions. Silk for the Romans was a civilian luxury: better horses for the Chinese were a military necessity.

Further up the Chinese panhandle, near the town of Tun-huang, is another distinguished ancient monument, commemorating a Chinese import of a different kind: the 'Thousand Buddha Caves', covered with paintings of Buddhist sacred subjects, done at various times between the fourth and fourteenth centuries AD. An enormous mass

The Flying Horse of Kansu.

of early Buddhist manuscripts was also found here, by Sir Aurel Stein; many of these are now in the British Museum.

Tun-huang itself had a position in the Han Empire analogous to that of Carlisle in the Roman Empire; it was the north-west outpost of civilization. Over the thousand-odd miles between Ch'ang-an and Tun-huang, the travellers had had the benefit of made-up roads, regular caravanserais and an efficient police force. Immediately west of Tun-huang, however, a place called Yü-men, the 'Jade Gate,' marked the end of the Great Wall and the beginning of the Western Regions, where Imperial authority had been asserted several times but never maintained for long.

The region in question, now called Sinkiang, is shaped like a huge shallow jug, or like one of the oil-lamps used in Neolithic times, in the classical world and more recently by Eskimoes. Having entered it through the spout, the caravan now had the task of working its way round to the opposite end, by the handle, and climbing out over the rim. To go straight across the middle was impossible, because of the waterless Taklamakan Desert; this had to be circumvented by keeping close to the mountain wall, where streams came down and created a series of oases. Before passing through the Jade Gate, therefore, the leaders of the caravan had to decide whether to go north or south of the desert, and bear in mind the latest reports on the weather and the political situation. For each oasis formed a separate state. At a given time, some might be genuinely pro-Chinese, others secretly or openly hostile, and others again having a revolution or civil war in which casual visitors were likely to be robbed or murdered or both.

Still more serious was the threat from the nomadic tribes, particularly the Hsiung-nu or Huns, whose attacks on China itself were mentioned in the previous chapter. It was the menace of these people that had led the Chinese to enter Central Asia in the first place, when Emperor Wu (141–87 BC) made a plan to weaken them by means of an alliance with their western neighbours and ancient enemies, the Yüeh-chih or Tochari (page 121). To further this, an ambassador named Chang Ch'ien went out to make contact with the Yüeh-chih, but had the misfortune to be captured by the Hsiung-nu and detained by them for over ten years. He escaped, bravely pushed on westward, and at last did reach his destination; the king of the Yüeh-chih, however, was politely unenthusiastic. Chang Ch'ien had to return home empty-handed – and endure a further year of Hsiung-nu captivity on the way. Though he brought back much new information about western lands hitherto unknown, he had failed to do what he had set out to do. A second expedition, however, brought better results. This time Chang Ch'ien reached a people called the Wu-sun, northern neighbours of the

Hsiung-nu, probably living on the river Ili near the modern border between Chinese Dzungaria and Soviet Kazakhstan; they may have been connected with the Issedones, visited by Aristeas several centuries earlier and repeatedly mentioned thereafter by Greek and Roman geographers. The king of the Wu-sun, though at first almost as unhelpful as the king of the Yüeh-chih had been, was at length won over to an alliance, and cemented it by marrying a Chinese princess. She was not pleased.

> My people have married me
> In a far corner of Earth;
> Sent me away to a strange land,
> To the king of the Wu-sun.
> A tent is my house,
> Of felt are my walls;
> Raw flesh my food
> With mare's milk to drink.
> Always thinking of my own country,
> My heart sad within.
> Would I were a yellow stork
> And could fly to my old home![9]

Archer firing a 'Parthian shot', from a brick of the Han period found in Szechwan province.

By combining such diplomatic enterprises with the use of direct force, Emperor Wu was able to control all the Western Regions right up to the Pamirs and what is now the frontier with the USSR. This control was maintained for some decades, but with gradually declining intensity; a strong party at court insisted that it was a pointless waste of money. The reign of Wang Mang (AD 9–23) saw general confusion in Central Asia as in China itself; 'the Western regions', we are told, 'were broken up and scattered like loose tiles'. They were reconquered in the seventies AD, under the auspices of Emperor Ming of the Later Han. A general named Pan Ch'ao anticipated the methods of Napoleon by seizing one western state after another, each time conscripting troops from the conquered one to help him attack the next. Unlike Napoleon, he also had a genius for playing everyone off against everyone else and forestalling all attempts to form a coalition against him. For nearly thirty years, till his retirement in AD 102, he was able to outmanoeuvre all the petty kingdoms of the Western Regions, as well as the two greater powers (Hsiung-nu and Kushans) who were trying to dominate the area, and in addition his own overlord the Emperor Chang, who had succeeded Emperor Ming in AD 75 and lacked his father's enthusiasm for foreign adventure.

Pan Ch'ao's operations, like those of Chang Ch'ien before him, greatly increased Chinese knowledge of lands still farther west than the Western Regions. One of his officers, named Kan Ying, visited some of these in person, passing through *An-hsi* (Parthia) and reaching *T'iao-chih* (probably Mesopotamia);[10] from here he planned to take ship to *Ta-ch'in*, the Roman province of Syria, but was dissuaded on hearing that the journey would take at least three months and possibly as much as two years. Why it should have been necessary to take this roundabout sea-route, rather than the much shorter one up the Euphrates, is not made clear. The direct route may have been jeopardized at the time by a civil war that was being fought between two claimants for the Parthian crown, but an equally likely explanation is that the Parthian middlemen were determined to prevent any direct contact between producer and consumer.

Parthian obstructiveness, however, did not prevent Kan Ying from finding out a fair amount about Ta-ch'in; nor did it prevent the Romans, at about the same time, from learning a little more about China than they had known before. Ptolemy's account is based on reports collected by a man called Maes Titianus, perhaps a contemporary of Kan Ying, whose agents in the silk trade sometimes penetrated as far as China itself. Though Ptolemy condemns them for producing too much fantasy and not enough hard information, they did at least have more to say about the 'Silk-land' than the mere fact of its existence.[11] One of their discoveries appears to be preserved in Pausanias' *Guide to Greece*, written at about the same time as Ptolemy's *Geography*:

> The threads the Silk people use for their cloth do not come from a bark or stem of any kind: they are produced in quite another way, like this. There is an insect in their country which in Greek is called the silk-worm [*ser*] though the Silk people themselves have some other name for it of their own. Its size is about twice the biggest kind of beetle, but otherwise it is like the spiders that weave their webs in the trees, and just like a spider it has eight feet . . . They look after the creatures for four years giving them millet to eat, but in the fifth year they know the creatures will die and they feed them green rushes: this is the most delicious food there is for these creatures, and they stuff themselves on rushes until they burst open and die, and you find the greater part of the yarn inside them.[12]

Though still wide of the bull, this is a far better shot at the subject than Virgil's notion of silk being combed out of trees.

*

Let us now return to the imaginary caravan which we left at the Jade Gate wondering which route to follow. Whichever one it chose, it would pass among people moulded by a remarkable number of diverse influences, and through a country that has yielded a remarkable number of ancient remains. The dry climate of Central Asia, and the way in which sites become covered with wind-blown sand, have preserved many perishable objects that would otherwise have long ago decayed. For example, when Sir Aurel Stein explored the region in the early part of this century, he found writings on such diverse materials as wood, sheepskin, birch bark, palm leaves, silk, and paper (a Chinese invention, dated to AD 105). The languages used were equally varied: they included Chinese, Sanskrit and its relative Prakrit from India, Greek, an early form of Turkish, and two other languages that had hitherto been unknown.

Religious beliefs also showed great variety. At one time or another in its history, Chinese Central Asia has been exposed to all the chief religions of the world except Japanese Shinto. The mystic beliefs of Shamanism arrived from Siberia in early times, and were noticed by Aristeas of Proconnesus in the seventh century BC. Classical paganism, particularly the worship of Apollo, was spread by the successors of Alexander the Great coming from the far west. Buddhism came north from India, promoted by such rulers as Asoka in the third century BC and Menander in the second, and brought with it many beliefs of Hindu origin. Confucianism and Taoism came up from the east with the armies of the Han dynasty. After the Roman destruction of Jerusalem in AD 70, many Jews fled eastward to Parthia, and some further east still to Central Asia and even China itself. Zoroastrianism, long established in Iran and Afghanistan, received a new boost with the rise of the Sasanian kingdom and its defeat of the Kushans in the third century AD. Christianity arrived through a complex chain of events, beginning in AD 431 when the beliefs of Nestorius were proscribed as heretical by the Council of Ephesus. His followers, many of them Syrian and familiar with lands east of the Byzantine Empire, moved into Persian territory and beyond; in AD 635 some of them gained the approval of Emperor T'ai-tsung of the T'ang dynasty, and Nestorian churches were set up in China alongside Buddhist monasteries and Zoroastrian fire-temples. Islam reached Central Asia about a century later still, and in due course replaced Buddhism as the dominant religion of the region. It is still important there today, despite competition from the newer creed of Marxism-Leninism.

The Buddhism of Central Asia was somewhat different from the Buddhism of India. The founder of this religion has sometimes been described (by Buddhists as well as non-Buddhists) as an atheist: it seems to have been a matter of indifference to him whether any gods existed or not, and he strongly opposed all suggestions that he himself was one. In Central Asia and China, however, not only was the Buddha treated as a god, but he came to be accompanied by an enormous host of heavenly assistants called Bodhisattvas, analogous to Christian saints. This kind of Buddhism, known as Mahayana or the 'Great Vehicle', remains important today in Taiwan, Korea and Japan, and contrasts in many ways with the more austere Theravada Buddhism ('Teaching of the Elders') found in India, Ceylon and South-East Asia.[13] Three important elements of Mahayana Buddhism have been described as 'postulation of an Absolute or Supreme Reality, the development of a pantheistic world-view, and the recognition of an individual 'soul' which survives death and may pass through various post-mortem states (heavens and hells) *en route* to final beatitude'.[14] Now, whereas pantheism was known in several parts of the Ancient World including China, the other two ideas have a Western air about them: an 'Absolute or Supreme Reality' was one of the fundamentals of Plato's theory of knowledge, and belief in a pilgrimage of the soul through various afterworlds was shared in Roman times by followers of Isis, Mithras and Christ. These two ideas may have been added to Buddhism through Western influence in Central Asia, before the religion became important in China.

Buddhist pictures and sculptures found in Chinese Central Asia show a remarkable mingling of artistic styles, as if to correspond to a similar mingling of philosophic ideas. The Buddha and his followers are portrayed sometimes as Chinese sages, sometimes as Greek gods, and sometimes with bushy beards and headdresses of Persian style. One set of paintings, found by Stein at a site called Miran near Charkhlikh, made him almost ready to believe that he was excavating the ruins of some Roman villa in Syria; not only were they done in the manner characteristic of the eastern Roman Empire, but the painter had signed his name on them as 'Tita' – almost certainly a variant of the Latin name Titus.[15]

On reaching the western side of the Sinkiang basin, in the neighbourhood of Yarkand or Kashgar, the silk-bearing caravans began to climb more steeply as they entered the High Pamirs. This range, reaching in places above 24,000 feet, now forms the boundary between Chinese and Soviet Central Asia. Among the ancient Chinese it had a sinister reputation.

> . . . Our envoys clasp the emblems of mighty Han and starve to death in the hills and valleys. They may beg, but there is nothing for them to get, and after ten or twenty days man and beast lie abandoned in the wastes never to return. In addition, they pass over the ranges [known as the hills of the] Greater and the Lesser Headache, and the slopes of the Red Earth and the Fever of the body. These cause a man to suffer fever; he has no colour, his head

Frescoes in the Roman style, found at Miran in Chinese Central Asia.

aches and he vomits; asses and stock animals all suffer in this way. Furthermore there are the Three Pools and the Great Rock Slopes, with a path that is a foot and six or seven inches wide, but leads forward for a length of thirty *li*, overlooking a precipice whose depth is unfathomed. Travellers passing on horse or foot hold on to one another and pull each other along with ropes; and only after a journey of more than two thousand *li* do they reach the Suspended Crossing.[16]

Ptolemy's account of the region is more prosaic: he calls it 'the country of the Sacae, who are nomads, and have no cities but dwell in woods and caves'. Somewhere here (its exact site is disputed) was a place called the Stone Tower,[17] perhaps one of the Buddhist monuments called *stupas* which play a part similar to that of minarets in Islam or spires in Christendom. This was an exchange-point, where caravans coming west from China would meet others coming east from Bactria and Persia. By land as by sea, commodities often travelled all the way from the Far East to the Far West, but only a few determined people ever tried to follow them throughout their journey.

*

The land west of the Pamirs, into which the silk then descended, resembles the Chinese side in consisting mostly of mountains and desert. Concentrated human settlement is possible only where rivers leave the one and enter the other. The contrast between desert and oasis is perhaps more intense here than in any other part of the world; within a matter of hours or even minutes the traveller may pass from a completely sterile landscape to one reminiscent of Mr Jingle's thumb-nail sketch of Kent – 'apples, cherries, hops and women'. The women of the region were renowned for their beauty; one of them, Roxana, married Alexander the Great himself, and another, Apama, married Seleucus I and had cities named after her all over the Near East. It was also a land of great and famous towns; Bokhara and Samarkand, unlike Timbuctoo, were at one time as impressive as European romance made them out to be.

   Russian Central Asia has four main rivers, all flowing towards the Aral Sea though only two succeed in reaching it. The most northerly of the four is the Syr-Darya, known in ancient times as the Jaxartes. Its upper course forms the valley of Ferghana, whose rich pasture nourished the 'Heavenly Horses' coveted by the Chinese. Next to the south comes a smaller river, the Zarafshan; the Greeks gave it a name in their own language, the Polytimetos or 'much-valued'. It waters the land known in ancient times as Sogdiana, with its capital at Samarkand. The third and largest of the four is the Amu-Darya, better known in the West by its ancient name of Oxus. Its upper course (now forming the boundary between Afghanistan and the USSR) formed the valley of Bactria, whose capital was sometimes called Bactra and sometimes Zariaspa; it is now sometimes called Balkh and sometimes Wazirabad. The fourth river has kept essentially the same name since the beginning of its history; it is now the Murghab, formerly the Margus. It gave its name to the land of Margiana, with its capital at Merv.

The whole area of the four rivers was conquered by Alexander in 329–8 BC, and afterwards settled with many Greek colonists. Whereas in Iran, further to the west, Hellenistic culture was never more than a thin veneer which soon peeled off to reveal the underlying Iranian tradition, the Graeco-Bactrian kingdom in the east maintained its Greekness for much longer. As was related in Chapter Seven, its most successful rulers dominated much of northern India as well as Central Asia; and many features of Greek life persisted even after the replacement of Greek rule by that of the Kushans.

The first Chinese embassy to Bactria was that of Chang Ch'ien in about 130 BC. He paid the country the same compliment that the Greeks had previously paid his own country; his name for Bactria was Ta-hsia, which had originally been the name of a mythical region somewhere in the far north. He had arrived a few decades too late, however, to see the kingdom at its best.

> Ta-hsia is situated over two thousand *li* southwest of Ta-yüan [Ferghana], south of the river Kuei [Oxus]. Its people cultivate the land and have cities and houses. Their customs are like those of Ta-yüan. It has no great ruler but only a number of petty chiefs ruling the various cities. The people are poor in the use of arms and afraid of battle, but they are clever at commerce.[18]

One example of this commerce is given immediately afterwards:

> 'When I was in Ta-hsia', Chang Ch'ien reported, 'I saw bamboo canes from Ch'iung and cloth made in the province of Shu. When I asked the people how they had got such articles, they replied, "Our merchants go to buy them in the markets of Shen-tu". Shen-tu, they told me, lies several thousand *li* southeast of Ta-hsia. The people cultivate the land and live much like the people of Ta-hsia. The region is said to be hot and damp. The inhabitants ride elephants when they go into battle. The kingdom is situated on a great river'.

Ch'iung and Shu were regions of western China, on the river Yangtze. 'Shen-tu' is the Chinese version of the name we met at the beginning of

Chapter Seven – Sindhu, *alias* Hindustan, *alias* India. The 'great river' is the Indus. It would seem, therefore, that the famous Burma Road between China and India was already open, despite its difficulties and dangers, and used to transport not only valuable silks and spices but also mundane objects like lengths of bamboo. It was the existence of this route, perhaps, that led Pliny to place the Attacori on the coast east of India, instead of in their usual place north of the Himalayas.

*

If travellers continued westward from Bactria instead of turning south towards India, their next important stopping-place would be the city of Merv, the capital of Margiana. This land was on the frontier between 'Iran' and 'Turan', between the settled peoples of the Iranian plateau and the nomads of the northern steppes, and was often the object of furious fighting. In the centuries on each side of the birth of Christ it was usually held by the Parthians, as the easternmost outpost of their empire. Chinese sources referred to Merv as Mu-lu (which literally means 'wooden deer') and assigned it to the kingdom of An-hsi, which was their name for Parthia.[19]

After their victory at Carrhae in 53 BC, the Parthians settled their Roman prisoners in the oasis of Merv, and thus gained the double advantage of strengthening a weak frontier and putting the Romans as far from their home as possible.

> The best thing about a patrol is that it gets us out of Margu, an unpleasant place. The district is densely inhabited, but no one lives here of his own free will. The farmers are serfs; and the garrison is made up of people like me, slaves or fugitives from the outer world, who must ride for the Great King or be drafted to toil in his copper-mines. Even the Parthian nobles who command us are exiles, posted to this edge of the Empire in honourable disgrace. We have all drifted here because this is the extreme limit of the world.
>
> What is odd is that Margu lies on the limit of more than one world . . .

The above quotation is not from an ancient source, but from an historical novel called *Winter Quarters*, by Alfred Duggan.[20] It relates the sad story of two young men from a tribe called the Elusates, in Aquitania. Having offended a local goddess, they are forced into exile; they join the army of Julius Caesar, are seconded into that of Crassus, and so find themselves at Carrhae. One of them is killed in the battle, the other taken prisoner; the story ends at Merv, when nine years later he hears of the death of Caesar, the only Roman who might have been able to conquer the Parthians and rescue him.

Winter Quarters was published in 1956. In the following year, a
work of non-fiction by Homer H. Dubs revealed that Alfred Duggan
could legitimately have put an extra twist into the tail of his novel.[21]
There is evidence that some Romans did succeed in escaping from
Merv, and not as isolated refugees but as an organized body which had
kept its weapons and its Roman discipline. Unable to go west, they
went east, perhaps with the object of reaching the Outer Ocean and
returning home by sea. Instead they found themselves among the
Huns, whom they agreed to serve as mercenaries. In consequence of
this they were to gain a small but fascinating place in the Chinese
annals. For the ruler of these particular Huns, named Jzh-jzh, was
persona non grata to the Chinese Empire, having killed some Chinese
envoys. In 36 BC a force went out against him, attacked him in a town
on the river Talass, and found it defended in a strange and most
un-Hunnish way. 'More than a hundred foot-soldiers', the annals
relate, 'lined up on either side of the gate in a fish-scale formation, were
practising military drill' – surely a reference to the famous Roman
formation known as the *testudo* or 'tortoise'. And later we are told
that 'outside the earthen wall was a double palisade of wood', as in the
standard layout of a Roman camp.

The Chinese were victorious, and Jzh-jzh was killed and beheaded.
The Roman mercenaries, however, survived and accompanied their
new masters to China. On the way, they may have explained another
old Roman military custom, the institution of a triumph, with pictures
showing the climactic moments in a victorious campaign; for the
account of the siege reads with unusual vividness, as if the author had
had illustrations as well as a text in front of him, and some of the
records attracted the interest not only of Emperor Yüan himself but
also of ladies in the Imperial harem. And the census of AD 1–2 records
a town in Chang-i commandery with the name of Li-jien or Li-kan,
which was also a generic name for the Graeco-Roman world at the far
western limit of Chinese knowledge.[22] Could this have been where the
mercenaries were finally settled? If so, we have the remarkable possibility that some Roman citizens not only visited the Chinese Empire
but ended their days as its subjects.

*

The disaster at Carrhae permanently poisoned relations between
Rome and Parthia; and as in later years Roman knowledge of the Far
East and demand for its products increased, repeated attempts were
made to collect these products by a route that avoided Parthian
territory. For if this could not be done, then every pound of silk bought

by Rome's luxury-loving subjects helped to supply her prime enemy with the sinews of war.

One way of by-passing the Parthians, the sea-route to the south of their country, has been discussed in Chapter Eight. Though a great success in some respects (it cut the cost of spices considerably), it was less important to the silk business. From China to the Roman Empire by sea was a long way, nearly twice as long as the overland journey, and the system of monsoon-winds meant that one often had to wait some time before making a particular leg of the voyage. Besides, several stages (such as the Red Sea, the west coast of India, and the Straits of Malacca) teemed with natural and man-made dangers to navigation. Direct sea-borne contact between Rome and China was always rare.

Another possible route, briefly noted in Chapter Three, went round Parthian territory on the other side, towards the north. Instead of taking the regular route through the deserts of Sinkiang, Turkestan and Iran, a traveller could follow the steppe belt through Siberia, north of the Aral and Caspian Seas, and so down to one of the Roman-controlled ports on the Black Sea. This was apparently the route followed by Aristeas in his quest for the Hyperboreans, and later by the anonymous people who supplied Ptolemy with his new information about the Volga (page 41); later still, it was the route followed by the Polo family on their visits to Kublai Khan. But it was always hard going for anyone not used to the way of life of a nomad horseman. The more southerly route, though steep and arid, did at least have permanent settlements along it, some of them very large and beautiful, where travellers could recuperate after a long march; the northern route had none.

A still more serious objection to the northern route was that most of the time it must have been more expensive, not less, than the southern one. No tribe, however primitive and disorganized, was likely to let a valuable cargo pass through its territory without exacting a toll; and when the steppe-belt was divided among a multitude of small tribes, as it often was, the cumulative effect of such tolls would have been more than those of the larger states on the regular southern route. Thus we find all the longest commercial journeys across the steppe being made when it happened to be dominated by a tribal group of exceptional size and power – the Royal Scythians in Aristeas' time, the Alans in Ptolemy's, the Mongols in Marco Polo's. And in the fluid society of the nomads no such group could last for any length of time.

A third route, the so-called Oxo-Caspian route often mentioned by older books on ancient trade, is now thought never to have existed. It came into print through a combination of ancient and modern misconceptions. The river Oxus today flows into the Aral Sea, and work in the USSR has made clear that it did the same in ancient times. There is no question of its ever having flowed into the Caspian instead, as used to be believed. The theory of an Oxo-Caspian trade route, from Bactria down the Oxus into the Caspian, and so across it, would seem to have been a Greek hypothesis, made at a time when the country was largely unknown to the Greeks. It may be compared with the seventeenth-century hypothesis that America could be crossed by following the Mississippi down to the Gulf of California; the argument was valid, but a false premise in it led to a false conclusion.[23]

There remains the question of sea-trade across the Caspian itself. There is a little evidence for this, but it is very slight. Most ancient geographical writings give the impression that the Caspian was a barrier rather than a highway, a kind of hole in the map which travellers went round rather than across. Even its south coast, though included in the Persian Empire and its successors, was never well known even to the Persians themselves. Not only is it cut off from the rest of Iran by high mountains, but its climate and landscape are unlike anything normally associated with Iran, and more reminiscent of parts of India, with much rainfall, a steamy atmosphere, jungles, paddy-fields and even tigers.

The most interesting evidence for the use of the Caspian as a highway comes from the reign of Nero, in the fifties AD. In pursuance of his war with the Parthians, Nero had sent a force under Domitius Corbulo into Armenia, and this achieved considerable success. An opportunity then arose to put further pressure on Parthia by making an alliance with Hyrcania, the land south-east of the Caspian, which had recently broken away from Parthian suzerainty and hoped to maintain its independence with Roman support. This was granted, and a trans-Caspian trade route may for a while have been practicable. But, calling as it did for an independent Hyrcania and a strong Roman force in Armenia, it must always have been precarious and is unlikely to have lasted for long. Like Nero's investigation into the sources of the Nile (page 70), the Hyrcanian adventure was probably a one-off sample in the history of exploration, with no fruitful consequences.[24]

Despite the expense and embarrassment, therefore, the usual way of bringing Chinese silk to Rome continued to be the way through Parthian territory. From the oasis of Merv the caravans made their way across the Iranian plateau, past Rhagae (Rayy, near Tehran), and Ecbatana (Hamadan) the capital of Media. From here they went down through the pass called the Median Gates, off the plateau on to the plain of Iraq, to reach the Parthians' capital at Ctesiphon. From here, if relations between the High King and the Emperor were reasonably good, the most convenient route to Roman territory was the one up the Euphrates. If not, there were other routes through Arabia Deserta, familiar to the local inhabitants and used by some of them to make themselves very rich.

And so, if any Chinese had persevered alongside the consignment of Chinese silk throughout its long journey, he would find himself in the land of Ta-ch'in or Li-jien, at the uttermost western limit of his known world.

> The inhabitants of that country are tall and well-proportioned, somewhat like the Chinese, whence they are called *Ta-ch'in*. The country contains much gold, silver, and rare precious stones, especially the 'jewel that shines at night' and the 'moonshine pearl' . . . They have fine cloth, called 'the down of the water-sheep' . . . they make coins of gold and silver; ten units of silver are worth one of gold. They traffic by sea with Parthia and India, the profit of which trade is ten-fold. They are honest in their transactions and there are no double prices. Cereals are always cheap. The budget is based on a well-filled treasury.[25]

What a wonderful country it seemed! Even more wonderful than China seemed, in the imagination of the Romans.

CHRONOLOGY

BC

753	Founding of Rome (traditional)
c.660	Greek founding of Byzantium and exploration of the Black Sea. First contact with Scythians
c.650?	Journeys of Aristeas in Central Asia
c.630	Greek founding of Cyrene. First contact with Libyans
c.600	Greek founding of Marseilles. First contact with Celts. Phoenicians circumnavigate Africa (?)
c.551?	Death of Zoroaster
539	Cyrus of Persia captures Babylon
530	Death of Cyrus, fighting in Central Asia
c.527	Death of Mahavira, the founder of Jainism
525	Cambyses, son of Cyrus, conquers Egypt but fails to conquer the Sudan
522	Accession of Darius I of Persia
c.512	Persian invasion of Scythia
c.510	Scylax circumnavigates Arabia
509	Rome becomes a republic
c.500?	Voyage of Hanno round West Africa (possibly fictional)
490	First Persian invasion of Greece, defeated at Marathon
486	Death of Darius
c.483	Death of the Buddha
480–79	Second Persian invasion of Greece (under Xerxes), defeated at Salamis and Plataea
479	Death of Confucius
c.470	Voyage of Sataspes round West Africa
431–404	Peloponnesian War, ending with Spartan conquest of Athens
390	Celts defeat Romans on the river Allia and sack Rome
c.350	Sarmatians begin to replace Scythians as dominant power in the Black Sea steppes
338	Battle of Chaeronea: Philip of Macedon conquers Greece
336	Assassination of Philip. His son, Alexander the Great, succeeds him
334	Alexander invades Asia
331	Founding of Alexandria. Alexander defeats the Persians near Arbela (Irbil)
329–25	Alexander's campaigns in Bactria and India. Nearchus explores the Indian and Persian coasts
323	Death of Alexander
312	Seleucus I captures Babylon. Beginning of Seleucid era
304	Seleucus abandons his Indian territories to Chandragupta Maurya
300	Founding of Antioch in Syria
c.300	Pytheas of Marseilles explores the British Isles and perhaps reaches Norway
c.297	Death of Chandragupta Maurya

280–75	War between Romans and Pyrrhus, king of Epirus. Romans successful
279–8	Celts invade Greece and Asia Minor
264–41	First Punic War, ending with Roman defeat of Carthage and annexation of Sicily
c.256?	Revolt of Diodotus; beginning of independent Greek kingdom in Bactria
247	Beginning of Arsacid era among the Parni
238	The Parni invade Parthia (and hence come to be called 'Parthians')
232	Death of Asoka, greatest of the Mauryan kings in India
225	Battle of Telamon: Romans defeat a Celtic invasion
221–210	Reign of Ch'in Shih-huang-ti, the 'First Emperor' in China. Building of the Great Wall. Conquest of South China. Burning of Confucian books
218–201	Second Punic War. Rome nearly conquered by Hannibal. Final Roman victory and annexation of southern and eastern Spain
c.207	Death of Devanampiya Tissa, king of Ceylon
202–195	Reign of Kao-tsu, founder of the Han dynasty
190	Battle of Magnesia: Romans defeat Antiochus III
c.185	Collapse of Mauryan rule in India
c.165	Yüeh-chih, defeated by Huns, begin to move westward across Central Asia
146	Roman destruction of Carthage. Polybius explores the west coast of Africa
141	Accession of Emperor Wu in China. Mithradates I of Parthia captures Seleucia-on-the-Tigris
133	Rome acquires western Asia Minor by bequest. Roman successes in Spain
c.130	Death of Menander, greatest of the 'Indo-Greek' kings. Operations of Chang Ch'ien in Central Asia
111	Chinese armies capture Canton. Fall of the kingdom of Nan Yüeh
c.110	Eudoxus of Cyzicus tries to circumnavigate Africa and never returns
105	Battle of Orange: Romans defeated by Germans
91	'Witchcraft Scandal' in China; many people executed
88	Mithradates of Pontus overruns Asia Minor
87	Death of Emperor Wu
74–63	Roman war with Mithradates, ending with triumph of Pompey the Great
58–51	Julius Caesar's conquest of Gaul. Germans defeated. Two expeditions to Britain (55 and 54)
53	Battle of Carrhae: Parthians destroy a Roman army under Crassus
48	Pompey defeated by Caesar at Pharsalus, and murdered in Egypt
44	Assassination of Caesar
39–33	Mark Antony's war with the Parthians and Armenians
31	Antony defeated by Octavian at Actium
30	Suicide of Antony and Cleopatra. Roman annexation of Egypt. Approximate date for end of Greek kingdoms in India
27	Octavian takes the title Augustus
25	Campaign of Gaius Petronius in the Sudan
25–3	Expedition of Aelius Gallus to Arabia
19	Triumph of Cornelius Balbus in the Sahara
15	Victories of Tiberius and Drusus on the upper Danube: destruction of Manching?

AD

1–2	Census in China
9	Fall of Early Han dynasty and accession of Wang Mang. Germans defeat Romans in the Teutoburger Forest
14	Death of Augustus; Tiberius succeeds him
14–16	Campaigns of Germanicus Caesar against the Germans
23	Assassination of Wang Mang
25	Emperor Kuang-wu restores the Han dynasty
c. 30	Crucifixion of Christ
41–54	Reign of Claudius. Roman conquest of Mauretania (42); Roman armies cross the Atlas. Roman conquest of Britain (43). Embassy from Ceylon to Rome
c. 48	Death of Gondopharnes, the Indo-Parthian king said to have been visited by St Thomas
54–68	Reign of Nero. War in Armenia. Revolt of Boudica in Britain (60–61). Unsuccessful expedition to find the source of the Nile
58–75	Reign of Emperor Ming, son of Emperor Kuang-wu. Buddhism reaches China. Pan Ch'ao begins to campaign in Central Asia
69	Civil war in the Roman Empire, ending with victory of Vespasian. Batavian revolt on the lower Rhine. War with the Garamantes in Libya
70	Roman destruction of Jerusalem
78?	Accession of Kanishka, Kushan king of Bactria and India
79	Deaths of Vespasian and Pliny the Elder
81–96	Reign of Domitian. Roman conquest of Scotland (Mons Graupius, 84). Wars on the Danube prevent this victory from being followed up
97	Kan Ying attempts to visit the Roman Empire, but is turned back in Mesopotamia
98	Accession of Trajan. Publication of Tacitus' *Agricola* and *Germania*
c.100	Roman exploration of the Volga region, the Sahara and East Africa. Publication of the *Periplus of the Erythraean Sea*?
101–6	Trajan's conquest of Dacia
102	Retirement of Pan Ch'ao
106	Trajan annexes the Nabataean kingdom and makes it into the province of Arabia
114–7	Trajan's Parthian War
117	Death of Trajan: Hadrian succeeds him and abandons his eastern conquests
122	Hadrian visits Britain and orders the building of Hadrian's Wall
128?	Another possible date for Kanishka
134–7	Roman and Parthian territory invaded by Alans across the Caucasus
138	Death of Hadrian: Antoninus Pius succeeds him
140	Census in China
c.142	Building of the Antonine Wall in Britain
c.150	*Floruit* of Rudradaman in western India. Publication of Ptolemy's *Geographia*
161	Death of Antoninus: Marcus Aurelius succeeds him
162–4	Lucius Verus's Parthian War
165	Plague in the Roman Empire
166	Roman embassy (?) to Emperor Huan of China
167–80	Wars along the Danube
180	Death of Marcus Aurelius

AD

193	Disorder in the Roman Empire. Accession of Septimius Severus
194–9	Severus' Parthian War
c.200	Goths enter the Black Sea steppe and defeat Alans
211	Death of Severus
220	Fall of the Han dynasty: China split into three kingdoms
226	Fall of the Parthian dynasty: Ardashir crowned as first Sasanian king of Persia
235	Death of Severus Alexander, followed by fifty years' anarchy in the Roman Empire
240	Accession of Shapur I, son of Ardashir. Victorious campaigns against the Kushans. Preachings of Mani
251	Emperor Decius defeated and killed by Goths on the lower Danube
260	Emperor Valerian captured by Shapur
271	Aurelian abandons Dacia to the Goths
280	Reunion of China under the Tsin dynasty
284–305	Reign of Diocletian (and colleagues). Order restored in Roman Empire. Many reforms
306	Constantine acclaimed emperor at York
309	Accession of Shapur II of Persia
317	Collapse of Tsin dynasty: renewed chaos in China
c.320	Founding of the Gupta dynasty in India by Chandra Gupta I
330	Founding of Constantinople
337	Death of Constantine
363	Death of Julian, fighting the Persians. Romans cede territory to Persia
367	Britain attacked by 'Barbarian Conspiracy' of Picts, Scots and Saxons
c.375	Huns appear on the Black Sea and defeat Goths
378	Battle of Adrianople: Emperor Valens defeated and killed by Goths
379	Death of Shapur II. Accession of Niall of the Nine Hostages, High King of Ireland
395	Death of Theodosius I: division of the Roman Empire between his sons
406	Suebi, Vandals and Alans cross the Rhine and overrun Gaul
410	Rome sacked by Goths
429	Vandals invade Africa
431	Council of Ephesus: Nestorianism denounced as a heresy
439	Vandals capture Carthage
c.450	Arrival of Saxons in Britain, and Hunnish tribes in India
451	Romans and Goths defeat Attila the Hun near Troyes
453	Death of Attila
c.467	Death of Skanda Gupta, followed by decline of Gupta dynasty
476	Romulus Augustulus deposed: Odoacer becomes king of Italy
493	Murder of Odoacer: Theodoric the Ostrogoth becomes king of Italy
c.500	Founding of the kingdom of Dalriada (Scotland). Victories of Arthur over the Saxons in Britain
511	Death of Clovis, king of the Franks
526	Death of Theodoric
527–65	Reign of Justinian. Byzantine reconquest of North Africa, Italy and parts of Spain
549?	Death of Maelgwn, king of Gwynedd
568	Lombards (a German tribe) invade Italy

AD

570	(traditional) 'Year of the Elephant': Abyssinians fail to capture Mecca. Birth of Mohammed
577	Battle of Dyrham: Saxons conquer all southern England
583	Avars and Slavs destroy Sirmium (Sremska-Mitrovica)
589	Reunion of China under the Sui dynasty
597	Mission of St Augustine to Britain
606	Reunion of northern India by Harsha
610	Accession of Heraclius at Constantinople
610–16	Victories of Chosroes II of Persia in Asia Minor, the Levant and Egypt
618	Sui dynasty in China replaced by T'ang dynasty
622	Flight of Mohammed from Mecca to Medina (the *Hegira*)
626	Persians and Avars besiege Constantinople
628	Victory of Heraclius. Death of Chosroes. Peace between Byzantines and Persians
632	Death of Mohammed. Beginning of Arab conquests.

NOTES AND BIBLIOGRAPHY

Chapter One: *The Celts*

Celtic history and customs are described by numerous ancient writers. For a discussion of these, see Piggott, S., *The Druids* (London, 1968), chapter 3.

For the Celts in general, see:

Chadwick, N., *The Celts* (London, 1970).
Cunliffe, B., *The Celtic World* (Maidenhead, 1979).
Dillon, M., and Chadwick, N., *The Celtic Realms* (2nd edition, London, 1972).
Harmand, J., *Les Celtes* (Paris, 1970).
Hatt, J.-J., *Celts and Gallo-Romans* (London, 1970).
Herm, G., *The Celts* (London, 1976).
Powell, T. G. E., *The Celts* (2nd edition, London, 1980).
Ross, A., *Everyday Life of the Pagan Celts* (London, 1970).

For Celtic religion:

Chadwick, N., *The Druids* (Cardiff, 1966).
Piggott, S., *op. cit.*
Ross, A., *Pagan Celtic Britain* (London, 1967).

For Celtic settlements:

Hogg, A. H. A., *Hill-forts of Britain* (London, 1975).
Norman, E. R., and St Joseph, J. K., *The Early Development of Irish Society* (Cambridge, 1969).
Wheeler, R. E. M., and Richardson, K. M., *Hill-forts of Northern France* (London, 1957).

1. Arrian, *Anabasis of Alexander* I, 4.
2. *Galatians* V, 19–21.
3. Quoted in Knott, E., and Murphy, G., *Early Irish Literature* (London, 1966), p. 125.
4. Polybius, *Histories* II, 28.
5. Livy, *History of Rome* XXXVIII, 21.
6. Scythed chariots in Persia: Xenophon, *Cyropaedia* VI, 1, 30; *Anabasis* I, 8, 10. In Africa: Strabo, *Geographia* XVII, 3, 7. *De Rebus Bellicis*: see Thompson, E. A., *A Roman Reformer and Inventor* (Oxford, 1952).
7. Caesar, *Gallic War* VII, 75.
8. Suetonius, *Gaius* 44.
9. *Gallic War* I, 18–20; V, 6–7.
10. Tacitus, *Annals* XII, 40; *Histories* 45.
11. Japan has two official religions, Shinto and Buddhism, See page 183.
12. Pliny, *Natural History* XVI, 249–51. Pliny specifically states that this was a rare ceremony, which it must have been since mistletoe seldom grows on oak-trees.
13. Forest of the Carnutes: *Gallic War* VI, 13. Anglesey: see below, note 16.
14. For other names containing the element *nemetum*, see Rivet, A. L. F., and Smith, C., *The Place-Names of Roman Britain* (London, 1979), pp. 254–5.

15. See, for example, Wuilleumier, P., *Lyon, Métropole des Gaules* (Paris, 1953), pp. 33–42.

16. Tacitus, *Annals* XIV, 30.

17. Gildas, *De Excidio* 34, 6; *cf.* Alcock, L., *Arthur's Britain* (London, 1971), p. 13.

18. Bibracte: *Gallic War* I, 23 etc. Gergovia: VII, 32–53.

19. *Ibid.* VII, 68–90. For the dispute about the site of Alesia, see *Popular Archaeology*, December 1982, pp. 22–7.

20. VII, 23.

21. On the river Sambre; *Gallic War* II, 16–28.

22. *Ibid.* V, 21.

23. Rivet and Smith, *op. cit.*, pp. 291–2.

24. Paris: Duval, P.-M., *Paris antique* (Paris, 1961). Besançon: *Gallic War* I, 38. Strasbourg: Forrer, R., *Strasbourg-Argentorate* (Strasbourg, 1927). Sisak (ancient *Siscia* or *Segestica*): Strabo VII, 5, 2.

25. Maiden Castle: Wheeler, R. E. M., *Maiden Castle, Dorset* (Oxford, 1943). Silchester: Boon, C. G., *Silchester* (Newton Abbot, 1974). Mont-Beuvray: Déchelette, J., *Manuel d'archéologie*, vol. IV (2nd edition, Paris, 1927), pp. 454–63.

26. Kraemer, W., and Schubert, F., *Die Ausgrabung in Manching, 1955–1961* (Wiesbaden, 1974).

27. *Antonine Itinerary* 250.3.

Chapter Two: *The Germans*

The chief ancient sources for the early Germans are Caesar's *Gallic War* (especially VI, 21–28) and Tacitus' *Germania*. For comments on these, see:
> Anderson, J. G. C., *Cornelii Taciti de Origine et Situ Germanorum* (Oxford, 1938).
> Much, R., *Die Germania des Tacitus* (3rd edition, Heidelberg, 1967).
> Norden, E., *Die Germanische Urgeschichte in Tacitus Germania* (4th edition, Darmstadt, 1959).
> Thompson, E. A., *The Early Germans* (Oxford, 1965).

For the Germans in general:
> *The Cambridge Ancient History*, vol. XI (Cambridge, 1936), pp. 46–76.
> Hachmann, R., *The Germanic Peoples* (London, 1971).
> Krüger, B. (ed.), *Die Germanen: ein Handbuch* (Berlin, 1976).
> Millar, F., *The Roman Empire and its Neighbours* (2nd edition, London, 1981), pp. 294–320 (by G. Kossack).
> Sitwell, N. H. H., *Roman Roads of Europe* (London, 1981), pp. 85–101.
> Todd, M., *Everyday Life of the Barbarians* (London, 1972; reprinted as *The Barbarians*, London, 1980).
> —— *The Northern Barbarians, 100 BC–AD 300* (London, 1975).
> Wheeler, R. E. M., *Rome beyond the Imperial Frontiers* (London, 1954), pp. 7–94.

For the later Germans:
> Blair, P. H., *An Introduction to Anglo-Saxon England* (2nd edition, Cambridge, 1977).
> Courtois, C., *Les Vandales et l'Afrique* (Paris, 1955).
> Musset, L., *The Germanic Invasions* (London, 1975).
> Thompson, E. A., *The Visigoths in the Time of Ulfila* (Oxford, 1966).
> —— *The Goths in Spain* (Oxford, 1969).

1. Tacitus, *Agricola* 30.

2. *Ibid.*, 21.

3. Tacitus, *Germania* 5 and 26.

4. *Ibid.*, 20.

5. *Ibid.*, 19.

6. *Ibid.*, 12.

7. *Ibid.*, 31 and 38. For Tollund Man and others, see Glob, P. V., *The Bog People* (London, 1969).

8. *Germania* 14.

9. *Ibid.*, 16; Caesar, *Gallic War* VI, 23.

10. Tacitus, *Annals* II, 62. Ptolemy (*Geographia* II, 11, 14) mentions the place as *Marobudon*, named after its founder.

11. *Gallic War* I, 34–6 and 43–7.

12. *Germania* 15.

13. *Annals* XIII, 57.

14. *Germania* 33.

15. *Ibid.*, 40.

16. *Ibid.*, 39.

17. Mount Zobten is probably the grove of the Naharvali, mentioned in *Germania* 43; and also the place which Ptolemy (II, 11, 13) calls *Limios Alsos*, the 'Elm-Grove'. Cf. Anderson (1938), p. 199: Schreiber, H., *Teuton and Slav* (London, 1965), pp. 37 and 52.

18. *Annals* I, 61.

19. Tacitus, *Germania* 29: *Histories* IV, 12–36, 54–80; V, 14–26.

20. *Agricola* 28.

21. Hermunduri: *Germania* 41. Chatti: *ibid.*, 30. Lugii and Marcomanni: Cassius Dio LXVII, 5, 2.

22. *Cambridge Ancient History* XI, pp. 349–65. For a list of the tribes involved, see *Historia Augusta, Marcus Aurelius* 22.

23. Gibbon, *Decline and Fall*, chapter 31; vol. III, pp. 251 and 258, of the Everyman edition.

Chapter Three: *Eastern Europe*

The earliest ancient account, that of Herodotus (book IV), is also the fullest and most interesting. Later writers often copied from him, with unfortunate results, since the steppe-dwellers did not stay long in one place and information about them quickly went out of date. Ptolemy, in particular, has a distressing habit of mentioning the same tribe in two or more places at the same time.

For the forest-dwellers of the north, see:

Gimbutas, M., *The Balts* (London, 1963).
—— *The Slavs* (London, 1971).
Kivikoski, E., *Finland* (London, 1967).

For the steppe-dwellers generally:

Cambridge Ancient History XI, pp. 91–104.
Grousset, R., *L'Empire des Steppes* (4th edition, Paris, 1960).
Harmatta, J., *Studies in the History and Language of the Sarmatians* (Szeged, 1970).
Millar, F., *The Roman Empire and Its Neighbours* (2nd edition, London, 1981), pp. 281–293 (by T. Talbot Rice).
Phillips, E. D., *The Royal Hordes* (London, 1965).

Sulimirski, T., *The Sarmatians* (London, 1970).
For their relations with other peoples:
Gajdukevič, V. F., *Das Bosporanische Reich* (Berlin, 1971).
Minns, E. H., *Scythians and Greeks* (Cambridge, 1913).
Rostovtzeff, M., *Iranians and Greeks in South Russia* (Oxford, 1922).
Teggart, F. J., *Rome and China: a Study of Correlations in Historical Events* (Berkeley, Cal., 1939).
For archaeology in the USSR:
Mongait, A., *Archaeology in the U.S.S.R.* (Moscow, 1959).
Rudenko, S. I., *Frozen Tombs of Siberia* (London, 1970).
For the later invasions of the steppe-dwellers:
Bachrach, B. S., *A History of the Alans in the West* (Minneapolis, 1973).
Maenchen-Helfen, O. J., *The World of the Huns* (Berkeley, Cal., 1973).
Thompson, E. A., *A History of Attila and the Huns* (Oxford, 1948).

1. Herodotus, *Histories* IV, 18 etc.
2. Tacitus, *Germania* 46.
3. Ptolemy, *Geographia* V, 8, 6–7.
4. *Germania* 45.
5. Pliny, *Natural History* XXXVII, 45.
6. Herodotus IV, 17–18; Gimbutas (1971), pp. 46–7.
7. Pliny, *Nat. Hist.* IV, 97; Tacitus, *Germania* 46.
8. Ptolemy, *Geog.* III, 5, 1 and 7; Jordanes, *Getica* V, 34.
9. Herodotus IV, 131–2.
10. *Ibid.* VII, 64 and 85.
11. Illustrated in Minns (1913), p. 139.
12. Herodotus IV, 13; Bolton, J. D. P., *Aristeas of Proconnesus* (Oxford, 1962). Proconnesus is the island now called Marmara, in the Sea of Marmara.
13. Herodotus IV, 71–2.
14. *Ibid.*, 53.
15. *Ibid.*, 117.
16. Pliny, *Nat. Hist.* IV, 44.
17. Minns (1913), pp. 460–61, 641–2.
18. Josephus, *Jewish War* II, 366–7.
19. Ovid, *Tristia* III, 10.
20. Tacitus, *Annals* XII, 16.
21. *Annals of the Later Han*, quoted in Teggart (1939), p. 199.
22. The *Ektaxis kat'Alanon* (*Order of Battle against the Alans*). A longer work, the *Alanica*, is now lost. For the life and works of Arrian, see Stadter, P. A., *Arrian of Nicomedia* (Chapel Hill, North Carolina, 1980).
23. Priscus, p. 277; Thompson (1948), p. 76.

Chapter Four: *Africa*

Except for the dubious *Periplus of Hanno* (see below, note 1), no ancient work devoted to Africa alone has survived. The chief authorities, as for most regions beyond the frontiers of the Roman Empire, are Herodotus, Strabo, Pliny and Ptolemy, supplemented by the *Periplus of the Erythraean Sea* (see below, note 30) for the east coast.

For a general account, see the *Cambridge History of Africa*, vol. II (Cambridge, 1978), and Deschamps, H. (ed.), *Histoire générale d'Afrique noire* (Paris, 1970). For the west coast and the Sahara, see also:

Bovill, E. W., *The Golden Trade of the Moors* (2nd edition, London, 1968).

Briggs, L. C., *Tribes of the Sahara* (Cambridge, Mass., 1960).

Carcopino, J., *Le Maroc antique* (Paris, 1943).

Carpenter, R., *Beyond the Pillars of Heracles* (New York, 1966).

Cary, M., and Warmington, E. H., *The Ancient Explorers* (revised edition, London, 1963), pp. 61–71, 110–31, 216–21.

Daniels, C., *The Garamantes of Southern Libya* (Harrow, 1970).

Davies, O., *West Africa before the Europeans* (London, 1967).

Desanges, J., *Catalogue des tribus africaines de l'antiquité classique à l'ouest du Nil* (Dakar, 1962).

Wheeler, R. E. M., *Rome beyond the Imperial Frontiers* (London, 1954), pp. 95–111.

For the upper Nile region:

Adams, W. Y., *Nubia, Corridor to Africa* (London, 1977).

Arkell, A. J., *A History of the Sudan* (2nd edition, London, 1961).

Cary & Warmington, *op. cit.*, pp. 202–215.

Crawford, O. G. S., *The Fung Kingdom of Sennar* (Gloucester, 1951), especially pp. 1–29.

Crowfoot, J. W., *The Island of Meroe* (London, 1911).

Emery, W. B., *Egypt in Nubia* (London, 1965).

Shinnie, P. L., *Meroe* (London, 1967).

For the east coast and Abyssinia:

Budge, E. A. W., *A History of Ethiopia* (London, 1928).

Buxton, D., *The Abyssinians* (London, 1970).

Crowfoot, J. W., 'Some Red Sea Ports in the Anglo-Egyptian Sudan', *Geographical Journal* XXXVII (1911), 523–50.

Kirkman, J. S., *Men and Monuments on the East African Coast* (London, 1964).

Oliver, R., and Matthew, G. (eds), *History of East Africa*, vol. I (Oxford, 1963).

Wheeler, R. E. M., *op. cit.*, pp. 112–4.

1. For the Greek text of Hanno, see Müller, C. (ed.), *Geographi Graeci Minores* (Paris, 1855), pp. 1–14; for an English translation and commentary, Cary & Warmington (1963), pp. 63–8. See also Mauny, R., 'La navigation sur les côtes du Sahara pendant l'antiquité', *Revue des Études anciennes* LVII (1955), 92–101: Germain, G., 'Qu'est-ce que le Périple d'Hannon? Document, amplification littéraire, ou faux intégral?', *Hespéris* XLIV (1957), 205–48: Ramin, J., *Le Périple d'Hannon* (Oxford, 1976): and the *Cambridge History of Africa*, vol. II, pp. 133–40 and 292–301 (where two authorities take diametrically opposite views).

2. Herodotus IV, 184.

3. Pliny, *Nat. Hist.* V, 6–7.

4. Sataspes: Herodotus IV, 43. Polybius: Pliny, *Nat. Hist.* V, 9; Mauny, R., 'Autour d'un texte bien controversé: le 'périple' de Polybe (146 av. J.-C.)', *Hespéris* XXXVI (1949), 47–67. Eudoxus: Strabo II, 3, 4–5. Juba: Pliny, *Nat. Hist.* VI, 202–5.

5. Desjacques, J. P., and Koeberlé, P., 'Mogador et les Îles Purpuraires', *Hespéris* XLII (1955), 193–202: Jodin, A., *Mogador, comptoir phénicien du Maroc atlantique* (Tangier, 1966).

6. Pliny, *Nat. Hist.* V, 14–15.

7. Mauny, R., 'Une route préhistorique à travers le Sahara occidental', *Bulletin de l'Institut français d'Afrique noire* IX (1947), 341–57; *Les Siècles obscurs de l'Afrique noire, histoire et archéologie* (Paris, 1970).

8. Herodotus IV, 183.

9. Pliny, *Nat. Hist.* V, 37: Desanges, J., 'Le triomphe de Cornelius Balbus en 19 av. J.-C.', *Revue africaine* CI (1957), 5–45.

10. Tacitus, *Annals* II, 52; III, 20–21, 73–4; IV, 23–6.

11. Pliny, *Nat. Hist.* V, 38: Tacitus, *Histories* IV, 50.

12. *African War* LXVIII, 4: Ammianus Marcellinus, *Roman History* XXVIII, 6, 5: Brogan, O., 'The camel in Roman Tripolitania', *Papers of the British School at Rome* XXII (1954), 126–31: Bovill, E. W., 'The camel and the Garamantes', *Antiquity* XXX (1956), 19–21.

13. Ptolemy, *Geography* I, 8, 4; IV, 9, 2.

14. Herodotus II, 32. For a map of the Lake Chad region, see *Cambridge History of Africa* II, p. 274.

15. Pliny, *Nat. Hist.* V, 44 and 51–3.

16. Ptolemy, *Geography* IV, 6, 4.

17. *Nat. Hist.* V, 30 and 53.

18. The expression *Aethiopia* could mean several different things. Usually, as here, it meant the land south of Egypt, the modern Sudan. Sometimes it was extended to cover all sub-Saharan Africa; sometimes, as in Herodotus' note on the 'Ethiopian troglodytes' quoted on page 64, it apparently took in much of Saharan Africa as well. One thing that it hardly ever meant, however, was the modern nation of Ethiopia. For this reason, with apologies to its inhabitants, I have referred to modern Ethiopia throughout this book as 'Abyssinia'.

19. See also *Genesis* X, 6–9, where Cush is mentioned as the son of Ham and the father of Nimrod. For ancient attitudes to the black Africans, see Snowden, F. M., *Blacks in Antiquity* (Cambridge, Mass., 1970).

20. The site of Meroe is now called Begarawiya; the site of Napata, confusingly, is very near the modern town of Merowe. See Shinnie (1967), 70–71.

21. Herodotus III, 21.

22. Pliny, *Nat. Hist.* VI, 181–2.

23. Seneca, *Natural Questions* VI, 8, 3–5: Pliny, *Nat. Hist.* VI, 181 and 184–6.

24. *Acts* VIII, 27–8.

25. But *cf.* Trigger, B. G., 'The myth of Meroe and the African Iron Age', *African Historical Studies* II.1 (1969), 23–50.

26. Paul, A., *A History of the Beja Tribes of the Sudan* (Cambridge, 1954).

27. Kirwan, L. P., 'Comments on the Origin and History of the Nobatae of Procopius', *Kush* VI (1958), 69–73.

28. Herodotus IV, 42.

29. There are two types of African elephant. The 'bush' type (*Loxodonta africana africana*) is larger than the Indian elephant, and is indeed the largest living land animal; but since it lives in eastern and southern Africa, only a few travellers from the classical world can ever have seen it. The elephants used by the Ptolemies and by Hannibal were of the smaller 'forest' type (*Loxodonta africana cyclotis*); this survives in western Africa, but is now extinct north of the Sahara. See Scullard, H. H., *The Elephant in the Greek and Roman World* (London, 1974), especially pp. 60–63.

30. For the Greek text of the *Periplus*, see the edition by H. Frisk (Göteborg, 1927). The most recent English translation is that of G. W. B. Huntingford (London, 1980). The translation by W. H. Schoff (New York, 1912), though more readable than Huntingford's and accompanied by many interesting comments, should be used with caution.

31. *Periplus* 4. Adulis is modern Zula; Coloe is modern Kohaito.

32. *Periplus* 5.

33. See Shinnie (1967), pp. 52–6; Kirwan, L. P., 'The decline and fall of Meroe', *Kush* VIII (1960), 163–73.

34. *Cf.* Miller, J. I., *The Spice Trade of the Roman Empire* (Oxford, 1969), p. 156.

35. *Periplus* 16: Ptolemy I, 9, 3–4; IV, 7, 4. Rapta has been variously located on the river Pangani, at Dar-es-Salaam, or on the river Rufiji.

36. Miller (1969), 153–172.

37. Ptolemy IV, 8, 1–2: Huntingford (1980), 173–6.

Chapter Five: *Arabia and the Incense Routes*

Arabia is a difficult land to explore, for political as well as physical reasons, and books on its ancient history and archaeology tend to be either very general, bringing in many other subjects besides, or else very technical and hard for the non-specialist to understand. Among the more general works are:

Bibby, G., *Looking for Dilmun* (London, 1970).

Botting, D., *Island of the Dragon's Blood* (London, 1958).

Hawley, D. F., *The Trucial States* (London, 1970).

Hitti, P. K., *History of the Arabs* (10th edition, London, 1970).

Ingrams, H., *Arabia and the Isles* (London, 1942).

Stark, F., *The Southern Gates of Arabia* (London, 1942).

Phillips, W., *Qataban and Sheba* (London, 1955).

—— *Unknown Oman* (London, 1966).

—— *Oman: a History* (London, 1967).

For a more detailed analysis, one very useful work is Doe, B., *Southern Arabia* (London, 1971). Grohmann, A., *Kulturgeschichte des Alten Orients: Arabien* (Munich, 1963) is worth consulting even by readers unfamiliar with German, for the sake of its excellent map. Groom, N., *Frankincense and Myrrh* (Harlow, 1981) is invaluable for anything connected with incense.

Some more technical works:

Altheim, F., and Stiehl, R. (eds), *Die Araber in der Alten Welt*, vol. I (Berlin, 1964).

Bowen, R. le B., and Albright, F. P. (eds), *Archaeological Discoveries in South Arabia* (Baltimore, 1958).

Glaser, E., *Skizze der Geschichte und Geographie Arabiens* (Berlin, 1890).

Müller, W. W., article 'Weihrauch' in Pauly-Wissowa, *Realencyclopädie der Classischen Altertumswissenschaft*, supplement XV (1978), 700–777.

Pirenne, J., *Le royaume sud-arabe de Qatabân et sa datation* (Louvain, 1961).

Ryckmans, J., 'Petits royaumes sud-arabes d'après les auteurs classiques', *Le Muséon* LXX (1957), 75–96.

Sprenger, A., *Die Alte Geographie Arabiens* (Berne, 1875).

Winnett, F. V., and Reed, W. L., *Ancient Records from North Arabia* (Toronto, 1970).

Wissmann, H. von, *Zur Geschichte und Landeskunde von Alt-Südarabien* (Vienna, 1964).

—— 'Himyar Ancient History', *Le Muséon* LXXVII (1964), 429–97.

—— 'Zur Kenntnis von Ostarabien, besonders Al-Qatif, im Altertum', *Le Muséon* LXXX (1967), 489ff.

—— *Zur Archäologie und Antiken Geographie von Südarabien* (Istanbul, 1968).

—— Articles 'Zaabram' to 'Zeeritae' in Pauly-Wissowa, supp. XI (1968), 1304–63.

1. Herodotus III, 106–113.
2. Pliny, *Nat. Hist.* VI, 143.
3. *Ibid.* VI, 162.
4. *Ibid.* XII, 69. For the East African Trogodytae (*sic*, rather than *Troglodytae*) see the article in Pauly-Wissowa (vol. VIIA.2, *Tullius-Valerius*, 2497–2500) and Huntingford (*op. cit.*, in Chap. IV note 30), pp. 143–6.
5. Bowen & Albright (1958), pp. 70–76.
6. *Ibid.*, pp. 215–300. 'Bilqis' (or *Bilkis* in the *Encyclopaedia of Islam, q.v.*) is the traditional Arab name for the Queen of Sheba. She is not given a name either in the Biblical account (I Kings X, 1–13) or in the Koran.
7. Pliny, *Nat. Hist.* VI, 155.
8. But *cf.* Groom (1981), 178–80, for a proposal by A. F. L. Beeston that the 'Catabani' and 'Gebbanitae' were different.
9. For a discussion of Timna and its destruction, see Doe (1971), p. 72.
10. For ancient accounts of Aelius Gallus, see Strabo XVI, 4, 22–4: Pliny, *Nat. Hist.* VI, 160–62: Cassius Dio LIII, 29. For modern accounts, the *Cambridge Ancient History* X (Cambridge, 1952), pp. 247–54 and 877: Pirenne (1961), 98–124: Cary & Warmington (*op. cit.*; notes to Chap. IV), 192–3: Groom (1981), 74–6.
11. Cleopatris was probably another name for Arsinoe, briefly mentioned on page 75. For a discussion of the site of Leuce Come, see Groom (1981), p. 261.
12. The site of Nesca (called *Asca* by Strabo) is now called Nashq; the site of Athrula is now called Baraqish. See the *Sketch Map of South-West Arabia* (Royal Geographical Society, London, 1976).
13. *Periplus of the Erythraean Sea*, 20. Cf. note 30 to Chap. IV.
14. *Ibid.*, 21–4. Ancient Muza is sometimes identified with the well-known Yemeni port of Mocha (from which Mocha coffee takes its name), and sometimes with a smaller place called Mawshij, further north.
15. *Ibid.*, 26.
16. *Ibid.*, 27.
17. *Ibid.*, 29.
18. For a map, with notes, of Roman roads between the Red Sea and the Nile, see *Tabula Imperii Romani* sheet NG 36, *Coptos* (Oxford, 1958).
19. Macoraba and 'Lathrippa' are mentioned by Ptolemy (VI, 7, 31–2). The name Medina, 'City', is short for *Madinat an-Nabi*, 'City of the Prophet': this name was given to Yathrib in honour of the important part it played in the career of Mohammed.
20. For Egra, see Strabo XVI, 4, 24: Pliny, *Nat. Hist.* VI, 156: Ptolemy VI, 7, 29. For the Nabataean kingdom, and its successor the Roman province of Arabia, see Glueck, N., *Deities and Dolphins* (London, 1965): Bowersock, G. W., 'A Report on Arabia Provincia', *Journal of Roman Studies* LXI (1971), 219–42.
21. Pliny, *Nat. Hist.* VI, 147. For a discussion of the site of Gerra, see the article by W. E. James in Altheim & Stiehl, vol. V.
22. *Nat. Hist.* VI, 149: *Periplus of the Erythraean Sea*, 36: Ptolemy VI, 7, 36.
23. *Nat. Hist.* VI, 160.
24. The site of ancient Najran or Negrana is still locally known as Al-Ukhdud, which means 'the trenches'.
25. But *cf.* the *Cambridge History of Iran* III, p. 606, where it is stated that the 'Year of the Elephant' must have been well before AD 570, and Mohammed's birth probably later.

Chapter Six: *The Parthians and Sasanians*

The main reference-work for these is now the *Cambridge History of Iran*, vol. III (ed. E. Yarshater, Cambridge, 1983). For a discussion of the ancient sources, see pp. 1261–1283 of this.

See also:

Colledge, M. A. R., *The Parthians* (London, 1967).

—— *Parthian Art* (London, 1977).

Debevoise, N. C., *A Political History of Parthia* (Chicago, 1938).

Frye, R. N., *The Heritage of Persia* (London, 1962).

—— *The Golden Age of Persia* (London, 1975).

Ghirshman, R., *Iran, from the earliest times to the Islamic conquest* (London, 1954).

—— *Iran: Parthians and Sassanians* (London, 1962).

Matheson, S. A., *Persia: an Archaeological Guide* (2nd edition, London, 1976).

Pigulevskaja, N., *Les villes de l'état iranien* (Paris, 1963).

Stark, F., *Rome on the Euphrates* (London, 1966).

For the operations of the Greeks in the east, see the references cited in the next chapter. For Armenia and the Caucasus, see:

Adontz, N., *Histoire d'Arménie* (Paris, 1946).

Allen, W. E. D., *A History of the Georgian People* (London, 1932).

Burney, C., and Lang, D. M., *The Peoples of the Hills* (London, 1971).

Der Nersessian, S., *The Armenians* (London, 1969).

Lang, D. M., *The Georgians* (London, 1966).

Manandian, H. A., *Trade and Cities of Armenia* (Lisbon, 1965).

1. For the Muslim attitude to figurative art, and its origins, see Okasha, S., *The Muslim Painter and the Divine* (London, 1981), chapter 1.

2. The word 'Persia' is hardly ever used by ancient writers. The inhabitants of the region called it *Parsa*; the Greeks and Romans called it *Persis* (with genitive *Persidos* or *Persidis*). The Arabs, whose language had no letter 'P', called it *Fars*; this survives as the name of a province in south-western Iran.

3. For the career of Crassus, see Plutarch's *Life* of him: Adcock, F. E., *Marcus Crassus, Millionaire* (Cambridge, 1966): *Camb. Hist. Iran* III, 48–58.

4. See Pauly-Wissowa, article 'Naarmalcha' in vol. XVI.2 (1935), 1440–49.

5. For Antony's Armenian campaign, see Plutarch's *Life* of him, and *Camb. Hist. Iran* III, 58–66. Phraata is now thought to have been at Maragheh, rather than at Takht-i Sulaiman as used to be supposed; the latter is more likely to have been ancient *Gazaca*.

6. Horace, *Odes* III, 5, translated by Hugh Macnaghten (Cambridge, 1926).

7. Tacitus, *Annals* XIII, 7–9, 34–41; XIV, 23–6; XV, 1–17, 24–31: *Camb. Hist. Iran* III, 79–86.

8. For these second-century campaigns, see *Camb. Hist. Iran* III, 86–95. No detailed account has survived of any of them. For the Roman province of Mesopotamia, see Dillemann, L., *Haute Mesopotamie orientale et pays adjacents* (Paris, 1962): Jones, A. H. M., *The Cities of the Eastern Roman Provinces* (2nd edition, Oxford, 1971), pp. 215–25: Oates, D., *Studies in the Ancient History of Northern Iraq* (London, 1968).

9. Bertrand Russell, 'Eastern and Western Ideals of Happiness', in *Sceptical Essays* (London, 1935). Whether the Chinese were happy with this state of affairs, as Russell maintained, is a difficult question and a very old one – at least as old as the fable of King Log and King Stork.

10. Pliny, *Nat. Hist.* VI, 112.

11. Mentioned by Ptolemy (V, 12, 8) as Thospia, the capital of a region called Thospitis.

12. Andrae, W., *Hatra* (2 vols, Leipzig, 1908 and 1912): Colledge (1967), 129–33.

13. Hansman, J., 'Charax and the Karkheh', *Iranica Antiqua* VII (1967), 21–58.

14. The famous ruins of Old Persepolis are locally called Takht-i Jamshid: the much less well-known ruins of New Persepolis or Istakhr are locally called Takht-i Tavoos. For their sites, see Matheson (1976), 220–34.

15. The name Veh-Antiok-Shapur was later corrupted into Gundeshapur or Jondi-shapur. For the site, see Matheson (1976), 156–7.

16. Adams, R. McC., *Land Behind Baghdad* (Chicago, 1965), 69–83.

17. For Mani and the Manichaeans, see *Camb. Hist. Iran* III, 965–90. For Kartir, see Frye (1962), 218–20.

18. Zoroastrianism reached China itself under the T'ang dynasty, but made few converts there. The Chinese believed that light and darkness (*Yang* and *Yin*) were complementary rather than opposed, and that it was foolish to identify one with 'good' and the other with 'evil'.

Chapter Seven: *India*

For the general history of ancient India, see:
    The Cambridge History of India, vol. I, ed. E. J. Rapson (Cambridge, 1922).
    Ghosh, N. N., *Early History of India* (2nd edition, Allahabad, 1948).
    Nilakanta Sastri, K. A. (ed.), *A Comprehensive History of India*, vol. II (Bombay, 1957).
    Raychaudhuri, H., *Political History of Ancient India* (6th edition, Calcutta, 1953).
    Smith, V. A., *The Early History of India* (4th edition, Oxford, 1957).
    Thapar, R., *A History of India*, vol. I (London, 1966).
  For historical geography and ancient sources:
    Cunningham, A., *The Ancient Geography of India* (revised edition, Calcutta, 1924).
    Law, B. C., *Tribes in Ancient India* (Poona, 1943).
    McCrindle, J. W., *Ancient India as described by Megasthenes and Arrian* (London, 1877).
    —— *Ancient India as described by Ptolemy* (Bombay, 1885: reprinted Calcutta, 1927).
    —— *Ancient India as described in Classical Literature* (London, 1901).
    Majumdar, R. C., *The Classical Accounts of India* (Calcutta, 1960).
  For the Greeks in India:
    Hammond, N. G. L., *Alexander the Great* (London, 1981), pp. 187–241.
    Lane Fox, R., *Alexander the Great* (London, 1973), pp. 331–402.
    Narain, A. K., *The Indo-Greeks* (Oxford, 1957).
    Tarn, W. W., *The Greeks in Bactria and India* (2nd edition, Cambridge, 1951, reprinted 1966).
    Woodcock, G., *The Greeks in India* (London, 1966).
  For some particular regions:
    Aiyar, K. G. S., *Cera Kings of the Sangam Period* (London, 1937).
    Barrett, D., *Sculptures from Amaravati in the British Museum* (London, 1954).
    Caroe, O., *The Pathans* (London, 1958).
    Gopalachari, K., *Early History of the Andhra Country* (Madras, 1941).

Iyengar, P. T. S., *History of the Tamils* (Madras, 1929).
Lambrick, H. T., *Sind* (2 vols, Hyderabad, Sind, 1964 & 1973).
Law, B. C., *Ujjayini in Ancient India* (Gwalior, 1944).
Nilakanta Sastri, K. A., *The Pandyan Kingdom* (London, 1929).
—— *The Colas* (Madras, 1955).
—— *A History of South India* (2nd edition, Oxford, 1958).
For everyday life:
Basham, A. L., *The Wonder that was India* (3rd edition, London, 1967).
Basham, A. L. (ed.), *A Cultural History of India* (Oxford, 1975).
Edwardes, M., *Everyday Life in Early India* (London, 1969).
Taddei, M., *The Ancient Civilization of India* (London, 1970).

1. In this chapter and elsewhere I use the term 'modern India' to mean the modern nation of India; 'Pakistan' to mean the modern nation of Pakistan; and 'India', unqualified, to mean what the ancients meant by it. There is no satisfactory modern synonym: 'Hindustan' sounds archaic, and 'the Indo-Pakistan sub-continent' sounds clumsy.

2. Megasthenes' original work is now lost, but long extracts from it are preserved in the works of later writers (especially Strabo, Pliny and Arrian).

3. Asoka's *Thirteenth Major Rock Edict*, quoted in Thapar, R., *Asoka and the Decline of the Mauryas* (Oxford, 1961), p. 255. The text has *Dhamma*, which is the Prakrit equivalent of the Sanskrit *Dharma*.

4. Chaucer, *Knight's Tale* 1298. For two very different interpretations of this Demetrius, see Tarn (1951), chap. IV; Woodcock (1966), chap. V.

5. Translated into English by T. W. Rhys Davids, *Sacred Books of the East*, vols. XXXV–XXXVI (Oxford, 1890, 1894).

6. For the legend of St Thomas and Gondopharnes, see *Camb. Hist. India* I, 578–80, 687.

7. Ptolemy VI, 16, 2 and 5.

8. Basham, A. L. (ed.), *Papers on the Date of Kaniska* (Leiden, 1968).

9. Ptolemy, VII, 1, 50.

10. *Comprehensive History of India* II, p. 245.

11. The name is conventionally spelt as two words, 'Chandra Gupta', to distinguish the Gupta kings from the founder of the Maurya dynasty.

12. See *Camb. Hist. India* I, 534–8, 683: *cf.* Ghosh (1948), 186–94.

13. Pliny, *Nat. Hist.* VI, 66–7.

14. Quoted in Thapar (1966), pp. 98–9.

15. The royal residence of the Cheras, according to Ptolemy (VII, 1, 86) was at Karura (Karur); their chief port was Muziris (Cranganore). The Chola capital was at Uraiyur, near Trichinopoly; the Pandya capital at Madurai. These are mentioned by Ptolemy as Orthura and Modura respectively (VII, 1, 91 & 89).

16. For Western ideas of the size and shape of India, see *Camb. Hist. India* I, pp. 398–402; for Indian ones, Basham (1967), pp. 488–9.

17. Herodotus III, 102–5. He states that the Euboean talent (about 57 lb. avoirdupois, or 26 kilograms) was the one used in this case. The price of gold quoted in *The Times*, 17th June 1983, was in the order of 411 dollars per ounce.

18. Herodotus III, 94.

19. Pliny, *Nat. Hist.* VI, 68.

20. The Nanda dynasty, overthrown by Chandragupta Maurya. See Curtius Rufus IX, 2: Diodorus Siculus XCIII: Plutarch, *Alexander* 62: *Camb. Hist. India* I, 469: Ghosh (1948), p. 81.

21. The Jains themselves believe that Mahavira was the last of a long line of founding fathers, collectively known as Tirthankars. The historical existence of the earlier ones, however, is doubtful.

22. Strabo XV, chap. 1: Arrian, *Anabasis* VII, chap. 3.

23. Depicted at the eastern end of the *Peutinger Table*. See Miller, K., *Die Peutingerische Tafel* (Stuttgart, 1962).

24. Strabo XV, 1, 36: Arrian, *Indica* X (both quoting Megasthenes).

25. Bashan (1967), pp. 218–20.

Chapter Eight: *South-East Asia and the Spice Routes*

For the general history of the region, see Hall, D. G. E., *A History of South-East Asia* (2nd edition, London, 1964).

For particular parts of it:

Aung, H., *A History of Burma* (New York, 1967).

Charoenwongsa, P., and Subhadrudis Diskul, M. C., *Thailand* (Geneva and London, 1978).

Groslier, B. P., *Indochina* (Geneva and London, 1966).

Moorhead, F. J., *A History of Malaya and her Neighbours* (London, 1957).

Wheatley, P., *The Golden Khersonese* (Kuala Lumpur, 1961).

For its 'Indianization':

Coedès, G., *The Indianized States of Southeast Asia* (3rd edition, Canberra, 1975).

Lamb, A., and Loofs, H. H. E., 'Indian Influence in Ancient South-East Asia', in Basham, A. L. (ed.), *A Cultural History of India* (Oxford, 1975), pp. 442–454.

For the spice trade:

Cary, M., and Warmington, E. H., *The Ancient Explorers* (revised edition, London, 1963), pp. 73–109.

Miller, J. I., *The Spice Trade of the Roman Empire* (Oxford, 1969).

Schmitthenner, W., 'Rome and India: Aspects of Universal History during the Principate', *Journal of Roman Studies* LXIX (1979), pp. 90–106.

Toussaint, A., *A History of the Indian Ocean* (London, 1966).

Warmington, E. H., *The Commerce between the Roman Empire and India* (Cambridge, 1928).

Wheeler, R. E. M., *Rome beyond the Imperial Frontiers* (London, 1954), pp. 115–53.

1. *Ch'ien Han shu* XXVIII.2, reproduced with translation and comments in Wheatley (1961), pp. 8–13.

2. *Periplus*, 63 (*cf.* note 30 to Chapter IV): Ptolemy VII, 1, 81. The site of *Gange* is unknown; it may or may not have been the same place as *Tamralipti* or *Tamalites* (modern Tamluk), which according to Indian sources was the chief port of ancient Bengal. Ptolemy (VII, 1, 73) treats *Tamalites* as a different place from *Gange*, but he may be mistaken.

3. Ptolemy VII, 2, 7.

4. Pliny, *Natural History* XIII, 1–25.

5. *Ibid.* XII, 82–4.

6. Celsus, *De Medicina* V, 23, 3.

7. Arrian, *Indica* XXIX–XXXI.

8. St Mark XIV, 3–5: St John XII, 3–5: *Periplus*, 48: Miller (1969), pp. 88–92.

9. *Periplus*, 46.

10. Pliny, *Nat. Hist.* VI, 84.

11. *Periplus*, 61: Ptolemy VII, chap. 4.

12. Ptolemy VII, 4, 10. For ancient Ceylon, see Boisselier, J., *Ceylon (Sri Lanka)* (Geneva and London, 1979): 'Zeylanicus', *Ceylon between Orient and Occident* (London, 1970).

13. *Periplus*, 60. Camara is Kaveripaddinam, at the mouth of the river Cauvery; Poduce is probably Arikamedu (see below, note 15); Sopatma has been identified sometimes with Madras and sometimes with Markanam. 'Limyrice' is an error for *Damirice*, 'the Tamil country'; *cf*. Ptolemy VII, 1, 8.

14. Wan Chen, *Record of Strange Things of the South*, quoted in Miller (1969), pp. 186–7.

15. Wheeler (1954), pp. 145–50.

16. For cinnamon, see Miller (1969), pp. 42–7; for ginger, *ibid*., 53–7; for cloves, *ibid*., 47–51; for nutmeg, *ibid*., 58–60.

17. Wheatley (1961), p. xxiv. There is silver in the Shan states of Burma, but it is hard to see how this region could ever have been regarded as an island.

18. Ptolemy VII, chapter 2.

19. Possibly to be spelt *Loanas* and linked with Pliny's river *Lanos* (see below, note 5 to Chapter X). For another example of confusion between the Greek letters *delta* and *lambda*, see note 13 above.

20. *Sina Metropolis*: Ptolemy VII, 3, 6. *Cattigara*: Ptolemy VII, 3, 3. The name should perhaps be amended to *Cattinagara* and interpreted as 'city of Chiao-chih'. The element *nagara*, 'city', appears in many ancient Indian place-names and some modern ones (*e.g.* Srinagar, the capital of Kashmir). For the Chinese commandery of Chiao-chih, in the Red River delta, see above, p. 138.

21. *Hou Han shu*, chapter 88: quoted in Schoff, W. H., *Periplus of the Erythraean Sea* (New York, 1912), pp. 276–7.

Chapter Nine: *China*

The three chief ancient sources for China in the Ch'in and Han periods are the *Shih chi* (*Historical Records*) by Ssu-ma Ch'ien; the *Ch'ien Han Shu* (*Annals of the Early Han*) by Pan Ku; and the *Hou Han shu* (*Annals of the Later Han*) by Fan Yeh. All three are very long, and none has been translated in full. For partial translations, see:

Chavannes, E., *Les mémoires historiques de Se-ma Ts'ien* (Paris, 1895–1905).
Crespigny, R. de, *The Last of the Han* (Canberra, 1969).
Dubs, H. H., *The History of the Former Han Dynasty* (Baltimore, 1938–55).
Watson, B., *Records of the Grand Historian of China* (New York, 1962).

Suggestions for further reading:

Cotterell, A., *The First Emperor of China* (London, 1981).
Cotterell, Y. Y., and Cotterell, A., *The Early Civilization of China* (London, 1975).
Cottrell, L., *The Tiger of Ch'in* (London, 1964).
Dawson, R., *The Chinese Experience* (London, 1978).
Grousset, R., *The Rise and Splendour of the Chinese Empire* (London, 1952).
Hay, J., *Ancient China* (London, 1973).
Herrmann, A., *An Historical Atlas of China* (revised edition, Edinburgh, 1966).
Loewe, M., *Imperial China* (London, 1966).
—— *Everyday Life in Early Imperial China* (London, 1968).
—— *Crisis and Conflict in Han China* (London, 1974).
Needham, J., and others, *Science and Civilization in China* (Cambridge, 1954–   ).

Pirazzoli-t'Serstevens, M., *The Han Civilization of China* (Oxford, 1982).
Rawson, J., *Ancient China: Art and Archaeology* (London, 1980).
Wang Zhongshu, *Han Civilization* (New Haven and London, 1982).
Watson, W., *The Genius of China* (London, 1973).
Willetts, W., *Chinese Art* (London, 1958).

1. So called because it is described in a work called the *Spring and Autumn Annals*, traditionally ascribed to Confucius.

2. The visible remains of the Great Wall today date mostly from the Ming period. The original Ch'in wall was even longer than the present one, and took a more northerly line.

3. Han Fei Tzu, quoted in Cottrell (1964), p. 99.

4. Also known as Wu Ti – but preferably not as 'Emperor Wu Ti', since the word *ti* itself means 'emperor'.

5. For the Witchcraft Scandal, see especially Loewe (1974), pp. 37–90.

6. As, for example, in the *Romance of the Three Kingdoms*, by Lo Kuan-chung (translated by C. H. Brewitt-Taylor, Rutland, Vermont, 1959).

7. For an account of the finding of this, see Hay (1973), 89–93.

8. The census of AD 1–2 is recorded in *Ch'ien Han shu*, chapter 28; that of AD 140 in *Hou Han shu*, chapter 65. See also the *Times Atlas of China* (London, 1974), p. ix: and de Crespigny, R., 'An Outline of the Local Administration of the Later Han Empire', *Chung Chi Journal* VII.1 (November 1967), pp. 57–71.

9. Sun Tzu, *The Art of War*, translated by S. B. Griffith (Oxford, 1963).

10. Mo Tzu, quoted in Griffith (*supra*), p. 22.

11. Anonymous: translated by Arthur Waley in *Chinese Poems* (London, 1946), p. 52.

12. Lin Yutang, *My Country and My People* (2nd edition, London, 1939), p. 97.

13. C. Northcote Parkinson, 'Lords and Lackeys', in *The Law of Delay* (London, 1970).

14. Emperor Wu, quoted in *Shih chi* 29 = Watson (1962), vol. II, p. 77.

Chapter Ten: *Central Asia and the Silk Routes*

The chief Chinese sources for ancient Central Asia are those cited in the last chapter. See especially:

Chavannes, E., 'Les pays d'Occident d'après le Wei-lio', *T'oung Pao* VI (1905), pp. 519–71.
—— 'Les pays d'Occident d'après le Heou Han chou', *T'oung Pao* VIII (1907), pp. 149–234.
Hulsewé, A. F. P., and Loewe, M. A. N., *China in Central Asia* (Leiden, 1979; a translation of *Ch'ien Han shu*, chapters 61 and 96).
Watson, B., *op. cit.*, vol. II, pp. 264–89 (a translation of *Shih chi*, chapter 123).
See also:
Boulnois, L., *The Silk Road* (London, 1966).
Herrmann, A., *Die alten Seidenstrassen zwischen China und Syrien* (Berlin, 1910).
Herrmann, A., *Historical Atlas of China* (*op. cit.*), p. 16.
Hirth, F., *China and the Roman Orient* (Shanghai, 1885, reprinted 1939).
Stein, M. A., *Ruins of Desert Cathay* (London, 1912).
—— *Serindia* (Oxford, 1921).
—— *Innermost Asia* (Oxford, 1928).

—— *On Ancient Central Asian Tracks* (London, 1933; reprinted Chicago, 1964).

For the careers of Sir Aurel Stein and his rivals in Central Asian archaeology, see also Hopkirk, P., *Foreign Devils on the Silk Road* (London, 1980).

For the nomads of the steppe, see the references to Chapter III; for the Graeco-Bactrian kings, those to Chapter VII; for the Parthians, those to Chapter VI.

1. Bolton, J. D. P., *Aristeas of Proconnesus* (Oxford, 1962), p. 180 and *passim*.
2. Pliny, *Nat. Hist.* VI, 55. Ptolemy (VI, 16, 5) calls them the *Ottorocorrhae*.
3. Pliny, *ibid.* See also Tarn (*op. cit.*, Chapter VII), pp. 84–5.
4. Virgil, *Georgics* II, 120: Horace, *Odes* III, 29, 27–8.
5. The Psitharas, the Cambari and the Lanos (*Nat. Hist.* VI, 55).
6. *Ibid.* VI, 88.
7. Ptolemy VI, 14 (Scythia within Imaus); 15 (Scythia beyond Imaus); 16 (Serica). For a translation, see McCrindle, *Ancient India as described by Ptolemy*, pp. 285–305.
8. Ptolemy VI, 16, 8.
9. 'The Lament of Hsi-Chün', translated by Arthur Waley (*Chinese Poems*, p. 43). See note 11 to Chapter IX.
10. *An-hsi* took its name from Arsaces, the founder of the Parthian dynasty; *Tiao-chih* perhaps from the town of Taoce (Tawwaz) in Persis. See Hulsewé & Loewe (1979), p. 113 note 255.
11. Ptolemy I, 11, 4–8.
12. Pausanias, *Guide to Greece* VI, 26, 6–8.
13. Sometimes known as Hinayana, 'the Lesser Vehicle', but its practitioners dislike this expression.
14. D. Bentley-Taylor and C. B. Offner, in *The World's Religions* (ed. Sir Norman Anderson, 4th edition, London, 1975), p. 181.
15. Stein, *Central Asian Tracks*, pp. 96–112.
16. *Ch'ien Han shu*, chapter 96A = Hulsewé & Loewe (1979), pp. 110–1.
17. Ptolemy VI, 13, 2.
18. *Shih chi* 123 = Watson (1962), vol. II, p. 269.
19. Hulsewé & Loewe (1979), p. 115, note 268.
20. First published by Peter Davies Ltd, 1956.
21. Dubs, H. H., *A Roman City in Ancient China* (London, 1957).
22. For the origin of the name Li-jien, see Dubs (1957), p. 26, note 8: Hulsewé & Loewe (1979), pp. 117–8, note 275. It is possible that *Li-jien* originally meant 'the land of Alexander', just as *An-hsi* meant 'the land of Arsaces'; and that, having first been applied to the Seleucid kingdom, it was then extended to cover all the nations (including Rome) whose rulers regarded themselves as the heirs of Alexander. It was a convenient coincidence that one of the largest cities of the West also bore this man's name; but, *pace* Dubs, it seems most unlikely that Roman soldiers would ever have described themselves as 'Alexandrians'.
23. See also Tarn (1966), pp. 488–93.
24. Tacitus, *Annals* XIV, 25; *Histories* I, 6: Teggart, F. J., *Rome and China* (Berkeley, Cal., 1939), pp. 162–3.
25. *Hou Han shu*, chapter 88, quoted in Schoff. See note 21 to Chapter VIII.

INDEX

Numbers in italics refer to maps